KILLER INSTINCT

RECOMMENDED FOR A BRAM STOKER AWARD

Dr. Jessica Coran tracks a blood-drinking "vampire killer" deep into the heartland of America . . .

"Just when you think there's nothing new to be done with the serial killer novel, a book as fresh and twisty as this one shows up. Strong horrific overtones and a real knowledge of hi-tech detection work turn this book into a genuinely spooky read."

—**Ed Gorman,** *Mystery Scene Magazine*

"Chilling and unflinching in its descriptions, technical without being heavy-handed, and brutal without glorifying violence or murder."

—*Fort Lauderdale Sun-Sentinel*

FATAL INSTINCT

Jessica Coran is summoned to New York City to find a cunning, modern-day Jack the Ripper nicknamed "The Claw" . . .

"A taut, dense thriller. An immensely entertaining suspense novel filled with surprises, clever twists, and wonderfully drawn characters."

—*Daytona Beach News-Journal*

But no killer in Jessica Coran's past can compare to the relentless, psychotic "Trade Winds Killer" in Robert W. Walker's brilliant new novel of psychological suspense . . .

PRIMAL INSTINCT

Other titles by Robert W. Walker

PRIMAL INSTINCT

ROBERT W. WALKER

DIAMOND BOOKS, NEW YORK

This book is a work of fiction
and purports nothing more. All
characters herein are the product
of imagination and research
finding a happy medium . . .

This book is a Diamond original edition,
and has never been previously published.

PRIMAL INSTINCT

A Diamond Book / published by arrangement with
the author

PRINTING HISTORY
Diamond edition / November 1994

ISBN: 0-7865-0055-7

Diamond Books are published by The Berkley Publishing Group,
200 Madison Avenue, New York, NY 10016.
DIAMOND and the "D" design
are trademarks belonging to Charter Communications, Inc.

PRINTED IN THE UNITED STATES OF AMERICA

10 9 8 7 6 5 4 3 2

This book is affectionately dedicated to Donna & Bill Leamy, whose love of Hawaii and whose support and kindness got me out of the office, off my *okole* and onto the grand isles of Oahu and Maui on my twenty-fifth wedding anniversary. In so doing, two special people played a major role in bringing this work to full-blown and flourishing life. *Aloha, aikanes.*

A special thanks to my *kanikele* (consul) Fran Katsuda Pennella, a godsend native-born, for invaluable help with the pidgin English and the myriad mysteries of the islands, which apparently no one knows all the answers to.

Thanks to T. I. Harris, Sally Carlson, Ed Humm, Beth Wilkerson, Julie Painter, Jena Bartlett, Jim Clark, Jon Bowden, B. J. Lantz, Lynn Zutler, Lori Campbell Baker, Lee Shargel, Francis Greppi, and innumerable students of mine whom I've learned from.

Thanks to author Theon Wright for *Rape in Paradise*, 1966; to Majorie Sinclair for *The Wild Wind*, 1991; to H. Paul Jeffers, author of *Who Killed Precious*; to Robert K. Ressler & Tom Shachtman, authors of *Whoever Fights Monsters*.

Thanks to the University of Hawaii Press and authors Mary Kawena Pukui and Samuel H. Elbert for the *New Pocket Hawaiian Dictionary* (another godsend). Helpful also was the *Illustrated Atlas of Hawaii* by Gavan Daws, edited by O. A. Bushnell and illustrated by Joseph Feher.

Finally, thanks to the Hawaiian people—U.S. citizens all—who were so cordial during our visit, and a heartfelt thanks to my *wahine* (wife), Cheryl, and my *kane* (son), Stephen, for putting up with *io'u* (me) on this criminally juicy crime novel for some two years now.

Hawaii, the island of Oahu, the outskirts of Honolulu near Koko Head crater . . . 1:35 A.M., July 12, 1995

He does a bad Elvis imitation, crooning aloud the words for "Don't Be Cruel" as it's pounding from his car-radio speaker on Hawaii's hottest rock station, KBHT—"Hot Hawaii!" He interrupts himself with a snicker and says, "Too late, hey, Kelia honey . . . tooooo late for doughn't be cruel, huh, baby?"

He chuckles lightly at his antics and the irony of the Elvis tune, and then he reaches out to his passenger, lifts the disfigured head from the bloodied chest, and stares into the vacant eyes of the dead girl he calls Kelia. He momentarily studies the fact her hands are missing, both severed at the wrists. He doesn't remember slicing them off, nor, for that matter, if he'd earlier taken time to put the hands on ice. If not, he will secure them later, when he gets back home.

1

Lopaka doesn't remember a lot of what he does while in the act itself; he is able only to piece things completely together after long bouts of depression and weeks of flashback. Looking at the dead girl's hands, for months afterward, allows him to relive the whole experience once again, the only thing save another kill that lends respite from his depression, even if temporarily. And he doesn't think the gods will really miss a pair of hands.

Kelia, he says mentally to the dead girl beside him, *you're so good for me now and forever.* . . . . A touching sentiment with Elvis as backdrop, he thinks.

He has taken his time with Kelia, all night now, and now it is time to send her over. He is secure behind the moonless Hawaiian night and the black interior of the Buick. He stares again into her dead, vacant eyes. To stare into the abyss, into the iris of death, is part of it, he tells himself.

Elvis is replaced by a Neil Diamond song: *"You got the way to move me."* The cowboy sings now in unison with Diamond, his gruff voice drowning out the mellow tones. "You got the way to move me . . . you got the way to move me . . . *ahhhh, ahhhh, owwwww!"*

The trade winds have swept over the island of Oahu and the city of Honolulu for several weeks now, the powerful caress like one long, unending, coiling draft begun high atop Mount Haleakala on neighboring Maui, arriving here in full force. Yet the unending wind is adored by the tourists as it allows for lovely, open-air seaside dining, moonlight walks along the beach and palm corridors, making love on the balcony without pesty insects swept up by the trades. It is the same wind that tells him to kill and kill again.

In the bleak darkness of a moonless sky, the wind now batters the trees that line the lavender-lit Ala Moana roadway; the trade winds threaten to lift and toss the car; so strong are the gusts that they make him think it might be the acrid breath of an ancient, tyrannical island god, perhaps Kaneloa, what the Christian religion calls Satan. Perhaps the great Kaneloa wants Lopaka to know that he approves of this night's work. Soulful voices in the "long" wind which careen down from *mauka,* the mountain side of the island, as always this time of year, speak clearly of the *kapus,* taboos broken over time.

He travels toward the waiting lips of a hungry sea that will lap up the remains of his prey. Maybe it isn't the wind that tells him to kill; maybe it's God.

His car finds the Kalanianaole, Highway 72 by the road sign, where the smaller tarmac parts with the Interstate, the main thoroughfare through Honolulu and all of Oahu's *makai,* or southern seaside.

He drives determinedly yet dreamily up the steep cliffs overlooking Hanauma Bay, fifteen miles south of Honolulu. About three miles further south and he'll be at the southernmost tip of Oahu, at the much-visited-by-day, deserted-by-night tourist snare called the Blow Hole. There, at this crevice in the volcanic rock extending in a cavernous ledge over the waters of the Pacific, he'll dump the girl's body.

The Pacific waves roll into the mouth of the cavern there with such force that it drives the waters skyward through the Blow Hole, giving it the appearance of a whale's plume, the terrific geyser effect sending the water up for over twenty feet. The spectacular dance between water and earth creates such a powerful force within the cavern that any object cast into it, such as a human body, is immediately pulverized beyond recognition, handily destroying all evidence of his crime, as it has before, in a matter of minutes.

The girl's clothes, tied in a soft, bloody bundle, will be disposed of elsewhere. She'll leave this world as she entered, with nothing whatever to identify her as the whore and prostitute that she was, a whore of Honolulu.

"Yeah," he mutters to himself as he turns off into the well-paved parking lot overlooking the Blow Hole, "trade winds're up."

When he steps from the car the wind sweeps about his legs, at first a playful animal encouraging him to carry on his work, now at his back like the hand of a benevolent father firmly pushing him forward. If Kelia were alive and walking around the car to meet him, the wind would be blowing her dress up so high that nothing would be hidden. All the Honolulu whores allow the wind to show their wares. But she no longer walks or talks or cries as she did the night before.

1:40 A.M., Koko Head Road

Officer Alan Kaniola was on patrol on the Waialae Road, the old main highway leading out of the city toward the southern end of

Oahu. He'd earlier gotten a not-so-unusual report of what appeared to be a street disturbance and a possible kidnapping; at one location a fight had erupted between passengers in two separate vehicles over some slight accident, and at another location along Ala Wai Boulevard there'd been a report of a young girl's having been manhandled and forced into a car apparently against her will. It might be assumed it was a lovers' spat, or an altercation between a hooker and her pimp, but who knows? There was little to identify the car or the attacker, which didn't sound like any pimp Kaniola knew. It was reported as a lackluster vehicle, dark in color, either brown or maroon, lightly tinted blue windows, a battered body but a "souped up" engine, a car otherwise without any distinguishing feature.

Now here was a maroon Buick sedan in ill repair heading out toward Koko Head, a volcanic promontory at the southern end of the island. The car was traveling at a fairly high rate of speed, and something about it made Kaniola curious. He radioed his position and told Dispatch that he was following a suspicious-looking car, and as he said the words he wondered himself how a car might "look" suspicious.

He got a buzz from another patrolman, Thom Hilani, also a Hawaiian cop. Hilani was a big motorcycle cop, and he, too, had noticed the speeding car that was touring toward Koko Head. Hilani fell in behind his friend Kaniola, saying that he would back him up. It was a quiet night except for ceaseless radio static and the knocking noises caused by wind through the coconut palms and monkeypod trees.

By daylight this was a beautiful ride, with the stark-white beaches and ceaseless emerald and blue stretch of water below in Hanauma Bay, which nestled between two claws of land jutting out into the Pacific. At this hour, it was a different matter, with no street lights to guide the patrol car as it twisted and turned its way up the precipice, further and further from the lights of Honolulu. But Kaniola liked old Hawaii and he knew the roads well, and he had backpacked into the mountains on many occasions.

Somehow in the twisting, upward spiral toward Koko Head, Alan Kaniola lost sight of the car he was pursuing, and then he almost passed it where it was parked in the lot overlooking the bay and the famous Blow Hole.

He abruptly halted his patrol car, thrust it into reverse and was backing it up just as Hilani's cycle came around the bend, nearly colliding with him, causing Hilani to swear over the police band and blare out with his cycle horn.

"Call in our position, Hilani," Joe told the other officer.

So much for the element of surprise, thought Kaniola. After having words with Officer Hilani, Joe veered off and into the parking area, which by day was jammed with visiting tourist buses and cars of every size and stripe so that it was a hazard to dare drive in. Here tourists, by the busload, fought for position along the man-made paths and rails to see the famous Blow Hole some thirty or forty meters below, the spray from it wetting their camera lenses.

Most of the tourists were Japs, lamented Kaniola. Like most Hawaiians, he had a lingering hatred of the Japanese and their attack on Pearl Harbor, which had killed many civilians as well as American enlisted personnel. Kaniola's grandfather had been a victim of that attack, and the stories surrounding that day were as fresh as yesterday's sea catch. Young Hawaiians and part-Hawaiians were taught to never forget the treachery of the Japanese, no matter how big the tip. It was confusing for Hawaiian boys and girls of mixed Japanese blood.

Nowadays Hawaii had become the Rio de Janeiro of the South Seas, playground of the wealthy Japanese who converged on the islands every year in greater and greater numbers. Newlywed Japanese couples actually married and honeymooned in the islands in order to save the enormous costs of a wedding back home, for if thcy married in Japan, they had to invite every single member of their far-flung, extended families on both sides. It was no dishonor, however, to elope to Hawaii. . . .

Of late, much of the property of the islands had fallen into the hands of wealthy Japanese business interests, replacing to a large degree the historically white economic choke-hold on the islands' wealth; at the same time, native Hawaiians owned little or nothing of lasting value in their own homeland, so disenfranchised had they become at the hands of the English and American *haoles* decades before. Still, like most Hawaiians, Kaniola preferred the Americans and British to the Japs. Through it all, few Hawaiian full-bloods were as happy as depicted in the tourist literature and *Birnbaum's Guide to Paradise*.

Many Hawaiians found solace in booze and forgetfulness; others worked hard to acquire Western paraphernalia to closely imitate the white man's ways, to become if not wealthy, at least capable of providing for their young in an ever more dangerous world. Still others found their native humor, dark and gritty at times, was the best medicine against Western progress, which had long since engulfed Oahu and the city of Honolulu, the Miami of the South Pacific, in particular.

Alan Kaniola had taken two years of college before enlisting in the police academy in an attempt to bring fortune to himself and his small family of five. Usually, he enjoyed the work and seldom had to use force against anyone, the uniform alone doing most of the talking for him. But Honolulu's crime rate rose steadily each year, now rivaling anything on the mainland. When necessary, he could deal with the toughest of the street element or the Pearl sailors on their own terms. He particularly liked arresting American sailors and Japanese tourists, but whenever he did so, he found himself admonished by his superiors for having too heavy a hand. It was likely this, along with his ancestry, that had kept him from making detective the month before.

"Much safer to arrest a Chinese or Japanese prostitute," he once told his father, who ran a small Hawaiian-language newspaper which was pro-native and pro-environmentalist. One of the last of its kind, the paper was called *The Ala Ohana,* The Pathway of the Extended Family. His old father was old-fashioned, and a dreamer, always with his face to the moon, thought Kaniola.

Alan flooded the lone vehicle before his patrol car with his searchlight and cautiously got from his car and inched toward the dark Buick with all due care. There appeared no one inside. Thom Hilani stepped briskly along the other side of the car and both men moved in silence.

At the same moment, each spied the bundle of oil-stained clothing in the rear seat. There were also multiple dark stains on a blanket in the front seat of the car. Hilani made as if to reach inside for the bloody bundle in the rear, the windows being wide open, but the more experienced cop halted him, lifting the garments in his own hands and smelling the coppery odor of the purple stain, realizing at once that it was blood so fresh that it wet his hand.

"Go back to your cycle, Thom, and call for backup. I think we may've caught the Trade Winds Killer."

"No shit, yeh, *auwe,* heh? Maybe, huh? Dis gonna make dem *okole*-holes at headquarters sit up, yeh, damn man!"

Thom always reverted back to the easy rhythms of pidgin English whenever there were no *haole* cops around to hear.

"Hurry, get help, Thom. This guy could be armed."

A blast rang out and Hilani's body hit the pavement so hard that Alan Kaniola heard his friend's skull crack. Kaniola searched for where the shot had come from, but saw only blackness all around, realizing that his own headlights made a perfect silhouette of himself. He dove for cover just as a second shot rang out.

He was unhit. If he could just get to his radio, call for assistance. The distance between the Buick and his radio car was too great. He had to think fast.

It figured that the killer was somewhere along the path to the Blow Hole, likely depositing his night's work, a body. What a place to dispose of it, the policeman thought. Damned clever bastard. He tried now to concentrate his night vision along the mouth of the path, and he began firing at what appeared to be the outline of a man. Another shot hit Kaniola in the right shoulder, the impact tearing his firearm from him. He lay helpless alongside the suspect vehicle, bleeding and weakened, clutching the blood-ied clothes he'd held in his left hand, pressing them into his wound, desperately trying not to pass out.

He heard the other man's footsteps nearing, and he saw from below the right fender of the Buick a pair of silver-tipped boots rounding the car. Kaniola had no feeling in his right hand, but he reached for the gun he kept strapped and hidden against his ankle anyway, guiding the hand like a stump. He could feel his strength draining with his blood. He felt his fingertips just reach the second gun when the man's boot came viciously down on his hand.

The killer stood over him, grinning, a jackal's laugh escaping him, the bastard's features dark and distorted by light and shadow. Kaniola met his dark, disturbing eyes, and in a flash of hope he imagined Thom getting up, taking aim, and killing the lunatic. Instead, a lightning flash occurred before Alan Kaniola's eyes, the flash of an enormous cane cutter, the huge blade sluicing easily through Kaniola's dark wide throat, painting it and his lapels with his blood.

The killer quickly tore Kelia's bloodied clothing from the dead cop's contorted fist and returned it, along with the big cane knife, to the safety of his car. There was no telling how many other cops were on their way, and so he hurriedly jumped into the car and wheeled out of the deserted parking lot, leaving the dead cops alone with their gods. He hadn't wanted it to come to this, but they shouldn't have pursued him here. They'd brought it on themselves, he reasoned.

He turned on the radio and found some soft Hawaiian traditional music, so soothing and real. He forgot about the incident with the policemen, and instead relived in his mind how he had made the girl suffer for what she had done.

The big sugar cane knife had been cruel and gigantic and shining against the light in her small black Hawaiian eyes. Now there was no light in those eyes, nothing left of her lithe little body, those creamy-skinned legs, or that mocking mouth, thanks to the sea.

Only a handful more to go, he silently reminded himself.

I will ransom them from the power of the grave;
I will redeem them from death. . . .

Hosea, 13:14

**Off the coast of Maui, below the ocean at Molokini
underwater crater, the following day . . .**

Schools of fat *kala* and *malolo* fish darted among the blue fire and
fan coral, and as Jessica extended a finger, the lovely, star-shaped
kihikihi slipped below the brilliant silver and golden-yellow coral,
which gleamed beneath the ocean in the refracted light in the
undersea forest. There were some six hundred and fifty different
varieties of fish in the Hawaiian waters, and Jessica believed she
had seen all of them this morning when she had dived from the
outrigger *Ku's Vision* into the famous Molokini crater just southwest of the Wailea coastline on the island of Maui. Here Jessica
Coran was scuba-diving with the local dive set, and her mind was
free, her body alive. It was the complete and utter feeling of
weightlessness and freedom from all things human that excited
her, along with the psychological distance from her normally grim

work as an FBI medical examiner, that she so needed and wanted. She had dived in the Bahamas, the Keys, Aruba, but there was nothing quite like diving amid a gentle old volcanic crater buried below the ocean to make one step out of oneself and realize the enormity of life on earth.

At the surface, a crescent-shaped tip of the crater formed Molokini Island; less than a mile in size, it was a marine sanctuary and a haven for divers. Nobody, not even the new Chief of Division IV, Paul Zanek, could touch her here. She'd even forgotten about Jack Westfall, a hardworking FBI grunt whom she'd begun to have strong feelings for just before he killed himself. Jack's last conversation with her had been a call for help which she had not heard.

"Ever been to the Smokeys?"

"Smokey Mountains?" she'd asked.

"Man can get lost in there; swallowed up."

"I get my kicks from hunting and diving, Jack, and when I can't get away, it's the firing range."

"I try to get there least once a year, to the mountains, I mean. . . ." he'd continued. "The bluest blues there."

"Take me next time," she'd dared him.

"Place swallows you whole. Got to know your way. People get lost in those mountains every year. Children mostly. They're like . . . swallowed up."

"I used to hunt all the time with my dad," she'd assured him. "I wouldn't get lost."

"I know the territory, Jess. And I'm telling you, anybody— *anybody*—can get lost in there."

He hadn't been talking about the damned mountains; he'd been talking about something darker, something scarier, but she hadn't heard. Then it was too late.

She had managed to forget about Jack Westfall and Chief Zanek and everyone else here, just allowing her eyes to intermingle with the world of light and dark below the planet, a world ruled by the same instinct for survival as that of the land animals; yet here even the struggle between hunter and prey for life and death took on softer, subtler hues.

She caught sight of the sentient spindly polyps, their full length searching for food and lodging among the coral. The rainbow of colors that extended from so many forms of sea life dazzled her.

Amid the brain coral and the fire-red coral, the fish sped,

dipped, rose and fell as if birds in flight, so at ease within their coral wood. A tubular, sleek trumpeter—a loner—swayed just above the bottom, so Jessica went down for a closer look. Near a bevy of sea fans an invisible flounder, buried in the sand, suddenly lifted and moved off, disturbed by the trumpetfish or her nearness, she could not tell. Like a leaf in an ocean wind, the flounder found a new home on the floor and bore into the sand and disappeared again.

A pair of sea turtles wafted into view, and she turned her attention on these playful creatures. They balleted about one another in perfect harmony, their movements synchronized like a pair of dolphins.

Jessica became part of the life of this new environment, allowing her body to be gently rocked in the ebb and flow of the surf as it spilled into and out of the crater reef.

The ocean here was a sunlit world even at forty feet below where the coral picked up the light and radiated a warm myriad of colors in return. The great crater, outlined in sunlight and shadow below her, seemed a cosmic symbol of life's unending cycle, a circle without beginning or end, and yet always there was a new beginning and a new end, ceaselessly and forever.

Maybe if Jack had been a scuba diver instead of a backpacker. Maybe if he'd not internalized so many of the unsolved cases of children disappearing. A world full of maybes waited for her on the surface.

The world caught up to Dr. Jessica Coran the moment she returned to her hotel room at the Wailea Elua Inn, where the desk clerk handed her a cryptic message that read:

Urgent. Call 1-555-1411

She recognized it as the local number for the FBI. She knew instinctively that something was up. She had purposefully avoided TVs and radios. She had no idea what the message might portend, but she guessed that Paul Zanek was somehow behind it.

She took her time in the shower and leisurely dried her hair, and then dressed in casual white slacks and a baby-blue pullover before calling. Zanek, the FBI, and the rest of the damned world could wait another hour. She still had several days left on her leave, so why couldn't they leave her the hell alone? Unless it wasn't Paul Zanek but Alan Rychman trying to locate her, to tell her that he was on a plane, on his way to her at this moment. Could it be?

Delight and dread chasing her, she finally made the call and was put on hold. She cursed and almost hung up before she heard a series of clicks. She was patched through to the main Federal Bureau of Investigation building on Oahu in Honolulu, a gruff voice breaking the long silence, announcing himself as Chief Inspector James Kenneth Parry.

Chief, she thought, impressed that the bureau chief should be calling. "So what can I do for you, Inspector Parry? You called me, remember?"

"We were informed of your presence in the islands some time ago, and when you failed to respond—"

"I just got your message today."

"Well, be that as it may, we'd given up on you."

"Good, then I'll get off and return to my peaceful and much needed R & R, if that's okay with you, Inspector."

"Two Honolulu cops were murdered last night," he said starkly.

She drew in a deep breath. "Reason or random?"

"It would appear random at first glance, but something tells us differently."

"Oh?"

"Radio dispatch had the two officers in pursuit of a suspicious vehicle. Both officers were shot outside their vehicles and tire marks indicate a third. Any rate, our most experienced forensics guy is in the hospital with a triple bypass, and when we began searching files and asking Washington for assistance, well, they came up with your name. Said you were nearby."

"But you just said you were leaving messages for me for days. Which is it, Inspector?" Zanek, she mentally muttered, angry that he'd put Parry onto her whereabouts.

"Sorry," he said. "I didn't make myself clear. I've been seeking your kind of assistance for a long time, Dr. Coran."

"Never mind," she said, inhaling deeply. "Look, it'll take me some time to get there. A two-hour drive to the airport on the other side of the island, and God knows what the flights are like, but with my badge, I suppose I can get aboard a plane for Oahu. Will you have someone meet me at the airport?"

"We can do better than that. We can have a plane at Kahului Airport when you arrive there."

"No, listen. I've got a return flight booked to Honolulu anyway and may's well use it. I won't be much longer and it'll save the taxpayers some jet fuel."

"If you like. Any rate, there'll be someone to meet you in Honolulu, and thanks, Dr. Coran."

"Meantime, no one's to touch the bodies. Understood?"

"They're at the morgue, under guard."

"See you when I arrive, then."

"I'm sorry for having to intrude on your vacation, Dr. Coran, but we've no one else to turn to."

"In all of Oahu and Honolulu? What about the Navy?"

"No one with your specialized expertise, Doctor, no."

"What about the state cops? They must have a good forensics man."

"We're trying to keep this in-house, as much as humanly possible."

"I see."

She thought him a bit cryptic until he said, "And cop-killers piss me off big time."

"Ditto to that much. See you then, likely at dawn sometime."

She was about to hang up when he added, "We've another problem plaguing the city and the island here you may've heard about?"

"No, I haven't heard anything. I've shut down: no TV, no radio, no newspapers . . . mostly just diving and shopping and tuning out."

"Well, Doctor, we've had a couple of unusual disappearances."

"Disappearances? What kind of disappearances? You mean children?"

"You might say . . . some were no older than children."

"Girls?"

"Local press is calling him the Trade Winds Abductor. Although nobody believes he's collecting them, so some have concluded that he's actually the Trade Winds Killer."

"Impossible to keep such news secretive, even for the purposes of an investigation, I know."

"It happened like this before, same way. Strange thing is, we've not recovered a single body."

"Then you don't know for certain that they are in fact dead, and even if you caught the guy, you'd need some damned strong circumstantial evidence to indict without a body."

He fell silent long enough for her to realize that she'd just told him all that he already knew.

"I think it's safe to assume that the missing in this case are also dead, Doctor. Any rate, this man is extremely thorough. Leaves no trace of himself or his victims, for that matter, whatever . . . until recently."

"Then you've got something to work with, good."

"We think that Hilani and Kaniola's deaths may be related."

"Your two cops? What makes you think so?"

"I'd rather not say on an open line."

"All right, understood. So, what's this until recently he's left not a clue? You've got something on him?"

"As I said before, I'd rather not discuss sensitive information over an unsecured line, Dr. Coran."

A little paranoid, are we, she thought. "Soon then, Inspector Parry."

Island-hopping was tedious, and lugging baggage and the hours spent traveling instead of enjoying the precious hours of vacation weren't her idea of fun, but then she was no longer on vacation. It was only fortunate that she loved to fly and the old birds of Aloha Airlines, like the 737 Jessica was now aboard, rattled and bounced in the updrafts so much that you knew—at all times—that you were flying. Parry's jet was likely a Lear, and while she enjoyed them for what they were, she much preferred something closer to a barn-burner ride than the feeling of being a well-sealed canned ham inside a Greyhound bus in the sky.

The plane came in low over Oahu from the east, the same pattern she imagined Japanese bombers used to strafe Schofield Barracks and Pearl Harbor. Long before finding the patchwork that was Pearl Harbor with its rows of naval ships so far below, she had seen the enormous, sprawling city of Honolulu, lush with the most opulent of high-rise hotels fronting the beaches. She saw miniature surfboards, yachts and sailboats off the Waikiki shoreline. Diamond Head looked from this straight-over angle no more special than any of the other mountain craters; there were huge mountain ranges on two sides of the island, its center a lush, tropical valley, like that on Maui, the prime land upon which all Western investment had been heaped.

Two million years before Oahu had become the pearl of the Pacific, playground to the world's millionaires, it had been two separate islands focused on the Koolau volcano in the east and the Waianae volcano in the west. Now these two turbulent volcanos were serene mountain ranges, known only to U.S. forestry officials, a handful of hikers, a few soldiers and air personnel engaged in military maneuvers, and maybe the Trade Winds Killer.

Like all of the Hawaiian islands, Oahu had been settled over a thousand years before by the Marquesans, who sailed the Pacific in huge outrigger canoes fitted with thatch rooftops. Tahitian immigrants followed, and as they mingled with the Marquesans, a distinct Hawaiian culture with its own language, traditions and ritual emerged.

As in all cultures there evolved gods of darkness who controlled much of village life and death. There was a complicated system of *kapus* or taboos, with intricately fashioned *kahillis*—made of bamboo poles with circular featherwork at the top, carried by bearers on special occasions—and elaborate leis whose design symbolized strict divisions in society, just as the elegant, feathered headdresses of the Ali'i, or royalty, symbolized the monarchy of each island. There was continual warfare between and among the islanders, skirmishes and human sacrifices, as the various chiefs sought to extend their power.

Since arriving in the islands, Jessica had learned much of the rich history, which was forever touted as colorful and splendid, spoken of by the bus driver, the porter and the waiter as well as the tour guides. She'd learned that in the 18th century, King Kamehameha, a chief from the big island of Hawaii, began an ambitious campaign to conquer all of the islands. He took Oahu in 1795 in one of the last and bloodiest of battles. All along, the king had been conducting a healthy business in firearms with Western ships arriving in Hawaii. Gunpowder and flintlocks were the King's new black magic.

When the islands were consolidated, the traders discovered a wealthy bounty in Honolulu Bay, the largest deepwater harbor in the islands. Ships began to arrive from all over the world, particularly Europe and America, and by 1820 New England missionaries were disembarking, eager to civilize and convert the native population to Christianity. Soon after came the great whaling ships, filled with randy, roughish seamen. By 1840 King Kamehameha III decreed that Honolulu on Oahu—*the gathering place*—would be the permanent residence of the up-till-then-nomadic royal court.

It was not long before Hawaiian women of nobility were wearing bustles, and the men were sporting epaulets. Palaces and summer retreats, the size of Georgia mansions, were built in the humid island capital. On the greens these same Hawaiians played cricket and held musical soirees.

As with all such pasts, time had erased everything but a few passing evidences of that life, so that Honolulu today was virtuous in a much different fashion. It looked for all the world to be Miami, Florida, if you could ignore the sweeping grandeur of the volcanic mountain ranges rimming it while the plane swept around the island and found the pattern, facing due east now, having come a full 180 degrees about. They were on final approach.

Jessica's ankles throbbed with the sudden drop of the plane, the sensation reminding her of the scars to her ankles, each Achilles heel having been severed by a maniacal killer she'd come here to forget. For a year now she'd had to use a cane, but thanks to remarkable reconstructive surgery, she leaned less and less on the damned inhibiting thing. In fact, secretly she believed it time to lose the cane.

Still, she carried it along with her on the trip as something of a crutch, expecting the old wounds to flare. Besides, she'd become somewhat attached to the cane, knowing that it kept men at bay, giving her an extra edge when coming into a new situation, like today. The cane gave her a more doctorly look, and it most certainly made her feel more like what people had come to expect, having learned of her accomplishments in previous serial killer cases, most of them looking for someone who might appear psychic, which she certainly was not. And not that she needed a crutch, she assured herself, but otherwise people looked at her and they saw only the superficial: a tall thin woman with flowing auburn hair and an hourglass figure, instead of an expert medical examiner whose victories with the FBI had already gone into the academy casebook files. Besides, the cane had become something of a comfort and a friend; it'd taken on a character of its own, and after all, it had been a gift from all those who appreciated her most, back at the crime lab in Quantico.

The plane landed with several shuddering bounces, a near-constant surge of wind over the runways here, but they were soon taxiing rather brusquely toward the terminal. Jessica waited for all the other passengers to deplane before she got up and started for the exit.

She wondered what King Kamehameha would've thought of air travel. Just as she got to the exit, lugging her carry-on and tapping her cane, the pilot stepped from his cockpit and offered her a warm smile and an apology.

"Sorry for the rough landing."

"Don't be silly," she replied. "I loved every second of it."

The pilot watched her go out of sight along the ramp, wondering about her and her cane.

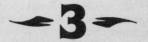

There is no more trusting in women.

Homer, *The Odyssey*

The Honolulu Airport was enormous and bustling, filled with travelers from all parts of the globe, giving credence to Hawaii's reputation as the Midway of the Pacific. Save for the leis being placed around tourists arriving from the mainland and the many *"alohas"* all about her, she might have been in a terminal in O'Hare Airport in Chicago, but a single glance at the window and the towering, cascading, green mountains reminded her of the island paradise outside. A large corridor of the terminal which she now passed was also open-air, so that the traveler passed outdoors in order to locate the baggage-claim area. It was a delightful airport for this reason. She passed a McDonald's along the way, and was wondering if she had time for a quick bite when she heard a male voice shout her name.

"Dr. Coran! Dr. Jessica Coran?"

She turned, expecting to find Bureau Chief Jim Parry in suit and tie. Her caller instead wore a flowered Hawaiian shirt, his face a deep ochre, his features those of a Hawaiian national creased with worry lines which seemed uncharacteristic of the race as a whole from what she'd seen on Maui.

"My name is Joseph Kaniola. My son was killed along with Officer Hilani."

"How did you know I—"

"I'm a newsman. It's my job to know. What I wanna know now is, are you gonna get the bastard who killed my boy, Alan, and left my grandchildren without a father?"

"I'll do everything in my power," she said, gripping her cane more tightly.

"From what I hear, that's a lot; that's all I ask."

"Kaniola!" shouted a second man, recognizing the bereaved father. "I told you to let us do our job." The more officious-looking man with suit and tie stuck his hand out to Jessica and firmly shook hers. "I'm Parry."

"Well, Inspector, so we meet."

"Parry," interrupted Kaniola, "you promise you won't let the Honolulu cops dust this under the rug?"

"Not a chance, Mr. Kaniola. Now, please, allow us the time and space we need to get under way."

"My boy was onto something up there at Koko Head. He was a smart boy, and he wasn't involved in no drugs like some are saying."

"We know your views, Mr. Kaniola . . . now, please." Parry, with a slight movement of his eyes, had two men intervene and usher Kaniola away. The aged Hawaiian's protests fell on deaf ears save for a few curious onlookers passing by.

"I'm not—goddamn you—here as a newsman! I'm here as a father!"

"He's hardly had time to get over the shock, I'm sure," she said to Parry.

"I'd like to hold his hand longer, but who's got the time? Besides, we need to talk privately."

She glanced around. "What'd you have in mind?"

He ushered her into an area marked private where a number of airline stewardesses were having coffee and chatting. He flashed his badge and asked them to give him the room, and they complied with only a few veiled looks and mutterings.

"We got some political problems here, like any big city. I just want you to know about the kind of pressure we're getting and will continue to get from the *kanakas*."

"*Kanakas?* The Hawaiians, you mean?"

"They've become quite vocal about the double standard they perceive—"

"Perceive?"

"—by which the cops here operate, one for whites, another for any other or mixed race, and now with two Hawaiian cops shot down in cold blood . . . Well, all hell's ready to break, and Kaniola's paper's right in the thick of the argument. Always has been."

"County and state mirror this same public image as the Honolulu Police Department?"

"To some degree, 'fraid so."

She assessed Inspector James Parry, a tall, sand-and-buff-haired man who'd somehow maintained his light features in this sun-bathed world. She guessed that he had been bureau chief only a short time because he was still doing things for himself, such as coming to fetch her. He was handsome in a Norse kind of way, clean-shaven, only a loosened tie left unattended, and his charismatic smile, which only fleetingly showed, might be enticing if there was more of it, and if the stakes here were different.

He pulled from his pocket a series of photos and spread them across a table. They were shots of young native island women, all smiling up brightly at the camera, all vivacious and squinting against the sun rays or the flashbulb. Each had dark, lovely features, frosty white teeth, smooth, tanned skin. One looked as healthy and carefree as the next. Any one of them might be a poster girl for Enoa or any of a dozen other Hawaiian tour companies. There were some nine photos in all.

"Seven disappeared last year without a trace and then the disappearances just stopped. None of them have ever been located, until now."

"So there've been two this year?"

"Yeah, with the return of the trade winds, 'fraid so."

"But you've located one of the bodies, yes?"

"Well, not entirely, no."

"What do you mean, not entirely?"

"We have a . . . a piece, a limb . . ."

"And"—she took a deep breath—"just what part of the body do you have?"

"Most of an arm."

"Most of an arm?" she repeated.

"Missing the hand at the wrist."

"So you naturally thought of me," she weakly joked.

He chewed on the inside of his cheek and lowered his eyes to her cane. "I've been trying to get D.C. to send someone like you out here for a long time, but since we had no physical evidence till now, well, your superiors reluctantly declined."

She scratched her forehead, snatched her cane and stood to pace. "Pacing helps me think. Where was the limb found?"

"The Blow Hole."

"Say again?"

"It's a popular tourist attraction, temporarily closed since the find."

"Blow Hole?" she repeated.

He explained the term and the location. "And it was at this site that Hilani and Kaniola's bodies were also discovered."

"Who made the discovery?"

"Couple of kids who drove up there to park and spark, same night. They reported seeing a car squeal off in the opposite direction, heading toward the city. They weren't paying attention to the tag, nothing distinguishing about the vehicle. Saw the two uniformed men under the lights of Kaniola's patrol car."

"Both dead at the scene?"

"Yeah."

"And the arm? These kids find it, too?"

"No, that came later."

Something in his tone revealed everything to her.

"I see. You found it . . . during a search of the area?"

He hesitated. "We fanned out. There was not a trace except for the tire marks that we photo'd. My men combed the area around. I went down along the path toward the Blow Hole. I was thinking this guy wasn't about to leave us a single trace, zip."

"Then you saw it?"

"No, it wasn't on the rocks. I looked down at that exact spot, saw nothing but the geyser, and then I walked back up. I was giving thought to the idea the killer was dumping here, but could tell nothing."

"Then who discovered the limb?"

"It was almost eight by then, and so we cleared out and allowed the first tourist buses to enter the park area."

"I see."

"Tourists—biggest business on the island, you know, and well, when they went to watch the Blow Hole do its thing . . . well, you can imagine the rest."

"The piece came spewing up?"

"That's about it. Landed on the rocks alongside. We had to rig up a safety line and get a rock climber to go down on that slippery surface after it."

"So the rest of the body, and likely all the others, could well be buried in that cavernous area below the sea at the Blow Hole?"

"Likely pulverized to Jell-O by now, but we got lucky this once."

She pointed to the photos. "So which of the girls is the most recent disappearance?"

"That's not the way it works; you're supposed to tell *me* who's on first, remember? I'll provide you with files on each of the women, you match the limb from there, if you can. Wouldn't want to influence your decision. Wouldn't look good in a court of law, and we are going to get this bastard before a court of law— whatever his nationality or color."

"What're you saying, that the crimes are somehow related to the social climate hereabouts? That our killer's involved in hate crimes?"

"What do I know? Social climate, maybe. Physical climate, most certainly. April to August last year with the coming of the trades. As far as that hate-crimes thing . . . I never understood that redundancy, Doctor. Aren't all crimes crimes of hate?"

"I suppose you're right, but I meant racially motivated as opposed to sexually motivated or due to some hatred of the gender."

"We don't know," he said simply, staring her in the eye. "Right now, all we've got is the arm, two dead Hawaiian cops, and nine missing Hawaiian girls, some of mixed blood, some Japanese. And we've got an island of jumpy people and the rumor mills are grinding daily along with the newspapers."

"So you want the investigation to remain tightly controlled. I understand, Inspector."

"I've been here for eight years, two as bureau chief, and I'll be honest with you, Doctor, I don't begin to understand the Polynesian or the Oriental mind, except to say that they respect and understand cold, logical justice, an eye for an eye, so to speak. Well, nine of their women have vanished, and now two of their boys are dead, and so they want justice, and they look to the sailors at Pearl, and they look to the high muckety-mucks on Diamond Head who've pretty well made a fortune a thousand-forty times over by parlaying their lands out from under them, and they look to us white cops for reasons and pretty soon, they'll be looking in the same direction for *compensation*."

"You got someone who can get my bags over to the Rainbow Tower?"

"Sure."

"If so, I'll go with you to have a look at the corpses and the girl's limb. Meanwhile, what're the chances of getting divers into the water and searching the area around this Blow Hole for more body parts?"

His laugh was without mirth, the laugh of an islander who is trying desperately to understand the logic of a *malahini,* a newcomer. "Any attempt to go near the Blow Hole could pulverize a diver in seconds. It's a vortex of water, the speeds of which have been clocked at hundreds of miles per hour, and it never calms. There's no way to dredge a volcanic hole in the sea like this one. It was dumb luck we got to the one gift before it was washed back inside."

"So there's little chance this hole'll be giving up any more such evidence?"

"Seriously doubtful. Still, we're maintaining the safety tows and I've got a man out there watching for just that."

"And he's also lying in wait for a possible return visit by the killer?"

"I've got tag teams out there, yeah, but since he left the two dead cops, we're not very hopeful of his return."

"Then get me to your morgue. I'll see what I can do to shed some light."

"That's all we ask."

On the way over to the morgue she assessed Parry. He was as tall as she, with firm-set features and piercing eyes. His facial expression gave little away, however, no doubt from years of dealing with press and public on sensitive cases. None more sensitive than this, the most delicate of all kinds: a mass murderer about whom the authorities had next to no idea.

Later that same day

Thom Hilani had been shot through the back of the head, the bullet entering at the base of the skull, indicated by a clean, round little hole, and exploding outward at the point of exit, leaving a five-inch circumference between the eyes, the epicenter of the outward explosion making mush of the soft tissues of both the frontal lobe and the man's eyes. He'd died instantly on impact, the large abrasion to his upper forehead and skull an obvious sign that he'd fallen like a tree onto the pavement there at the promontory overlooking Hanauma Bay. At least he'd not suffered.

Jessica's trained eye told her that the killer knew something about marksmanship and ammo, that he'd intentionally used what was termed on the streets as a "cop-killer" cartridge in a cowboy's gun, a .44 or a .45-caliber weapon.

A thorough autopsy offered absolutely nothing more, other than what Officer Hilani had had that evening for dinner on his night watch.

Kaniola was a different story. He'd been shot but not mortally, and a hidden "throwaway" gun was still in its secret holster tied about his ankle. Parry had promised that absolutely nothing had been disturbed about the body of either man, and perhaps he could be taken at his word. It was unusual, however, that other cops, friends, hadn't seen fit to discreetly remove the illegal "throw-down" weapon which cops used whenever they might find themselves in a situation requiring them to quickly place a weapon at the side of an assailant to warrant the use of deadly force; the second gun was also seen as backup on the street, should a cop lose control of his service revolver.

It appeared from the trajectory of the bullet, which ripped through Kaniola's upper right shoulder, bursting forth near the left shoulder blade, that he would have had a difficult time unholstering the second firearm, and if he had reached it, it might have been impossible for him to apply the pressure necessary to fire it.

The killing wound sustained by Kaniola had come as the result of an enormous blade that had cut an entire swatch of throat from him, severing the jugular and very nearly the head. Without instruments, Jessica gauged the blade to be between two-and-a-half and three inches in width, making the weapon something along the order of a sword or machete.

She presented the picture of science now in her white lab coat, her hair tied tightly back. She clicked on the overhead tape recorder and announced the time and date of the autopsy, the name of the deceased and his morgue identification number, followed by her own name before beginning the autopsy on Joe Kaniola's son.

Momentary flashes of Kaniola's father entered into her thoughts as she worked: the man's leathery face, the folds of his skin like aged crinoline, the rugged wrinkles like caulk lines on an ancient vessel. She imagined him in his late fifties. Most likely he'd worked tirelessly his entire life to better the lives of his children, and now one of them had come under her grim care. Despite what Parry said to her or the senior Kaniola, she had the distinct impression she would see the tough newsman again.

She continued to meticulously probe now the two major wounds to Kaniola's body. No longer eyeballing it, but taking precise measurements, keeping log on it for anyone who might follow up or relieve her of this onerous case, she began to wonder how long the assailant stood over the uniformed officer, delighting in his helplessness, before sending the pendulum of death across his throat. She wondered if the killer had taken unusual delight in watching the man then convulse in shock and bleed to death. Or did he only take such pleasure with the women whom Parry suspected of being his victims of choice?

She had yet to do the internal on Kaniola, a big, strapping, proud-looking man, taller than his father. But she first went to his hands, as she had done with Hilani, to explore the possibility of skin fragments or hair below the nails, which would indicate that he had scuffled with his killer, reached up and tore at him. Kaniola's left hand was caked with dark blood, his own, she assumed.

Describing this finding, she spoke aloud for the sensitive microphone overhead as she worked.

"Left hand is bloodied; blood may be assumed to be that of Officer Kaniola's, as he likely would instinctively reach up to his wounded shoulder."

As she said these words, she heard her father's voice at the back of her head. "When you assume, you make an *ass* of *u* and *me*." Her father had been the best medical examiner to ever grace a military uniform, and he'd constantly warned her that many an M.E.'s hard-won career had gone the way of the toilet on the basis of a hasty assumption, that assumptions were for the public and floundering gumshoes.

Suppose the blood covering Kaniola's left hand was that of Kaniola's killer. Suppose he had also been injured in the gun battle. It was a big leap, but only the microscopes could prove it was Kaniola's blood alone on his palm. So far this killer—if it was Parry's Trade Winds Killer—had left not so much as a molecule of evidence to incriminate himself. She could dazzle Parry instantly if Kaniola had got one hand on the monster who'd murdered him.

Most likely, however, it was the officer's own blood on his hands. Still, Jessica quickly amended her remarks for the record by adding, "By the same token, if the assailant were injured, then the blood on Officer Kaniola's hand could belong to the assailant."

She took scrapings for the microscope of both the blood and the matter below the nails, hopeful it would not all be for nothing, realizing once more in her state of fatigue that her father would say, "Thoroughness is its own reward."

She now arched her long legs and back, yawning over the slab, stretching, feeling too tired to go on. Her assistant, a man named Dr. Elwood Warner, was several years her junior, a pathologist with Honolulu General on call for the state; a second pathologist for the county had also turned up somewhat late, and apologized, asking Warner to duplicate any samples he'd be taking for him. This fellow, Dr. Walter Marshal, was also affiliated somehow with the military at Pearl Harbor, the military having taken a decided interest in the case of the two dead Hawaiian cops—"boys" Marshal had called them. He was particularly interested in the blood samples, obviously convinced that the two cops were involved in drugs and anxious to prove it so, thereby extinguishing any future *kanaka* complaints coming out of the community about Pearl sailor involvement in the deaths.

It was obvious that Marshal and the Pearl brass wanted to tell the community that the two cops had flirted with a cobra and that the cobra had bitten them; *no one's fault but their own.* It seemed neither the military, the state nor local cops knew as much as Parry, and that perhaps Parry was alone in his suspicion that the dead cops and the missing "prostitutes" as she'd heard them called were connected.

But the big discovery at the Blow Hole had some people hanging closely onto Parry's shirttail now, not to mention hers.

The Honolulu City Medical Examiner, Dr. Harold Shore, had routinely stepped in as M.E. of record for FBI cases when called to do so here on Oahu, and he had a fine reputation; however, he'd recently undergone open-heart surgery and wasn't expected back soon. Jessica, in effect, was standing in for Shore. If he could drag himself from his bed, no doubt, Shore would have been on hand today as well, to represent the city and the HPD. The deaths of the two cops had stirred up a lot of agencies, opened a hornet's nest of festering wounds and reminded people here of hurts both real and imagined.

"If you're too tired to go on, Dr. Coran," said Dr. Marshal, "I should be happy to take over for you."

Jessica's eyes were instantly boring into Marshal, but below her mask she gave him an easy smile. "I'm fine, Doctor, and I'll finish."

"Two autopsies? In a single day? Seems grueling even by military standards, Doctor. As professionals, I think we can all recognize that?"

She recognized militarese when she heard it. Marshal liked being in command, and he no doubt felt ill at ease playing second fiddle to a female M.E. "Yes, well . . . just the same, as the representative of the Federal Government here, I think I'd best continue as lead here, if you don't mind."

"We both work for the same boss, Doctor," he replied coolly. "And with Dr. Shore unable to be in attendance, I'm also here on behalf of the Honolulu Police Department."

Marshal seemed like a man who might have walked out of a thirties film with William Powell and ZaSu Pitts. He never let an expression cross his face, and the military bearing with which he presented himself didn't necessitate a uniform. The military showed right through his white gown.

"You obviously wear a lot of hats here, Dr. Marshal."

She continued with the scalpel in her hand.

Warner, the junior here by comparison, seemed a boy, anxious to be done so that he might return to a date on the beach where he'd spiked and left his surfboard; Jessica even pictured him in a bathing suit, stretched out with a buxom friend. A pair of dark glasses dangled around his neck even in here. *Moon-doggy,* she thought.

It always annoyed her that everyone at an autopsy wanted more than just a "piece" of the corpse, that each man in particular had to jockey for a position of authority over the deceased. She remembered a similar scene two years before in a small Midwestern city where an exhumation had caused every petty official in the state of Iowa to jump. The exhumation had moved her closer to catching a killer who collected human blood the way a vampire bat might, but this killer here in Hawaii was quite a different breed. He didn't collect blood, but rather marveled in spilling it, bathing in it as it cascaded from the bodies of his victims, if Kaniola's corpse was anything to go by. She imagined the so-called Trade Winds Killer using his enormous knife like a deadly phallus against his female victims.

She continued with the autopsy, making the familiar Y-section cut to the chest and abdomen, laying bare the viscera, and with Warner's help they lifted the organ tree whole and intact, leaving the carcass hollow. The eerie silence was quick to fill the void of inner space left by the awful dredging of the body, leaving the room even more deafeningly still than before. Only Jessica's voice seemed strong enough to overcome the silence.

It was some hours later before she saw the dismembered limb that had frightened tourists at the Blow Hole. Parry had met her when she'd exited the autopsy room, her neck and shoulders giving way to great pain now, so intense had been the work. "You might've told me about Marshal."

"Thought I'd let you two get on on your own."

"We managed, but just barely. What an ass. I take it you haven't informed him about the girl's arm."

"Did I say it was a girl's arm?"

"I . . . assumed after showering me with those pictures . . ."

"In answer to your question, at this point I saw no reason to involve anyone else, particularly Marshal."

"What story'd you circulate for the tourists? That it was a prank? A mannequin, maybe?"

"Alert of you to guess."

"Problem is I'm far from alert now to do much good here. I'll take a quick glance at the body part, but I'll have to beg off till tomorrow."

"Deal."

"Mamma said there'd be days like this."

He lightly chuckled. "Mamma was a smart lady, too?"

"Actually, it was my father who said there'd be days like this. He was an M.E., too. Mother died when I was fairly young. Daddy raised me on his own after that, never remarrying."

"Find anything of interest in there with Hilani or Kaniola?"

"Early to tell; now we run tests. I hope you've got good lab people."

"The best. Don't worry there."

They entered a laboratory where a few white-coated techs greeted Parry with broad smiles. One or two faces were distinctly Polynesian.

"Mr. Lau," called Parry, "this is Dr. Coran, from Quantico, Virginia."

"Ohhhh," said Lau, coming quickly to her and taking her hand. "I have read much about you, Doctor. Extremely impressive, extremely. I tol' Parry, we need somewon like you."

"How about someone exactly like her, Lau? How about her?"

"That's what I mean."

Parry laughed good-naturedly. "So, where's the muttonchop, Lau?"

"In safekeeping, this way."

He led them to a refrigeration chamber and pressed a button, and a drawer eased outward sending a cascade of smoke as the super-cooled air hit room temperature. Below the cloud of cold a thick glass container held the object of Parry's concentration. Jessica, too, stared at the lone, thin, pathetic shoulder, elbow and forearm. The fact that the hand was missing only added to the gruesome object. It was a mangled hunk of flesh, pounded, bruised, blue not simply from the cold but from dark patches where it had been battered, parts of bone showing through.

"Tomorrow, I want you to determine the age, sex, height, race, time of death—and anything else you can decipher from that, Dr. Coran."

She gave Lau a look that told him he could close it up, and the short, stocky young man did so, a sad look in his black but radiant eyes. She saw that Parry was staring at her, and this made her a little uncomfortable. What did he want from her, a magic act? To make immediate pronouncements about the body part in the freezer?

She caught a glimpse of Lau telling the other technicians who she was. Lau was in charge of the techs, the equipment and the lab in general, and it was to him that the techs had brought the various test materials from the adjoining autopsy room, each labeled in Jessica's meticulous hand.

"Tomorrow, then," she croaked. "Meantime, Lau and the others here can work on the slides and samples taken from the police officers."

"Well, so far, so good," Parry said. "Allow me to see you to your hotel."

"Thanks, but I'm sure you have more important things to attend to."

"Right now, Doctor, you're the most important thing on the island. We're very aware of your track record, what you did last year in New York City in the Claw case, and the time before that . . . that sicko vampire in Chicago."

His eyes had come to rest on her cane. "We're hoping you'll *stick* it to this guy, the way you did those others."

"Don't get your hopes up. I don't think I found anything useful today, and I'm not sure that muttonchop as you call it in there belongs to any of your missing girls."

He nodded, biting his lip before presenting her with nine manila folders. "Homework," he said, shrugging apologetically.

"How soon you want these back?"

"They're duplicates, so no sweat."

"Have you had a profile of your supposed serial killer drawn up?"

"It's included, but I'm not so sure I trust it entirely."

"Don't trust your own profile team?" She halted and stared at him for a direct answer.

He cleared his throat and said firmly, "There's no team on it. *Ahhh,* just me."

"You're kidding."

"Wish I were. We've been understaffed and well . . . see, to date, it's been of low priority for the bureau. Back burner all the way. I haven't got D.C.'s backing, only a nod from your pal, Zanek, to pursue it."

"Paul Zanek," she said aloud. Thinks he'll put me back to work, take my mind off myself. "Indeed a pal." Her sarcasm, not meant to escape, had bolted free.

"We've just had so damned little to go on—"

"And since no one but the *kanakas* were missing women," she interrupted.

"Whoa up there! Hold on. We just didn't have the facts or the manpower to move on it. You trying to tell me it's different in D.C.?"

She bit her lip and nodded. "Touché."

He walked along with her. "Just look over what I've managed to scrounge up on my own and you tell me . . ."

"Tell you what?"

"If I'm on or off the mark here."

"I'll look it over."

"My car's in the garage. Come on," he said. "I'll see you to your home away from home."

"If you insist," she replied, making as if to take the folders from him, but Parry insisted on carrying the hefty load for her.

"So who amassed all these files then?"

"Agent Gagliano—Tony and myself—with the help of the HPD missing persons bureau of course."

"For back burner, you've been working pretty hard. HPD looking the other way on this?"

"Some might say so."

She nodded. "What do you say?"

"You wouldn't know it to look at Honolulu from the standpoint of a tourist, Dr. Coran, but it's teeming with lowlife, crime's rampant, drugs everywhere. We've got our ghetto wars, poverty, ignorance, beastiality, our brain-dead, our wanna-be victims, just like Baltimore or New Orleans or a thousand other American cities."

"*Paradise Lost* comes to mind."

"Exactly so, Doctor."

"A place of such beauty and opulence—"

"So's New York, L.A., Chicago or D.C. if you don't have to look at it from a radio car or through the eyes of a ghetto kid. Like all cities, there's two faces to Honolulu. There's the glittering coastal palaces along Diamond Head and Waikiki, sure, but there's also the seamy side."

" 'Look under any yacht and whataya got?' my father used to say. 'Slime and barnacles.' "

"Sounds like a sensible, practical person, like yourself?" Parry ventured, but then he quickly returned to the subject. "Yeah, it would be a paradise, these islands, if it weren't for the people."

Parry's tone spoke of a deep wound, she imagined, but he quickly squelched any further words, indicating the direction they had to take along a final corridor, and then to his unmarked Ford LTD, where they got in without another word. He quickly busied himself with seat belt and radio, tapping into the system and reporting into FBI Dispatch, informing them of his whereabouts and movements.

Jessica stared across at him, studying him without his knowledge, wondering about James Kenneth Parry, his past and his current dreams.

4

Dark Care sits enthroned behind the Knight.

Horace, *Odes*

"So, where's home, James Parry?" she asked as they bullied their way through the thickening afternoon soup of traffic in downtown Honolulu.

"Grew up in West Bend, Indiana. Most of the family's still there, 'cept for my brothers and a sister. All of us wanted bigger 'n' better and far away. West Bend was great as kids, but as we got older, it turned into the pits."

"It would appear you won."

"Won?" He was puzzled.

"You don't get much farther away than this."

"Actually, I've got a brother who lives in Auckland, New Zealand, and my sister's in Tokyo!"

She laughed. "Wrong again."

"Hey, look, I'm sorry if we've made you feel as if you're, well, on trial here. We just . . . we don't have anywhere to turn. We're used to dealing with white-collar crime, street crime, rape, even murder, but this . . . this is different . . . something bizarre about this whole thing, something . . . I don't know . . . can't finger it . . ."

"Something ritualistic, maybe?"

He stared across at her. "Funny you should use that term."

"Why's that?"

"Just that it occurred to me and Tony on separate occasions. I think there's a connection between the victims, something ritualistic, patternistic."

"Sounds like you two've given up a few nights' sleep over it. When do I meet Tony?"

"Tomorrow, and damned straight we've lost sleep." He fell silent for a time before opening up again. "I figure it this way. Seven disappearances last year over a three-month period. Here it is July again, the trades are peaking, and two already missing, two that we know of . . . and I expect there'll be five more before season's end."

"That what you mean by ritualistic? A killing season, you figure?"

"Like he's gone and bought his license, yeah."

"I've heard of slave rings operating out of this part of the world. You sure these girls just didn't fall prey to various methods of shanghaiing? With no bodies turning up, it's got to be a possibility."

"We've scoured the wharves. Shaken out spiders 'n' lizards 'n' rats, sure, but it doesn't play that way, Doctor."

They arrived at the beautiful Rainbow Tower in the Hilton Hawaii Village in Waikiki, and Parry drove into the winding circle drive, dropping her at the door. "Listen," he said, his voice taking on a near-conspiratorial tone, which was both curious and pushy at once, "if you need an escort, someone to have dinner with . . . well, give me a call at either of these numbers." He handed her his card and sped off.

Her eyes took in the heady, exciting capital city of Hawaii, the seemingly unreal mountain faces carpeted with lush, dense green, reminding her of a visit to Ireland only on the sunniest of days there. Pivoting to her west, she could see the deep azure blue of the Pacific peeking from between the skyscrapers, and she felt the firm touch of the trade winds as they swept over her skin. The winds were so strong that she imagined it would be easy to lift her arms and fly off to wherever winds ran away to.

She felt an urge to rush out to the sand and surf of the beaches here, a desire to return to the sea from which Parry had plucked her, to run from the city, from Parry, from the FBI and her responsibilities here in Oahu. Why not, she desperately wondered. Hadn't her shrink told her that quitting the FBI was one option she could exercise? That such a change in her lifestyle might help quell her bouts with depression and fear?

But her father didn't raise a quitter, so instead she marched briskly into the hotel where she was immediately caught up amid the bustle of tourists both coming and going. She wasn't surprised when, asking for her key at the desk, she was informed of several messages from the mainland—from Quantico, Virginia.

Maybe later she'd get down to the pool, try out that new bathing suit she'd found in that little shop in Lahaina, Maui . . . maybe . . .

Somewhere in Honolulu the same night

He shuffles around his place where the furniture is ancient and large and heavy, the end tables made of old crates used to haul grocery items, crates he once thought to turn into rough-hewn works of art, except that the stain had gone too dark and he never could get the polish to take effectively. The lamps are likewise homemade, built of sturdy wood he's gotten for nothing, scrap parts at the mill. The old canvas-covered couch nestles between two enormous lamps carved with the faces of Hawaiian gods, lamps that seldom see use since he is adverse to the light. The floors are gummy with dirt and filth, blood and other seminal matter. He isn't much of a housekeeper and part of the stickiness and the stench is endemic now, ground into the floors, particularly one corner caked with blood.

He is antsy, angry with himself and with circumstances. For so long now he has gone undetected, his work known only to the dark lords of the islands. But now everyone in Honolulu is either reading of, or listening to, news reports on their TVs about his latest work, the killing of two local cops, both Hawaiian—as bad luck would have it. This means an uproar that isn't likely to soon die away. The only hope he has is that someone else might be arrested for the crimes. Local police are now hinting that arrests are forthcoming.

He enjoys learning about the politicizing of his crimes, the furor he has caused between the races. Still, not a word about the disappearance of his latest Kelia. He's read one or two items about the so-called Trade Winds Killer, a phantom stalker on the islands between April and August, but to date nothing has linked him to the crimes, and police have not recovered one shred of evidence to prove the murders have actually taken place. They can only point to "disappearances." So long as they find no bodies, he reasons, they can never find nor prosecute him, even if they know! With the lack of physical evidence and eyewitnesses, nothing whatever to link him—or anyone, for that matter—with the deaths, a U.S. court of law would not dare touch such a case. God bless the Blow Hole and the U.S.A.

Policemen, a white guy and a Samoan, spoke to him once, for a statement, when they were canvassing the district for any possible witnesses to a killing he'd committed the year before, but they never returned.

They still don't know how he does it, or the kind of weapon he uses on his victims. He means not to make the mistakes of other killers. He means never to give his enemies the least satisfaction or opportunity or magic to hold over his head. . . .

Have to get some sleep, he tells himself now. His dreams have been disturbed by roaring gods since his stupidity: drawing the attention of the two Hawaiian police in the first place, and then having to kill them. He dreams of landscapes littered with his own serated flesh and blood, of cavernous tunnels into which he's been cast, where demons of bizarre shape, size and lurid color give chase, trampling him and tearing parts of him away. These caverns are interconnected, the walls running with a yellow, stewy gruel, and the moment he escapes one, he finds himself trapped in another, sliding down a wall, unable to stop his spiraling progression downward toward yet a deeper prison, a filthy hole. Dante's *Inferno* or someplace only the Hawaiian gods knew of, *Kehena*?

Such troubled sleep will not help him on the job tomorrow, or when he goes cruising. He has a number of other sacrifices to make between now and when the trades decide to leave the islands. The winds could be capricious. They might leave at any time.

Maybe warm milk with a dollop of cocoa, tinged with a tad of vanilla extract, he thinks. He's read somewhere that sleep is helped along by some chemical in hot milk. Trypteeo-something.

He steps into his ramshackle kitchen in the dingy and cramped bungalow, its black memories and dark corners echoing in his consciousness. He snatches open the small icebox and pulls forth a quart of aging milk. He pays no attention to the odors emanating from his icebox, closing it on the collection of hands he's kept as souvenirs of his conquests. He now quickly warms his milk to a temperature most men could not tolerate. Once the cocoa is prepared as he likes it, he wanders about the empty, wailing house he once shared with Kelia. The shadows, even the wood and the wood grain in the walls, are alive with Kelia's many ghosts who scream at him.

Kelia has long ago left him, deserted him. She had to die for that indignity and she has. . . . At least in his mind, he has killed her many times over now. He would like to kill the real Kelia, but he knows he can't, at least not now, perhaps never unless she comes back home. . . .

He fervently misses their former life together on the island of Maui and later here on Oahu. She was alive and well, living with friends on the mainland in California, afraid one day that he would come for her. But if Kelia were ever to be murdered, the family—everyone—would know who had killed her.

So he kills Kelia by killing the others who are—or were—*like* Kelia.

He occasionally wonders if Kelia hasn't at some time snuck back onto the island of Oahu without his knowing. He gets reports from relatives now and again, but they arc vague, unsure. His people don't come around him. Most think him strange. Most of them think that he lives too much in the past.

He is a big man, although short at five-ten, stout and strong, proud of his strength, his barbells always nearby. His living room is taken up by his equipment and he routinely works out here until his muscles bulge. He must keep in shape for his self-esteem and for the passionate work he does for his gods.

He likes to keep the house dark. Without A.C. or the hope of air-conditioning, he keeps the place cavelike and cool, accepting the dankness over the heat. He once had a dream of building a house into the side of one of the mountains, for natural cooling and heating. He'd dreamed of building it for Kelia. God, that was so long ago, when he and Kelia first lived together on Maui. He realizes the old dream is in ruins; only his new dream can come to pass now.

He lifts his long sugarcane knife, his favorite of several he owns. He has a rack of such knives along with several Japanese swords he has purchased over the years. He has a fascination for shiny steel blades; he likes their feel, the cool evenness of the metal as it is ripped from its scabbard, the way it cleanly slides into flesh and out again without disturbance to the metal. A powerful knife is like the phallus a god dangles between enormous legs, and lately, he has begun to think of his own body as a steel blade to be put to use by the gods of Oahu and the islands.

"Have to get rest . . . sleep," he anxiously tells himself now. He has suffered now for two years with bouts of insomnia; it is one of the reasons he willingly accepts night-shift work from 2 to 10 P.M. He's become used to sleeping three or four hours a day, scouting the downtown area for a while before going on duty, and then returning afterwards to the streets of Oahu to continue his hunt. But today is his day off.

He is not easily satisfied. His princesses all must be elegant, at least in appearance, to appease his gods. They must be strong-willed, not the pliant, easy pickups that will get into a car with just anyone. He likes them to stand up to him, to fight. It shows their courage, that they're worthy of his plan to re-ignite the powerful lords of the islands who speak to him, speak through him, urging him along the path he has chosen.

"Lopaka," they each in turn call out to him.

"Lopaka . . . son of chiefs before you . . ."

"It is you . . . Cowboy Lopaka."

They each reach out to him through their sonorous voices. Their voices all mesh into one when they chant his name. The sound of it reverberates through his brain. They claim him as one of their own.

"Lopaka . . ."

"We, your gods, need you . . . beg you . . ."

". . . feed the hunger . . ."

". . . hunger that is great . . ."

". . . feed the blood-sky-fire that feeds you . . ."

". . . empty yourself into us . . ."

". . . into the unbearable fire coursing through us . . ."

". . . find us . . . give us your fire heart . . ."

". . . give us our daily red . . ."

He stands it—*the suffering of those ethereal voices, dripping with unimaginable sorrow, stabbing at his brain*—until he can stand it no more.

This is how he remembers it in the beginning, with the first life he ever sacrificed to the voices. It had begun with the noises in the wind, voices only he could hear, even long before he ever knew Kelia. He'd tried to change after meeting Kelia, whose presence at first ended the lamenting voices inside his head. For a time the voices were silent and held in check.

After Kelia had left, he slowly came to a startling realization: The gods had chosen Kelia for him, to grant him a special insight into their spectral world. Kelia was really the kind of sacrifice they wanted. And finally, he'd known what the gods wanted of him, why he had been born, why he had come here from his true homeland, what his purpose, after all, was . . . and why he killed.

All part of a plan beyond even his full comprehension.

He is so focused by them when he kills that it happens independently of him, as if his limbs and his mind are overtaken by the powers who speak through his actions, as if he is no more than an arrow of his gods, as if he is not even truly present in the normal sense.

The next day, after he kills, he's awakened into a new body and being, refreshed and feeling clear-headed, remembering only the final moments before she finally expired, her blood spewing about him, painting him as he carves on and ejaculates on the body.

His ingenious method of disposing of the bodies he also owes to the inspiration of his gods.

In time, under the most common of circumstances, he will remember snatches of what he has done—or rather, what *they* have done, until eventually flashes of memory will reveal everything—*absolutely everything*.

He recalls only one name for all his victims, Kelia—for they are all one and the same when they belong to him; they are no longer Lindas or Kias, but Kelias. He knows they are all alike; that they are all shallow little creatures, interested only in pop music and rock stars, in mindless magazines and makeup, in instant gratification—*"What's between their legs"*—in becoming yet another dark-skinned *haole*, loving all things white, Western and decadent. Kelia—the real Kelia—is a full-blood Hawaiian, rarer these days than a virgin, but the Kelias he has sent to his gods were all of mixed blood, and now the gods are repeating their demand for a full-blood Hawaiian. He has tried to get it right, but the intermarriage between the races makes it near impossible here in Oahu to find such a flower for his gods.

To him, there seems little difference, just so they look like Kelia, so that when he begins to hack away with the cane knives or the swords, he might voyeuristically enjoy Kelia's torturous death again; it seems of no importance what *kind* of blood it is while he is catching it in his hands, sending it to the ceiling and walls or rubbing it into his nude body in an ecstatic orgy of body art.

His little bungalow's walls bear the marks of many such deaths now. It is fortunate that he lives at the end of a dead-end street against a vacant lot, his closest neighbors the clannish Portuguese down the block. No one ever seems disturbed by the noise or the odors coming from his home.

But now with the killing of the two Hawaiian cops, he worries. They are not killings he planned or wanted, particularly since the men killed were Hawaiians, and most certainly he was not told to take these lives by his Hawaiian gods, who have, for the moment, abandoned him. His gods speak continually of regeneration and rebirth, of a great empowering of the Hawaiian race far beyond what the Hawaiian politicians and newspapers scream for. How then do they feel about his having killed two strong Hawaiian warriors? he now wonders.

Warriors, hell . . . he rationalizes his last killings. They were working for the man, playing white cop.

He now puts his head against his pillow on the bloodstained couch and tries desperately to pretend that his eyes are weary, that he is sleepy. The drugs he uses have helped to bring him down; still, his eyes roam about the little place, marking where the previous night's fresh blood, brighter in color, shining in the glow of the oil lamp, has splattered the ceiling fan. He is effectively painting his interior in crimson, all since Kelia's leaving.

He wonders again if Kelia will ever return. Wonders if he will ever again find her. *Again* . . . perhaps a pointless time frame as long as she refuses to understand. Still, he wonders and wanders over the shards of his past, the moments when he tried to convince her, what he might have said to otherwise convince her to accept her fate, to become a sacrificial lamb. Now the what-ifs cram into his mind. He wonders if he can gain her back, what then? Might she understand now more than she did? Would she ever willingly share his newfound religion with him? Or would she again run . . . again too afraid to allow him a single cut, much less willingly sacrifice her life for his beliefs.

He stares at the still-blaring TV set. Reporters are jockeying for position around the federal building downtown, trying to get some joker in a beige suit to talk about the deaths of two *kanaka* cops. It looks like a re-hash of the earlier news programs, and so he pretty well ignores it, just letting the voices wash over his brain, their tedium hopefully helping him to get the sleep he so needs, when suddenly his ears perk at the mention of a supposed human body part found at the Blow Hole.

"*Ho'ino wale*, damn! *Kuamuamu!*" he curses.

He instantly sits upright, staring at questioner and questioned. The FBI man wears expensive Costa Del Mar dark glasses and has handsome *haole* features, is tall and ruddy-complexioned. He quickly denies knowledge of any body parts dredged from the Blow Hole.

"It's impossible," Lopaka tells himself.

The TV voice continues. "Seems some boys were playing a prank, a practical joke, with some mannequin parts," says the FBI man named on the screen as Parry. "Scared a few tourists using broken parts of a mannequin. That's all."

They got part of her out. They found part of Kelia. . . . He cringes, stares about at the evidence of multiple murder all around him. He wonders what he must do. Wonders what his gods want him to do. He can't possibly go on as if nothing has happened, as if all is right with his world, as if they don't know anything about him anymore, and aren't actively searching for him this fucking moment. Before now authorities knew only what the gods wanted them to know, only that a shadowy "maybe-man" called the Trade Winds Killer whom they hadn't a clue about was abducting whores. But now? Now they know something about him, and they know something about Kelia; they have a part of her, something that belongs to Ku . . . and they'll have the Blow Hole staked out.

The thought terrifies him.

He imagines they know his name, his place of work, where he lives. That they have the living Kelia in custody and under questioning, grilling her.

Hc imagines they have the dead Kelia's head, and the damned thing is speaking to them from its parched lips.

He envisions them crashing through his door with huge animal nets and a cage to put him into; imagines them dragging him before the TV cameras now focused on a second FBI man named Gagliano. He imagines being dragged into a court of law, being sentenced to a life behind bars unless he is executed by some angry cop or relative.

"Hell," he tries to convince himself, "such a quick end mightn't be so bad, really."

It'd mean an end to all his unrest, to the fevered state of his soul; maybe in the next life he'll be a god, a real god . . . not some make-believe god, or at least *somebody*. In this life, what chance did he have with his father always standing over him? His bloody father was the reason he chose to leave home to seek out a place of his own, and perhaps why he hears the voices in the trade winds, and perhaps why he helps the evil ones to feed upon the Kelias of the world. His father was one of the sharks, and so was he. . . .

In this life, if he'd never heard the voices telling him what to do, what would he be? Nothing, less than the sand on the beach, dirt. Besides, now on the rare occasion when he dares disobey his gods, they torch his brain with a searing red poker that scorches with a great fever of disquiet. It is the worst kind of torture imaginable, like super-heated, jagged knives being slowly placed into his eyes and ears, and the only release comes with slaughtering sacrifices in the manner of his own torture, as if Ku is showing him the way it is done.

He remembers heating the sword the night before, thrusting it, searing flesh.

The gods warn constantly of tortures far in excess of anything mankind might do to him, that these god-directed tortures wait for him should he fail to do what he is told. If he were locked up and unable to provide for his gods, what then might *they* do to him? He shudders at the thought.

Now a moment of calm washes over his brain. What does he have to worry about? he asks himself. No one has the first idea that he's guilty of anything, that he's the Trade Winds Killer, and they never will. He closes his eyes and sleeps his fitful, drug-induced sleep until a calm peace descends like an unexpected gift. . . .

He dreams of a lush forested backyard and a hiding place where once he felt safe, a place where Father can't find him. The dream lulls him into deeper and more peaceful sleep at first, but then the forested area is stripped away, the soft, billowy dream colors turning crimson and black, the dream itself replaced in a sudden eclipse of images. . . .

Another dream or another's dream? A dream out of the mind of a god? A vision? his subconscious is asking. It's an unfamiliar landscape; it's not his dream . . . coming from someplace else, someone else . . .

. . . deceptively simple and pleasing, a pair of enormous hazel eyes looking squarely into his brain, as if . . . He gasps on realizing the woman's soft eyes are looking into his brain, slicing with a laser, his removed scalp pulled over his eyes. The eyes are those of a giant Kelia, larger than Diamond Head, larger than the island itself, boring into him and lifting everything from his mind and *knowing*. She always knew.

He must find Kelia . . . must destroy her.

Pale Death with impartial tread beats at the poor man's cottage door and at the palaces of kings.

Horace, *Odes*

Paul Zanek at Quantico told her in no uncertain terms to remain in Oahu and cooperate completely with Parry, and to keep him and the Psychological Profile Team in Virginia informed and abreast of developments, and that they would do all in their power at long distance to help profile and track the supposed killer.

"I was supposed to be taking it easy here, having a vacation, you know, how do they spell it, r-e-s-t?"

"Sorry, Jess, but Parry's in straits there, what with his main guy out. Trust me, nobody planned this."

"Sure, Chief. I'm just feeling tired and a little sorry for myself."

"Remember, anything you need, Jess."

"Don't you get on a plane and start out just yet. So far I've seen nothing to indicate we've even got a serial killer here."

"Parry's an experienced bureau chief, Jess, and I'd—"

"He could be blowing smoke this time tomorrow, Chief. I'll let you know. My regards to J.T. and the team."

"Thorpe's in Detroit."

"Oh?"

"Something nasty cooking there; series of slum killings, mostly homeless."

"Well, if you hear from him, tell him I send my regards."

After she hung up, she gave a few moments' thought to John Thorpe, her next-in-command at the criminology lab at Quantico in Sector IV. He'd recently undergone a difficult bit of surgery, and this on top of a tough divorce that had separated him from his kids. It sounded like J.T. was a man of his word, burying himself in his work. She had a choice now of showering, calling room service for dinner or going through the nine files staring at her from the table across the room. She'd just as soon go to sleep, but her mind wandered back to New York City and Alan Rychman, whom she'd still not forgiven for forsaking her here. He had promised her for months that he'd get away with her to Hawaii and that everything was set, but now that he was angling for commissioner, he had very little say-so about his own schedule or life, it seemed. So they'd argued again. As it looked now, she supposed it was perhaps best that Alan had missed his flight after all, since things were shaping up here as they were. She imagined his rage had he been here, seeing her sucked into the island case. If he were in her company when all this occurred, he'd be as upset with her as she presently was with him.

She toyed with the idea of calling Alan, as he'd have no idea where she was by now. If he did call, he'd be trying to find her in Maui. Maybe he'd left word at the hotel there. She made a quick connection and learned that there'd been no word from Alan after all.

Maybe she'd just let him stew.

She decided to shower, and was soon under the relaxing spray. Fresh now, she put on a robe and stepped out onto the balcony to watch the brilliant orange, lavender and purple spray of sun and cloud out over the ocean on this gorgeous Hawaiian night settling lazily over the city. It was beautiful and exotic, this place so many thousands upon thousands of miles from Quantico, Virginia, which she'd called home since her days in the FBI academy.

As beautiful as Hawaii was, her heart was heavy. She'd come a hell of a long way just to be alone. She thought again of the moment in San Francisco when she finally got it: the fact that Alan Rychman wasn't going to be meeting her there to fly on to the Hawaiian islands with her after all. His city, New York, had won again, just as on earlier occasions. Still, she was honest enough to agree that her own profession had called her away from him more than once.

Perhaps their relationship had been doomed from the start, as her friend J.T. had said in his less-than-comforting certainty when she'd called to cry long-distance on his shoulder, inviting him to join her and knowing how foolish it sounded the moment the words left her. She just didn't want to be alone so far from home. It wasn't like she was trying to muscle in and take advantage of J.T.'s recent change of status to single and less-than-carefree. Nothing was certain in a world where even J.T.'s supposedly perfect marriage had gone aground on the jagged rocks of divorce. There hadn't been a single clue, so closed-mouthed had he remained about it.

"Life as medical cops," she muttered to herself, sipping at some wine she'd found in the dry bar. She had an M.E. after her name, and she was an FBI agent, but it all boiled down to the work of a cop, after all, and it left little in its wake for what others might consider a *normal* life.

"A relative term at best," she reassured herself with another of her father's favored phrases. She recalled him saying these words when, as an army brat, she'd protested his lifestyle as *less than normal;* so uprooted were they time and again.

"But when do you get to slow down, enjoy life, Dad?" she'd asked.

"I do enjoy life, Jess. I love my work."

"And what about me and Mama?"

"I love you guys, too."

She felt a tear well up at the memory. It was not long after that her father was filled with regret at not having loved her mother *enough,* at not having spent more time with them both. She had had to reassure him thereafter until his death that he'd been a terrific husband and father, and he had. He had raised her to be independent, to be a self-starter, a hard worker, a self-thinker, and to be obsessive about caring. He had taught her the tactics of the deer hunter, the methods of the hunt and how to deal with the prey once you caught it. He had taught her strength and gentleness in the same lessons.

She wiped away her tears and stared out at the expanse of ocean, getting dreamily caught up in the ebb and flow of the current far below her balcony. Lovers walked among the palm-lined paths in the distance where Waikiki Beach was lit with the torches of a luau just getting underway. The trade winds blustered about the balustrades and rattled the small outdoor furniture, threatening to lift her robe to reveal her nudity beneath, but the feel of the wind against her skin was warm and pleasing as if it were alive and interested in her alone.

"More than I can say for Alan Rychman." Her sad little joke was followed by a pout.

She allowed her mind to play with the wind as it poured over and through her, at first not hearing the phone, which was ringing insistently inside her room.

Blowing out a long thread of exasperated air, she stepped back inside, out of the wind and stars to lift the receiver.

"Have you eaten?" It was Parry.

"No, I mean, yes . . . I mean, I was about to order from room service."

"I'm downstairs . . . and if you'd care to have someone to dine with, well . . . I just thought . . ."

He sounded like a nervous boy. She cleared her throat. "I'm awfully tired."

"Maybe a little wine and some decent *opaka-paka* will—"

"*Opaka-paka?*"

"Best fish dish in the islands, the way they do it here."

"Downstairs, you say," she considered aloud.

"At the restaurant."

She sighed, gave him time to worry and then said, "All right. Give me a moment to dress."

"C-casual," he intoned.

"Island casual?"

"And I promise, no shoptalk."

When she hung up, she wondered if she'd made the right decision, and if he'd stick to his word about no shoptalk, or if he was chomping at the bit to glean as much information as possible from her about the earlier autopsies. Still, she wasted no time in dressing in a light, rainbow-colored, muumuu-style dress she had picked up at a hotel shop in Maui. As she quickly blow-dried her hair, using a little gel to style it comfortably and nicely, allowing the gentle, auburn curls to flow freely to either side, she wondered about his intentions. She also questioned her own. Then again, why shouldn't she enjoy herself here in the world's most lovely resort city; why shouldn't she have a place to wear her new dress; why shouldn't she taste this *opaka-paka* delicacy? And Alan Rychman and Paul Zanek be damned—for different reasons. And by God, why shouldn't she enjoy the company of another man?

She found her cane and took a moment to appraise herself in the full-length mirror before stepping out, glad she'd bought the pullover island wear with the tie about the waist as opposed to the one without. She quickly cautioned herself about Parry, reminding herself that all men were the same the world over, and that despite his good looks, she didn't intend to get romantically involved with any goddamned, workaholic bureau chief, Hawaii or not.

Dinner was delightful, served in an open-air atmosphere on the rim of the Pacific, tracings of lavender and purple aproning the horizon as the sun abandoned sky for sea. Remarkably, Parry remained a man of his word, not once broaching the subject of the double autopsy earlier or the case he was building against a phantom killer stalking Honolulu's Waikiki resort area.

After a delicious dinner of thick, fresh *opaka-paka* served up with wine, he took her for a walk along Waikiki's busiest strip. Life teemed here on the streets and in the hotels as it did below in the ocean, the schools of people in their weaving groups swimming in relaxed but controlled fashion, going in, out and among the doorways and concrete pillars, the shopping on Kalakaua Avenue going on all night.

Parry needn't have pointed out the dazzling one-of-a-kind shops lining the way. Here shops known worldwide competed with local oddities. To her uninitiated eye, it seemed as though the people were mad; having come halfway around the globe, most of them were fixating on an activity they could do at their local malls in Upper Sandusky or Idaho, or Tokyo. People seemed both astonished and pleased to find familiar shop names alongside the unfamiliar, the gaudy neon alongside the tasteful designs that announced such places as Endangered Species, The Wyland Art Gallery, and exotic Korean, Japanese and Hawaiian restaurants; there was also Woolworth's, Burger King, Hilo Hattie's, ABC Liquor and Pharmacy, Thom McAn Shoes. There were three-tiered shopping malls in the International Market Place in the heart of Waikiki. It was all dizzying, exciting and a good deal disheartening, she thought. Maui, too, had high-rise hotels dotting its coasts, but there was nothing to compare to this for the atmosphere that only a major world city might provide.

"You could spend a hefty fortune here before you got halfway down the block," he said in her ear as they walked casually along the brightly illuminated street.

Her thoughtful *"Hmmmm"* was a purr. She'd drunk a bit more wine than she ought to have. "I can see that," she managed. "But it's not what *I* came to Hawaii for."

"It's certainly an allure for a good many others, though, Doctor. Big bucks, big time . . . Honolulu attracts millions each season."

She looked across at him as they continued to stroll along amid the bustle, adroitly maneuvering about the human quagmire they now found themselves in when they came to a standstill in front of a small grocery that specialized in Vietnamese goods. "Some unusual delicacies in there," he assured her.

"You were in Viet Nam? Acquired a taste for the food?"

"Didn't everybody?"

"What sort of a unit did you serve with?"

"I was just your ordinary grunt."

"A grunt, and you came out alive. I'm impressed."

They continued along the avenue, the gentle trades whooshing along the man-made valley of asphalt, concrete and steel all around them, the millions of windows winking down over their progress as a street vendor offered them paper leis so he could take their "honeymoon snapshot."

Parry waved the vendor off and she shook her head a bit self-consciously, each of them laughing, both amused and a bit uncomfortable. She instantly recuperated, however, asking, "Must have a hell of a lot of pressure on to keep this city's reputation sparkling?"

"FBI's supposed to be above all that kind of bullshit, but yes . . . your little understatement is quite correct. You're quite observant, Dr. Coran, but if you remember, I did promise *no talk shop, remember*?"

She ignored this. "Some of the young women disappeared from this very area, didn't they?"

"Yes, but that's not why we're here."

"He may's well have taken them in daylight as here. He'd be surrounded by people and the street's as lit up as Times Square on New Year's."

"People haven't been known to disappear on Times Square at New Year's?" He laughed lightly and then breathed deeply, shaking his head, the carefully combed hair now tossed by the wind. "I promise not to talk shop for your benefit, to show you around town a little, and here you are talking about precisely— "

"A shrink would call it obsessive-compulsive, a fixation I have on my work, a fatal flaw for any relationship."

"Well, I admit to symptoms myself. I don't mind telling you, from what I've seen so far, I think we're lucky to have you . . . compulsions and all. Nothing wrong with devotion to duty, all that . . ."

"Jesus, you're not going to break out in a patriotic Lee Greenwood song, are you?" she said while thinking, *What the hell does he know about my compulsions?*

He laughed from the gut at her joke, singing, "God bless America and the U.S.A." He drew stares and laughter.

A seriousness crept into her voice. "You haven't any idea what I'm all about, Chief Parry."

He smiled at her thinly veiled remark, their eyes momentarily meeting before he responded. "All cops are fanatical—if they're doing their jobs. Call it what you will."

"Most people are obsessive about something, or someone," she countered. "Crazy is one of the key words in most country-western songs, isn't it?"

"Everybody's crazy about something," he agreed, "sure. For some it's a movie star's lips— "

"—or hips— "

"—comic books, baseball trading cards, stamps— "

She kept pace. "—trashy novels, green lawns— "

"—antiques, money, cars . . ."

With a salutation toward the crowd, she added, "Shopping."

"Exactly."

"We haven't even touched on porcelain junkies, sports nuts, dog enthusiasts, cat lovers, collectors of the weird and the arcane."

He began a bantering laugh.

"From book matches to little stone dolls with large reproductive organs," she added with her own laugh. "And some people just can't get enough of fire. You like to play with fire, Mr. Parry?"

"Sure, certain fire, who doesn't?"

"Controlled fire, you mean. Well, perhaps you'd better be cautious, because even the most controlled fires tend to get out of hand in a wind like this."

They continued onward until they stood outside an unusual shop that carried items from New Guinea, the walls and windows filled with headdresses and masks with stoney, bulging eyes, fanglike teeth and enormous ears. She stepped inside to browse the unique store, and he followed. There was something completely raw and uninhibited about the items on display for sale here, items that appeared better suited to a museum showing than a capitalistic enterprise. Spears and ancient tools adorned one wall, rustic artwork the other, and as they moved from one display to another, the eyes of the ancient, one-of-a-kind, handmade masks seemed to follow their steps.

"An archaeologist would be right at home here," she commented.

"Another kind of fanaticism?" he asked. "The desire to stare into the past, to understand the dead?"

"Not so different from what we M.E.'s do, only our dead are usually of a more recent vintage."

"So a good medicine man, or woman in your case, is still worth her weight in papayas, at least in these islands," he said with a wide and infectious smile.

"Have all the victims disappeared from this area?" she asked.

"No, not all. Several have been abducted from our Chinatown area."

"Chinatown?"

"One of our oldest districts where the oldest profession is still the oldest profession."

"I see. Were all the women prostitutes?"

"You haven't had time to go over the files, I take it."

She shook her head to indicate she hadn't.

He ushered her back out onto the street before saying, "Several were university students, possibly plying the trade to continue at the university, but others seem to have simply been in the wrong place at the wrong time. Some of last year's disappearances were working night-shift jobs, supposedly on their way home, when they vanished."

"And all of them fall within a certain age range?"

"Sixteen's the youngest and nineteen's the oldest."

"Pretty tight range."

He agreed, adding, "He appears to like them with long, free-flowing black hair, and he obviously prefers island girls, never a *haole*—a white."

He walked her back to her hotel lobby where a short, stocky man in a raucous, multicolored Hawaiian shirt, dashed up to Jim Parry, pulling him away, speaking in hushed and rapid fashion. The other man was dark-skinned, a heavy sweater. His hair had once been jet black, but now it was streaked and peppered with gray; tossed by the wind, it scuffled about his creased forehead and worried eyes. She heard Jim call him Tony. He'd brought some urgent message to Parry, who was doing his best to rid himself of the heavier fellow.

It then appeared that Parry wasn't going to get away, so Jessica made a move for the hotel entrance, to go to her room, but this spurred Parry back to her; he stopped her with a hand on her shoulder, the older man beside him, frowning, a natural scowl distorting his features.

"This is Special Agent Anthony Gagliano, Dr. Coran." Gagliano was so darkly tanned that his Italian features had turned to that of a dark Latino. *Swarthy,* she thought.

"Gagliano," she said, "I might've guessed," trying to muster a smile, feeling wrung out.

"We've got a line on the missing girl," Parry said. "Honolulu Missing Persons notified Tony right after their two Hawaiian cops fell, but its only been a few hours ago that Tony's been able to get her family to agree to see me. It's been twenty-four hours, and the girl's description fits our victim profile."

"Then you *have* worked up a *victim* profile?"

"In the files I gave you, remember?"

"A victim profile without bodies. That may be a first, Inspector. I'm impressed."

"Don't be. It wasn't too tough. They all might've been sisters, they look—looked—that much alike."

She sighed heavily, nodding, realizing that this was one more point of evidence that made Parry believe that a demented mind stood behind the disappearances.

"I've got to go. Tony and I'll question the relatives, find out what we can."

"Be sure to get any and all *medical* information you can," she urgently told him.

"Sure, sure," said Gagliano, sounding a bit offended.

"Don't stop at dental. *Anything* medical," she persisted to Gagliano's best we-know-how-to-do-our-job glare. "All we've got is that awful arm in Lau's freezer, and that's not much to work with. We'll need every shred of information from the girl's doctor, from measles shots on. Be nice if we had medical records and long-bone X-rays on all of them."

Gagliano, a hefty man, had the eyes of an impish boy. He stared at Jessica for a moment before replying. "Not much to attach to that ham hock we found, huh, Doc? Sure, we'll grill her family for any medical records."

"Get a good night's sleep. You'll need it for the morning," Parry said to her as Gagliano faded toward his car. "I enjoyed dinner and the walk," he confided.

"So did I. See you sometime tomorrow then, Chief Parry."

"Might just as well call me Jim. We're going to be working very closely together."

"I'm not sure we're going to be working that close, Jim, and I don't know how long Zanek'll let me remain. Maybe *Chief* is best for now."

He frowned, but it quickly disappeared and was replaced by an elegant smile. "All right, Doctor. Have it your way."

"I usually do."

"I can believe that."

He allowed himself to linger over her disappearing form, not caring what Gagliano made of his behavior. Even with the cane, or perhaps because of it, she was a unique and intriguing combination of beauty and brains, femininity and strength. He decided he very much liked her and that he wanted to get to know her better.

Gagliano rejoined him, saying, "Helluva looker for an M.E., Jim. Couldn't figure it when they told me you were at the Rainbow having dinner with a coroner, but Christ, nobody told me she was such a doll. I figured her more the 'Iron Matron' in the lockup type, if you know what I mean? Still, I never figured you to go for a chest cutter."

"Tony, tonight was strictly business."

"Hey, if you got to do business, it's a hell of a lot easier if the dame across from you looks like something between Marilyn Monroe and Lauren Lo-and-Bacall!"

Parry laughed. "Shut up and get in your squad. I'm under the bus terminal and I'll follow you out. Let's get whatever the doctor wants."

"Strictly business, huh?"

"Go!"

Parry had worked on and off with Tony Gagliano for most of the eight years he had been in Hawaii. Tony was a good man, a tough cop and a straight friend who had several times tried to fix Jim up with one of his many relatives who visited from the mainland from time to time. Most of Tony's family remained in the San Francisco Bay area. Tony, the black sheep of the family for most of his life, had stumbled into police work only after running off to Hawaii to be a beach bum. That had been almost twenty years before. He had come up through the ranks of street cop in Honolulu, had done every conceivable job through detective-shield status and had finally applied for the FBI at the ripe old age of twenty-five. Now thirty-eight, prematurely aged and balding, he had covered a lot of ground with Parry, and they instinctively trusted one another as they could no one else either in the HPD or the FBI. Aside from the work, they had spent many a backyard barbecue and ball game together.

Tony had also watched James Parry fail at every relationship he had ever had with a woman over the years. Sometimes, Jim Parry thought as he slid in behind the wheel of his unmarked car, Tony knew too damned much about him.

Parry's car cut sharply from beneath the bus terminal at the Rainbow Tower and out into the traffic of Ala Moana Boulevard. He tried now to concentrate on the work at hand. He'd seen a photograph of the last supposed victim of the Trade Winds phantom, a lovely petite young woman with shining black hair that cascaded down to near waist-length, and while the others hadn't hair quite so long, they all wore tapering hair in similar fashion. Linda, or Lina as her closest family called her, this nineteen-year-old, hadn't much of a file yet, just a photo and the particulars of her home situation and place of work. Her employer had been questioned without result, having been the last to see Linda before she was believed to have gotten into a car with a dark figure on Ala Wai Boulevard, where she'd walked from the job to home, just opposite the canal. She'd been working nights in order to pay her tuition at the university.

"Bloody shame," he muttered to himself, turning now into a cramped little driveway as Tony pulled ahead and parked on a steep incline. The two cops were met by Linda's father, a short, crusty full-blood Hawaiian with the characteristic large features and thick folds of skin that marked his age and race. His small Portuguese wife was on the porch, sitting in a stupefied daze on a swing, humming a tune which harkened back to another time and place. The house both outside and in seemed draped in an impenetrable darkness.

Parry introduced himself, shaking the man's hand, but his eyes roamed the porch and the black interior of the house.

"It's da way she no want it for now, no lights, nobody inside. She no want you goin' in and goin' through our daughter's stuff, you unnerstand?" He sounded almost apologetic, trained to accept authority.

Parry nodded, and immediately asked the father if there were any medical records on Linda. "It could help," he assured Mr. Kahala.

"When you guys ask for medical and dental records dat mean bad t'ings," replied the sad-eyed father. "I know dat. But my wife, Miya, she knows mo 'bout where da kine paper bettah, so let me talk to her 'bout dat." He fell silent a moment and stared at Gagliano and Parry. "You got any mo questions?"

"Yes, quite a few."

"And it would really help, sir, if we could get into your daughter's bedroom," added Gagliano. "You never know what little item might prove useful in an investigation."

"We told the cops everything we know."

"But you didn't let the cops inside either. Now we have a warrant, but we'd prefer your cooperation instead."

Parry apologized for his partner, taking on the role of the good guy in all this while Gagliano got right into the man's face and continued. "We need to hear it straight from you, sir, for ourselves. We get it second-hand from HPD, who knows . . . we might miss something."

The old man nodded and began a soliloquy tinged with monotony, until he mentioned that his girl was going to the university. A light turned on inside him for a moment and his voice rose. But the wife shouted from her shadow on the porch, "That's what got her killed! Trying to be Miss High-Mighty and pay for that school! If my Lina had stayed home—"

"Quiet, woman! You don't know Lina is killed!" As he chastised her, he ran to her and put his arms about her. Tears shone in reflected light from the street lamp, now the only thing they could see of the bull-shouldered, short man's features. "You go in; do what you gotta do," he told Parry and Gagliano.

Inside the sparse space of the bungalow, Parry jammed a shin against a coffee table before Gagliano found a light to guide them. The light shone on a comfortable, clean house with throw rugs over a parquet floor, countless pillows which soaked up so many cooking odors as to be comfortable with them these days. A large couch, a smaller settee, an easy chair for the old man, along with the TV/VCR/stereo center filled the place — *the American Dream*.

Pictures adorned the walls, cabinets, any open space, photos of the family on picnics, outings, at parties with friends, but most of the photos were of Linda, a lovely, smiling creature whose innocent brown eyes were huge, so trusting and curious.

Satellite rooms went around the living room: kitchen/dining area, a master bedroom and a smaller bedroom. Linda's was easy to find. The light here revealed a teenager's cave, filled with posters of rock stars. Sting, Guns & Roses, Ice-T fought for space with a silly replica of a Hawaiian warrior, the mascot of the University of Hawaii, alongside beautiful seascape posters, Save the Whales posters, pictures of dolphins and the like. A large bookshelf was littered with paperbacks of every stripe, size and shape, as many science fiction titles as romance, and it appeared she loved horror tales as well, her obvious favorites being Dean Koontz, Geoffrey Caine and Stephen Robertson.

Parry always felt like an intruder at such moments, like some morbid vulture interested in digesting the "remains" of a life. On the girl's nightstand was a book of poetry, a page marked and a few lines of a poem highlighted in red marker, possibly something she was studying at the university. The book was *Shakespeare's Sonnets,* the lines were from Sonnet 94 and as Parry read them, they spoke deeply to him:

> The summer's flower is to the summer sweet,
> Though to itself it only live and die,
> But if that flower with base infection meet,
> The basest weed outbraves his dignity;
> For sweetest things turn sourest by their deeds;
> Lilies that fester smell far worse than weeds.

Parry flipped through the book and saw that other lines were marked. "No time for a poetry reading, Chief," said Gagliano. "These people're going to kick us out on our asses any second now."

Parry slipped the book into his pocket and went on with the search of the girl's room. It turned up nothing unusual or telling or helpful. Gagliano was going through the underwear drawer when the father appeared at the door.

Parry stepped between asking, "Was your girl seeing a boy? Anyone in particular, I mean?"

"She too serious for most boys; she had mind made up to finish college. No boys, no, 'cept sometimes she went with George, but broke it up."

Both FBI men immediately wondered about George, and if this wouldn't simply turn out to be a lovers' spat and Linda would show up on her doorstep tomorrow.

"George got a last name, sir?" asked Gagliano.

The father looked perplexed and shouted to his wife for the name.

"Oniiwah, George Oniiwah," she moaned through the window from the porch, where she'd remained.

The father cautioned, "But dey didn't see each other for long time."

Parry instantly thought Hawaiian on hearing George's last name, as it was a familiar island name. In fact, many in the Oniiwah family were well-to-do by any standard. "Do you know where this George Oniiwah lives?"

The father called to his wife, who muttered to him in Portuguese before he came up with a street name and number. It was in a much nicer section of the city. The two of them had met during her freshman year at the university, he said. "But Lina broke it off when he got too serious for her."

"Too serious?"

"You know, get married, have home and children."

The mother came in and stood in her missing child's room, her hands filled with papers and a little book, the medical records. Parry accepted them with his heartfelt thanks, and Gagliano took the moment to say they might return again at another time. The father began to protest, but then he let it go. Parry and Gagliano said good night to the distressed parents, whose neighbors were now swarmed about the bungalow and the unmarked FBI cars in a show of support for the bereaved family. Parry wondered where George was, and he asked Linda's father if the boy had gotten in touch since the disappearance. The answer was no.

Gagliano's glint met Parry's knowing look. "We'll have to pull Georgie boy in for questioning."

"Tomorrow, Tony," Jim Parry replied, weary-eyed and searching the dial on his watch, trying to focus, only to find it was already one in the morning. It had been a full day. He patted the book of poems in his pocket and said, "I'm going home, catch up on some reading and some sleep. See you tomorrow."

Suddenly one of the concerned neighbors, a large, healthy Hawaiian woman who came at Parry like a rhino, said in a voice that shook even Gagliano, "You bastards bettah fine-dat little honey Lina, sin her home to her momma, you got-dat, Mr. United States FBI Mans? If you don't, there goin' to be big trouble in Oahu for you."

"You threatening Chief Parry, lady?" Gagliano began. But Parry held up a restraining hand and shouted to the crowd, "We're going to do everything within our power to locate the girl, but we're not superhuman. We can't work miracles."

He'd as much as told them the girl was dead. Parry and Gagliano got into their separate cars and wasted little time in moving off, but they did so at a snail's pace, all but daring the crowd to throw a rock or fire a shot. Both men were glad when nothing further developed. Parry looked back via his rearview mirror the whole way down the block, feeling frustrated, angry, and weary all in equal measure.

6

Philosophy is written in this grand book—I mean the universe—which stands continually open to our gaze, but it cannot be understood unless one first learns to comprehend the language and interpret the characters in which it is written. . . .

Galileo

Jessica had sat up with Jay Leno and the rest of the *Tonight Show* gang via satellite, but she'd lost all but the back-scatter noise of the show in her concentration over the series of files left her by James Parry. Each photo and bio spoke of a young woman with a full life ahead of her, each of the victims coming from a large extended family, a few with children of their own. They weren't the typical big-city prostitutes one might expect. They weren't hardened or beaten or haggard, anorexic or overweight; they didn't have broken noses, scars or pimples, and from their photos most of them looked clean of drugs, their eyes clear and vibrant, speaking of souls filled with life and interests. Several—as Parry had intimated—were part-timers, supplementing their income in order to finish out a term at the university, while still others had no record of prostitution and had last been seen at a regular place of work.

Linda Kahala, also known as Lina, of mixed Portuguese and Hawaiian blood, had been a dark-skinned beauty with radiant round eyes that seemed, from her photo at least, to be filled with an island innocence that likely got her killed.

She wondered if this most recently vanished girl, had actually become the killer's ninth victim by Parry's count, or if she'd turn up at a boyfriend's house or telephoned from the mainland, having run away. Parry had made some big leaps, trying to connect a series of earlier disappearances on the island of Maui, a far less developed and more rural isle, with the disappearances in Honolulu on Oahu.

Jessica wondered if the sweet-faced woman-child in the photograph was as innocent as she appeared; whether she had gotten sucked into the seamier side of Honolulu's cesspool. Every city, no matter its outward beauty and wonder, nourished a seductive, erotically appealing underbelly, all the more alluring to the poor, and it would appear that Linda Kahala might well have been caught in the quagmire, desperately in need of funds to continue at the university . . . and if her friends could turn tricks for tuition, why not her?

The victims had commonalties among them, each one itemized in Parry's hand. First was appearance and race, then the fact they all worked in service-type jobs catering to tourists, even the ones labeled prostitutes. All of them had at one time lived in or near Kahului on Maui or here in Honolulu City, in and around a tightly woven ghetto surrounding Chinatown and an ancient neighborhood of mixed and Hawaiian families, where rows of squat little bungalows hugged the Ala Wai Canal. According to Chief James Parry, thin little Linda Kahala had last been seen on Ala Wai Boulevard the very night that Officers Hilani and Kaniola were murdered by gun and machete. Coincidence or connection?

If the two incidents were connected, she reasoned now in a half-dazed state, the mangled limb in Lau's freezer could well be Linda Kahala's.

She fell asleep to the sounds of Leno's band as he wrapped for a commercial, her subconscious seemingly grateful for the noise of life. She fought her own mind for control of her dreams, determined that they be pleasant and relaxing, and soon she was back beneath Maui's coastal waters at the incredible underwater

Molokini crater where she'd been diving before she was called to Honolulu. The sights were as breathtaking as when she was actually there, but what was even greater than this was the absolute feeling of freedom in the water; weightlessness brought its own rewards, a sense of absolution. It was the same high she'd heard fliers speak of when they left the ground, the same adrenaline rush that mountain climbers felt and that sky divers loved.

She looked around to find herself completely alone in the water save for its teeming life, reflecting all the colors of the rainbow amid the fanning, waving coral. She saw a school of exquisite silver-blue fish disappear into a cavern below her. Darting after, feeling playful and alive, Jessica swam without hesitation into the black hole of shadow below her, where the beauty of the place took on an entirely new face; still lovely, it was an abiding deep blue turning to midnight in the cave. It was a mysterious and teasing midnight world into which the fish had simply vanished.

She might have slept comfortably with this image, but suddenly the strength of the current which she'd glided on pinned her, forcing her forward into the blackness ahead of her, its strength ten times her own. She could not escape by the route she'd entered, unless the current receded and she caught the force as it returned, but it was growing, and became so turbulent now as to have taken on the character of a killer, capable of smashing her against the jagged rocks she saw silhouetted in the darkness.

She felt a cold chill break out beneath her diving suit; felt gooseflesh slither along her body; heard the symbiotic human and mechanical sound of her own labored breathing through her regulator growing in intensity, now dangerously erratic as she sucked frantically on what little oxygen was left her. She felt dizzy, disoriented, confused as the water tumbled her about in the now-blue-black cavern, trapping her here, a powerless paper doll. The cutting, jagged edges of rock tore into her, ripping her suit and flesh, rending her life support from her mouth, crushing her tanks. Her body was held against the rock surface above her and she could feel both her blood and her breath slowly taken from her.

Floating past her were bones and fleshy body parts, the long-haired, severed heads of dark-featured women, and one of them came to rest before her, pinned with her against the volcanic cave wall here below the Blow Hole, and this one's eyes were those of Linda Kahala. The girl's wide eyes filled both the cavern and Jessica's mind.

She sat bolt upright, desperately fighting for breath in the phantom cave below the sea, fending off the dead girl who had come into her bed. "Christ!" she shouted at the room and at herself, angry for allowing herself even a subconscious moment of fear. She had fought long and hard to overcome the scars left upon her by the madman named Matisak, now safely locked away in a maximum-security prison for the criminally insane, but she knew that she'd never again be the same Jessica Coran she'd been before he had maimed her, that weakness and doubt shadowed her every step. It was the kind of frailty she did not want Parry, or anyone else for that matter, to ever see in her.

A bittersweet taste of perspiration found her lips as beads cascaded tearlike from her forehead and down her cheek. She gave another moment's thought to Matisak, who even from behind bars had managed to get word to the press that he, from the confines of his cell, had meticulously led Jessica ever closer to the identity of the cannibalistic Claw in New York the year before. The story, finding print in the worst rags, claimed that she had used "Professor" Matisak's considerable powers of deduction in her remarkable manhunt to locate and destroy the Claw. Matisak, who was once a teacher, known also as "Teach," had a well-fed ego thanks to the incompetence of her superiors and the tabloid press. Two years of incarceration had only inflated his self-image and his lunacy.

She wanted nothing more to do with the maniac who had killed Otto Boutine, and she'd made this clear to her superiors at the close of the Claw case when *that* bastard saw real justice done him: a paralyzing bullet she had sent through his skull, allowing him plenty of time for the kind of suffering and pain he'd inflicted on others before he went completely catatonic and died.

Now, with a new section head, the overtures on the part of the new chief to keep gleaning information from Matisak left her cold. She'd told Zanek never again.

Still, while she knew that rationally Matisak was thousands upon thousands of miles away and imprisoned, he was somehow here with her, his chilling astral spirit bringing down the temperature in the hotel room. He was with her now . . . along with Linda Kahala . . . tonight in Honolulu.

Several days later, July 15, 1995

After several nights of fitful dreams and nightmare visitations by Matisak, the Claw and their phantom evil here in Honolulu, the Trade Winds Killer, the toll was beginning to show on Jessica. Between 3 A.M. nightmares and all-day stints at the lab with Lau, she was exhausted. Still, she pushed herself harder than anyone on the team, anxious to fill in as many gaps as possible for Parry and his people, expecting any day now to get an evac order from Paul Zanek. She was just beginning to make progress, finalizing tests which Lau's people had prepared the way for, and the results were remarkable. From this fact she drew strength and pride.

It was determined early on that Officer Kaniola's gunshot wound had not been fatal, and that he was alive and possibly conscious when the killer, using great force, sent what amounted to a machete or cane cutter into his throat, nearly severing the head. Tests proved this assumption valid. More importantly, perhaps, she'd discovered that blood found covering Alan Kaniola's left palm was determined to belong to someone else. While another medical examiner might simply have assumed it was Kaniola's own blood, instinct told her that Kaniola, in his death throes, might possibly have gouged his killer, possibly with the man's own knife. She was elated to gain this small prize of information. At least it gave her some degree of hope, for now the *killer's* blood could be tested, and they'd be that much closer to their prey, for no one knew the outcome of a blood test. Anything might be forthcoming about their killer: blood type, race, age, sex.

But now, closer examination of the blood proved confusing. It was the blood of a young woman, possibly Linda Kahala's, and if so, it meant that somehow Officer Kaniola came into contact with either the body or a blood spatter somewhere up there on Koko Head. Seeing this turn of events beneath her microscope lens, Jessica set her teeth and clenched her fists. This information changes things, she thought, wondering at the possibilities.

Earlier she had seen Agent Tony Gagliano, who'd come by to drop off all the medical documents he'd been able to lay hands on; wonderfully enough, he'd located useful medical information on Linda Kahala, an entire medical history from birth. Jessica began a routine blood-matching scan between what was found on Kaniola's palm and what was known about Linda Kahala's blood, which was considerable since she had a rare blood disorder and several easily identifiable characteristics. The testing took most of the morning, but the difficult part was extracting blood from the shoulder and forearm removed from the freezer. Meanwhile, the arm itself was undergoing a battery of tests, and so far the results all pointed to its belonging to a young woman between the ages of fifteen and twenty, as close as Jessica could tell, the age when the bone marrow was fully extended, at its peak in growth and maturity. The size of the bone also matched that of a girl Linda's age. With the help of a forensics anthropologist on loan from the University of Hawaii, a Dr. Katherine Smits, it became increasingly clear that this was the limb of a young woman in her late teens whose ancestry was Hawaiian, at least in part. Had there been an X-ray of Linda's arm in her history or any DNA samples to match against, Jessica was certain they could undoubtedly match the body fragment to Linda Kahala. As things stood, a blood match had to suffice.

She returned to the blood matching, and by mid-afternoon she was completely convinced that not only was the limb's owner Linda Kahala, but that the blood on Officer Kaniola's palm *had also been Linda's.*

The now-*sure* revelation made her sit down and lean back into the folds of the easy chair in the office that had been turned over to her. Lau alone, among all the assistants, seemed to suspect or know. He had helped her do the blood matching. He came in, and saw her confusion over their findings.

"Odd, no?" he offered. "I mean about the arm and Kaniola's palm?"

"Don't go jumping to any crazy conclusions, Mr. Lau," she admonished. "This is just the kind of information that, in the wrong hands, could cause no end of confusion, embarrassment to your lab and our combined reputations, not to mention what I've been told is a volatile situation here in your city. We don't want the wrong people to know about this, understood?"

He looked stricken. "You do not trust me as a professional to keep silent about what is inside our house? I have been here long time before you come, Doctor, and I have to be here long time after you gone. No, you don't worry 'bout me telling people outside house what kine work we are here doing . . . no."

She was immediately apologetic. "I only meant to say that the press can be awfully good at skinning people like me as well as

you, Mr. Lau, so it was a cautionary remark, that's all. Chief
Parry's going to want it hush-hush, top secret, I'm sure. At least
for now."

"I understand. *Haole* press headline read: 'Kanaka Cop Is Trade
Winds Kill'a, He Kill All Hawaiian Girls.' A Hawaiian man do
this. I see it now, and then what happens?"

"Exactly," she agreed. Although she hadn't seen it happening in
the same way, she knew as he spoke it that he was absolutely right.
The whites, especially those in power, would assuredly like
nothing better than to pin the killings of the Hawaiian women on
a Hawaiian national, thus ending any suspicion that the monster
was a white man—as Jim Parry believed. She'd read his profile of
the likeliest age, sex, race and lifestyle of the phantom. And it
made complete sense, based as it was on statistical averages. Still,
statistics didn't always pan out; that was why they were called
averages.

"Not to worry one bit," Lau assured her. "So what is next step?"

"Late lunch," she monotoned, dropping her head in her hands,
fatigue now a constant companion.

She stood, stretched and stared out the huge windows for some
time without saying a word, Lau becoming fidgety behind her. She
stared fixedly at the western rim of Oahu, the gorgeous flood of
green foothills spilling from out of the volcanic rim of the vast
Waianae Range. If she could not look out the windows and see this
sight, she might imagine herself back at her Quantico lab which
overlooked the academy and training grounds. She'd learned that
the greenness of Hawaii was actually man-made, created by the
many canals built into the mountains to bring water down from the
uppermost heights in order to irrigate an otherwise barren landscape that, if not so nurtured, would be the color of teakwood. She
now wished that no one had told her, that the illusion was intact
and whole.

"Lunch a good idea," said Lau, breaking the silence. "You work
too hard, Dr. Coran. Not good for nobody."

"Lunch! My thoughts exactly," said James Parry, who'd appeared at the door so stealthily that even Lau was shaken.

"You're some G-man, Chief Parry . . . sneak up on a person
like that," said Lau.

"Sorry, didn't mean to get on your nerves, Mr. Lau."

"No bother," Lau lied, and started to leave, saying, "I think you
guys have much to talk about."

"Our Mr. Lau reads minds," said Parry as he made himself comfortable across from her, sitting in an office chair.

"Whatya mean, reads minds?"

Failing to answer her, he said, "There's something we've got to talk about."

"Oh, something come up I should know about?"

"I took the whole thing, what we know, what we suspect—all of it—to Dave Scanlon, the Commissioner of Police, Honolulu. Now he's sweatin' it."

"Sweating what? Why?"

"Let's just say the commissioner's a good politico, and he simply wants to cover all his asses. Any rate, all the different districts of the HPD are pouring over their missing-persons case files for the past several years. No telling how long this thing may've been going on, you see?"

"You think the disappearances could've gone undetected for much longer than we already suspect?"

"No one's sure at this point."

"But you dug up some old cases that're suspiciously similar in addition to last year's here and two years ago on Maui?"

He nodded. "Guilty as charged."

She realized that Parry was of a breed of men who looked differently at whatever fell under his purview, that while countless other cops on the island had seen the same information, it was Parry who'd put it all together. All of the material had been studied by others, but Parry and his team had looked at it in a fresh if twisted light, in the dark light cast by a stone-cold killer. Parry was what the FBI was all about. To him a crime scene wasn't simply a place where the evidence might be collected, bagged, collated and tagged, but a blight of the darkness within a killer's mind. Why had the killer chosen this place, this time, this person? It was the kind of approach pioneered by the late Otto Boutine, whom she had both admired and loved very much, a man who had died to save her from a terrible death at the hands of the infamous vampire killer, Matt Matisak.

Parry didn't work a crime scene backwards in an effort to reconstruct the crime, as the typical street-level detective might, formulating a mock-up of what might've occurred and then launching a neat and tidy investigation along a line of presumptions. Parry, like Jessica, knew that there are some clues left at a crime scene, which by their very nature do not lend themselves to a sane orbit. Parry obviously would be interested in items of tangible evidence left by the killer if there were any, but even if there were, he'd be even more interested in the implied clues lingering at the crime scene, each a passport to the mind of the killer. In the case of the Trade Winds Killer, or what the lab people had begun to think of as the Cane Cutter, there'd been no tangible clues—not a scrap—until Linda Kahala's misshapen arm had appeared; furthermore, there still was no crime scene as such, only a dumping ground, and even that was no ordinary dumping site, for it remained inaccessible.

Now James Parry wanted to know for certain, "Is there any sign so far's you can tell of ritualistic, sadistic, pseudo-sexual acts performed on the victim?"

"What in God's name do you think I am, Parry? A magician? No way I can tell all that with what little I have to work with. Get me more of Linda Kahala's body and maybe . . . just maybe . . ."

Still, she understood his burning need to know the answers to all the questions: Did the murderer take his time, or was he hurried? What insight into the mind of the maniac haunted the killing ground? What was he thinking before, during, after?

As her father had once put it, "To understand the 'artist,' you must first truly look at his 'work.'" Otto Boutine's profiling team had taught her that the killer must be defined as either an "organized" or a "disorganized" murderer, and that these traits were "symptoms" of orderly or disorderly behavior at the scene of his crimes, further defining the fiend far more than the type of weapon he used or the caliber of the bullet he preferred. Cane cutters on these islands were a dime a dozen.

"What I can tell you now for certain is that given the severity of the mutilation to the arm alone, the ritual nature of the slashes, the blade marks against the bone itself, he definitely cut into her while she remained alive; we are also confident that such brutalization means that he's certain to continue. He enjoys it."

"So that's the reason for the consistent victim profile. He seeks women who have that certain look." Parry stated it as a verification of what he'd already come to believe.

"When killing involves such butchery, it is either a crime of passion or psycho-sexual passion."

"Psycho-sexual passion?"

"A term we've just coined recently at the bureau for all the sociopaths who destroy people based upon some predisposition to an ideal or fantasy that is all mixed up with their emotional crisis."

"Passion seems a dirty word to use with this bastard."

"Two sides to every passion, Inspector."

"Yeah, I suppose so."

"We've got to locate his lair, find his killing ground, where he plays out his fantasy," she said, her right hand running the length of a stiff neck.

"Don't get your hopes up on that score."

She looked at him with a wondering gaze.

"You know as well as I that chances favor our serial killer going the way of most, meaning he'll never be caught," said Parry. "More likely than an arrest, he'll reach a state of complete mental breakdown."

"And quiet, private institutionalization," she softly agreed.

"It's what most believe happened to Jack the Ripper, who was also 'down on whores.'"

She bit her lip thoughtfully, placed her head in her hands and asked, "Do you think they were all prostitutes? Including Linda Kahala?"

"If not, she was mistaken for one. Hard to tell if she was into that scene just yet."

She showed him proof positive that the errant limb had once belonged to Linda, and then she told him about Kahala's blood on Kaniola's palm. This information shocked him into uncharacteristic silence.

"Then old Joe Kaniola was right about his son's having been the only man to ever see this bastard up close. If it's her arm, the killer must've been at work getting rid of the body when Kaniola and Hilani surprised him."

"It appears so."

Parry continued to ruminate. "But how'd the Kaniola boy get *her* blood on *his* palm?"

"That *boy* was thirty-four, Jim," she corrected him.

He frowned, realizing he'd been caught in a verbal slip that could have cost him had he been on camera. "Of course," he quietly agreed. "So how did he get her blood on his hands?"

"You figure it out. He was following a suspicious-looking vehicle, right?"

Parry thought back over the radio signal tapes he'd listened to countless times now of Hilani and Kaniola sparring with one another, their friendly banter culminating in their last words on earth. "Yeah, the car they followed."

"The car, the dead girl's clothes, the dead girl's body—anything's possible," she suggested.

"So Kaniola reaches into the car, touches the dead girl or her clothes, sure . . . sure."

"Your guesswork is quite probable." There was a little girl's glint in her eye and a lilt to her voice.

"You've found something else, haven't you?"

"There were some cloth fibers found on his uniform and adhering to his left palm, in the coagulated blood. All the fibers match. Now all we've got to do is find Linda Kahala's clothes, have the relatives I.D. them and we cross-match."

"Is that all?"

"Get Scanlon's people to comb the countryside up there around Koko Head, see if something gets shaken loose."

"Why wouldn't he have simply tossed the clothes into the Blow Hole with the body parts?"

"Too much chance of their going awry, lifted by the wind, missing the hole; besides, if he's a purist, I think he'd send his victims over nude."

"Purist? Purist what?"

"This guy's into some kind of la-la fantasy world I don't pretend to understand, but suffice it to say that sacrifices appear to be his thing. Usually sacrifices are sent from this world in the manner in which they came into it, nude."

"Is that how you see it?"

"Kaniola comes along, finds the clothing in the car and while he and Hilani are examining it, realizing too late what they have in their possession, *he* surprises them. That's the way I see it."

"Pretty shrewd," he replied, a hand going to his chin.

"Damn sure the first giveaway clue from this guy in all this time, and completely unintentional. He's cool and calculated, quite organized in the way he eliminated your two HPD cops, and in not drawing attention to himself over the years. He obviously is quite intelligent."

"That'd figure." Parry paced the office, his mind racing now that he had the first forensic truth to back his up-till-now-flimsy net of assumptions.

Because the killer was in the organized category, they could predict with some confidence that, once caught, he would match the profile, at least in part. Unlike psychics, they weren't professing to "see" into the heart and mind of a killer, but utilizing known facts and information gleamed from serial killers in captivity, such as John Wayne Gacey, Jeffrey Dahmer, Gerald Ray Sims before he'd killed himself while in captivity, the executed Ted Bundy— all serial killers who'd been far more forthcoming and cooperative than Mad Matt Matisak cared to be. Although for her money, Jessica believed Ted Bundy had merely filled in blanks to presupposed questions placed before him by the State Attorney's office in Florida, providing little more than what they wanted to hear.

The Trade Winds Killer would come from a dysfunctional family. His father's work would be stable, but parental discipline would have been inconsistent at best. Child molestation in one of its myriad forms was likely a staple of family life. He would have an average or better-than-average I.Q., but was likely working at a menial job which he felt was far below his designated rank or calling or talented abilities; his work history would be sporadic, even chaotic.

"He could be a student at the University of Hawaii, most likely with an uneven average," she suggested.

"Perhaps, but then again not."

"Several of the girls were attending the university," she reminded him.

"One of the few connections we've made among some of the victims," he agreed. He briefly told her about George Oniiwah, Linda's boyfriend, who happened to be a student at the Monoa campus at U.H.

"It would seem likely that the killer may have some connection with the university, given what little we know, that is." Jessica lifted a warm can of Coca-Cola off her desktop and poured what remained of its contents down a drain in the lab, rinsed the can and tossed it into a recycling bin below a table. Lau watched her movements from a room three doors away through a series of glass partitions separating the portions of the lab and offices. She was a little unnerved by Lau's interest in her and Parry, and she couldn't help wonder what was cooking behind his black eyes. Is good gossip in the lab hard to come by? she wondered.

"Yeah, and that means forty-six percent of the student population," Jim Parry was saying as he followed her about.

"Come again?"

"The precise number of male students at the Manoa campus hovers around five thousand nine hundred eighty."

"Concentrate on part-timers first," she suggested.

That'd be something like two thousand two hundred fifty."

"No," she corrected him. "Less the females, say forty percent, one thousand two hundred fifty to thirteen hundred."

"Hey, not bad. Now there's a figure we can work with," he said with a little salute of sarcasm. "I'll set Tony to work on it."

"Just remember, our guy—if he is a student and not a bottle-washer out there—he may've dropped out or flunked out before now. You may want to get backlist enrollments as well as current ones."

He nodded, telling her she was right, and then he quietly added to her repertoire of knowledge about the killer, saying, "This creep probably lives, or has lived most of his life, with a partner or spouse."

"Or parents," she replied.

"Maybe one parent."

"Stress would factor into his violence."

"Stress is brought on by the trade winds, maybe?"

She quickly agreed. "Something symbolic in the wind, perhaps? Maybe our guy got left out in a nasty storm as a child, who the hell knows."

"Probably hears voices in the damned wind."

She nodded admiringly, continuing the game of automatic thought. "Violence could also be triggered with a sudden problem— finances, job, marriage, or a romantic relationship."

"Alcohol and/or drugs are apt to figure in," Parry added, casually rising to the challenge. "A person who's usually no threat, nothing to take a second look at, socially capable, visibly acceptable, but he doesn't stand out."

"Approaches his victim in an open area, uses a non-threatening manner in a friendly, even familiar place."

"Picks 'em up at malls, in shops, at the bus station."

"Prefers verbal manipulation to physical force as he hunts for his prey. From the police reports, sounds like Linda may have known him from an earlier time, didn't want to go with him, and so he had to resort to physical force to get her off the street and into the car."

"Exactly . . . she knew him, and perhaps some of the others also knew him."

"Control over his victim is a vital part of what he does, and fantasy—"

"Ritual dominates his actions; the murder itself an acting out of a long-held fantasy, I know."

"He brutalized Linda. It was no pure accident the geyser sent her arm up from the spray."

Parry looked quizzical. "Whataya mean?"

"Close examination of the tear shows that it was sliced off at the shoulder, not torn off by natural forces. There're striated marks at the bone."

"Bastard . . ." he said.

"He transports the bodies in a vehicle," she said, continuing the unofficial killer profile they'd begun together.

Parry, pacing now, nodded and said, "Yeah, and his car's in fairly good condition. He won't risk being pulled over or caught with a dead engine, especially after Koko Head."

"Still, something about his car that night attracted the HPD cops."

"Kaniola."

"What?"

"Alan Kaniola first noticed the car . . . called it 'suspicious-looking.' I've only listened to the dispatch tape a thousand times." Parry's obvious anguish over the case showed through. "There's nothing there. They never called in a plate; never had the chance."

"Look, I think the killer takes souvenirs from each victim, squirrels them away, possibly clothing and jewelry, but most assuredly the hands."

"Cut at the wrist?" he asked.

She nodded, her eyes boring into him. "He . . . he takes his trophies out later . . . re-counts them, relives the fantasy over and over, until he does it again. And one more thing. He likely enjoys reading about the accounts of the missing girls and any news coverage devoted to their disappearances."

Parry nodded. "He's always out there looking for prey, the girl who looks like Linda Kahala."

"He knows what he likes . . . what he wants, and he feels comfortable doing it here. He's on his own turf. He knows the terrain well."

Parry agreed. "And when he sees that look-alike victim, he strikes."

"He ensnares, perhaps with words at first."

Parry thought of the Shakespearean sonnets he'd picked up from Linda's room, taken home and glanced over.

"Then he renders his victim helpless," she went on, "as when a snake sends venom into a mouse, immobilizing it. We found traces of a drug called curare, not present in the usual street drugs."

"I see . . ."

"He next assaults, kills and disposes of his victims."

"And he hunts nightly during the trades, looking for his victim of opportunity."

"Exactly," she agreed. "And when he fails to find her, he goes home and opens his box of precious collectibles—a collection of keys, hairpins, lipstick vials, underwear, earrings, necklaces and body parts."

"HPD has a lot of red-eyed detectives back out on the streets, particularly along Ala Moana, Kalakaua, Kuhio and the Ala Wai, interviewing pimps, johns, taxi drivers, employees in stores and restaurants in the vicinity, you name it. My own people have already logged three hundred man hours out there and zip. It's like this guy's a magician; makes 'em disappear before everyone's eyes."

"Yeah, I saw how crowded the streets were the other night when we were strolling. He meets her at a bus stop or a supermarket, convinces her that he has something she needs, that they have to go to his place to get it."

Parry grimly replied, "He has that lethal combination of desire, passion, lust and an inability to satisfy that need through any normal means."

"Impotence," she agrees. "Dysfunctional, and squeamish over the thought of pain and suffering—his own, that is—and the sight of blood—his own, that is. But at the first sight of blood from his first slash when he lost control with his first victim, he learned that the feel of anguish and torture, and the sight of blood streaming down the body of a helpless victim, creates in him an epiphany of pure pleasure, an orgasm like nothing he has ever experienced before, that for the first time in his miserable life he is sexually fulfilled."

"Yeah, understood . . . not only does overpowering a helpless woman give him an erection, it makes him ejaculate."

"Blood and pain . . . that's what he's into, and whoever this guy is, he's slowly come around to the conclusion that murder's not only easy, it's sexually gratifying," she continued. "The sight of blood, the struggle against him, the ultimate empowerment he feels, his goddamned erection, it all combines when he cuts into his victim and dangles her life over the edge."

"Her life or death in his hands alone. Makes him feel like God, I'm sure."

"For once in his life he's in control. That's what matters to him."

Parry swallowed hard, thinking of young Linda Kahala, of her father and mother, of how he was going to break the news to them that their daughter was now, for a certainty, the first positively identified young woman of the many missing who were all assuredly dead. It followed that since the last of the missing was murdered, the others were more than likely just as dead. There was no telling how many bodies this madman had accumulated below the waters of the Blow Hole.

"Not so sure I can eat lunch now," admitted Jessica.

"How about a stiff island drink?" he suggested.

"That I can't refuse."

"Maybe after a drink, you'll feel like something to eat, maybe a sandwich. I know a place close by."

She got up, grabbed her cane and came around to where he'd remained standing. "You're certainly taking good care of me."

"Zanek's orders," he said casually.

"Is that it? And what did Paul tell you about me?"

"Only that you're the best, and now I understand why he says so."

She stripped away her lab coat, put her jacket over her shoulders, and tapped with her cane ahead of him, privately pleased at his attentions. In D.C. she had a reputation as something of a cold "cutter," a typical M.E. rubric. Some there still called her the Scavenger—always on the hunt for clues. People, and men in particular, were usually standoffish, unsure around her, often threatened by her. The irony of it was that, despite her education, her medical training and her time at the FBI academy, and despite the fact she was an excellent markswoman, she thought herself the least intimidating person she knew. At least, she didn't intentionally intimidate men; still, like an aura one is born with, she was seldom viewed as anything other than Dr. Jessica Coran, M.E., FBI. There had only been a handful of men in her life who had gotten beyond their initial hangups about her qualifications and degrees, and even this usually required close working conditions and long hours to reach what ought to be an easily accessible plateau.

Interestingly, this hadn't been the case with Inspector James Parry. Here, with him, she'd been treated like a lady from the moment they'd met.

"You seem to do pretty well without the cane," he commented when they'd gotten into the elevator. "I looked in on you earlier. You were busy in the lab, so . . ."

"Sometimes I need it more . . . depends on how long I've been on my feet," she managed.

It was a lovely, silver-handled thing, given her as a coming-home present from J.T. and others at her Quantico labs when she had "come home" after her long ordeal with rehab. The trial that had placed a maniac into a psycho ward in a federal pen for the criminally insane had also been a treacherous ordeal. To this day, Mad Matthew Matisak held sway over certain of her emotions. As Donna, her well-paid psychologist whom she knew on a first-name basis now, had told her, "When you stare into the abyss, it sometimes stares back."

The healing process, for the brand of distress which Matisak had put her through, had taken years, and even now she was far from any cure or freedom from the scars, particularly the invisible ones. Matisak had cut into her for reasons not unlike those of the Trade Winds Killer, and here she was, staring again into the pit, looking for answers to questions most people pretended never to hear . . . searching through the rubble of the ugliest side of the human condition which netted rape, bloodletting, torture, mutilation and lust murder.

She wondered if Jim Parry's solicitousness was due to his measured concern for what had happened to her in the past, due to what he knew of her encounter with "Teach" Matisak. He knew that she had looked even deeper into the abyss than he, and that for her it was Matisak's insane eyes that stared back. Parry was intelligent and keen and sensitive. Was he interested in her, she wondered, or what she knew firsthand about serial killers?

Like all of the FBI family, Jim had to be well informed about her ordeal, aware of her near-death experience at Matisak's hand. How she'd lost Otto to Matisak . . .

At his car, he took her cane and offered a hand as she eased into the seat, and for a moment he lingered over the beauty of the cane itself, commenting on the ornamental craftsmanship. It wasn't a

Rolex, but it had to have cost some bucks . . . and he must have known that it was the same cane which had thwarted the demonic efforts of Simon Archer, a.k.a. the Claw. She could read it in his lingering gaze.

"You want to know about Simon Archer and about Matthew Matisak, don't you?" she asked.

"No, no," he said.

She didn't believe him. By the same token, she knew that Parry thrived on knowing facts, and that feeding on case-file information was not enough for a thorough investigator such as he. This was his strength and what made him appealing, and she also knew that he was dying to know all the inside dirt.

"If it'll endear me to you," she said with a crooked smile, "I suppose I can tell you about Matisak and Archer." *It might even be therapeutic,* she heard Donna Lemonte say.

He came around to the driver's side, the cane still in his hand. Placing the cane onto the rear seat and sliding in, he said, "Jessica, you don't have to talk about it."

His sincerity was tinged with a healthy dose of cop curiosity which she both understood and respected. "No, no," she began, "it's pretty obvious what's on your mind."

"Really," he insisted, "we can talk about other things."

"Yeah, maybe," she replied, "after this is out of the way."

"Jess!" he said, feigning annoyance.

She launched into the subject of Mad Matisak by way of an autopsy and a double exhumation which led her along a twisted trail to Matisak's lair.

We heed no instincts but our own.

Jean de La Fontaine

Jessica's whiskey sour with a twist of lime had arrived alongside Parry's gin and tonic, and she was taking in the incredible expanse of the turquoise Pacific, about to taste her drink there in the lounge atop the Aloha Tower, when Jim Parry lifted his glass in a salute, pointed to Diamond Head in the distance and said, *"Okole maluna."*

She accepted the toast, touching her glass to his, asking, "And what does that mean?"

"Bottoms up, in this instance."

"What do you mean in this instance? It has a double meaning?"

"A vulgar one."

She was intrigued. "Really? I love vulgar—what?"

"I'd just as soon—"

76

"No, please, what else does it mean?"

"Well, the literal translation means 'stick your bottom up toward the moon,' kind of moon the moon, a practice which most Honolulu cops let pass unless the drunk gets completely out of hand."

She shook her head and frowned, "*Luna*, like the Italian moon."

"Suck 'em up." He made it sound like sock 'um op, as he downed the rest of his drink. "That's another island expression, generally to do with alcoholic beverages, but this could also be taken as a cry of need, an invitation . . . depends upon the speaker and . . . circumstances."

"As circumstances warrant? It sounds as if the Hawaiian people are a flexible lot, if you go by their language." She felt a bit uneasy with the innuendo, looked around and asked aloud about the time.

He laughed lightly and said, "It's Hawaiian Time."

"Meaning?"

"A bit late. Anywhere from several hours to several days late, that is."

She smiled again, relaxing. "You know the island people well, don't you?"

"No *haole* ever completely knows them, and when you speak of the island people, well, that includes a lot of varied nationalities. What with all the imported labor for the sugarcane and pineapple fields over the years—Chinese, Portuguese, Japanese. Did you know there were one hundred sixty thousand Japanese on the islands at the time Pearl Harbor was attacked?"

She realized of course that he was right; she'd heard nine languages being spoken in the space of time it took for her to gather her bags at the airport in Maui and get to her hotel—Chinese, English, Filipino, Hawaiian, Japanese, Korean, Portuguese, Samoan, and a smattering of Spanish.

"The diversity," she told him, "simply adds to the romance of the islands."

"For the visitor, sure. For the working law-enforcement official, it can cause a lot of problems. For instance, the big Samoans, many of them huge monsters, keep an annual holiday which when translated is 'Kill a *Haole* Day.'"

"Kill a White Day," she repeated. "I see."

"Still, English has been the spoken language of Hawaii since the 1850s and it's taught in all island schools."

"I've heard a pidgin English among the bellhops, cabbies and others."

"Mo betta leave da kine talk 'lone."

She laughed at his charming accent.

"Hawaiians liberally lace their language with pidgin; kind of a tapestry of Hawaiian words, English words and something in between. Tony, me, others working the law here have had to learn it as a matter of survival."

She knew that the Hawaiian alphabet was the shortest in the world, using five vowels—a, e, i, o, u—and only seven consonants—h, k, l, m, n, p and w. All vowels were pronounced and there was a vowel at the end of each syllable, and a vowel always between consonants. An eighth consonant was a glottal stop, pronounced the way the breathy pause in "oh-oh" was created. The w after an i or e made the sound of a v as in Ewa.

"And I should warn you about asking a Hawaiian about directions," he added.

"Oh, and why's that?"

"You've got two main directions here: *mauka*—towards the mountains—and *makai*—towards the sea. Even on their maps you'll be hard pressed to know north from south, east from west. A *kamaaina* refers to landmarks rather than to points on a compass."

"Give me an example."

"All right, to reach Iolani Palace from here, 'da kine trip, you go *mauka* four blocks, then *waikiki* three blocks, li' dat. Now geev um, brah—go for it, friend!"

Jessica's full, warm laughter filled the cocktail lounge. She stared out at the unending sea and back to Diamond Head. Parry watched her gleaming eyes.

He said almost in whisper, "Leahi."

Her eyes returned to him, her lips parting, asking him to explain himself with a mere look, almost certain he was paying her some sort of Hawaiian compliment.

"Wreath of Fire."

"What?"

"Leahi—that's what the Hawaiians called it—Diamond Head. They called it Wreath of Fire because long ago signal beacons were lit up there, or possibly because in Hawaiian mythology, Hi'iaka, Pele's little sister, compared the crater's shape to the brow—*lae*—of an *'ahi* fish, the yellowfin tuna."

"Then how'd it become Diamond Head?"

"It was first called Diamond Head by British seamen who mistook the calcite crystals they found there for diamonds. At night sometimes, when the light is right, the calcite crystals resemble—at least for the Hawaiian romantics—the tears of Pele, goddess of the crater. Her tears were formed into diamonds, so to speak, by the force of the lava. Anyway, makes for great copy for the island promos."

"It is beautiful," she said, "and so are the legends, *wherever* they come from."

"Sometimes hard to distinguish fact from fiction here," he replied, lifting his empty glass at the waitress. "People think that grass skirts and ukuleles were invented here, but not so."

"It still sounds to me as though you love the islands, Jim."

He smiled at the use of his name. "I do. It's become home for me now. I've gotten accustomed to their ways."

"Guess I feel the same about my place in Quantico. We certainly grow attached to our surroundings—people in general, I mean."

"People in our line of work in particular," he added. "You try to build a safe wall of protection, a place to finally get away from what your normal day—if you can call it that—brings you. I don't have to tell you."

She shook her head. "Sometimes I wonder why I stay in the FBI."

"So do I, but then I get up in the morning and go straight back in. Some of the cases I've worked have been so brutalizing, dehumanizing, awful—for me, I mean. Guess . . . guess from what you've said, you're not wanting in that department."

She shifted uncomfortably in her chair, thinking of the nearly nine months of intensive psychological trashing she had taken at the hands of her therapist. "Guess it's in my blood," she replied, telling him about her father instead, a man who had been an M.E. for the Navy for most of his life. She didn't want to admit to any failures or scars, either physical or psychological. She didn't want Parry to think her less than perfect, for despite the cane, he seemed, at the moment, to think highly of her.

Parry now ordered an island daiquiri, explaining that the locals made the drink two and three times as potent as normal. "I earned it," he proclaimed. "I'll need it for the trip back to the Kahalas'. Time to inform the parents . . ."

"I'll go with you," she offered, extending her hand, her jaw set firmly, eyes fixed onto him. "I've dealt with grieving parents before."

"I'm sure you have."

"Having a female along might help."

"It might at that, but you've had enough for one day."

"Worried about my stamina or Paul Zanek?"

Instead of answering her, he pulled out a small, tattered-looking book of poems which might have come from an ancient pawn-shop. "Found this in Linda Kahala's room several days ago." He handed it over.

The title read *Shakespeare's Sonnets*. He indicated the high-lighted lines, flipping through to Sonnet 73, where Jessica scanned the morbid lines underlined in red, made more curious by the circumstances of Linda's death:

> In me thou see'st the twilight of such day
> As after sunset fadeth in the west;
> Which by and by black night doth take away,
> Death's second self that seals up all the rest.
>
> In me thou see'st the glowing of such fire,
> That on the ashes of his youth doth lie,
> As the deathbed whereon it must expire,
> Consumed with that which it was nourished by.

"I've checked with the university and she was involved in a Shakespeare class," said Parry. "Most of her grades were pretty mediocre, except for the English, with the exception again of the Shakespeare course. So thought I'd take a pass at her instructor. See what shakes out there."

"Not a bad idea. She certainly seemed melancholy, but that's true of most teens. It's the age when they groove on Edgar Allan Poe and H.P. Lovecraft, too, so maybe you ought not to take these red marks too seriously."

"Just a hunch, a feeling."

"I still think you ought to get some divers as close to that Blow Hole as possible; see what may have flushed out from the bottom," she suggested.

"Didn't suppose you'd let that go. But it'll be dangerous, even for the most experienced men. Still, I guess we'll have to go hunting down there now for sure."

"I'm not interested in a media show, just forensic evidence. If this bastard's ever caught, we're going to need all we can get on him."

"Whether you like media circuses or not, we've got one on our hands. No way to duck it, and maybe we shouldn't. Maybe we ought to use the media to our advantage."

"That kind of thing can be risky. People can get hurt."

"I'm aware of that, Jessica. I wanted you here for good reason. You've used the press to advantage in the past."

They sat in silence for a moment while she tried to decode what he was getting at. Failing this, she repeated herself. "I meant what I said about the Kahalas. If you'd like me to, I'll go with you as moral support."

He almost took her up on her offer, but shaking his head, he replied. "You've been through enough today. I'll take you home and maybe you can sample Waikiki Beach."

"If you're sure."

"Tony's meeting me later. We'll manage." He got to his feet and she followed suit.

"Well, thanks for the drink and the foreign-language lesson."

"My pleasure, really. Thanks for . . . for sharing, earlier."

She forced a marginal smile, recalling all that she'd told him about the Mad Matisak vampire case and the case of the Claw. Quickly reverting back to the lighter subject, she said, "Going to have to get a dictionary if I stay much longer. I think I love the language and this place."

"Good, maybe we'll make an islander of you yet."

She smiled genuinely now, accepting his hand on her arm. Parry gently guided her toward the exit. It'd been a long time since a man assumed she might like such treatment, not that she couldn't find her way solo from the table to the door.

They left the lounge unaware that they were being discreetly followed by a native man in casual Hawaiian shirt and shorts, keeping at cautious distance. The man was darkly tanned, his skin the color of red earth, his clothing loose and fluid. He took a separate elevator and at ground level, when he saw the two FBI agents get into Parry's car, he rushed to his cab and got on his C.B. radio and announced that Parry and Dr. Coran were leaving the Aloha Tower going south toward Waikiki, most likely the Rainbow Tower, where she was staying.

A voice returned on the C.B. radio, saying, "Aloha, Toma. Excellent work. I'll take it from here."

"You got it, *aikane*."

"*Hele* on outta deah, and say hello to Nola."

"Shaka, brah."

"And no talk story, eh?"

"Garans, brah!"

The C.B. went dead.

Parry balled his fist up and allowed his pinky and thumb to stand upright, and twirling this peculiar fist at her, he said, "Shaka, shaka, brah. It means everything's cool, friend!"

"See you later," she called out.

Parry left her at the entrance circle by the Rainbow Tower where cabs scurried in and out, tour buses trundled past and people lolled about, mostly tourists whose steps told others that they had all the time in the world. It was what Parry called the "tourist gait." In the crowd there were a number of Japanese women, and one, with a little skin toning, might for all the world be another Linda Kahala, her long trailing hair near her hips, the bone structure fine and petite, the twist at the edge of the mouth, the dark eyes. This young woman, traveling in the company of her parents, it appeared, looked like the ideal target for the killer.

Something inside Jessica made her want to rush up to these strangers and warn them, but she was too practical for such a step. They would think her mad, and they most likely would understand nothing she had to say, given the language barrier and the morbid nature of her message. Warnings were seldom heeded anyway, and if a warning were to be of any use, it might perhaps be done better via the media as Jim was thinking. The investigation into the Cane Cutter case was leading in that direction. There was no artist rendition of the killer, but there most certainly were enough faces and evidence to make a rendition of the typical victim. A Linda Kahala-type pencil drawing could be flashed over the TV channels throughout the island and presented in the press. It might be the right thing to do at this point, but Jim Parry had said that it was too soon, that with her coming in on the case, he didn't want to have the killer suddenly fleeing the jurisdiction, vanishing as most serial killers did.

From the corner of her eye, she saw someone watching her, a lone figure who stopped suddenly short, turned and was pretending to hail a cab. When she turned back and started for the hotel, he quickly pursued. He was a short, stocky Hawaiian whose step was lively and quick. She was about to lift her cane and strike when from the doorway stepped Joseph Kaniola, the newspaperman and father of the slain cop. She recognized him from their brief encounter at the airport.

Kaniola shooed the other, younger man off before saying to her, "I have come for some answers."

She stared into his unwavering, dark Hawaiian eyes at a smoldering light there. "There's really not much I can help you with, Mr. Kaniola."

"As a father? Off the record," he pleaded. "I've got to know what's being done."

His anguish clearly undeniable, she suggested they go inside.

They entered the open, airy lobby of the hotel, where the trade winds were allowed to dust everything in the place, going straight through to the seaside exit, where they found a table. Birds flew so close she might reach out and touch one. A waitress asked them if they'd like to order something to drink. She asked for iced tea and Mr. Kaniola asked for a beer.

"There's truly not much I can tell you," she began.

"That's not good enough," he challenged.

"All right, but this is in strictest confidence, sir."

"Accepted."

"It cannot go beyond this table."

"Accepted."

"Your son's murderer is the same man who has been killing young island women."

He sat in silence, the news sinking in. "To finally hear it from someone in authority . . . that Alan's death . . . that he didn't die for nothing, shot by some stoned drug-head . . . that he was so close to solving the Trade Winds killings . . . I knew it . . . felt it here." He finished by beating his chest with his fist.

"We believe your son stumbled onto the Trade Winds Killer."

"Stumbled? That's not exactly right. He followed the case closely. He knew every detail about the victims. He was on the bastard's trail."

"Perhaps . . . at any rate, the killer surprised him; got the upper hand."

"There's more you're not saying."

"I can't tell you any more. I've already overstepped my bounds just by talking to you."

"Did Parry tell you that you could not speak to me?"

"No, to the press in general."

"I tell you I am here as a father."

She cast out a long breath of air as if this might return some investment. He continued to stare, his eyes glistening over with the loss he had suffered. He reached for a napkin, dabbed his eyes which were red and swollen.

"His mother and I . . . his wife and children . . . we have all suffered a great deal. We have to know all that we can learn. We have to know that his killer will be brought to justice."

"He will," she said, knowing she could make no such promise.

He continued to bore through her from a purely Hawaiian visage with the eyes of a man seeking truth. She wondered momentarily about his ancestry.

"You must promise that nothing I say will find its way into your newspaper."

"I swear on the graves of my ancestors that nothing revealed here, from you alone, will be made newsprint."

"That's an old newsman's trick, Mr. Kaniola. Take what I tell you, run it by another source and then claim it came from the secondary source whom you fooled into nodding yes or no. I guess Parry was right about my not talking to you." She got up as if to leave, but he stopped her with a firm hand on her wrist. Nearby, she saw the Hawaiian man who'd earlier been following her, and she saw the glint of metal where a shoulder holster bulged beneath the Hawaiian shirt. She sat back down.

"Please, I must know, as a father."

She sighed heavily and sat back down. She told him about the profile of the victims, hoping this would suffice. She also confirmed that Linda Kahala was the first of the missing women to be identified and that this came as a result of a limb spewed forth by the Blow Hole. It was information that was generally circulating anyway, she rationalized.

"God, that could've been one of my grandchildren." He was horrified, his eyes wandering far from the table now. "Please, anything else about my son?"

She then added, "At some time your son was in close proximity to the killer, it appears because—"

"I knew it."

"—because—and this for certain you don't want to get around, Mr. Kaniola—your son's hands made contact with Linda Kahala's blood, either from the body or clothing."

His small eyes pinched at this. "What're you saying?"

"I'm not saying that I think he had anything to do with the Kahala girl's killing. He put his hands on some item that was covered in her blood. Most likely her clothing."

He thought about this, how close his son had come to being the hero in this story without heroes.

"News like that could be twisted," he said.

"I'm well aware of that, and so are my lab people."

"But they're not your lab people, are they? They're Parry's people. How can you trust strangers?"

She gazed questioningly at him. "You knew the exact time when I landed at the airport, and now you've learned where I'm staying. Mr. Kaniola, maybe I should be frightened of you."

"You have nothing to fear from me. I want only that my son be honored, and his killer brought to justice."

"In the meantime, what're you paying Mr. Lau for information?" She'd taken a calculated shot. His reaction was bull's-eye, not in words but in body language.

"I pay Lau nothing." He clenched his teeth as if insulted.

"Not even in beer?"

"Lau is my sister's son."

"Your nephew?" She dropped her gaze and drained her tea, which had turned to water. "I think I've said enough."

"But you've told me nothing. How soon will you and Parry find this madman?"

"What's really going on here, Mr. Kaniola? Island vigilantes at work?"

"You shock me!"

"You find the name of the killer, and then you and your pals can work a little island justice? Is that it?"

"I have a right to know what is being done about this matter!" His shout startled people all around them. She got up to leave, ignoring his repeated apologies and his bodyguard. As she walked away, he said firmly, "I will see vengeance done. I have a right to see it done. I am an American, too, Dr. Coran."

She rushed toward the elevator and her room, strangers on all sides of her now taking on a sinister form. How many of them were working as Kaniola's eyes? How many people were watching her? She had thought someone back at the Aloha Tower was watching her, but she had cast off the notion as preposterous. Now this.

She wondered how deeply Joseph Kaniola's frustration and anger ran. Just how far might he go if he learned who the killer was before she and Parry did?

When she got to her room and locked the door behind her, she wondered if perhaps she hadn't overreacted. Yet something in Kaniola's eyes, his manner, told her otherwise. She wondered if she should not tell Parry about the incident.

She undressed and showered, the tension draining from her, leaving her pleasantly empty; empty of thoughts of homicide, autopsies and Kaniola, of Lau's obvious deceit, and other pestering, thorny problems she'd have to face tomorrow. For now she'd get the sleep she had missed the night before, wake refreshed and be prepared for the next day far better than she had been equipped for this one.

God, why'd I say anything to Kaniola? she chastised herself. "Might've known better." He was, after all, a newsman, and no matter his race, the story was more important than food, water and truth. Sure, he professed a father's concern, and no doubt he was absolutely sincere in this instance, but he still remained a newspaperman.

She half expected and feared that tomorrow's *Ala Ohana* newspaper would run a story telling everyone of the FBI suspicions she had shared with Kaniola. Parry would have her head. It was too soon to release such information, and it might backfire on all of them, including Joseph Kaniola.

She toyed with the idea of trying to reach Jim Parry, to tell him of her encounter with Kaniola and what she had foolishly revealed to him. She thought about it but decided doing nothing was, for the moment, best.

It was early yet, 6 P.M., but she was exhausted, and the single drink she'd shared with Parry, at island proof, had left her mellow, perhaps why she'd been such easy pickings for Kaniola. She wondered now how worried she should be. Either way, she'd locate the pool, do some laps, come back up and sleep on it.

8

There is in God, some say,
A deep but dazzling darkness.

Henry Vaughan

After dropping Dr. Coran at the Rainbow, Chief Parry met Tony
Gagliano a block from the Kahala residence, where they sat for a
moment in Tony's unit. Tony was wearing a freshly cleaned,
midnight-blue flowered Hawaiian shirt, his usual attire, along with
loose-fitting dungarees.

"So what's new?" Tony asked. "Anything developing I ought to
know about? Anything at all? Like are you or are you not seeing
Dr. Coran on other than work-related business, Boss?"

"No, no and no," Parry replied. He changed the subject to the
victim's boyfriend. "How'd you fare with the background check
on George Oniiwah?"

"The kid's squeaky clean, Jim?"

"Too clean or just clean?"

"Well, as clean as it gets, let's say. He's *hapa Japa,* as they say."

"What's his being half Japanese got to do with anything?"

"Jim, when's the last time you arrested a Jap?"

"What?"

"Think about it, seriously."

Parry gave it a moment's thought. "Can't say that I ever have."

"That's what I realized after talking to this kid. I bet the HPD wouldn't find many arrests of Japs on their books either. It's not that they don't do crime like everybody else, but when they're good, they're very good, if you know what I mean."

"If they're into crime, they cover their behinds, I know, but what about the other half of this guy?"

Gagliano pulled his wallet out, absently checked how much cash he had on him and put it away. "Any rate, Georgie's clean. I mean he may be into smoking weed, doing a hit once in a while, maybe selling burn bags out of his dorm room, maybe; but he doesn't come over as any sort of maniac or hard-assed killer."

"Christ, Tony, neither did Jeffrey Dahmer to the cops who interviewed him just before he killed and fried up parts of his last meal."

"Hey, you maybe have to trust me on this one, Boss."

"You like this, don't you?"

"What?"

"Yankin' my chain, damn you."

"Come on, Jimbo. All I'm sayin' is that this guy don't shine like a hardcase. Japan's home for his father's parents, but the kid was born here, an American, the good ol' U.S. of A. Mother is Hawaiian, some sort of social worker; father's big in the computer programming business, makes a bundle for—get this—General Fucking Electric."

"And so the kid's well off and attends the university, the big campus?"

"Right, and get this: He not only knew Linda but also another of the victims, Kia Wailea."

"She was also attending classes."

"Right, and according to the kid, it was Kia who led Linda into the part-time-prostitution business down on the strip. Linda got off work at nine. So what's she doing on Ala Wai at midnight the night she disappeared? It's pretty sure she was tooting, Boss." Tony had called it "tooting" for years. "According to Georgie boy, Kia told Linda that hooking was her ticket to get through school, all that.

George says when he learned about what she was doing that he went a little crazy. They had a big fight. He slapped her around some . . . she scratched hell out of him."

"Any fresh marks on him that you saw?"

"No, but they split some time ago. Says he broke it off and hasn't seen her since. That was three months ago, he said, but he lied. It was less than a month ago he last saw her, according to the girl's parents."

"Gag, if the punk's lying about that, what else's he hiding, huh? Is he half clean or half dirty?"

"I think he's hiding plenty about his relationship with the girl, but I think it's small potatoes."

"Then why's he lying to you?"

"It's not small-time shit to him; to him it's important shit."

"Well, if it's important to him, and he's the only thread we got, then it's important to me, so out with it. What is it he doesn't want to get around?"

"For one, he's worried shitless that the girl's relatives are going to come after him, you know, the way we have, and if they do, they're not likely to be so gentle."

"What else?"

"Just a lot of crap, Jim."

Tony's guessing games sometimes annoyed Parry, who stared hard across at his subordinate now.

Gagliano finally said, "His pride."

"His pride? What the hell do we give a shit about this punk's pride?"

"Nothing, just that you know . . . he goes to bed with her again—"

"Again?"

"After he'd learned she was tooting, after he'd had time to cool off."

"You don't think he's angry enough over this to kill her?"

"Getting ahead of yourself, Jimbo. No, now he's had time to think, and he's asking himself how he really feels, down and deep, you see. Maybe it'd be kinky and fun to sleep with a dirtied, soiled dove, and Linda's a perfect way for him to find out. She takes on a whole new dimension since she's become a prostitute, more rounded, more complex, more interesting to his *hapa Japa* brain. Know what I mean?"

Parry followed Tony's reasoning. "It's risky. She's taking risks with AIDS and all, and now *he's* taking risks."

"He gets a hard-on he didn't expect, a rush to jog his safe, little world."

"I see."

"Only, he doesn't want anyone to know that he's got back together with her, not on the outside, anyway. Still, her parents aren't completely blind, and it seems every kid at the college knows who's on and who's off who, just the same as they know who's on drugs, who's selling, and who's tooting whatever down at Waikiki."

"So when did Georgie last see her alive?"

"Just a few days ago. Friends saw them together."

"Then maybe he did her."

Tony frowned. "Don't think so, Chief."

"Why not?"

He continued shaking his head. "No stomach for it. He's Mr. Clean, like I said; Hawaii goes preppy."

"So that clears him?"

"That and a lie detector, yeah, in my book."

"Lie detectors aren't foolproof. Anybody know we've questioned the kid?"

"Not a soul. The test was done in an out-of-the-way fashion, strictly hit and run. I did the test myself working out of the case. Convinced Krueger to turn over the machine to me."

"Good . . . good," replied Parry, popping a mint. "Keep it that way."

"I'm telling you, Chief, another go at this kid's a waste of time. And it could expose him to some ugly feelings in the community."

"Maybe, but I've got to ask him a few questions. After we're finished with the Kahalas, you can run me over there."

"Waste of time."

"Maybe, but perhaps I can shake loose something from the kid."

"Something I missed?"

"Something you weren't aware of."

"Swears he knew nothing about how she was living in between the time he dumped her and last saw her."

"Ted Bundy swore a lot of 'truths' too. Come on, Tony, the kid freakin' lied to you about the timing."

Gagliano shrugged. "Whatever you want, Boss."

"What I want is some answers. So far, we got shit, Tony."

"What about the doctor lady? She come up with anything?"

Parry brought his agent up on the news from the lab. It was enough to light Tony's eyes up. "Then those *kanaka* cops *were* on to something. Too bad they failed to follow proper procedure."

"They were good men, Gag."

"First thing they ought've done was call in the damned plate. Had they done that, we'd have their killer, the Trade Winds Killer, locked away for life right now."

"Maybe there was a good reason they didn't call it in immediately. Plate might've been obscured."

"So they inspect the car instead?"

"Yeah, like that and—"

"—and they find blood on the interior, maybe the girl's clothes, but before they can make another move, they're under fire."

"Like sniper fire from the brush. Never saw it coming."

Both the FBI men had served in Viet Nam and both understood how sudden death could strike.

The time in and out with the Kahalas to inform them of the positive I.D. made on Linda's torn limb, making it a certainty that their daughter was at peace with her Maker, was a mere twelve minutes, but it seemed like an hour. The mother crumpled under the weight of the news, supported only by her husband, who also slid to the floor. In their dark house of mourning, the couple reminded Parry of the twisted, sad figure in Picasso's *Blue Guitarist*.

The FBI men left a card and quickly disappeared, leaving the grieving parents to themselves.

"Get me to this Oniiwah kid," Parry said in an acerbic voice.

Gagliano knew the tone and what it meant. He said nothing as he and Parry, boarding Tony's car together, drove for the University of Hawaii. After a few miles, Tony said, "The kid lives in the dorm. We may not catch him. Could be out at a pizza joint, a dance, a party, a rat's-ass gala, anything."

"Tonight, Tony."

"We'll find him . . ."

Just then the usual clatter and clutter of the police ban radio in Tony's unit caught their attention, the dispatcher calling on a city squad car to investigate a disturbance on Paani near Kapiolani

Boulevard. It was coincidentally the same street on which the Kahalas lived and where Parry had left his car.

Each of the men looked at one another. "What do you think, Jim?"

"Dispatch gave it a 10–6. Couldn't be anything too big. Let's push on for the college."

As they did so, Parry thought of Linda Kahala's small, tight-knit community, thought of her hanging out on the corner at the drugstore where she and other children bought their crackseeds and Coca-Colas, thought about her walking the few blocks to Iolani School as a child, about her later catching the bus for Kapiolani Community College, which she'd attended for two years before going on to the university. She'd seemed a determined young woman with a plan. Parry had to know what had happened to end that plan.

They were now entering the Manoa Campus of the University of Hawaii, its peaceful, serene setting at the base of the mountains where the lush, green blanket of the Honolulu Watershed Forest Preserve marked its boundary, making it appear a place where nothing bad in the world could ever happen. For the FBI men such a fantasy world did not exist; they knew that no matter the place, so long as there were people, evil was very much in attendance.

They located George Oniiwah, pudgy and smug, squatting in a rat's nest called Paniolo's, a cave into which the patron had to climb down and in, sheltered from any street light or noise. From the sign outside it was ostensibly a bar and grill that existed just off campus as a place for students to get a pizza and a beer, to shoot some pool and hang out. To Parry's trained eye it was much more than this.

Oniiwah sat in the gloom far to the rear and close to the pounding jukebox, which was blaring out the most recent death-metal tune, an ear-shattering mix of high-tech guitar, screams about sex with corpses and a pretty fair drum section. The lyrics would make any maniac proud.

Everyone in the place had marked the FBI men as exactly what they were the moment they'd entered the dark entrance to this lair: cops. Still, George feigned indifference and simply continued to sip his Hawaiian homeboy brew, a beer called Kona, with a girl at his side and another couple across from him.

An amorphous spirit floated about the place, going in and out of what little light was afforded by a Schlitz beer sign, cigarette smoke that'd been trapped there forever. Paniolo's, or Cowboy's, was outwardly a typical Hawaiian watering hole, its patrons' faces all dark-skinned and leathery. Tony knew a little bit about the owner, who had been a Hawaiian cowboy for years over on the island of Maui, working with free-range-fed cattle and horses there until he got tired of eating dirt. Before establishing himself here, he had been arrested on drug-trafficking, but he'd not served time due to technicalities brought about by an improperly obtained search-and-seizure warrant with probable-cause violations and violations against his civil rights. Since then, his lawyer, a man looking for places to invest, had set him up with the tavern.

The disreputable owner, a full-blood Hawaiian, went by the name of Halole, Hal to his friends, better known to police as Harold Ewelo. It looked to Parry that the "Cowboy" was still eating dirt, only of another kind, as the place was an obvious front for drug-dealing, with Hal set up to run the operation from both the front and the back door. Somewhere in the bowels of this underground labyrinth where not even the trade winds could penetrate, Parry had no doubt you could get just about anything on your mind.

Tony needn't have pointed out George Oniiwah. Something about the kid called out to Parry. He looked out of place, a child among thieves. "Thought you said he was squeaky clean," Parry shouted, having no need to whisper over the roar of the music.

"I'm tellin' you he is."

"Then what's he doing here?"

"His crowd comes for pizza, the jukebox, the beer, I tell ya. They're not what you'd call heavily into drugs."

What about prostitution? Is Georgie above that? Parry wondered. *And what possible reason was there to attract Linda Kahala to this turkey?* As Parry approached the young people at the table, he could believe Tony's assessment. They were all clear-eyed and intelligent and quite aware of the two cops bearing down on them, their nervous necks twitching, eyes casting about at one another like ping-pong balls, hands alternately opening and closing, stock defensive gestures. In fact, Oniiwah's thumbs were closed over by his clenched fists, a sure sign of more than just nerves. Even the girls gave off body language that told the cops they were guilty of something. So did the man behind the bar, and another at the grill, each eyeing the other until the first one disappeared into a back room.

"Hello, young people," said Gagliano to the group in a mock show of grandfatherly concern.

At the back door Parry caught a glimpse of a pair of onyx eyes that had followed the bartender back in; the eyes now stared out at the FBI men. *The owner whom Tony had described to him?* Jim wondered.

Parry let the jet black eyes know, with his own gaze, that he knew that they knew. As soon as the onyx eyes disappeared, a commotion could be heard in the rear, the music having died.

George Oniiwah recognized Tony Gagliano from their earlier talk. Now George stood, making a show of it, saying, "Awww, man, haven't you pigs got anything better to do? Damnit, I'm sorry 'bout wha' happen' to Lina, sorry as all hell, but I didn't do it, and I don't fuck-king know who did! You cops're like maggots. I've got you crawling all over my ass. First you, den the Honolulu cops, now you again? Shit, man!"

"Beat it," Parry told the other young people.

"Hey, man, you don't tell my friends what to do."

"Get out," Parry shouted, and the three others vacated without a word.

"Now, Georgie boy, we're going to talk."

From one corner of his eye, Parry saw the bartender return with a heavy carton and begin to refill shelves already stocked to overflowing. He heard Tony belatedly introducing him to Oniiwah. "This here is Chief Parry, George."

"I already told this FBI mother—"

"Watch your mouth!" ordered Parry, his eyes burning into the kid.

"I . . . ah, already tol' Agent Gagliano all I know."

Parry instinctively disliked Oniiwah, knowing him for a selfish, priggish type of islander who had spent his entire life trying to be cool and to put on a good show, to look, speak and act Western in the MTV sense, and to pretend he had some political leanings that didn't show him for the sapling-blowing-in-the-wind that he was.

"Search your soul, Georgie," Parry said, realizing this kid didn't have much of a search ahead of him. "Search it and tell me about this." Parry handed the book of sonnets across a blackened wood table that'd been carved with the names of hundreds of students who'd sat here before George Oniiwah.

"Check out the marked pages," continued Parry. "I think—no—I know that Linda was trading poetry with someone. She mailed letters almost every day. Was she sending these to you?"

George Oniiwah was a thickly built young man with a handsome face; he wore the most expensive designer clothing. His father was a merchant, doing extremely well on the strip. "No, she never sent nothing like this to me, man. She never talked like this, ever. She . . . this isn't the Lina I knew, man, no way."

"She had her dark side," Parry began. "Least she was interested in the darkness, death maybe, maybe had suicidal tendencies, maybe?"

Oniiwah sat before him like a stone, expressionless.

"Well, damnit, did she?"

"No, she didn't ever talk that way round me, man, never."

"All right then, who do you know that might've encouraged her in this?"

He set his teeth, understanding where Parry was going, grateful that Parry's questions didn't center on himself. "I don't know. Kia was like that sometimes, depressed, you know. Maybe it was her."

"But she disappeared, too."

Kia Wailea, the other university student who'd disappeared and who was the subject of another of Parry's case files, continued to be listed as a missing person.

"George, you've got to see why we are suspicious of you; the fact you knew two of the victims? That kind of news gets around."

"Hey, man! If people think I killed those girls . . . Geez, I could find myself in a body bag. Why don't you guys leave me alone?"

"Killed? Who used the word killed? Did you say anything about these girls having been killed, Agent Gagliano?"

"No, not once," replied Gagliano.

"That's bullshit," cried Oniiwah over the sound of the heavy metal of Poison coming out of the box now. The guy at the bar, trying to appear busy by wiping it down, leaned in to try to hear more of the conversation between the government men and Oniiwah, who continued to protest.

"Everybody knows them girls gotta be killed. They been missing too long, and nobody was fooled about that business at the Blow Hole, about that leg being a store dummy's."

"Leg? Who said anything about a leg? Tony?"

"No, Boss, not a word. Besides—"

"Besides, it was an arm, Georgie boy," continued Parry. "Supposing it was Linda's arm, you want to tell me about it?"

"What?" he nervously blurted out. "I don't know what you want."

"Know anything about something missing from her arm, Georgie? Something you keep in your little fridge in the dorm?"

"Goddamnit, man, I don't know what you're talking 'bout, man!"

"Supposing Kia and Linda were tortured to death, their bodies horribly disfigured and mangled. Don't you know that we need somebody to put away, to show that we're doing our job? Suppose you won our little *lottery,* Georgie?"

"This is nuts! I didn't do anything like that to Linda or Kia or anyone else!

"There's got to be someone you know that Linda and Kia also knew, someone who could have kidnapped, tortured and murdered them. Among your friends, Georgie . . . someone you fucking know. It's in you, this knowledge, buried but it's there. Now, I want you to search for it. Try . . . try, damn you, you little fuck!"

The music in the box ended just as Parry swore out his threat. Parry was almost across the table, his eyes flaming with intensity, his fists white and pounding the table for splinters. Tony tried to calm him. The college boy put his hands to his head and gave the appearance of trying to tear from his mind the information Jim sought. "There's nobody like that, not that I know, no one that could make all those women disappear like—"

"Mutilate, Georgie, try mutilate, disembowel, eviscerate. They teach you all them big words here at the university, Georgie?"

"No one . . . nobody I know could do a thing like that, none of my friends."

The music came back up, a freakish clatter of horns over steel guitars and a screeching rapper that Parry could not place.

"Friends? Who the hell said anything about friends? Did I say that the bastard had to be a friend?" Parry asked Gagliano, turning to his partner for help.

"All right, maybe he's not a friend," suggested Tony, easing the situation a bit.

George considered this as if he'd been told for the first time that the world wasn't flat.

Brain-dead, Gagliano was thinking. *We're dealing with a*

brain-dead. "Just someone you would all have had to come into contact with at some time, maybe somebody employed here at the college?"

"Well . . . no," he reconsidered. *"Naaah."*

"What *naaah*? Who? Give or the chief going brok' yo' face, kid," pressed Gagliano.

Oniiwah looked stricken now. "Claxton."

"Who's Claxton?"

"Dr. Claxton just popped into my head, but no, that's not possible."

"Who's this guy?" pushed Tony.

"Her English professor," said Parry. "Shakespeare, right?"

"Shakespeare?" asked Tony.

"Yeah, Shakespeare. Tell me, George, why'd you mention Dr. Claxton?"

"Well, he's sometimes kinda scary, you know what I mean?"

"No, why don't you explain to me what the hell you mean?"

"He's a huge man, for one, but it's not even that; it's how he talks when he gets the least mad at you; makes bad, awful jokes, sometimes about your family, your nationality, stuff like that; and the guy's morbid, real graveyard-bound, man."

"Give us an example of graveyard-bound, George."

George squirmed in his seat. "I don't want this getting back to me, man."

"Don't you worry, George," said Tony.

"Well, he's into heavy-duty heavy metal, satanic shit, really."

"So's a lot of people," Parry pressed.

"And once, I swear, I was an eyewitness to this, once he took a kid and threw him out of class and—"

Tony laughed. "Real bad dude."

"—and smashed his face into the door first; said it was all an accident, but it wasn't an accident. And nothing was done about it, and a time before that he . . . he made a move on Lina."

"What kind of a move?" Parry was instantly interested, as was Tony.

"I only heard about it from her after."

"Go on."

"Called her in . . . something to do with a grade he said. One of those late afternoon conferences, man, and the building's as empty as a crypt. He forced Lina into a corner of his office, tore her clothes before she got outta there. Lina claimed he didn't get far, that she brought her knee up right into his nuts. Nex' day I did notice him staring at her like he was going to kill or rape her if he ever got a chance."

"This is beginning to sound like bullshit," said Gagliano, unconvinced.

"It was him who gave her the poem book! I saw him give it to her. And those passages that're marked? Lina didn't mark 'em; he did, he did!"

"George, you lied to us about the last time you saw Linda," said Parry, immediately waving off Oniiwah's objections. "I think I'm hearing some lying going on now. I can tell when a man lies. I'm a walking detector. Now, do you want to amend anything you've said about this Professor Claxton before I go after his ass?"

"What I said was the truth . . . only . . ."

"Only what, George?"

"The part about his having marked the pages. I don't know that for sure. Could've been her that marked the pages. I don't know. She was in his ten o'clock class. I had him at nine, an hour earlier."

"Anything else you wish to amend?"

"I tol' you what Lina tol' me. What reason did she have to lie? She was real upset. I think it was one of the things that led her to the street; I mean, think of it. Someone in a position of trust and power over you, someone like a teacher that you look up to all of a sudden trying to put his hands all over you and shit like that?"

"Yeah," Tony agreed, "the bastard."

Trying or succeeding? Parry wondered. It was an all-too-familiar story in these days of sex, scandal and betrayal in the American classroom.

"I want to meet this guy Claxton," said Parry.

"He's got morning classes only. Disappears at night. Nobody knows where. . . ." George's Sherlock Holmes intonation didn't help his credibility.

Outside, Tony said to Parry, "Damned if you didn't shake something out of that punk, but what's with the book? You copped it from Linda Kahala's room, didn't you? And why'n hell didn't you tell me about it?"

"Picked it up from Lina's room the other night, and—"

"Now you're calling her Lina?"

"She went by Lina, the Hawaiian equivalent. Guess she preferred it. So maybe we should, too."

"If it'd make a difference . . ." Gagliano began, but let it go.

"I took the book home with me that first night."

"You might've told me about it."

"Did a little bedtime reading. Wasn't sure how I might use it until I saw Georgie's smug face. But after laying it on him, I agree, he's not our killer."

"I knew that much."

"Now we locate this Claxton character."

"I wanna know why you didn't tell me about the Shakespeare, and why you didn't hash it over with me, Boss."

"I didn't know if it was relevant or not, and the case didn't need another confusing dead end, Tony; simple as that, all right?"

"You're raising your voice, getting angry at me for asking about an oversight on your part?"

"I thought it best to keep her private thoughts private if they held no bearing on the—"

"Private? Christ, Jim, private?"

"Yeah, private, you remember the word?"

"There's nothing in this world that's private when it comes to a murder victim, Jim. You know that!"

"Yeah, yeah, I know that . . . sorry, Gag."

Like silence broken the moment you said something, privacy was shattered the moment a crime was committed.

The state of man: inconstancy, boredom, anxiety.

Blaise Pascal

Midnight, July 16, 1995

Claxton wasn't in the phone directory. They found the name of the Dean of Faculty on a placard in front of a closed and darkened administration building of gleaming steel and glass. Parry telephoned the dean, identified himself and asked for the whereabouts of Dr. Claxton. The dean, shaken by the late night call, finally gave him the home address for a Dr. Donald G. Claxton. He lived within walking distance of the campus and they were soon on his doorstep, pounding away like a pair of Nazi Occupation troops.

Claxton was a big man, filling the doorway. He was also a belligerent bastard who refused to allow them inside where the sound of some less-than-classical music blended with heavy breathing, the telltale blue cast of a video screen rising and falling. Parry caught sight of someone hastily dressing and stumbling

100

around behind Claxton's large frame, no doubt another of his students catching up on some late assignment.

Claxton was bearded and balding with the appearance of a man once active and involved in sports. Nowadays it appeared that boredom, beer and coeds made up his sporting life, and if his students were good sports, they'd receive good grades; otherwise, they got what was considered in college the ax, a grade of C. Parry recalled that Linda Kahala had gotten a C in her Shakespeare course, but had done superbly well in all of her other English classes.

Parry quickly introduced himself and Tony. "I want to talk to you about Linda Kahala."

Claxton was immediately on the defensive. "Yes, of course, I'd heard about her disappearance. Tried to locate her about a grade conference but, well, some kids don't want to be found. Has she? Been found, I mean?"

"Found, yeah, she's been found." Parry watched intently for any reaction to this news.

"Thank God. It must've been a nightmare for the parents."

Either Claxton was an extremely cool character, or a socio-path—which their killer must be—or the man had no idea that Linda Kahala had been brutally murdered. At this point, Parry didn't want to disturb his line of questioning with the fact the girl was found dead. "I understand she had a problem with you, Dr. Claxton?"

"Problem? Oh, well, she wasn't too bright; she failed to do well in my class, but—"

"Why's that, Doctor?"

Tony snidely asked, "She didn't do well on her orals or what?"

"Because she didn't pass your goddamned sex exam?" Parry bluntly added, having agreed on the ride over to press the man this way.

Claxton visibly reddened there in the dark doorway. "What the hell is this? I'll thank you to leave now, you gentlemen of the law."

"We know all about your classroom tactics, Claxton," Parry retaliated. "And now one of the girls you sexually molested has turned up dead, mutilated beyond recognition and—"

"Dead? Mutilated?"

"—and that's a bit too much to overlook, Doctor, even for a man of your refinement and reputation. Now, are you going to cooperate, or do I have to get a warrant to search, and maybe a second to arrest?"

He stood there breathing heavily, pondering his options. "All right, all right, what the hell do you want from me?"

"We'd like to come inside, look around," said Tony. "'Less you got somethin' to hide."

He looked over his shoulder, eyeballing his guest. "It's really a bad time for me. What about coming back tomorrow, say two in the afternoon?"

Parry pressed on. "You gave Linda a book of sonnets?"

"I give a lot of books away."

"Did you or not?"

"What if I had? What's it to you?"

"This book?" Parry's sleight of hand with the book impressed Tony, whose eyes bored into Claxton, his fists clenched.

"Yeah, maybe . . . I suppose I may've given her a book. I give away a lotta books."

"When? Before or after you raped her?"

"Raped her? Are you guys nuts? What rape? There was no . . . never any rape. She . . . consented."

"Yeah, right," muttered Tony.

"Right there in your office, Doctor? Where you backed her into a corner?"

"Goddamnit, do you know how many of these kids with poor grades go shouting sexual harassment these days?"

"She's told others about the incident," Tony added.

"It's her word against mine."

Tony instantly corrected him. "Was . . . was her word against yours."

"And who's a court to believe, Doctor? You or a poor dead girl whose life was shattered first when her professor put his hands all over her, from where she spiraled down to the street?" asked Parry.

"What exactly do you fuckin' cowboys want from me?"

Parry and Tony heard the noise of a back door closing. "Go get that person, Tony. Maybe we'll have a talk with her, too . . . corroboration, maybe."

Tony started away. Claxton called out. "All right, all right."

Tony stopped at the foot of the stairs. Parry motioned for him to return.

"Now, Dr. Claxton, I want you to tell me where you were on the night of the 11th when Linda Kahala disappeared."

Claxton backed from the door and pushed it open for them to step inside, saying, "Look around. Does this look like the house of a maniac?"

Parry stepped in, followed by Gagliano, who said, "You got any coffee?"

Claxton ignored the request.

They went through the necessary questions and as they did so, Parry began to feel that Claxton, while a scum, was no killer. He finally asked Claxton, "Have you any students, particularly male students, that Linda gravitated to in class? Was there anyone she worked with in particular, studied with, say on a class project, anything?"

"She was dating some guy in my nine o'clock. That's all I know."

"We know about the boyfriend, Oniiwah," replied Tony. "He's clean."

"Anyone else she might have shared a book like this with?" pressed Parry.

"A guy, huh?" He had lit up a cigarette and now he blew out a long stream of smoke. He sat back on his lounge chair in his robe, naked beneath, rolls of fat making a spiral of snakes about his relaxed midriff. "I couldn't say . . . I don't know . . . I'm no mind reader . . . Don't pay that much attention to these kids, you know. Besides, I have a lot of classes and students."

"Sounds like the Albert Schweitzer of academia, don't he?" asked Tony.

Parry said, "This would be a guy in her class."

He shrugged. "I can give you the roster; you take it from there. I didn't notice anything in particular going on with her and another student. Course, I don't pay that much attention to the private lives of my students."

"No, I guess you wouldn't. You're just interested in their private parts."

Claxton started to protest but thought better of it.

"Let me have the roster. Fact, let me have all your rosters."

Claxton nervously bit at his inner jaw, but went to a desk and ripped several computer printouts from a book. "Here, take them. I got others."

"Jesus," moaned Tony as he stared over Jim's shoulder at one of the lists which numbered three hundred students.

"This the way Shakespeare's being taught nowadays?" asked

Parry rhetorically as he made for the door, anxious to be rid of Dr. Claxton.

"It's a fucking introductory level course." Claxton pursued them, as if it were important for them to understand him better. "It's bottom-line, product-centered, factory mentality in the bloody womb of academia, thanks to the bureaucratic assholes in administration whose primary concern is to suck every cent out of their pockets! Whataya want from me?" Claxton bellowed as the door slammed in his face.

At the car, Gagliano began a coughing and spitting jag. Parry asked him if he was okay, his right hand pounding Tony's back in mock concern. "Come on, it wasn't that bad."

"I'd rather deal with the rats on the wharves than a puke like that. Guy turns my stomach."

"You carry Rolaids; use 'em. For now we'll split the lists into four evenly divided, Tony. I'm getting additional manpower and if the Trade Winds Killer is on that list, I intend to get to know him up close and personal."

Parry then took the list from Gagliano and ripped off the first of the four sections.

"You've got to be dead on your feet, Boss," offered Tony. "What can you do tonight?"

"Narrow the list to all Caucasians first. It's a good bet our killer is white; also look for the killer to be older, a good deal older than Oniiwah, upper twenties to middle age marks the kind of organized, controlled killer we're dealing with here, if the statistics mean anything. It's unlikely this guy's a kid. He's too deliberate, too careful to be a kid strung out on drugs, or some hot-tempered punk who'd leave a trail any idiot could follow."

"Given the deliberateness of his remaining in the shadows, the fact he's left no crime scene for us to work, yeah, I got to agree on that score."

"He seems to know enough to cover his ass, all right. Tomorrow, start with the registrar's office, get every bit of vital information on every male on the list their damned computer has, and have it play kiss-face with our mainframe, got that?"

"It's called in-your-face, Boss."

"You mean innerface."

"Who'll you be recruiting?"

"Haley's expressed an interest and so has Terri Reno."

"Kalvin Haley, that big Aussie?"

"He's had experience with serials, and he was practically born here, part Hawaiian even if he won't admit it. Could really be of help to us."

Tony remained skeptical. "Yeah, but Reno, a mainlander?"

"Tony, you're going to have to work with her, all right?"

"Whatever you say, Jim."

"She's got to get experience somewhere, and who knows more than you, Tone?"

"Whatever you say, Jimbo."

"I say don't call me Jimbo, okay?"

"Whatever you say," he repeated.

"I say get me back to my unit so I can take myself home. Tomorrow noon, I want to feed the computer the breakdowns on these names—sex, age, height, color of eyes, nationality of each person on the list. Run 'em all through the Honolulu Police I.D. files, our own files . . . see if we get lucky."

"Whatever you say, Jim."

Tony sensed the foul mood Jim Parry had fallen under, and so he wisely fell silent. The drive back to the street where the Kahala house stood didn't improve either of their moods as they looked past the lifeless, darkened house to where Jim's car stood stripped and smashed. It looked as if there'd been a block party, everyone issued a sledgehammer and given a license to attack Parry's car. But first the more prudent had ripped out the radio, popped the trunk and made off with a pair of expensive Kevlar bullet-proof vests along with several boxes of ammunition for his .38 and an expensive Remington 12-gauge shotgun; his tires had been punctured, the moon hubcaps gone, every window smashed, the street littered with the raining pellets. The hood and top of the vehicle were destroyed beyond recognition, and beneath the hood expensive necessary parts had been stripped away. A siphon hose extended from out of the gas tank, likely the only reason the car hadn't gone up in flames, as several bullet holes had cut paths through the metal.

Parry was stunned. "That call we heard," he said, the words tumbling out as hard round marbles, Parry not feeling his throat muscles, tongue or lips moving.

"You sons of bitches," Tony bellowed to the night.

Parry cursed the street as well and gained as much response as Tony had. The two FBI men felt eyes on them, imagined the glee in the hearts of those watching, and in a moment began to feel vulnerable. "Where were the city cops when my wagon was being annihilated? It must've taken twenty or thirty minutes at least to do this kind of damage, damn!"

"We can't do squat about it now, Jim," said Tony.

"The hell we can't!"

"Come on. We'll send a wrecker for it tomorrow."

"Gutless bastards!" shouted Parry, shaking his fist.

"Jim, standing here and shouting at the pavement's not going to get us anywhere."

"Where are you now?" Parry continued to shout, venting his anger.

The dark little street responded with a few lights going on here and there, but no one came outdoors to claim any victory. Parry scanned the windows, Tony tugging at him.

"Forget it, Jim. Come on."

"Don't take it so personal, huh, Tony? Well, fuck that!"

"Jim, these people're frustrated. They struck out at what we stand for, not who we are."

Parry paced around the hulk of his destroyed vehicle, gritting his teeth over the sight of its stripped interior and slashed seats, mutilated with machetes and knives. He realized it was just over a century ago that native sovereignty had been wrested from Queen Liliuokalani in a bloodless takeover backed by 162 sailors and Marines from the *U.S. Boston,* then docked in Honolulu Harbor. It was on January 17, 1893 that a group of powerful white businessmen and plantation owners took up arms, calling them- selves the Hawaiian Rifle Militia. They forced the queen to abdicate, and soon after Hawaii became a U.S. Territory, and in 1959 the fiftieth state in the Union. To a sizeable number of Hawaiians this was not ancient history, and although the white mind could not conceive of ever rending the intricate tapestry of economic, industrial, technological and cultural fabric woven out of this tortured paradise by returning Hawaii to its sovereign status, as Hong Kong was slated to be returned to China, there were many prominent Hawaiians actively seeking just that, along with ten billion dollars in reparations, an apology and a return of their lands used as U.S. government holdings, including Pearl Harbor.

Now the grand and long-standing debate between the U.S. and Hawaiian nationals, coupled with the recent spate of disappear- ances and probable murders of Hawaiian women, seemed to have all congealed here on this street tonight and the frustrations of several generations had come down heavily on Parry's unfortunate vehicle.

"The unit's ruined."

"It can be repaired."

"I've had that car since I became bureau chief."

"I know . . . I know . . ."

Tony managed to dance him back to his own car and Parry got inside. "Where the hell you suppose the police were?"

"Probably no one called it in, Jim."

"We heard a disturbance call, remember? Christ, should have responded ourselves."

"The disturbance call was a 10-6, remember? No big deal, but this—this had to've happened after the cops came and went, is all I can figure, unless—"

"Isn't this sector routinely patrolled by Hawaiian cops? Right, and all they saw was a block party, right?"

Tony, who had pulled from the curb only to hit the opposite curb with his wide U-turn, drove away now. He was trying on a smile when he said, "Hey, Chief, it could've been worse."

"Oh, how so?"

"You could've been in the frigging car when it happened . . . or worse . . ."

"Or worse?"

"It could've been *my* unit."

Parry shook his head and held back a laugh. "It's just a machine, I know, but you do get attached to what's yours. Even if it does actually belong to the bureau, you know."

"We aren't talking horses here, Sheriff. At least the machine didn't feel any pain."

"So what, Tony? Does that mean I shouldn't? It pisses me off, all right?"

"Let's just get out of this area before someone takes a shot at us. Feel like a sitting duck here."

He put his foot to the floor, the engine roaring. Tony nervously glanced in the rearview where he saw a crowd of dark-skinned youths gathering like corporeal shadows behind them, thankful that Chief Jim Parry didn't look back or hear them.

"Lot of anger building up out here, Jim."

"The damned police aren't cooperating, Tony. They had George

Oniiwah two days before us, and yet they chose to say nothing about him."

"Wrote him off as a suspect, I'd say, so why bother you with him, Jim. You're overreacting."

"Goddammit, Tony, do you know how long I've tried to get an island-wide task force put together on the Trade Winds Killer?"

"I know . . . I know . . ."

"I was told by the commissioner of police of Honolulu— guaranteed, mind you—that whatever they know, we know."

Tony sat up at this. "And we'd extend the same courtesy?"

"Which I've been damned careful to do."

"Oh, like you've told Scanlon every single result of the two autopsies on his cops?"

"Fully informed Scanlon, yes."

Tony nodded approvingly. "And the girl's arm?"

"They've got it, as does the military, thanks to Marshal, and the county, and the state." Parry's voice began to drag along with the list of need-to-knows. "This case is turning into a political soccer game."

"So you've held nothing back?"

Parry thought of the bloodstains found on Kaniola's hands, the blood belonging to Linda Kahala. It was the one item of information he had withheld. "Nothing," he lied.

"Then I guess those bastards are shafting us, Chief."

"Wouldn't be surprised if they didn't have a hand with the sledgehammers."

"Only an off-duty cop on a drunk would be that reckless to risk his job, Chief."

"Yeah, maybe."

They were at Parry's house, where they exchanged their good nights, Tony assuring him that he'd pick him up at eight sharp. Parry trundled off to his door, a small ranch home, well manicured and out of the mainstream of Honolulu life in an area between Fort Shafter Military Reservation and the Likelike Highway on a dead-end street named Kiloni. It was quiet and serene here, no bustle or distractions, attractions or madness. He had had opportunities to move into a condo fronting Honolulu Harbor, but he'd never taken the step.

Inside the house there was a friendly emptiness, a solitude and stillness that were both warm and needed for his frayed nerves. The walls were lined with photos and paintings, primarily of mountain scenes he'd collected over the years, which shared space with a few citations.

He tore away his shirt and wandered through the well-furnished living room to the refrigerator in the kitchen, searching for something to quench his thirst and to nibble on. He couldn't decide which was more pressing, his hunger, his fatigue or his need for a shower to wash off the filth of a day that seemed steeped in grime. He gave a thought to Claxton, to George Oniiwah, to the pair of eyes that belonged to the cowboy proprietor of the drug-fronting bar and grill, and then he recalled the slinking rats who'd destroyed his car.

He opted for the shower when he saw that his refrigerator needed re-stocking.

Prices in Oahu for such items as cereal, $6.99 for a twelve-ounce box, $4.00 for a gallon of milk, had become routine for him, acceptable, but keeping his place well stocked had always been a problem. Still, the beer was cold and chilled. He took one into the shower with him and drank as he lathered up.

Once he began to relax, the tension draining from his aching muscles and limbs, he thought of Jessica Coran, thought how wonderful it would be to step out of the shower and find her somehow magically transported here, waiting for him, her arms open, her lips inviting.

"Crazy fantasizing bastard," he admonished himself, stepped from the shower and halfheartedly toweled off, the muscles of his chest heaving with the effort. It was past midnight. Honolulu was wide awake and Honolulu cops were on the prowl for the Trade Winds Killer, on the lookout for young women who matched the description of those already brutalized by the killer. FBI agents, too, were posted at strategic locations along the strip. Every disturbance call was being taken seriously, at least everyone but those involving an FBI vehicle demolition.

Tomorrow, he'd shift to nights, to help out in the street surveillance operation. Tony would join him, spelling other agents he'd sent out.

The phone rang; he didn't want to pick it up; didn't want to hear any more bad news today; wasn't sure he could take any more. No one but Tony knew for certain that he was home. He let it ring. On the fourth ring, he gripped the receiver, started to pick it up, but cursed instead. When he did pick it up there was only a dial tone.

He had made a lot of mistakes tonight, he told himself, and not answering the call might have just added to them. Suppose there was another disappearance. Suppose a kidnapping had been foiled. Maybe a candidate for the Cane Cutter'd been apprehended. It could have been Kal Haley and Terri Reno calling with good news.

"More likely bad news," he muttered to himself, trying to shrug off the phone call when the damnable thing rang again. This time he picked it up on the second ring.

"You sonofabitch, Parry!"

It was Dave Scanlon, police commissioner of Honolulu, angry as hell.

"Something bothering you, Dave?"

"You, you bastard! You fucking held out on me. One of my cops has the victim's blood on his hands and you don't see fit to tell me? And now it's going to be all over the goddamned morning papers, thanks to that goddamned *kanaka*!"

"Kaniola?"

"Who the hell you think called to corroborate the information?"

"How the hell did he get it?"

"You tell me, Mr. FBI. Frankly, Parry, I don't give a mongoose shit how in hell he got it. I want to know why I wasn't informed."

"No one had that information outside our lab this morning. I was going to alert you when—"

"When! Yeah, when it suited you. And what about this hypothesis that the Trade Winds Killer is a white male between the ages of twenty-seven and forty who's wielding a cane cutter? How did the papers get that?"

"Not from my office."

"No, I suppose not. I suppose your hands are spotless."

"Believe me, Scanlon, it didn't come from this direction."

"Sounds like you've got a leaky valve somewhere, pal. *And I understand you're on foot these days.*"

The delight in his voice gave Jim Parry a visual image of the smirk on Scanlon's face. It dawned on Parry that every cop in the city knew about his vehicle.

"Any information withheld from the public and your office, Scanlon, was done for the good of us all, for the sake, goddamnit, of peace. Now you're telling me that the headlines in the *Ala Ohana* are going to read that a white man is stalking Hawaiian women with a cane cutter?"

"And the goddamned English papers'll be running a counter-story, saying that Alan Kaniola was Linda Kahala's murderer!"

"A little information in the wrong hands." Parry's words tumbled out in a sigh. "Dangerous as a cornered mongoose in a cradle."

"I had a right to know beforehand, Parry. We had an agreement, I thought. You broke faith."

"Faith hell, Scanlon! You've been withholding information since day one on this and—"

Scanlon hung up.

"Christ," moaned Parry. Things were fast getting out of hand.

A half hour later he was sound asleep, but rudely awakened by the insistent phone ringing at his bedside. This time it was the melodic, whiskey-voiced Dr. Coran, her tone tinged with an icicle of agitation as she told him about her earlier meeting with Joseph Kaniola.

He was instantly angry with her. "But why'd you tell him anything, Dr. Coran? It should have occurred to you that you were talking to the most irresponsible newspaperman on the island. One of the most vocal lobbyists for Hawaiian sovereignty, a leader in the nationalist party here."

"He promised it wouldn't be used in the paper."

"It'll be all over the island tomorrow. I've already had calls on it. Damnit."

"I'm sorry, but he is the father. He had a right to know as next of kin, and he promised what we spoke of was off the record."

"And you believed him?"

"I did, at the time."

"The man must've been following your movements the whole time and you trusted him?"

"I did what I felt best, under the circumstances."

"Well now the circumstances have changed, drastically."

"Thanks to me," she replied.

He softened his tone. "Look, I suppose it would've had to have come out in another twenty-four hours or so anyway. Don't lose anymore sleep over it."

"Did you have any luck at the college?"

"We have a lead, but it's going to take time to pursue, learned a few details about the last days of Lina . . . Linda Kahala's life."

"I see."

"Funny, I'd hoped to hear from you," he managed to say, "but not about this."

"Oh? And what had you hoped to hear about?"

"About how you enjoyed spending the late afternoon with me, that's all. Listen, you said you used to go deer hunting often with your father?"

"Well, yes," she said. "I did."

"I know a place in the islands where deer season is just opening."

"Here, in Hawaii? You have deer?"

"Imported, but yes, real live deer. On the island of Molokai."

"Sounds like a great trip. Have you hunted on the island?"

"Yeah, once. I have to warn you: It's a wilderness section."

"No problem. I love the wilderness."

"I mean, it might be difficult getting around."

By her silence, he knew that she understood his concern was with her bad leg and the cane. Finally, she said, "Don't worry. If you can arrange it, nothing'll stop my accompanying you to Molokai. Well, I'd best say good night now. Let us both get some rest."

"Expect to read about our case in the papers tomorrow," he warned her.

"I hope I haven't completely ruined things."

"I hope we don't have a race war on our hands."

Silence for a moment. "Do you really think it could get so . . . out of control as to—"

"Like L.A., we have our minority held pretty much in economic bondage; these people are very close, very strong in their family ties; it's really all they have. I've already seen evidence of their frustration and anger played out on my car tonight."

"Oh, no," she gasped into the phone. "You weren't hurt, were you?"

"My car was totally dismantled and destroyed while I wasn't looking, but otherwise, I'm unhurt."

"You think that some of Kaniola's well-meaning friends may've been behind it?"

"No, not likely, although who knows for sure . . ."

"Christ, I wish I'd kept my mouth shut around the man. I hope I haven't screwed things up to the point—"

"I don't fault you, Jessica," he said. "You couldn't know the depth of feeling between the whites and non-whites here in paradise."

"Shoulda known better."

Her deep, breathy voice alone made it all worthwhile, he thought, listening to her every word.

"Forget it. We go on from here."

"Dammit, Parry, you're being too goddamned nice. I just fried you and all you can say is—"

"Night, Jess."

He hung up, not allowing her another word, glad to have the last word, pleased to have heard the sound of her voice again, and totally frustrated on learning that the leak Scanlon referred to had indeed come home to roust at his doorstep. As upset as Scanlon was, he knew there'd be a great deal more hell to pay come sunup.

Suddenly, he could no longer sleep. He got up, fixed himself a cup of steaming-hot tea and switched on a tape player that'd remained on his table all week. Once more he listened to the voices of Thom Hilani and Alan Kaniola from the moment Kaniola picked up the "suspicious"-looking, dark or maroon Buick sedan barreling up toward Koko Head at a fairly high rate of speed at 1:43 A.M.

"HPD 12, this is Hilani, Unit 2E, Sector Bravo. I have you and the sedan in sight. Can I be of assistance, since you're such a fucklick?"

"This is Dispatch Officer A312. No can make dat kine talk on dis frequency, Officer Hilani."

"Friendlies're hard to fine out heah," replies Thom Hilani.

"Fall in behind me, 2E." Kaniola's invitation gives no sign of agitation until his next words. "Shit, Dispatch I've lost sight of him off the hairpin just before the Blow Hole."

Hilani's reply is clipped and angry, a blaring motorcycle horn providing a backdrop to his curses. "Damnit, brah! Whataya doing backin' into me fo'? Almost run my ass over!"

"Call in our position, Hilani."

"No readin' this mother by no book. HQ, this is HPD 12 and 2E, leaving unit to investigate abandoned suspect vehicle. Our location is the Blow Hole, over."

"Roger that," replies Dispatch.

Neither man mentions why he fails to call in a DMV check on the plates. The transmissions simply end. After an uncomfortable amount of time Dispatch tries to hail the two dead cops.

There was already much criticism circulating about how Hilani and Kaniola didn't properly execute procedures, that they should have secured the area around the car, got that license plate, called it in, and called for reinforcements up there. But Parry, who'd now listened to the tape sixteen times, was convinced that these two men had not been given an opportunity to respond and had had good reason for their every action, because the plate was intentionally obscured. "No readin' this mother by no book," Hilani had said.

Hilani, Kaniola and Lina Kahala's deaths were all linked as closely with their Hawaiian blood as with anything else. Hawaiians, by nature, were open and honest to a fault, like the Eskimos, inviting terror into their lives without even recognizing it for what it was, he thought. For now he allowed the tape to replay, but his attention floated away to the book lying next to him on the table, Lina Kahala's book of sonnets.

He lifted it, felt its heft in his hands, squeezed it in a fantastic hope that in doing so some clue would ooze from the damned thing, but the book remained as silent as ever.

In the still of the Hawaiian night, he feels time slow to a crawling, halting stop. He opens the pages and reads as he has each night from the dark passages the young woman, now beyond this life, had once marked for him to find.

Shakespeare's words . . . her words flow off the tongue easily, like a timeless riddle, and he wonders anew if he hasn't been placed on this earth to unite Lina with her prophet, Shakespeare, whom Jim Parry has never before thought of as a poet of darkness and despair. He wonders, too, what he has missed, what has escaped his eye and his consciousness.

He keenly feels that he is being haunted by Lina, that she pleads with him from every crevice and dark corner of his universe, that she is asking him specifically to untie the twisted ribbon of darkness that somehow links Lina with an embittered, saddened poet and her killer. What is the link that binds a white man who lived hundreds of years before in a place alien to all that Lina knew — England — and an adolescent teenaged girl trying to find herself in modern Hawaii, who instead finds a killer?

Does the book belong to the killer? Whose name, spoiled by water damage, has been all but erased? The killer's? Or someone close to the killer?

Why has he been so reluctant to turn the book over to the lab, to let the analysts conduct tests, to restore the badly damaged ink, to re-invent the name in the dark smudges? Why hasn't he let go of the book? Is it his only connection with the killer, or with Lina? If he loses this connection, does he lose all connection with her?

His tea is gone. He stares into the dregs wishing he could read something into them like some psychic, some fictional sleuth who, in the absence of reason, acts on instinct alone and wins. *But heroes often fail,* like the song says.

The night offers little more than an empty feeling inside him now—nothing more. He is left to pace, to think of his heavy responsibility, his burden to put an end to this madman. He paces until exhausted, until he again finds himself staring into the mirror and wondering if the killer, too, is awake at this ungodly hour, if he is pacing and staring at himself through a looking glass, questioning himself, his next step, wondering if he can go on, doubting his resolve to reach seven murders this season. Parry stares longer into the looking glass, and knowing the killer to be out there, he wonders if the killer is staring back at himself, pulling at facial stubble, washing white skin, or rinsing brown skin?

Unable to account for or remember his night's slumber, Parry, stupefied, awakens to the sound of military aircraft beating a thunderous approach and retreat overhead, as if he and his modest home are under siege. It is as if he has not slept at all.

—10—

O Rose, thou art sick.
The invisible worm
That flies in the night,
In the howling storm,

Has found out thy bed
Of crimson joy,
And his dark secret love
Does thy life destroy.

William Blake, "The Sick Rose"

July 16, 9 A.M., FBI Headquarters, Honolulu

"Joe Kaniola's put your shit, my shit, everybody's shit on the street, in print, front page of his rag!" shouted Scanlon at the top of his lungs. "Only good news is nobody reads it and it's in Hawaiian. Course, it's going to be picked up and translated by every paper in the islands and on the fuckin' radio and TV and the mainland anyway, a story like this . . . Christ, Parry!"

Scanlon was a bear of a man, broad-shouldered and barrel-chested, whose once-hard, chiseled face had collapsed in and was now jowly and square, a near-hidden cleft chin below the folds, and a surprisingly thin nose no longer at ease with a pair of near-closed, squinting colorless eyes. There was a history between Parry and Scanlon, Jim Parry's office having embarrassed the HPD in the past on more than one occasion, but particularly on the

116

Daiporice murders when Parry had, after extensive examination of the facts, quickly linked several island scams which had led to a brutal professional killing. It turned out the hit man was contracted for by a high-ranking city official who was dirtier than most Mafia types Parry had known.

Meanwhile, the HPD blithely followed a path that netted several suspects, all of whom had nothing whatever to do with the crime. The HPD districts weren't communicating well on the case, and each area had arrested separate individuals for the scam and the killing, maintaining the two incidents were unrelated, filing separate reports bearing no relation to each other.

Another body surfaced and this time the FBI, acting on a missing-persons report, got involved. As bureau chief of the FBI, Parry didn't need a formal invite from Scanlon or any of his captains to come in on a missing-persons report, especially if it involved a minor, and Daiporice's own son, aged seventeen, had somehow gotten in the way and been eliminated. The loss of his son brought Ted Daiporice to his knees.

Parry's take-charge style had been viewed as abrasive by some HPD personnel before Daiporice, and it was likely for this reason he'd been "unaccountably" left out of the loop on the seventeen-year-old's disappearance. Parry charged in and crashed HPD's party anyway, when they couldn't find a trace of the missing young man anywhere.

Then came the Wilson Lewis case. Parry studied forensic reports and police reports on the case, along with the so-called confessions of those men being held in connection with a string of brutal slice-and-dice mutilations. Those arrested were mental defectives, down-and-outs and PSOs—previous sex offenders. When Parry came in on the case, he immediately saw the links between the victims; wounds to the eyes in particular showed such force as to indicate uncontrollable rage and hatred. Even the bones around the eyes had been damaged by the hilt of a knife; sexual organs too were gutted and turned out, as if the killer had to look and touch inside them, not unlike the Trade Winds Killer in this regard.

To be fair to Scanlon and his detectives, the bodies were always found weeks later in deserted areas of the forests, far off the main roads, and in the summer heat, that year reaching into the nineties, a cadaver was stripped to skeletal remains within ten days. So Scanlon's people didn't have much in the way of evidence either to identify the victims or to reconstruct the crimes. Like the Trade Winds Killer, Wilson Solomon Lewis, an otherwise mild-mannered insurance salesman by day, didn't leave his victims where he had killed them, so there was no crime scene to analyze per se; all they had to go on was where the bodies were dumped—a stone whodunit, in police parlance, the hardest kind of case to resolve.

Parry went to work, orchestrating a surveillance, his people watching every drop point for a full month, while he and Tony, spelled by others, watched what ought to be the killer's next and last drop point, according to the computer program tracking the bastard. They got lucky one night when a large vehicle consistent with the tire marks found at the other locations drove calmly off U.S. 61 passing the darkened surveillance vehicle on the far side of the road, placed at some distance away. Parry and Gagliano called for backup and drove into the woods, following at a safe stretch until their headlights hit on Lewis, his arms filled with overstuffed garbage bags, the trunk of his car popped, the light from the trunk setting off his features into a mosaic of contortion.

For a moment he looked relieved, waving to them as if he'd expected them long before. Still, he stuffed what he'd lifted from the trunk back into the vehicle and slammed home the lid.

Gagliano turned the spotlight on the man, who was wearing a pullover sweater and jeans, his hands smeared with a red substance that was unmistakable. A body was indeed inside the spacious trunk of his roomy Lincoln Town Car, the one he did regular business in. Wilson Lewis put up no resistance, standing aside like a child staring down at the valuable vase he'd broken, the damage irreparable.

"Whhhhhh-y'd it take youuuuuu so . . . so . . . so long to . . . to st-st-stop me?" He stuttered.

"Read him his fucking rights, Tony," Parry had said, his eyes riveted to the horror encased in the man's trunk, his mind going over the question put to him by the insane.

Why had it taken them so long to stop him? he wondered. How could they've been so blind?

All of Lewis's victims had been prospective clients, many taken right from their homes at midday, all of them single and living alone. Records indicated that Lewis had no previous police record, but a careful scrutiny of his life later unearthed the troublesome nature of this man whom no one liked, not his neighbors, not his relatives, not his former bosses, of whom there were many. He had a long list of jobs from which he'd been fired, often for "odd, lewd or strange" behavior in one form or another. He had all his life been building toward vengeance against women, for women were, in his estimation, the cause of all sin on earth, the mothers of ruination, since his own mother and the mother of his children were satanic.

Parry's handling of the case effectively threw out several HPD "convictions" and so-called confessions, which both the press and the public had been screaming for. A police detective in any state in the land lived or died by the number of cases he closed, so Parry's victory was not as welcomed as it might otherwise have been by detectives who had followed the other, now patently useless leads. Not only were the detectives below Scanlon embarrassed, but so too were the ranking officers, Scanlon included, who had okayed the arrest, confession and indictment of a partially retarded itinerant pineapple farmer.

Since then Parry had begun a secretive crusade of sorts, aimed at indolence and incompetence within the HPD. He began with unsolved missing-persons reports, carefully reviewing the case of Sinitia "Cynthia" Toma the year before, which led to Kololia "Gloria" Poni. The trail led to a list of seven missing within a span of a few months. He'd heard of a similar situation on Maui the year before this. In Maui he learned the girls' names: Ela, Wana'ao, Kini, Merelina, Kimi, Lala, and Iolana. Of course, there were other missing persons, even during the period of these vanishings, however, all of these young women were not only natives, but they shared a common appearance, down to the long-trailing black hair and light-filled wide eyes, as well as size, general age and weight. Parry had made it a pet project, reviewing all information authorities had on the cases, searching for any pattern, any link between them. The first obvious such link was that the victims in Honolulu vanished along a trajectory that was bounded by the National Memorial Cemetery of the Pacific known as the Punchbowl, the University of Hawaii and the Waikiki Beach resort area. Searches among the foothills, along deserted mile markers off the Pali Highway and elsewhere, turned up no clues at the time. The proximity to the air force and naval bases continued to lead Parry to suspect someone in uniform. Whoever he was, this guy left no trace either of himself or his victims. Yet the geography was always the same, that rectangular wedge of island centering on busy Waikiki. The killer must spend a lot of time there, possibly working in the area, living on its perimeter.

Now Dave Scanlon stopped his lionlike pacing, gave a glance to Dr. Marshal, who'd come in with him, leaned over Parry's desk and got in Parry's face, saying, "We're not going to allow any history between us, Jim, to color what we do here now, are we?"

"History? History's history," Parry replied sharply. "All I care about is what we're going to do about this damnable business now."

Parry stared down at the *Ala Ohana* newspaper. He could make out enough Hawaiian to know that everything Scanlon had said about Kaniola and his paper was true—and then some. It was a story so hot it fairly burned the hands to hold it.

"Just read the crap there about the HPD's not doing a damned thing while two of our own cops are murdered in cold blood." Scanlon pounded his fist over the newsprint as if to do so could change things.

"Get hold of yourself, Dave," Parry said, trying to counter the bull's rage. "It's just a pile of innuendo and half-truths gathered up by a grieving father who—"

"The appearance of impropriety, the mere appearance of wrong-doing, Jim, and we're in the stocks down at HPD. You damned well know that, and so does Marshal here."

Dr. Walter Marshal tried to console his old friend. As the U.S. M.E. from Pearl, he had a lot invested in the case as well, but he wasn't having any luck in calming the HPD Commissioner of Police, so he turned to Parry instead and added kerosene to the fire by saying, "You can bet your ass the mainland'll get this."

"Christ," continued Scanlon, pacing for emphasis. "We've got every uniform, pulled every detective, every sergeant and lieutenant in on this, but old Joe Kaniola makes it sound like we're all sitting around masturbating ourselves! And he's got the inside dope, that top sources with the FBI claim the only man ever to get near the killer was his son who didn't have proper backup! Christ, what a lot of horse shit! And how'd he get information about the blood, Parry, news you didn't even share with me! And what's all this about the supposed killer being most likely a white male? And possibly having some connection with the U.S. military? Christ-a-minny!"

Parry tried to defuse Scanlon as much as possible by repeating himself. "Kaniola's got nothing. A handful of assumptions and innuendos any number of people've been slinging around, Dave."

"You just tell that Dr. Coran of yours to keep her mouth shut, or we'll have a full-blown race riot on our hands in the south central quadrant," Scanlon hotly replied. "I thought she was a pro! I thought she knew what she was doing. I thought you knew what you were doing when you called her in on the case, Jim."

"Scanlon, Dr. Coran's remarks to Kaniola were off the rec—"

"Not any fucking more!" Scanlon paced anew.

Parry went instantly to Jessica's defense. "Dr. Coran did not disclose anything to Kaniola intentionally, and so far's I know not a word about the arm, the racial makeup of the killer, or that he could be military. We don't any of us know that."

"Bullshit! Then who did?"

"I don't know." He privately wondered about Tony, but instantly ruled him out. "Kaniola's just canny, that's all."

"Christ, she ought've known you don't expose yourself to an experienced—"

"She took him to be the bereaving father."

"Son of a bitch is bereaving all right—bereaving right down our throats, Parry. He's got nothing kind to say about your bureau either. Read on!"

Parry shook his head, remaining calm. "He's blowing smoke and he knows it. There's no evidence the killer's a white man or that he's from the naval base, none whatever."

"But every Hawaiian thinks so now," challenged Dr. Marshal. "There doesn't have to be any real evidence, not with these types who're just looking for an excuse to torch this city like L.A. in '92."

"It isn't going to happen here."

"You want to make bank on that?" shouted Scanlon.

Jessica Coran pushed noisily through the door, her cane thumping out a requiem, Parry's secretary chasing gooselike after her, quite unable to stop her. The secretary was making excuses over Jessica's words:

"I'm so sorry, Chief Parry, but this woman—"

"Chief Parry, gentlemen," Jessica began, "I believe I should be in on this roundtable since I am the guilty party here and—"

"—I tried to stop her, but she's so rude and—"

Parry motioned his secretary off and the woman stepped back, without turning, obediently closing the door in front of her, leaving Jessica Coran in the center of the big office full of men.

"All right, Dr. Coran, please join us," Parry said, trying not to show his displeasure and the dark circles around his bloodshot eyes. "Have a seat."

She remained standing. "I'm sorry for my ill-timed words of yesterday to Kaniola. I won't be surprised to hear from Quantico, perhaps find myself replaced."

Parry realized now that she thought she was doing the valorous thing, that she'd come to his rescue, somehow learning of the meeting.

Dr. Marshal cleared his throat and said, "Gentlemen, Dr. Coran, of one thing you can be assured, all leaves to servicemen will be temporarily canceled and every man confined to base at least until the news simmers down."

"Good thinking," muttered Scanlon. "Now whata we do with all of the other white males living in the city? I'm telling you, Jim, your car the other night was just the beginning."

"If the newspaper leaks came from within my organization"— Parry fell short of admitting it—"I'll deal with the problems at this end."

"And from here on out, I want full cooperation, Jim. No more behind-the-back shit, like alla this crap about how the killer maybe is using the Blow Hole as a dumping site and maybe he's using a U.S. regulation-sized bayonet or machete on his victims."

"I said nothing of the kind to Mr. Kaniola," insisted Jessica.

"Joe's just feeding his people a pile of *kukai,* as they say, huh?" asked Scanlon. "For what reason then?"

"Who knows," Parry fired back. "To make his son look less like the asshole your department painted him for getting himself killed in the line of duty, maybe?"

"Or maybe it's become a political thing with Kaniola. Everything's political with him," suggested Dr. Marshal when the two lawmen had locked gazes. "Now everyone in this room has got to be supportive of each other, gentlemen. We have got to cooperate and stick together on this."

"I'll keep my hands on the table if you will," Parry relented.

Scanlon at first said nothing, then frowned and said, "It becomes clearer the longer this thing goes on, Jim, that we need each other. To pool our resources."

"I realize that, Dave."

"Good . . . good . . ." Marshal, acting as referee, seemed delighted—missing something here, Jessica thought. There was bad blood between Jim Parry and Scanlon. She'd sensed it from the first moment she walked in, and now it was ripe and odorous.

"Kaniola's facts are wrong and his story's full of shit, like you say, Scanlon, and I think most thinking people, white and Hawaiian alike, will see it for what it is." Parry held tightly to a heavy paperweight in the likeness of a pair of handcuffs, squeezing hard as he spoke. Despite his words to the contrary, even the new girl on the block, Jessica Coran, knew that the newspaper story was partially accurate: that thanks to men like Scanlon at the top, the HPD nourished a certain amount of inbred prejudice against its own Hawaiian and minority cops, cops who'd been hired to fill quotas fifteen years before, cops who'd never see promotion in the ranks. Nor was Joe Kaniola far from the mark when he suggested that Scanlon's department wasn't pulling its weight in the investigation, that at best they'd fallen into familiar patterns of organizational behavior by arresting derelicts, the homeless, previously known sex offenders, all without the slightest clue as to who the Trade Winds Killer might be. She could almost hear Jim's seething thoughts below his painted smile: Hell, the HPD brass hadn't seen the strange pattern of disappearances of young women of Hawaiian and Oriental extraction over the past two years here in Oahu . . . nor the link with the missing Maui women before this.

Marshal cleared his throat and spoke up. "Jim, I've heard you call this killer the Cane Cutter, and now Kaniola himself says his favored instrument of death is a huge machete of the type used in cane cutting. We all know that information, leaked properly to the press, can lead to only one conclusion: that our killer is a field worker, one of *them*."

That information, thought Parry, had been confidential, held in abeyance for the day when a suspect could be brought in and presented with the facts, hopefully to press the man into a confession. Men were known to break during long interrogations when the interrogators had a series of facts in evidence that a killer could not ignore, facts which might cause a guilty man to gasp, fidget and raise an eyebrow. Interrogation only worked if the investigators could carefully walk a suspect along an inexorable path lined with the truth; only such overwhelming evidence might push a recalcitrant sociopath into a corner, awed by the light shone on his actions and secrets. A good interrogation meant laying out all the pieces of the case along the table, in full view of the suspect, like an archaeologist looking over the day's cache of relics and artifacts, but the artifacts of murder didn't lie silent on the table, at least not to the killer or the hunter who had cornered the killer; no, the artifacts of murder literally screamed out at them both.

Now the information regarding the killer's favored weapon, or at least what he'd used on Linda Kahala, was rendered weak and ineffectual by virtue of the fact it'd become part of the public domain, useless as an interrogation tool. Every madman in the city who chose to confess to the crimes could now state that he was the Cane Cutter, that he used a cane knife. Many would bring a weapon in, wasting hours of lab time in which each instrument had to be checked against Linda Kahala's wounds along the one arm.

At the moment, thanks to Kaniola, who no doubt believed in his heart that his news story could only help and never hinder the search for his son's killer, any nut with a big knife might walk into a station house and turn himself in.

Scanlon was right on this score. Joseph Kaniola's story ultimately meant more false leads, more trails to nowhere.

"I didn't say a word about the weapon, Jim," Dr. Coran swore.

"Kaniola says the source of that information came from someone extremely close to the investigation, so if you didn't reveal the fact, who did?" Scanlon persisted.

Her eyes widened at the accusation, the fact the commissioner of police would not accept her word. "Dr. Marshal, here for one—"

Marshal was outraged at the suggestion, shouting, "You can't for a moment believe that I had any—"

"Elwood Warner, the County M.E., any number of lab techs, cops and agents who are notorious gossips," she continued, "and now Dr. Harold Shore, your own Oahu M.E."

"Dr. Shore? That's preposterous," countered Marshal, defending the absent M.E.

"He's been sitting up in his hospital bed, demanding the details of the autopsies done on Hilani and Kaniola, as well as the pathology workup on Kahala's arm. I submit to you, gentlemen, that all these people have had access to the information. Information leaks come from any number of directions and sources, and no one's more skillful in getting someone to verify suppositions and filling in half-truths than a crafty, experienced newsman like Kaniola."

Parry mentally ran down the list of his agents, anyone remotely connected with the operation. Haley, Reno, Gagliano, Mr. Lau and his people in the labs. He also wondered about himself, if he'd foolishly left anything of a confidential nature lying about for the cleaning lady at the office to pick up. He wouldn't put it past Kaniola to use tabloid techniques to get a story and sell papers.

News leaked . . . as if it were obligated to. Especially in the case of a red-ball like this, especially in the fishbowl of an island community, with everyone's eye pressed against the glass. U.S. military brass was interested, the state, the county and the city of Oahu all wanted to know the latest yesterday, as did the State Department and D.C. It was the reason Paul Zanek was so free with advice and with Jessica Coran.

Now they could all read about it in the papers.

Not altogether satisfied, Scanlon abruptly left while Dr. Marshal lingered behind. Jessica watched the officious military doctor step to the window and stare out at the mountain mosaic in the distance, patches of it cluttered by homes that seemed to creep ever closer to the summit each year.

"I've lived here for nearly twenty years, Inspector, and in all that time I've never felt afraid."

"Afraid, sir?"

"Never afraid of the volcanic activity, the occasional tropical storm or hurricane, the serpentine traffic, the congestion or the growing tourism . . . not even the worst backwater streets in the worst sections of the city ever really frightened me. But now . . . this . . . this scares me, Parry." He turned from the window to emphasize his point, staring hard at the FBI bureau chief. "This city could go up in flames tomorrow. We all know that."

Jessica stepped toward him and firmly said, "I understand your concerns, sir, but I assure you, we are doing everything within our power to bring an end to the killings."

"We need more, Parry. We need an arrest, a suspect, a . . ."

"A scapegoat?" asked Parry.

"It would take the heat off; give you room to, you know, maneuver, shall we say? Time to get at the root of the problem. I have it on good authority that the boyfriend of the latest victim has been under interrogation."

Christ, thought Parry, how many eyes were watching the fishbowl? Marshal was an old man who had watched Honolulu grow, and he, like most *haoles,* had invested a great deal in real estate here.

"I'm not prepared to arrest someone just to appease the likes of Joseph Kaniola or any other newsman, Doctor."

"No one's asking you to appease Kaniola." He looked sternly into Parry's eyes, shocked that Parry didn't understand him. "But there are many who would be appeased by an arrest at this time."

"I'll let Scanlon do your dirty work for you, Dr. Marshal. The FBI doesn't knowingly make false arrests."

"I have friends in the State Department, Inspector, and you can be assured that everyone back home"—America was forever home to the older generation of whites in Hawaii—"everyone is watching this case with extreme curiosity and interest, I assure you."

The veiled threat wasn't lost on Parry or Jessica. He'd only become bureau chief two years before, and a case such as this, left open too long, or worse, defying solution, could cost him dearly. Jessica guessed now that whatever people "back home"—no doubt senators, congressmen and other high-ranking officials— didn't know about the case, Dr. Marshal was only too happy to provide.

Parry, with obvious disdain, said, "I appreciate and understand the nature of your concern, Doctor, but please, leave the investigation to the experts. It's what we're here for."

Marshal only stared for a long moment, Parry returning the cold glint until finally Marshal said, "Of course, and perhaps we at the base can be kept informed? Just as the HPD is informed of the progress you and Dr. Coran are making?"

"Of course."

Marshal extended a hand, and for a moment it was poised between them before Parry reached out and vigorously shook it, saying, "I'll keep you posted."

"That's all I ask. Thank you, indeed."

With that Marshal disappeared and Parry looked thoughtfully up at Jessica as she waited for him to speak. Instead, he scanned Joseph Kaniola's story once again, and there, in black and white, was George Oniiwah's name, just a line, saying that "Oniiwah has been repeatedly questioned by police," which meant that the *hapa Japa* was by innuendo a suspect and that he clearly knew something.

"So," he finally spoke, breaking the unhappy iciness between them, "our good Dr. Marshal thinks it'd be a wonderful idea to lock Oniiwah up, play the Hawaiian population against the Nip population, thereby skirting the FBI profile, which points ever more to a white male, late twenties to early forties. For Oniiwah's own safety, maybe it's not such a bad idea, but it sticks in my craw."

"We did it in New York, you know, on my last case," she offered, falling into a cushioned chair before him.

"Did it? Did what?"

"Arrested a known sex offender, you know, to appease the public mind," she admitted.

He frowned at this. "If it were that easy, I might consider it, but Marshal's only half the problem. While he's trying to save the boys in white and blue from Pearl, any number of whom could be our killer, the governor of Hawaii, the mayor of Honolulu and your boss, Paul Zanek, are all screaming for somebody's head."

"Zanek's on your case? That's some nerve! I'll have something to say to him. Hell, he's not even your direct super—"

"Jess, everybody in the military wants to believe our killer's one of *them*—Hawaiian or, of mixed island blood, that is—while everyone in government wants us to catch the Caucasian killer. You see, such an end to this would show good faith, so to speak, take a hell of a lotta heat off every level of government, and—"

"That's one asinine way to conduct an investigation!"

"—and our so-called 'good faith' move'll clear law-enforcement agencies throughout the islands of the stain of prejudicial proceedings. Get it?"

"In one fell swoop. It's coming clearer, yeah." She shook her head, disbelieving even as she understood.

"Ironic as hell, isn't it?"

"Reverse discrimination, so to speak?"

"At its worst, yeah . . . something like that."

"So what're you going to do?"

"Nothing."

"Nothing?"

"For now, *nada*. See which way the wind blows."

"As will our killer I'm sure, Jim."

"I didn't say we're going to sit on the investigation." He lost control, shouting, "Just on the goddamned politics surrounding the bloody case!"

She dropped her gaze, nodding. "I'm sorry. I know that, Jim. I didn't for a moment mean to imply anything other—"

"Look, forget it. I'm wound like a top today. Look." He tried desperately to tread lightly now. "How're things going in the lab?"

"Torturously slow, but we're moving onward. As soon as I know anything new, you'll be the first."

"Well, thanks for coming down on the white charger."

"Only hope it helped."

"Helped clear the room sooner, that's for sure."

Together they laughed at this.

But their laughter was short-lived when she lifted a copy of Kaniola's paper, written in Hawaiian, yet crystal-clear from the photos of each of the missing young women bordering the story, and a crude sketch of a human forearm with upper muscle and shoulder, ruptured at the wrist, gracing the bottom of the page.

"I told him nothing about Kahala's arm." She didn't want to point a finger, but she didn't want Jim Parry to think any worse of her than he already did either.

"Kaniola's shrewd. He's weaseled out a hell of a lot of details about the crimes. See this?" He pointed to the word 'a'apl.

"What's it mean?"

"He says the blade used on the Kahala girl was warped or curved. Here he speaks of tragic misfortune, 'awa, and of persons dying before their time, 'a'aiole. And that it happens with the a'e."

"The a-eee?"

"The northeast trade wind."

"Geeze . . . so what else does the story say?" she asked.

"Depicts Thom Hilani and Kaniola's son as a couple of heroes—the only two cops in the whole of Oahu who'd ever gotten near the Cane Cutter. Describes the rest of the HPD as something far less admirable; depicts the bureau as a confederacy of bungling idiots."

"It says all that?"

"See this word, here, hawawa? Its literal translation is unskilled, awkward, blundering and incompetent."

"Sounds like the papers back home."

"So how'd he get the drawing of the dead girl's limb? If not from you, that leaves someone in Lau's lab, perhaps, or one of my agents, all of whom I'd thought I could trust."

She told him of Kaniola's connection to Lau. "Look, when the limb rose from the Blow Hole, people witnessed it. Cops were called on scene and got there before your guys, right? Everyone in Oahu knew about the limb."

"Guess so . . . Damn tired of having to fight my back, though."

"I hope you don't think that includes me."

He shook his head. "No, no. You, I think, are genuine. Look at this," he said, changing the subject, pointing once more to the *Ala Ohana*'s Hawaiian words. "Our pal Kaniola talks about you, too, here."

"What?"

"Calls you an anchor stone for the investigation."

"Anchor stone?"

"*Heleuma*," he replied, using the Hawaiian term, and then he read on. "'Dr. Jessica Coran has been called onto the case by top-ranking FBI officials'—that'd be me—'to oversee the forensic investigation in the absence of Dr. Harold Shore. Coran has solved a number of puzzling and bizarre serial-murder cases on the mainland, the most famous of which culminated in the capture of the mad vampire slayer, Matt Matisak, in Chicago, and also the case of the Claw in New York City last year.'"

"I see," she said, staring to where he pointed.

"The placement of your name at this juncture is direct innuendo that the information following this came from you."

She looked quizzically at the Hawaiian words before her. "What information?"

"That the suspect is believed to be a white male between the ages of twenty-seven and forty."

"I told him that was just probability, that it is statistically likely that—"

"The Hawaiians are looking for the least provocation to shut down Pearl as a base of U.S. operations; word of this spreads, we're going to catch hell from both sides, and we know Marshal's going to spread it—not to mention the racial tensions which are running quite high right now."

"Kaniola's playing on these emotions?"

"Like a virtuoso, yes. That's how native political power works." She shook her head. "I can't entirely agree."

"Sure, sure, he genuinely wants his son avenged first and foremost; for all their inherent good nature, the fact that Hawaiians are lovely people does not lessen their sense of justice and faith in vengeance."

"Like most of humanity?"

He gave her a knowing look and a smirk. "Okay, but Joe Kaniola's also fanning embers that've been smoldering for a long time, over a hundred years to be exact. He's got a whole population of disenfranchised people to blow off to, to vent his spleen with, over this issue, which leads him and his people straight back to the fundamental issue of who governs here and who carries the big stick of enforcement."

"Oh, God . . . I hope I didn't really mess things up for you, Jim."

"Well, the worst of it has nothing to do with what you told Kaniola."

"What's that?"

"Like I said, this mention of George Oniiwah. Putting his name into this story made him a target for anyone remotely interested in avenging Linda Kahala, Thom Hilani, Alan Kaniola or any of the other women. Shit, if someone reading this decides that Oniiwah is the Cane Cutter, some bad *pilikia*'s going to follow."

"Is Oniiwah white?"

"Half Japanese."

"Surely that's inconsistent with Kaniola's innuendo that the killer is suspected to be a white male."

"Kaniola characterizes the kid as half 'white' by virture of his and his family's so emulating the white man—dressing white, dancing white, eating white, all that."

"Surely that's not enough to condemn him. Nobody could possibly decide that the FBI profile states the killer's whiteness is just mock white behavior, could they?"

"We got some pretty big, pretty nasty and pretty dumb Samoans and Hawaiians on this island who put *pilau* like that together all the time, and proud of it."

"Is the man under arrest, in protective custody?"

"Neither, and he's missing."

"What're you saying? That he's gone into hiding? That he's fleeing, what?"

"No one's sure at this point."

"You're not saying . . . he's not been abducted? Has he?"

"Possibly."

"Jesus . . ."

"Minute I saw the paper, I called to have him picked up, but it was already too late. Oniiwah's roommate tells a story about three heavyset Samoans bursting into their dorm room—middle of the night—at the college. The roommate was knocked senseless, or so he maintains, but we're not sure his story is a hundred percent accurate."

"You suspect he was in on the abduction?"

"Bruises he sustained are minimal; could've been inflicted by someone, but certainly not enough to knock him unconscious as he states. Anyway, his story has these big Samoan dudes taking George out by the hair, kicking and screaming. Tony's continued to grill the guy and—"

"Neither Scanlon nor Marshal know a thing about this development, obviously, and you're not telling?"

He ignored her and continued. "An APB's being put out on the kid, but it doesn't look good for Oniiwah. All in all, nothing's turned out quite right."

"Hell, I didn't even know about Oniiwah when I spoke to Kaniola."

"I know that. Look, it could get ugly," he stated.

"If the boy's hurt . . ."

"Oniiwah's being half Japanese and dressing the way he does . . . that's all some Samoans need to know. The typical dyed-in-the-wool Samoan believes in 'act now, think later,' and that's why there're so many of them in the state pen. Samoans are worse than the native Hawaiians in their hatred for the Japanese and the whites. They're the ones who initiated and now annually hold the Hawaiian version of Hell Night here, the 'Kill a *Haole* Day' festivities which annually lands many behind bars. So, don't go whipping yourself over this."

She sensed that he was doing exactly that to himself all morning.

"Anything happens, it's Kaniola's fault and mine," said Parry. "I should've listened to Tony last night. He tried to warn me about the mood of the people. Damn . . ."

"What next?"

"We've got a notion we're playing out. Tony's working on getting paper for a search warrant as we speak. I'd be over at the site myself by now if I hadn't got hung up with Scanlon and Marshal." He looked at his watch. "Should be about time now. When's the last time you were in on a bust?"

"A bust? Me?"

"Sure, why not. You want to see some real local color?"

She took it as a challenge.

"Want to join me or not?" He buzzed his secretary and called for his car to be brought around. "Well?"

"All right, all right, maybe I will."

Lopaka's hands are busy over the wheel of the bus he drives, a small, versatile twenty-four-seater for Enoa Tourist Industries. The bus makes stops at predesignated hotel locations to load more passengers till filled to capacity today. A typical Tuesday on the island. But while his hands and eyes are occupied here, Lopaka's mind is elsewhere.

His eyes scan the city streets for his next victim, for someone who resembles Kelia, someone who may walk like her, and whose pattern of life he can approach and intercept. Once their paths cross, he might easily fit into her world, which is his world, too. He's on the same streets every day, doing his job, carting tourists back and forth along the same avenues from the hotels—making some six to seven stops depending—to the sights at Pearl Harbor on his run. Along the way, he must spout the history and culture of the islands to the hungry tourists, who seem to have tattoos over their eyes that scream, *"Tell me something I don't know, excite my curiosity, wake me up."*

"Over to the left, the large building you're looking at is the Bishop Museum, Hawaii's largest and oldest museum. A day's visit in its friendly confines is a delight for all who visit the islands, a real must!" he tells his passengers, but even as he speaks in rote memory of his lines, his mind shifts between past experiences with the Kelias he has known and killed, and the future Kelias he *will* slay, and he wonders what life will be like after he reaches the final number, seven times seven, the one which will make him immortal.

"The Enoa Bus Line can of course accommodate you on a separate and unique trip to the Bishop Museum, if you wish to see the archaeological treasures of the islands," he says over the P.A. just as they pass the turn for the famous museum. "Should you wish an extended trip into a truly Hawaiian world of gala festivities, topped off by a traditional evening luau, Enoa buses run daily to the Polynesian Cultural Center on the other side of the island. Read about it on the back of your free Enoa Tours map and plan for a six-hour tour."

The bus came to a shuddering slowdown with traffic jamming

up ahead. "No worry, folks," he tells his charges. "Just a little accident up 'head on da freeway." At just the right marker and moment, he adds, "Coming up on your right is the world-famous Hula Bowl, host to the world's finest young athletes, the All-Stars of college football each year after the regular season. The Hula Bowl is also known for being the home of . . ."

He no longer hears himself, having so often done the stock spiel. His mind is partitioned and while the left side takes care of business in the here and now, the other is considering his choices after dark. He might simply go to Alakana's ABC Liquor and Pharmacy on Ala Moana, the street of abundance, where he'd gotten to know the sales clerk enough to call her by her first name, Hiilani, and while she was younger than Kelia by a few years when Kelia had left him, she was all Hawaiian—no mix. At least she'd claimed to be a full-blood native when he'd jokingly asked if there were any full-bloods left. He had bought his newspaper as usual and had been careful not to overstay his welcome, but he did ask her what she'd do if he showed up that evening to drive her home.

"In the bus?" she had asked, amused.

"No, I have a car of my own, a nice car."

"Really? But I have a boyfriend."

"Is he coming to pick you up?"

"No, he's too lazy. I have to take the bus usually."

He'd quickly countered with, "If you were my girl, you wouldn't never ride no public bus."

She'd only smiled coyly at this. So he had repeated his offer to drive her home, finishing with, "What do you say?"

"Maybe yes, maybe no. I'll see when I see," she'd teased.

He recognized bait when he smelled it, and he easily assumed that Hiilani was just as loose and fast as Kelia had been; she just hid it well behind her white smock and long braids, which, if allowed to fall, would trail to her back like Kelia's.

While not terribly bright, Hiilani held down a regular job. She wasn't a college girl or a streetwalker like some of the others. She was different from Kia and Linda from the university, who'd both ridden for free in his bus when he'd taken another driver's route for two weeks. They'd teased him about being a bus driver, because earlier in class, he'd bragged about working on a big ranch nearby, saying one day he'd become a lawyer or possibly a doctor.

A simple check with the registrar might have told either girl that he was barely capable of paying for one class, let alone a full load, and that he was a failing part-timer at the university.

He had flirted with Kia Wailea, telling her all kinds of stories about himself, building himself up to her. She had seemed disinterested until he suddenly surprised her on the strip, where, after several nights of hunting for a new Kelia, he saw her taking on johns for money. It wasn't long before her friend Linda was doing the same. He saw them in broad daylight doing this; he saw it all from the big tinted windshield of his bus.

It was then that Lopaka began to steadily watch his two classmates to learn their routines. He knew from experience that everyone had a routine, that people walked through patterns of existence that dug ruts as deep as canals, and these two girls were no exception. He counseled himself to be patient, to present himself to the girls whenever and wherever possible as a harmless but interested fellow. He was careful not to pressure either of them, but at the same time to learn their likes. Linda, for instance, was a poetry lover and wanted to write poetry, so he located the only book of poetry he owned, an ancient relic left him by his mother, the only item he'd ever known that belonged to her, a book of Shakespeare's sonnets. It endeared him somewhat to Kia, and greatly to Linda, to give her his mother's book of poems. Some years before giving Linda the book, he'd read the sonnets himself, and he'd underlined passages that appealed to him. The underlined passages spoke to him and to her, the hunter and the hunted in intimate conversation, he thought. Surely, she must know to stay away from him after that, he thought. Meanwhile, he continued to hold an inordinate power over the girls, for he knew their daily routines as well as they. It was only a matter of time before he struck. At the exact right moment, he meant to intersect Kia's and Linda's pathways, so that their meeting by chance beamed brightly like a flash of fate, a surprising crisscross of serendipity, when in fact it was well timed and practiced.

Even when Kia, the more streetwise of the two, questioned that fate, and he confessed to following her, she found it *romantic* that he should go to such lengths. She teased at first, calling him a stalker, then laughing at her own joke, never really believing him capable of anything but total adoration and awe. Then, too late, she learned the truth of his hunt.

Not for the first time does he realize that the very anonymity of his job, and of the large city of Honolulu, makes success in his hunt possible. The fact he has no friends, no relatives any longer—for they have long since abandoned him—and the fact he is considered an introvert and an *'ae'e,* a wandering, shiftless, rootless, unstable soul, an awkward *'ano'e,* and odd duck as the whites say, shying from crowds, parties, relatives, presenting a stiff arm to others—all of it aides in the hunt.

No one has *willingly* come to his bungalow since Kelia left years before.

Still Hiilani, he tells himself, is a high risk. She has close family ties from what he can tell, and already the island families are outraged about the disappearances of Kia and Linda. It may be safest to go elsewhere tonight in his hunt. He might just return to the Waikiki strip to meet for the fourth or fifth time that heavily made-up streetwalker named Terri, but there's something not quite right about her. There's no way she's a native, despite her dress and that horrid, long black wig she wears, but she does—*in her costume*—look something like Kelia, and if he were to ignore the fact Terri has no Polynesian blood whatsoever, he might *imagine* her to be another Kelia.

She could be a cop posing as a hooker, he fears. If not, she's obviously an American girl who's gone native. Terri is slender, petite—Kelia's size—pretty, willing enough if the price is right, but he wants her to come regardless of any transaction. He wants her to open herself to him, to make herself vulnerable to him the way Hiilani already has, the way Kia and Linda did. But there's a hard edge to this Terri that speaks of experience.

Linda was different. Lopaka had to lure and bait her over a longer period of time, and even when he did strike, she'd been weakened more by the sudden disappearance of her friend Kia than by him. She didn't particularly wish to go with him that night. While many others followed him like stray dogs to their deaths, Linda did not go so peaccably. She fought. She hurt and even scarred him. She was more like Kelia in that way than any of the others. So, he wonders now, which Kelia is it to be tonight? The streetwalker or the liquor-store clerk who likes to peek at the dirty magazines?

Either way, he will be doing the work of gods. . . .

He often daydreams on his route, even as he tells the tourists what they want to hear; it is one of his few pleasures. His daydreams surround his killing fantasy. He re-invents the moment

of attack, binding the limbs, attaching them to the rack he has built
especially to hold Kelia helplessly against the wall, a rack like that
used by his father against those who broke the law in the village.
He relives those dark-time moments with Linda, with Kia, with all
the Kelias he has sent over to Ku and in whose destruction he has
found gleeful satisfaction, far beyond sexual fulfillment, he
assures himself, for with each killing he comes one step closer to
his own godhood.

Sometimes his daydreams become inextricably mixed with
memories; memories he'd just as soon forget, reshape or counter-
feit, memories of hurt and humiliation so intense they must be
forged anew if any of it is to make sense. Yet it was in those early
years—even as an infant, humiliation and all—that he was first
contacted by the running-wind gods to become their servant. The
trade winds rocked his cradle.

Remembrance is painful and he hides from it always, yet it finds
him, creeps into his daydreams, slithers into his bed, catches him
at the wheel and at his weakest moments. Since he is unable to
fully escape, a black and inky depression pours over his soul,
blotting all else out. Childhood: No matter how he tries, his huge
father finds him. His father still wants him to one day *become* him,
but Lopaka has decided on another fate, one offered by a higher
power than his earthly father. He escaped his father's tyrannical
domination, escaped the place of his birth, the backward life of his
youth, when his father sent him away, ostensibly to gain a deep,
abiding understanding of the world through a Western education.

His freedom won, he found himself venting his pent-up rage on
the unsuspecting in his midst, first on Maui, until his marriage to
Kelia when, for a time, he was in control of his primal urges. Still,
his angry father, never understanding the depths to which Lopaka
had sunk, was enraged on learning that his son had married
without consent or traditional ceremony. His father not only cut
off all funds for him, but all contact as well, banishing him from
ever returning to his island home of Molokai. He had dared to
marry below himself, to marry a mixed-blood at that, to take a
noanoa, a common peasant, for a wife. Hypocritically, the old
man, chief of his puny tribe, had taken in a white woman, living
in sin, giving birth to Lopaka, but she had been, according to his
royal father, a "high-born *haole.*"

As a boy of four, he had seen his twin brother die when the
ministrations and incantations employed by his father failed

miserably to save the boy from a disease that had spread across their homeland. Lopaka, like his deformed brother, Lopeko, was infected with the contagion and very nearly lost his own life at that time. Often now, as in the past, he wishes it had been him whom the gods had taken.

He saw his brother's body taken away by the woman his father would later take as his second wife. He felt the flames of the fire as the little body of his brother was placed upon a stack of others and burned. He cried out that his brother was still alive, that he could *feel* the flames scalding his living flesh; Lopaka had the welts on his body to prove it, but no one listened; they assumed it was the fever talking. Lopeko's bones were cast into the sea for fear they would contaminate the burial ground.

Later, as he grew older, Lopaka began to see his father's cruelty, hidden as it was behind a veneer of civility, law and custom, yet clearly present. He also began to slowly realize that his father and he did not look at all alike, and that his father was desperate to have more sons, to replace the misbegotten one, the one without the *'ele'ele,* the luminous black color of the Hawaiian eyes, but rather with pale blue eyes, so it was not long before Lopaka realized that he was an embarrassment to his father, a defilement. That while he was the son of the *mokoi,* he'd been conceived by a *haole* who'd brought death and disease to the people. Lopaka's mother, too, had succumbed to the devastating disease which she had brought to the village.

His father's attempts to have more children became common knowledge, and everyone in the village spoke behind Lopaka's back about the evil the white blood in him had brought to the village, and how the chief could not possibly pass on his powers to this pale son.

An outsider who never fit in, he became a misfit at an early age, keeping to himself, living an all-but-mute existence, hearing not the voices of loving parents each night, but falling asleep to the whispered curses of anger, disappointment and distrust coming out of his own father.

For years he tried desperately to change his father's mind and the mind of the community, attempting to be him, mimicking the man, following him around like a dog, gazing up at him with admiration and feigned love. He wore the ceremonial lei and garb of the son of a chief, carried the ceremonial knives and clubs, and generally played the part fate had meted out to him in a pathetic attempt to win acceptance from everyone around him. At the same time, he secretly cursed his stepmother and asked the gods of the air and the earth to make her barren. Unable to have children, the stepmother was soon replaced by another, but she, too, could not give the chief another child, for Lopaka's evil magic was powerful. It was the first time the gods granted him his wish, and they opened his eyes to the true nature of his brother's death. It was a death that Lopaka knew in his heart had nothing whatever to do with the disease.

That healing lotion of his own brain that hid such horrors from the conscious child had placed the terror so far away that he'd lost *all* memory of it until the wind voices came to remind him. They opened his eyes to what his mind had closed on, that young, deformed Lopeko did not die of his illness but by the ceremonial sword belonging to his father. The gods told him that the hand wielding the sword had been his father's, that Lopeko had been an embarrassment to him.

No matter how he tried, Lopaka—a constant, brooding reminder to his father of all the taboos he'd broken—could never fit in, and in fact had good reason to fear for his own life; he was marked from birth and by the death of his twin, and there was no changing the public mind about him. There were other children in the village considered perfect, the epitome of the race, the last vestiges of it, in fact—children who were full-bloods, with rich smiles and warm, radiant *'ele'ele* eyes that told of an ancient ancestry, their little bottoms and sturdy legs thick, their baby skin swarthy and their lives filled with freedom and happiness. And when one of their pet birds or dogs disappeared, found later to have been brutally slain with a long blade, it was held up as a warning to them to never tempt the demons of the night and the forests.

Lopaka's earliest memories of creating a state of non-existence in a living creature were now like the playful struggling and curiosity of a child over a complex jigsaw puzzle. Yet those first experiments in creating death where there had been life had stirred in him feelings and sexual emotions he'd never before touched. It was a kind of crude baptism for him, and his newfound religion quickly escalated when he began to lure smaller children into the forests, where he delighted in humiliating and hurting them, until one day a little girl named Alaya was found dead, her body brutally savaged and fed upon by the forest beasts and perhaps some supernatural demons known to lurk in the black shadows amid the mountains.

No one suspected that the demon was the boy who'd lured Alaya into those woods with promises; no one suspected—least of all the other children—not even those whom Lopaka had practiced his little tortures on. No one but his father. Yet Lopaka simply braved it out, strutting about, pretending to be his father, the little *keiki ali'i,* doling out justice and punishment at the court of his peers just as he'd seen his father, the *ali'i kane,* do a thousand times.

The gods sometimes told him that his father was not his true father, that *they* were; that Lopaka was spawned from the seed of the supernatural. He didn't at first believe this, but as he grew older, more and more signs pointed to the fact that he was not in any way like his father.

His first killing was unintentional. He was hardly into his teens at the time, and Alaya was a trusting eleven-year-old. He might not have killed her had she not had such a vile temper and nasty tongue, had she not screamed out what everyone else thought of him. . . .

He recalls now with a cold and clear memory, like a photographer interested in light and shadow, just how slowly he eased the knife into the child's limb only to maim. She fainted immediately, and he, using one of his father's ceremonial blades, continued to cut. He had learned much from his father, how to get the most out of a torture victim. Still, it surprised him to learn when the little girl's blood gushed forward that he was moved to a higher plane of feeling. The next wound and subsequent ribbon of red lace over her throat so excited him that he was filled with delirious joy, a kind of ecstasy that forced a ritual dance from him.

He was *sexually* aroused by the little girl's pain, the suffering making him stiffen in his private parts, the blood begging him to taste of death, to take it on his fingers and lap it up. . . .

The entire attack lasted only a few minutes, but within that compressed moment he'd stabbed the girl thirty, perhaps forty times before he was completely spent, using his blade as his penis, totally destroying her. The act blotted out all of her kind—anyone who dared question him or despise him.

It was the first time that his subconscious had *authenticated* the trinity, the three-way link between the voices in his head, his need for sexual arousal, and the fact he could only reach it through physical violence. Before this, any sexual arousal had been lukewarm and minimal at best, but now it was fiery and full-blown.

Memories, he thinks now, sitting behind the wheel of his clean, air-conditioned bus, have a place, but he prefers memories that arouse him sexually, so he draws most on memories of his recent bloodlettings.

The little bus he drives now bumps off busy H-1, Kamehameha Freeway, and runs the familiar and crowded off-ramp to Pearl Harbor. The bus winds its way around to the lawns of the well-kept entrance of Pearl Harbor, toward the site of the *U.S.S. Arizona* Memorial, with its bones entombed underwater. Lopaka's passengers, fully two-thirds being curious Japanese citizens with cameras in hand, are prepared to record what they consider their history, regardless of what American textbooks say about the war in the Pacific.

So together, American and Japanese tourists, along with Australians, New Zealanders, Europeans and others from around the globe, will go by solemn Coast Guard cutter out to the sunken World War II battleship. There, shoulder to shoulder, they'll read the list of names in alphabetical order on a "wailing wall" monument, the names of privates and noncoms, officers and marines, from H. Aaron to M. Zwarun, Jr. Then the tourists will stand over the underwater tomb of over eleven hundred men, a 184-foot crypt of shattered metal seen clearly through the crystal waters of the harbor only four feet below the concrete platform built over the forecastle of the sunken ship, a liquid rainbow of leaking oil still rippling over the stern after fifty years.

The bus comes to a jerking stop, and the door opens with a swishing sound; Lopaka gets off the bus with his passengers, leads them like children to the gate and haggles with the ticket-handler for twenty-four discounts for his tour group, discounts they're to receive for riding the Enoa Bus Line. He sleepwalks through the process and then tells his passengers where and when to meet after the sightseeing is finished. This done, he returns to his bus and takes it out of the entrance lanes, to park and wait and think more about tonight, about Hiilani, whom he has finally chosen.

11

Fate sits on these dark battlements and frowns. . . .

Ann Radcliffe

1:05 P.M. July 16, 1995, Paniolo's bar, Honolulu

The raid on Paniolo's bar and grill near the university netted some suspicious blood spatters and other stains lingering after what appeared a hasty cleanup, but no ready evidence of George Oniiwah's having been held hostage there was turned up. Nonetheless, employees and any *standing* clientele were all arrested on drug charges, as both cocaine and heroin on the premises were sniffed out by dogs trained in the art. A little time in interrogation, a little wheeling and dealing, and someone in Paniolo's employ or sphere of enfluence would give the cretin up, or at least spill something about the missing boy, or so Parry believed.

Somebody heard something. Somebody saw something. Somebody knew something. Meanwhile, Professor Donald G. Claxton was offered protective custody but refused it, leaving Parry to put a couple of men on him, reckoning that if Oniiwah had given up Claxton as the possible killer in the Linda Kahala case, then Claxton would next disappear. And if a white man, however despicable of character, happened to be beaten or killed by *kanakas* . . .

All efforts at locating Oniiwah looked bleak until news came over the wire that the body of a young Hawaiian male was found floating in relatively remote Waimanalo Bay just northwest of Makapuu Beach Park and the Sea Peace Museum and whaling village at Waimea Falls.

Parry grabbed Jessica and drove as if possessed through the Pali Tunnel on State Route 63. The tunnel, carved through the dark bowels of the mountain, took them to the other side of the island. There they sped southeast on State 72, Parry praying they wouldn't find the body of the *hapa Japa* he'd rousted at Paniolo's the night before.

They arrived at a scene already secured by uniformed officers from the district, finding the usual curious onlookers edging closer to have a better look, necks craned, the crowd absurdly held at bay by hundreds of yards of black and yellow plastic ribbon. The streamer tape formed a series of U's and W's where it dangled and flailed in the wind, extended at intervals between coconut trees along the mile-long stretch of beach.

Jessica could tell two things at a distance: Her cane would be useless in the sand, and the body was extremely fresh. She left her cane and heels in Parry's new vehicle—a sporty-looking new Dodge Stealth—pulled a lab coat over her blouse and slacks, grabbed her medical bag and trudged after Parry, who'd not bothered to wait, anxious to know the truth he feared.

She'd sensed his growing anxiety as the day had worn on, and with no sign or word of George Oniiwah until this, Jim was understandably concerned.

If it was Oniiwah's body out on the sand, Jim would bury Hal Ewelo. Jessica had caught a glimpse of the man in lockup, and had found Halole "Paniolo" Ewelo not at all like Joe Kaniola. Joe, despite grief over his son, despite his frustration and the fact that he'd lied to her, had never displayed a fraction of the malevolence found in Ewelo's eyes. Paniolo was a big, burly man whose leathery face—never the same twice—folded with light and shadow as he walked through the dimly lit corridors between holding cell and interrogation room. He looked powerful enough to snap a boy like George Oniiwah in two, and his smile, which could not be wiped away by his predicament, was that of a crocodile.

They'd learned that he had, for most of his life, been a working cowboy on a huge ranch on Maui, of which there were several centered around the town of Makawao, where the famous Makawao Rodeo was held each year on July 4th, where cowboys of every size, shape, color and hue of Hawaiian ancestry or otherwise competed in a day of wild sport. From the look of him, Ewelo rarely lost, but scars on his face, hands and arms were reminders of a rugged life in which he more than once was stepped on by a Brahman bull. It was quite conceivable that the man could easily lose control, go over the top and kill Oniiwah while trying to get the *truth*—that young George knew *something* about the disappearance and death of Lina Kahala, at least according to the *Ala Ohana,* which Ewelo, an illiterate even in his own language, had read to him each morning.

Parry didn't need any further reason to suspect Halole Ewelo after learning of a rumor that the rugged cowboy was carrying out a vigilante search for the sadistic killer of a native girl. Parry had desperately tried to make this clear to Donald Claxton, but the man wouldn't listen to reason.

As Jessica now approached the body on the beach, dredged up by a local man's net, she feared the worst; Parry's instant reaction to the body lying face down in the sand, the head turned to one side, the mouth agape and playing home to a sand crab, told the story.

Jim's eyes spoke clearly of his hurt, and for a moment she searched his gaze deeply, trying to share the pain, to feel with him, and for an instant she snatched at and caught all the emotions that had cauldroned between them since their first meeting. The empathy surged through her heart.

"I'm sorry, Jim."

His terse response was cool, even defiant, a pretense. "I want to know exactly how he died, when he died, what he ate a half hour before he died—down to the last ugly detail. I want all the I's dotted and the T's crossed on this, Jess. I want this sonofabitch Paniolo like I've never wanted anybody before. You understand that?"

She understood it was personal, that he felt guilty, that he believed himself as culpable as Hal Ewelo and the likely others who'd killed this boy. "I'll do what I can," she quietly said, going to her knees, creating an indention in the sand alongside the body. She began her superficial examination of Oniiwah's remains. She was keenly aware of the incongruity here between the beautiful landscape and the ugly death at her fingertips, and that all around her stood the island authorities, equally puzzled and bewildered by death's ability to end life at so young an age.

The men shuffling about and around her were nervous ambulance attendants, uniformed county cops and detectives, some just arriving to have a look, others responding to the alert. Even here, in paradise, men ruled and men squandered and women picked up the pieces, she thought.

The boy'd been deposited in the ocean without clothing, and his bruises were everywhere over the torso, head and limbs, many of the purple bruises and gashes no doubt inflicted by the coral reefs here, but many also bearing the unmistakable mark of human cruelty. . . .

On first glance, with the body face down, she could not say for sure which blow might have killed Oniiwah, although there was great trauma to the head.

"All right." She firmly gave the order. "Let's roll him."

With Jim's help, she turned the body in a controlled, easy manner so as not to add any new injuries, such as a broken neck from wrongful handling of the dead weight. With the turning of the corpse, a collective gasp went around the men standing over her to combine with her own when the real damage came clear: Oniiwah had been literally emasculated, his sex organs gone, the scrotum washed clean of blood and loose matter by the sea. This alone might have been enough to send him into shock and thus eventual death. Multiple contusions about the eyes, nose and mouth were also contributing factors, along with a horrid gash to the left temple by a blunt instrument, most likely a hefty paperweight, brass knuckles, a ball bat or the butt of a revolver.

"He was severely tortured," she said uselessly just to break the eerie silence that had materialized all around her.

"You saying he was butchered before or after he was killed?" Parry asked, his jawbone set and quivering.

"I'd need some lab work to prove either way."

"Your best guess?"

"If I were guessing . . . *before*. All part of the intimidation and interrogation. Strip him and threaten and cut him."

Parry stalked off, unable to stare down at what remained of George Oniiwah a moment longer. She shouted to the waiting ambulance attendants, "Bag the hands—for all the good it'll do—and finish up here. See the body gets to the FBI morgue in Honolulu."

She caught up to Parry, who was leaning over the hood of his car. "You can't blame yourself for this, Jim."

"Damnit, I should've known better. I should've seen it fucking coming."

"Christ, an act of depravity like this? How do you see that coming, Jim? What? You're supposed to be psychic or something? Give it a rest, and give yourself a break, Jim . . . Jim!"

He pulled away, not listening, climbing into the car. She gave him some space, going to the passenger side and sliding in beside him.

He wheeled on her and pointed his finger in her face. "We're all walking on a tinderbox here. Of all people, Jess, I shoulda known. I shoulda foreseen this. I shoulda been more careful. Tony tried to tell me; hell, the population over in the canal district tried to tell me when they dusted my car, but I'm thick! I'm goddamned thick and stupid. I keep thinking the best of people; keep thinking people've got to see right from wrong, but that's crazy. . . . It gets people killed."

"Damnit, Jim, we've got no time for this . . . this self-pity crap! If what you say is true about the Trade Winds Killer, he's still searching for another victim, and the sun'll be down in a few hours."

His jaw firmly set, he said, "So what the hell do you suggest, Dr. Coran?"

"I suggest to you that Ewelo be held as long as possible on as many violations as you can get him on, and in the meantime, we do a blood typing on Oniiwah's body, and maybe we'll have a match that will put Ewelo at the scene of the boy's death. But that won't be enough. You've got to have a finger pointed in the right direction. I suggest that finger be the roommate. Lean on him."

"Way ahead of you on that score. Tony's working on him as we speak."

"And in the meantime, run a check on any possible connections Ewelo may've had with any of the victims. If you find there are any threads there, that he knew Kahala and perhaps Kia, if they frequented his place, and if he put them on the street, that gives him a ticket to the show."

He considered this in quiet reflection until the ambulance sirened for clearance and sped out of the sand. A cascade of pebbles responded as the ambulance careened onto the tarmac, taking Oniiwah's body off with little fanfare.

"Better keep the ambulance in view," she suggested. "No telling how long Ewelo's reach is."

"This Paniolo guy disgusts me, but I don't think he's the Trade Winds Killer," he flatly observed.

"Aren't you being a bit premature?"

"He doesn't fit the profile."

"Sometimes the profile doesn't fit, so? You can't be a slave to it. Let your instincts guide you. Besides, the color of his skin certainly fits." She hesitated, doing battle with her seat belt. "Serial killers tend to kill within their own race. At least you've got probable cause which, even if it doesn't stick, may get Ewelo on Oniiwah's murder, not to mention the fact it'll give you some breathing room."

"Ever the opportunist, aren't you?"

"Drive," she replied.

He tore out and flipped the switch to his strobe light, in hot pursuit of the ambulance. Bodies had been known to get lost before, and if Ewelo did have friends in high places . . .

Jessica, still with her lab coat over her shoulders, and tearing away the surgical gloves she'd used in examining the body, now said, "Ewelo's mean enough and ugly enough to please Pearl, the city, county, state and the boys back home in D.C. Hell, his eyes alone'll convict him. Just see to it the newsies get his photograph—preferably a mug shot."

"I like the way your mind works, Jess."

"And Jim?"

"What?"

"It's time to warn the women of this island in complete detail just what turns the Trade Winds Killer on, just in case Ewelo's not the real thing, which given our doubts . . ."

Jim, thinking aloud, said, "You think Ewelo used a cane cutter on George Oniiwah?"

"Possibly, but whatever he used, if the evidence supports it, you'll have him on the boy's murder."

"But you agree with me; you don't think he's the Trade Winds Killer, do you?"

"My luck doesn't usually run that well. How 'bout yours?"

"I've seen overly helpful men volunteer, join in search parties, work day and night on a case—"

"Sure, and shout the loudest for police to do their job," she added.

"And go ballistic and self-righteous and do the vigilante thing as a cover."

She considered this a moment as the lush island landscape flew past. "It'd make for a hell of a cover. Yeah," she conceded, "I've been involved in cases where the killer revisited the crime scene, relived the events over again, fantasized about his emotional release at the point of killing, all without the least worry of being caught by a stakeout, because he's part of the damned stakeout."

Parry, nodding, added, "Not to mention the fact he becomes privy to the investigation."

"Sure, Ewelo *could* be our guy, but we won't know that unless we can make the connections. One is his proximity to the university where the women were going to school; a second is the fact he may've feared what Oniiwah knew, and in a show of civic duty, he offs Oniiwah, as a lesson to those who dared to harm Hawaiian women. A third connection, Oniiwah's blood, will give us an opportunity to revisit Paniolo's, his den, not to mention his home. Hopefully locate other blood samples. We need to know everything there is to know about this man: who his friends are, who does business with him, where he's worked before on the island, and if he likes to cruise the strip where the women disappeared."

Parry liked what he heard, and he gunned the Stealth until they were a hundred yards behind the ambulance, which was now cutting off 72 for 63 and the Pali Tunnel. Once they were back in Waikiki they'd tighten up to be sure the driver knew he was being watched. Never again would Parry assume anything when it came to the mind of a Hawaiian national. He gave a thought to the political power of the PKO, the Preserve Kahoolawe Ohana, which had come into greater prominence in the nineties.

Parry radioed ahead that they were coming in with George Oniiwah's body, and said that information should be conveyed to Claxton for his own safety and that Claxton was to be picked up.

"On what charges, sir?" asked Dispatch.

"Contributing to the delinquency of a minor."

"Roger that, Number 1. We have your orders." Even Dispatch liked the sound of it.

"You think you can make it stick?"

"Maybe not, but when we wheel Oniiwah's body past him, maybe he'll change his mind about protective custody and a change of scenery."

"What about Claxton as a possible suspect in the Trade Winds killings?"

"No, won't wash."

"Why not?"

"He's a lover; likes pretty young women, can't keep his hands off them, but he doesn't get his jollies by beating or humiliating them, no . . . and he's not into carving them up for sexual arousal as obviously our boy is."

"So, what're the Cowboy's sexual proclivities?"

"Closer to our killer's, I'm told."

Jessica could never quite fathom the sadistic sexual urge that led to a primitive need to destroy a sexual partner completely in order to ejaculate and thereby conquer wholly the being of another. Murder and sex, an ancient story. The Cane Cutter didn't murder to cover a rape, however; in fact, what he did was not classified at all as a rape by FBI standards, but rather he raped in the ultimate sense by raping life from his victim in order to fulfill his peculiar, deviant sexual urges. The Trade Winds Killer punished his victims because they had something he did not: a normal sex drive; he tortured them and cut into them to prove himself a man, to prove that he could overcome his own impotence, showering them no doubt with his sperm when it finally came forth, ending the ritual of foreplay and ejaculation only to open the door to the final ritual of death, the last act played out between victim and killer.

Having enjoyed the victim's pain and blood, which "turned him on," blinded by a mad desire for more, the final raining blows and cuts—which Jessica postulated from the Kahala arm must number in forties and fifties—filled the killer with a mystical and religious release from this plane of existence.

Not everyone could comfortably contemplate or fully comprehend such a religion; it wasn't everyone who had to examine such diabolical acts to make sense—however twisted—of sexually motivated mutilation murders. But she and Parry had to do exactly that.

Tenderness, caresses, kisses, soft touches, all that love meant for normal, God-fearing human beings who found a healthy lust in mutual respect, care and fondling, were turned to their opposite extremes by the sado-masochistic Cane Cutter and others of his kind. The Cane Cutter preferred brutality to tenderness, punches and knife wounds to caresses, a disgorged tongue to a kiss, a clawing, tearing rake of nails to a soft touch, madness to a healthy lust, tearing and rending to fondling, humiliation to respect. He wanted total domination over life, to completely bond with and take another life. Ironically, he preferred pain to pleasure, death to life. Subconsciously wanting death for himself, but too cowardly to destroy himself, he instead becomes the carrier, the reaper.

The more Jessica thought about him, the more she both recognized and despised the Trade Winds Killer, and the more she believed him still out there, despite the Claxtons and Paniolos of the island or other deviants behind bars at the moment. For not only was he a psychopath, the Cane Cutter was quite cunning, planning out his every move, cautious to a fault and invisible even when seen.

It still remained true that Officers Thom Hilani and Alan Kaniola were the only two lawmen who'd come even remotely close to ending the terror of the Trade Winds Killer.

4 P.M., July 16, FBI Crime Lab, Honolulu

Back at Lau's labs, as they'd come to be known since Dr. Shore's extended departure, Jessica prepared Oniiwah's blood to be tested against that found at Paniolo's. Each specimen was carefully processed, but it would take time to know for certain if they had a match or not. In the meantime, she had to know whether she could or could not trust Lau, who would be overseeing the tests.

Lau had not been present when she'd arrived with the samples she had taken from Oniiwah's corpse. It was 6 P.M. and Lau had gone home, but now his sudden return surprised her.

"You've heard the news?" she asked.

"The Japanese-Hawaiian boy, George Oniiwah, yes," he admitted.

"Then you knew of him?"

"Only what I have read in the papers."

She knew he was lying and from the speed of his darting black eyes, and the pretense with his hands over a rack of test tubes and slide trays he fiddled with, Jessica knew that he knew she'd just assessed his body language.

"You are closely related to Joseph Kaniola?" she asked.

"Closely? No, not closely."

"But you are related?"

"By blood, no."

"Marriage then?"

"Yes."

"You know your work here must remain confidential at all costs; you know that, and yet you told Kaniola details that should not have left this office."

Lau's brow creased and he found a stool to sit on. Shaking his head as if to say no, he replied. "I only told what was already public record."

"No, you told him about our cane-cutter theory."

"And *you* told him more than that," he said defensively.

She stared back at the impenetrable black eyes of the small man. "I am an investigative member of this team as well as a forensic expert, Mr. Lau. You are the manager of a lab. Are we clear on that?"

His jaw tightened, but he said, "Yes, of course."

"Chief Parry knows that it was you who divulged the fact the killer uses a cane cutter."

"Kaniola promised me it was off the record, that he would not use such information."

"Right," she said, but she could believe the little man, too. "So what're you saying, that Joseph Kaniola was *forced* into printing all that he knew?"

"Who do you think funds his paper? You know business? Politics?" A little shrug of the shoulders and Lau felt he had explained all.

She nodded. "All right, so far, so good. Kaniola is pressured by the nationalist party members to tell all to the people. Who's twisting Kaniola's arm?"

"The Honorable Provisional Government of our people, the PKOs, those who will take over power of the islands when your government has lost our many standing suits in your courts."

She could almost forgive Lau his idealistic and naive dream that the U.S. Government would one day benevolently return all native lands and properties to the Hawaiians. It was about as likely as one day seeing Arizona returned to its native population there. With the capital invested in Oahu alone, in the Waikiki strip alone, the islands of Hawaii were inextricably bound to the economic and social fabric of the U.S., and nothing would ever change that, despite the agreement to return Hong Kong to China by Great Britain in 1977—or perhaps because of it.

Jessica could almost forgive Joseph Kaniola now, knowing that his own "provisional government" ties could make life hell for him and the rest of his extended family, and that such a government wasn't above using a man like Halole Ewelo anymore than her own might. As for Ewelo's part, he must've been promised much for the role he'd played in the drama—his attempt to lead the investigation to a white male suspect, namely Professor Claxton, knowing that hanging a white teacher for the murders of island girls would spell out a victory for the nationalist party. But perhaps no one could know just how far Paniolo Ewelo might take his deadly interrogation techniques.

"Who are the PKOs?" she curiously asked.

"Kahoolawe preservation society. They want everything to return to traditional ways."

Jim had mumbled something about this PKO group in the car on their way back. She had to get Jim on the line, explain her newfound knowledge to him. See if he did not concur that both Kaniola and Lau were being squeezed, and that these men were both in an impossible position. But for now she had Lau to deal with.

"Now we have another dead Hawaiian, Mr. Lau, thanks to politics. Do you really think the deaths of all these young women have anything to do with political matters on the island?"

"No, of course not, but *your* government—whom you work for—is desperate to use the killings, to point to the heathens living here—"

"I've got no such orders!"

"—to bring home the fact we can't conduct our own affairs—"

"I've had no such instructions, Mr. Lau, and neither has Parry," she scolded.

"—that we are little more than pagan children still to be Christianized and colonized and Westernized and homogenized."

"You can't believe this, Mr. Lau."

"If your government can show this, then they take back

Kahoolawe and all lands and titles we have fought to regain over the years." A kind of native islander's paranoia had infiltrated the man's voice.

"Damnit all, Mr. Lau, we—people such as you and me—we have an obligation to the truth first and foremost. In the laboratory there are no bloody politics, only science . . . only fact. That's true in every state of the Union, including this one!"

"Noble words, sister American," he said calmly, "but all we do, all we say, *they* wait to pounce upon and twist to whatever expediency may suit them. Read the Congressional Record."

Christ, she silently admitted, *he did understand the Great White Way*. "You can trust Parry."

"Can I?"

"Yes, damnit, and you can trust me. The only question remaining is, can either of us trust you?"

He hesitated answering. "It is a small island still in many ways. We have modern skyscrapers, Western high-tech businesses, the computer revolution confronting us, all this speeding change in a handful of years, change which your country and people have had a hundred years to assimilate to. We still struggle and stumble. And I must live here after you and Parry and others are gone."

"I need your help to catch a killer, Lau; that's all that matters inside this lab."

His steely eyes bore into hers, and she allowed her own to send forth a vivid fire of determined anger. "Are you willing to give your full support to this investigation? And to keep what is confidential in-house? I must have your word, your guarantee; otherwise there will be more George Oniiwahs."

"No one wished Oniiwah dead, least of all me."

She saw the pain he'd concealed. "Mr. Lau, if anyone's to blame for Oniiwah's death, it's the man they've jailed for it."

"No, the fault belongs to us all," said Lau, "to the climate we've all contributed to here, one of fear and desperation and political unrest."

"Yes, I believe so," Jessica agreed, extending a hand. "I want to trust you again, Mr. Lau."

"Now it is *Doctor* Lau," he replied, taking her hand and vigorously shaking it, "as of today. I received news of my final review and dissertation acceptance."

"Congratulations." Her smile was genuine.

"It was being held up . . . for *political* reasons."

She shook her head over this, realizing that it was due the ineptitude, mistrust and jockeying of Lau's so-called superiors—white men—that he had become the enemy beneath their noses.

"Then we are *all* guilty after all," she conceded. "Will you trust me, Mr . . . ah, Dr. Lau? And can we work as scientists, together, amid this turmoil, keeping no secrets from one another?"

"I would like that very much, yes."

She demonstrated her trust by giving him the details of the death of George Oniiwah and asking him to finish the lab analysis of Oniiwah's blood type, so she could be in attendance at a meeting of all the FBI agents involved in the ongoing search for the Cane Cutter.

Lau took the samples and promised to have results back to her as soon as humanly possible. She knew now that they could start over, on firm ground.

As she was about to leave, he said, "Oniiwah was not supposed to be killed. How it happened? Only this man, Paniolo, can say."

"He was not under orders to kill the boy, we know."

"No, no such orders, ever."

"But he was ordered to interrogate the boy?"

"For information, that is all."

"Dr. Lau, you tell these people for me that, under U.S. law, it is they who are legally responsible for contributing to the boy's abduction, violations of his civil rights, and ultimately his death."

"These people, Dr. Coran, do not recognize U.S. law, unless to do so helps in their cause."

"These people, Dr. Lau, will recognize it when they see it from behind bars."

"You will never find them to lock them up. They are *'umalu* and *'uhane,* shadows . . . spirits."

"You just tell your brother-in-law that I want to meet with him, that I want to talk."

"He will contact you," Lau assured her.

"Good . . . good. Then can I expect results on the blood in the next twenty-four hours?"

"You can."

"And you expect it will match the stains taken from Paniolo's place?"

"I am certain it will."

"Prove it then, and what happens to you, Dr. Lau?"

"The same as Kaniola. I am in the middle. We are all of us Hawaiians in the middle."

She nodded, stripped off her lab coat, grabbed her cane and walked from the lab, somehow confident that Lau could be trusted for the truth.

12

Something has licked my heel
Like a sturgeon
And I have a problem
With my right foot and my life.

James Dickey, "Snakebite"

FBI Headquarters, Honolulu

At 8 P.M., a late evening meeting was called by Parry, who'd rounded up the principal agents working the case. With Jessica looking on, Parry warned that they were a far cry from a conviction against Hal Ewelo as either Oniiwah's murderer or the serial killer who'd been terrorizing the city.

"Having any of you rousted Ewelo before? Have any of you given consideration to the possibility that Ewelo could be the Trade Winds Killer before his arrest on the Oniiawh charges?"

Amazingly enough, several had pursued leads along this line after tips and informants had suggested the notion, including Tony, but he, like the others, had come up empty-handed. "Except for his petty crimes, drugs and prostitution," said Tony, "Hal Ewelo's clean. No murder charges. Always has an alibi that checks, and he doesn't own a history of violence reserved for women only, since he spreads it around."

Jessica had to agree that Ewelo did not fit as neatly as they'd all like to make him fit. "The nature of his type of violence is considered to be within normal parameters by any law-enforcement standard, and certainly well below the 'norm' of mutilation set by the Cane Cutter."

"Whoa up there, Doctor," said Parry. "This man had George Oniiwah's sex organs sliced off while the boy was bound to a chair."

Jessica had found traces of blood and feces in the hastily wiped chair when gathering evidence at Paniolo's.

Parry's statement silenced the room, but still no one who'd responded to Jim's call tonight believed Ewelo was the Cane Cutter. Parry went on like a desperate prosecuting attorney, trying to convince the others of Ewelo's guilt as a serial killer with a lust for mutilation murder. "The man's record places him in Maui during a period when seven women there disappeared, their bodies never recovered."

This got a few rethinking Paniolo Ewelo.

"The man also worked for a time in a cane field."

"Beggin' your pardon, Chief," said Haley, a big Australian-born American agent, "but what *kanaka* hasn't worked a cane field at some time in his bleedin' life?"

This brought laughter to the group, all except Jim.

"Something's got to break," shouted Parry to his people in the debriefing room. The wall was lined with the photos of young victims. "We've got to share our snitches, pool our knowledge. Is there anyone here who has any leads whatever they have not shared with command?"

"What about this business in the press, Chief?" asked Terri Reno, the well-formed blond agent who'd been walking the Waikiki strip in a brave effort to bait the Trade Winds Killer. "Any truth to it?"

All eyes went to Terri, who was in full dress as a hooker. Parry replied cryptically at first, saying, "Some, yes." He then quickly separated fact from fiction in the *Ala Ohana* article.

As Parry spoke, Terri combed out her long, black wig. Then she paused and said, "You know, Chief, I've been getting nibbles, but no bites; we got quite a few lockups for solicitation, but nothing of the caliber we're looking for, not that I'm complaining. On the other hand . . ."

"What?" pressed Parry.

"There's this one guy . . . kinda strange."

"Strange how?"

"We got tapes on him, if you want to listen. Just that he never does anything. Flirts, says he would rather not have to pay for sex. Wants it given to him freely. Imagine that, telling a working girl that. So I brushed him off the first time, but he keeps sniffing around like a dog in heat."

"But he never does anything except talk," interjected her partner, Haley.

Parry was interested. "Did he ever give out with a name, Terri?"

She blinked and shook her head, saying, "Robert, I think, yeah, Robert . . . that's all, Boss."

"Nothing more?"

"Sorry."

"He never invited you elsewhere to 'talk'?"

"Sure, every time. Wants me to walk to his car with him, go to his place, he says. Says he thinks I'm pretty; say's he'd like to take care of me, shit like that, but when I mention money and tell him he can have me for an hour, he backs off and repeats himself. Then he tells me I shouldn't sell myself on the street like common garbage, tells me that I could be happy being taken care of by a man like him."

Her partner, Haley, laughed at this. "Pip-squeak."

"Compared to you, Haley, everybody's a pip-squeak," replied Gagliano.

Reno went on. "And last night I answered with how I could use a place for the night, because my pimp's been looking for me to beat the shit outta me, and he says he knows the guy."

"Knows the guy?"

"Yeah, and get this . . . says his name is Paniolo. You believe that?"

Parry's eyes lit up. "You didn't say Paniolo first?"

"No, I swear."

"And you were wired? You got this on tape?"

"Damn straight, mate," said Haley.

"Any film on the guy?"

"No, we're not budgeted for film," Haley said with a moan.

"All right . . . go on, Terri."

"Course, at the time, I didn't know Paniolo from shinola, but I said sure, that's the guy, so Robert says that he'd be happy to put me up for the night."

"What happened then?"

"Weirdest thing."

"Yeah?"

"He wanted to know what I was."

"What you were?" Jessica asked before Parry could.

She nodded, the comb in her hand at a standstill now. "My nationality. Wanted to know if I was even part Hawaiian, and I told him I was one-quarter Hawaiian, part French—'cause I thought that would turn his burners up—and part American." She was punctuating with the hairbrush now. "I figured he'd never believe me if I told him I was Hawaiian, you know."

"So what happened then?"

"Nothing."

"Nothing?"

"He didn't come back. Said he had to go get his car, which he said was over by the park, and—"

"The park?"

"Fort DeRussy, I took him to mean. Anyway, I asked the guys on the mike what rating they'd given the guy."

"Rating?" asked Jessica.

"On the nut scale. One to ten. Anyway, they just gave him a mild rating, so I waited, not particularly interested, and when he didn't come back, I figured he'd thought better of crossing this guy Paniolo."

"How many times did he come back to speak to you on the street?"

"Last night? Just the once, but others, *whew* . . . and if he wasn't speaking, he was watching. Spooky guy, really, but I took him for a mental, and since they're generally harmless, well . . ."

"How many times in all did this guy approach you?" asked Parry, clarifying Jessica's question.

Reno pursed her lips and thought about this for a moment. "*Hmmmmm* . . . four, maybe five different nights."

"Consecutive nights?"

"No, no . . . scattered."

"You haven't been out there more'n a week," said Tony Gagliano, getting the picture.

"And he'd come up to me two or three times a night to just

make small talk until I brushed him off, telling him I had business to attend to and how he was cramping my style. Now I hear about this guy Paniolo here, and suddenly I'm wondering all over about this guy I thought was a nerd, that maybe he could be the Cane Cutter."

Parry was instantly at her. "I want you to sit down with Don Myers, get as good a sketch of this guy as possible to put in Kaniola's paper and the *Union Jack News*. And Tony, you and I are going to be backing Terri out there tonight, and if this toad shows, we're going to corner his ass. The connection with Paniolo is just too sweet."

"It's the bottom of the ninth and two outs," said Jessica, "and we're due for a little luck."

"I don't get this," said Haley. "I've seen this guy. He's a *kanaka* worm."

"Then he's Hawaiian?" asked Jessica.

"Would figure if he's acquainted with Ewelo," Tony Gagliano put in.

Parry asked, "A worm in what sense?"

"Slinks like a goddamn worm, Chief. He's hefty, eats well, I'd say, works out maybe, but he's low to the ground and he's mealymouthed. Hell, even Terri scares him."

"Terri scares me," joked Gagliano, breaking the others up.

Terri threw her carefully brushed wig at Tony.

Haley continued after all had settled down. "I figured the Trade Winds Killer for a ladies' man, Chief, not a worm."

"He's dysfunctional where women are concerned," corrected Jessica.

"And he bides his time like a damned spider," Parry stated. "Crawls in and out of the darkness to locate food, goes back in, comes back out again. He spends hours, no, days, laying it out, planning, lulling his victims into the same complacency you and Terri're in, Haley, making his intended vics think he's a harmless little shit. This guy's exhibiting the very traits of our killer, Haley, and you don't even recognize him. He's like a street lamp to you, a garbage pail, and he's damned glad you see him that way."

The room was silent after Jim's emotion-laden lecture, thick with Parry's accusation that the hardworking agents weren't thinking clearly, weren't seeing even though they were looking.

Terri Reno swallowed hard, thinking of what might have happened had she gone to this thick-necked, thick-armed creep's place with him last night. According to information Jessica had released to them on the killer, once he had his victim where he wanted her, he struck so ferociously and quickly that she could be killed or maimed for life before anyone could break in a door.

Jessica could see the pained expression on Terri's face from across the room, and she could well imagine what was going through Terri's mind at the moment. She flashed on a time when she was defenseless against a maniac bent on taking her own life.

Parry continued. "While you two are busy with a sketch artist, Haley, the rest of us want to hear those surveillance tapes. Terri, you get started with Don Myers. Haley, fetch those tapes."

"Will do, Boss." Kalvin Haley needed no second telling, relieved to be going out of earshot of his chief.

"The guy knows Hal Ewelo," Parry said thoughtfully, "and Ewelo ironically kills an innocent kid in an attempt to learn the killer's identity!" He shook his head. "Sometimes people do prove the stereotype, and Ewelo's one stupid *kanaka*. We push Ewelo harder, find out who his friends are, who his goddamned relatives are, who he knows that's kinky or strange or sexless in his estimation, anything out of the norm. Promise the bastard a deal. Tony, you're on that, and don't hesitate to use this information to get some leverage with the bastard."

"He's called in a lawyer."

"Then do it with his lawyer present, but do it."

Tony hustled off, disappearing as Haley had before him.

"We're going to end the killing," said a resolved Parry.

Every wheel went into motion. Parry, along with Jessica, listened intently to the taped meanderings of their latest mystery suspect, and she found Robert all that Haley had said and more. He sounded like a pitiful soul, a poor castaway wretch, just searching the city for a little kind word, a soft touch, a pleasant smile. He talked of everything and anything, almost nonstop, as if Terri were a long-lost relative, and with each contact, he became more and more familiar while maintaining a mewing, whimpering voice, conspiratorial actually, in which he maintained that he was a lot like Terri, a down-and-outer, misunderstood by his parents, his friends and relatives, not to mention his bosses, and that he had kicked about from one job to the next, always being pushed around by some bully or a boss, and always fired or let go because someone didn't like him. *Politics,* he called it.

On subsequent tapes he let Terri know more about himself, or about his false self, one could not tell for certain. He spoke of his favorite job once as a *cowboy*.

This made both agents sit up after the long and tedious rendition of the previous tapes.

"Oh, really? A cowboy." Terri's leering laughter followed, and then: "Ever ride a cowgirl? Want to break this mare? Huh, *cowwwww-booooy*?"

"You don't believe me?" he asked her.

"Sure . . . sure, cowboy. I believe you."

"It was a big ranch on Maui. I was in charge of strays and fence-mending. I did an excellent job."

"Then why did you leave your pony on Maui, cowboy, for this? Bright lights, big city and pretty things like me?"

"You are pretty."

"You want me? You got the money, cowboy?"

"I . . . I tol' ya, I don't cheapen a lady like that. If you just come with me, I . . . I can take care of you, make you eternally happy. It's not about money."

"Honey, everything's about money."

"No, not everything. I tell ya, I can set you up with everything. Maybe, in time, you get to know me better, you might wanna marry me or something. . . ."

Terri laughed uproariously and contemptuously, which effectively served to end the conversation, but still he came back for more the following night.

"Now we've got two cowboys who know each other, both from Maui. This guy and Ewelo," Parry said. "Let's go see how Terri and Kalvin are doing with the sketch artist."

The sketch artist, Don Myers, with Terri Reno's help had accomplished a great deal. Myers was better than the usual police sketch artist and was in fact an accomplished painter on the island, doing Hawaiian scenes that sold in the boutiques around Honolulu. The rendition here was a true creation with pigmentation and shading, detailed and sharp. Obviously, Terri Reno had remembered far more of her strange night visitor than even she'd realized. With Haley's additions, the portrait of the killer was remarkably clean and distinctive, the eyes like emotionless blue stones.

"If we're going to see him tonight or tomorrow night, why

bother with a sketch?" Terri, the junior member of the team, wanted to know. "Why not just pick him up?"

Haley raised a hand asking that he be allowed to field this one while the others looked on. Haley told his partner, "You see, dearie, it's like this. If we have the sketch of the suspect ahead-a-time, before we nab 'im, it's just one more nail in his bloody coffin."

"One more item to stack onto the evidence side when a judge and jury get at him," added Parry.

"But it's just our suspicions, now isn't it?" she replied in a mock Cockney accent. "How's it going to hold up in a court of law these days?"

"Police suspicions are still worth a little something in a court of law, and FBI suspicions even more. Add the fact we were concurrently working on this sketch along with what we got from the connection with Hal Ewelo, and every bit helps," Jim Parry explained. "I just hope Tony can get something out of Ewelo before we have to use the sketch and taped voice on him. It'd sit better if the bastard would implicate our man *before* we flash a picture or run a tape in the interrogation room, believe me."

Jessica only half heard the legal discussion among the others, becoming lost in the sad, doe eyes of their possible mass murderer, marveling at the features, so mild on the surface, not the least resembling a Halole Ewelo; rather this was the face of anonymity here in the islands, the face of a half-breed, a *hapa haole,* of which there were literally hundreds of thousands, many with the telltale wide cheekbones of the native, the somewhat slanting eyes, the thick neck and nappy, native red-brown hair and the softened nose and bone structure of the white race. The only feature that marked him as remarkable were those cerulean eyes in the native face. There was no telltale distinguishing scar or birthmark, nothing but the vacant blue coals for eyes and a slight *haole* tinge to his skin. The natives had called the first whites they'd encountered *haoles* because of their pale skin, assuming they were the dead ancestors come back to roam the earth in ashen and anemic form, risen as it were from the grave. There was certainly something dead about this man, Jessica thought, and much to mark him as partially white. His Hawaiian features dominated, but there was a muted understatement that spoke of his mixed-blood ancestry, possibly part American, certainly Caucasian.

"At least now we've got something real to rattle the snake with, heh, Chief?" asked Haley, whose infectious smile and bright Aussie eyes had lightened the intense work.

Everyone in the room knew the value of actually having hard information before walking into an interrogation room, and knew that at the moment Tony was only working a bluff with Paniolo. "Get a copy down to Tony right away, Don," Parry instructed the artist. "And spread 'em around. Call Dave Scanlon and share it with him. Tell him he can take it to the nightly news guys tonight if he wants."

The decision to allow Scanlon to give it to the press represented a gamble. Parry was damned if he did, damned if he didn't. They could sit on the suspect's description or put it out as an APB. If they withheld the information from the public, it could end up costing another life; by the same token, if they published it along with the sketch, the killer was also likely to know, and his first reaction most likely would be fleeing and going into extended hiding, possibly escaping the island. Because Parry wanted him off the streets of Oahu at any cost, he chose to put out an APB and to involve the TV and radio stations as well as the press. At the same time, he had all the airlines, passenger ships and Port Authority points notified.

Myers picked up his art materials and promised to get copies around as ordered, took a bow to a standing ovation and quickly left.

"Now, let's get back out on the street, and this time, Haley, I'm going to be there with you when Junior here shows up. As for you, Terri, just play the creep the exact same as always. Bat it right back at him. He says he's a cowboy, stomp on his horse."

She smiled at this. "Got it, but what if he wants me to go bye-bye with him? Not so sure I want to be alone with the Devil, if you know what I mean."

"We'll escort you to the door, and as soon as he's home and closing the door on you, we'll kick it in and search the place on probable cause."

"The tape and the sketch?" she asked, wondering if that was enough to make probable cause.

"That and the connection with Ewelo, yeah. But we need to know where his den is, and unless Ewelo comes clean with it, well, it's up to us."

"Been a hell of a night for discovery," commented Jessica.

"Quantum leap!" Parry replied, smiling for the first time all day.

Jessica agreed with Jim's moves. Something had to end. Either the killings or the killer's life had to stop. Something had to shake loose. Something had to give.

No more women could be abducted, mutilated and cast into the sea by the Cane Cutter.

The description alone would cause a great ripple effect across the islands: Hawaiian male of mixed ancestry, light-skinned, thickly built, five-nine, 165 pounds, age twenty-seven to thirty, dark blue eyes, driving a Buick sedan, possibly black to maroon in color.

It wasn't much, but it was, along with the sketch, far more than they'd had before now.

13

The Prince of Darkness is a gentleman.

Shakespeare, *King Lear*, III, iv

Midnight, July 17, near Fort DeRussy, Honolulu

Beneath multicolored signs and lights, Lopaka prowls the streets of Oahu's Waikiki area, blending in easily with the ebb and flow of tourists. At one with his surroundings, wearing a billowy Hawaiian shirt, he lets his tattooed arms hang free and unencumbered. The only thing that marks him as different from everyone else on the street is that he isn't in a group, that he strolls alone, yet he might easily be regarded as a bellhop for one of the dozens of hotels along the strip, or even a clerk from one of the countless shops here.

He's pacing outside the ABC Liquor and Pharmacy, waiting for Hiilani's shift to end. She is his newest Kelia who has yet to feel his brand of final absolution. She half expects him, after all. She wants it, even though she doesn't completely understand why. He hopes not to disappoint her.

He has seen some other possibilities tonight, but with the store clerk he has a history, and that will make for small talk and a rapport he has yet to build with the other girls he has marked. With Hiilani, who is easily flattered and easily amused, he can be more *natural*. He'll offer her some of his weed. She can take it or leave it, he'll tell her, but either way, he finds her beautiful and he wants to be alone with her. In his car a hypodermic filled with a narcotic is awaiting her arrival.

She'll come away with me, climb into my car without argument, and go with me, a lamb to my slaughterhouse. Once inside . . . the thought makes him swell and bulge. He swoons with a flush of heat and power that is too much for his neurons to take, exciting his blood, and tingling his private parts in a way that ordinary sex had never done.

He is intent on his prey now, and the circling perimeter of his stroll is coming in tighter and tighter loops as the time for Kelia's appearance approaches.

Timing, like the smoke, mirrors and sleight of hand of a magician—diversionary actions—all become the tools of the hunter. Everything is fair; everyone is fair game; nothing is *kapu* so long as the result feeds his god, for it then becomes a sanctifying, a *ho'okapu*, and no more taboo. . . .

It had been so with Linda Kahala, his last Kelia. She was surprised to see him at first, perhaps even embarrassed a little, although he'd had her in his sights for several weeks by then. It was obvious she was turning tricks on the avenue. It was the only way she could possibly come up with the money she needed for tuition, and she wanted out of her house in the worst way, so she needed rent money as well. She had confided a great deal before they got to his place. When she'd first laid eyes on him, a failure and a dropout in her eyes, she hadn't wanted anything to do with him, but then he wore her down with his attentions, returning nightly to shower her with high praise, telling her that she did not need to prostitute herself, that if she came to live with him, he could take care of her and defray the costs of her tuition as well, that he was the answer to all her prayers. Remembering how she loved poetry, he reminded her of the book of Shakespearean sonnets that had belonged to his mother, which he'd given her.

He pressed her, begged, pleaded, not for her services, but for *her* . . . saying he was lonely and that he could free her of the streets, if only she would just be *his*. This offer gave her pause, but at first she still remained recalcitrant, saying she had no usual price, and that she was no whore. After five weeks of this, he threatened her with exposure to her parents, whom he'd met once when she'd brought him home with another friend. Then he begged her apology for being so low to even suggest such blackmail.

She hadn't actually wanted to go with him that night, but when he grabbed her and she felt the strength in his arms as he forced her into his car, his grip caused her to relent, to in fact freeze for a moment.

She let out a little cry and said, "All right . . . all right, you don't have to get rough. Damn it, Lopaka, look, you've brought up a bruise. If you're going to get rough, I'll never speak to you again."

He apologized. "Once you see how nice my place is, and once you have a little *pakalolo* with me, you'll know you're in heaven. You'll never have to work the street again, I swear."

"How're you going to do that? Pay for me every night? And what about Paniolo?"

"To hell with that bastard. One day, I'll cut his throat." He had half expected her to leap from the car before he could pull away from the curb, but she seemed to have resigned herself by then. Perhaps she liked the idea of his coming to her "rescue," or the thought of his slitting Paniolo's throat. Either way, that night he lived up to his promise: She never again had to return to the streets. Now she was with all the previous Kelias and with Ku, the great god of the seas, the winds, the fire and all things.

As always, his mind wanders back to Kelia. She was his wife, and they had met in bustling, busy Lahaina on Maui. Both of them had aspirations to go to Honolulu and the University of Hawaii, but neither had enough money at the time. They talked freely with one another and found much in common, and soon they made a pact that somehow, together, they would one day make it to Honolulu and the university.

Kelia had sacrificed so much for him, working and saving, and while their sex life was unfulfilling—due his inability to perform without some type of sadism involved—they managed to maintain the relationship.

Kelia was good for him, never judgmental, always supportive, never angry or upset or afraid of him. Soon she was even allowing some sadism to be played out on her for the sake of their relationship. She was the first and only woman to understand that his craving was a compulsion. She pretended to enjoy it, the humiliation he heaped on her, but her love for him was no pretense, not at first anyway. Then he found her with another man.

All the memories of childhood flooded back in on him, the memories of torment and the inadequacies he had felt all his life. Unable to cope, he locked her in a closet, her hands and feet tied, her eyes blindfolded, for a day and a night before he went to her with one of the many swords he kept in the house, fully intending to do to her what he'd done to other women who had hurt him.

He removed her blindfold, wanting her to see his anger. He slapped her repeatedly and brandished the long blade, slicing parts of her clothing while telling her how he had killed the little girl named Alaya in his village so many years before, and now the disappearances of young native women reported on the Island of Maui were due to him.

He watched her squirm against the cold touch of the blade, and he felt himself becoming sexually aroused. She pleaded, struggled against him and this only made him harder and hotter, and he ejaculated into his pants, and he grabbed her roughly by her wild black hair and shoved her face into the growing wet spot, his blade raised above the soft nape of the neck, prepared now to fall.

But at the last he stopped himself, unable to punish her further, fearful of what the sight of her blood would do to him. He knew that if he drew the least blood, he would revel in spilling all her blood.

He instead loosened her bonds, kicked her hard, and ordered her to get away from him. She didn't need to be told a second time. She tore from the house with the shredded clothing on her back. He never saw or heard from her ever again—*except in his fantasies,* when he finds her again on a street corner in Waikiki.

And tonight Lopaka's eye falls on the lovely, little sales clerk Hiilani as she steps from the brightly lit store to wait outside for her boyfriend to arrive and pick her up. But no luck for her means much luck for him; his patience is rewarded, for now she's going straight for the bus stop. There are some others at the stop, but this does not deter him.

"Ho, Hiilani, hi!" He startles her from behind, but she laughs at her own fright, her eyes sparkling, trusting and smiling.

"Lopaka? Whatchu doing here?" she asks coyly as he smiles back, displaying his crooked front teeth.

"I tol' you, I come fo' you." Lopaka falls easily into pidgin English to further put his prey at ease.

"But I gotta go home."

"To dat lazy boyfriend? He no can bother to pick you up, even with a killer running round da island, killing girls who look like you?"

"All of the girls didn't look like me. I saw the papers."

"They were all like you," he disagreed.

She shook her head, not wanting to hear this.

"I mean all of dem was Polynesian girls with long, dark hair like yours, and beautiful eyes like yours, and all about your age. Dat's why I'm frightened fo' you, and I will happily drive you home."

She considered her options: an hour on a wretchedly smelly old bus without shocks, or Lopaka's kind offer. His smile is handsome, his eyes are a blue volcanic rock with a hint of shining mystery lurking there; promise and danger all rolled into one, she thinks.

"I . . . I don't know, Lopaka."

"Please. I wanna do dis for you, Hiilani."

"But my boyfriend. He's a hothead, he's Samoan."

"Don't a bit worry me. I carry a weapon fo' protection."

"A weapon?" She is instantly curious.

"Fo' protection only. Can't be too careful nowadays. I've got"—he hesitates, then whispers in her ear—"several knifes, swords even, some ceremonial ones but others quite useful, some Jap stickers." Then he whispers, "I've also got some French and Colombian stuff, if you get me, some good smack, if you like—get high? I can make it happen fo' you, babe."

"No, no . . . I don't do dat kine stuff."

He shrugs. "I don't either," he lied, "but I keep it round fo', you know, my *aikanes*."

"Here come my bus," she says. "I betta say good night."

"Why're you afraid of me, Hiilani?"

"Afraid?"

"Yes."

"I'm not."

"Den why you no come wit' me?" He begins to whisper, seeing nearby a curiously large, wide-shouldered white woman with a lantern jaw listening intently to their conversation.

"I'm not, really. I just don't wan-no problem with my boyfriend, you know?" she says.

Lopaka at first gently presses her in their native tongue, and then begins an insistent tugging on her arm, trying to lead her away from the stop. He pleads almost childishly for her to come away with him, saying that she'd be surprised at what he could show her.

"She said no, fella!" The surprisingly gruff voice, coming as it does from the heavyset white woman beside them, shocks Lopaka, as does the big woman's burrowing, searching eyes.

"What?" he asks without thinking.

"So buzz off," replies the old lady.

"No, please." Hiilani quickly intervenes. "All right, Lopaka. I go with you, but you put me out a block from where I live and no argument?"

"No argument, I promise," he lies.

Lopaka places an arm about her, and they stroll off down Muluhia Road toward Kalia Road and his car, Lopaka looking over his shoulder, curious to see the heavyset woman with the horse face stare after them. The bus arrives, however, and the nosey bitch gets aboard, so Lopaka turns his full attention to young Hiilani.

The big woman who'd lumbered onto the bus and out the back door before it pulled from the curb now quick-stepped her awkward way amid the crowd of tourists and thrill-seekers who routinely milled about Waikiki's streets. Beneath the dress and makeup, she was Sergeant Nathan "Bigfoot" Ivers. The HPD undercover cop now followed Lopaka and Hiilani, expecting nothing really to come of his hunch. He'd followed similar hunches now for days, working on his own time as well as the department's, his ear to the ground, anxious to learn anything he might regarding the sonofabitching Trade Winds/Cane Cutter who, it was rumored about police circles, was also responsible for the deaths of Officers Thom Hilani and Alan Kaniola.

The getup Ivers wore tonight was particularly uncomfortable, his knee-length hosiery riding down while his skirt, a tent for anyone else, was riding up his hips. He hated decoy work, and he particularly hated wigs and makeup, but he'd do whatever necessary to get a line on the man who killed Alan Kaniola.

The double murder of the two Hawaiian cops out at Koko Head

had been a great personal loss for Ivers, who'd trained both of the dead men. Being Hilani's and Kaniola's training officer made it personal.

Hilani was wet behind the ears, as was Kaniola, but both men had been levelheaded. Kaniola, in particular, was a deadly shot with his weapon, even from the hip! He was quick, intelligent and cautious, all traits which should have kept him alive. Ivers wondered if Hilani hadn't done something stupid to compromise Kaniola's good judgment and natural ability to handle himself. He'd really liked young Kaniola. There wasn't a prejudicial bone in Alan's body and he was always laughing, his eyes eternally smiling. He represented the best of the native Hawaiian, both open and friendly while shrewd and aloof when necessary, not to mention his physical virtues. Ivers believed his young protégé would be angry if he'd survived to read the kind of crap that was being printed in his father's newspaper these days.

Both Alan and Thom were dyed-in-the-wool police officers who didn't deserve what they'd gotten that night up at Koko crater.

Ivers had been working a one-man crusade to get a line on Alan's killer, but it was as if the ocean had swallowed up the shooter/slasher who'd disfigured Kaniola so badly with that cane cutter. None of the usual tactics of shaking down known street lowlife had worked; no one knew the lone killer. The fiend was a modern-day Jack the Ripper who left no bodies and nary a clue, and he was apparently, as Ivers's FBI contact said, a loner, without attachments, either friend or foe.

Hearing the guy called Lopaka call out the girl's name, Hiilani, had first caught Ivers's ear only because her name was so similar to Thom Hilani's. Then the guy just kept at her to take a ride with him, and while that alone might've been annoying enough, Ivers realized that the creep had been waiting for her to come off work, and that his car wasn't even on this block. When the hair on his neck stood on end, Ivers knew to listen to it. On a hunch, a kind of sixth sense, Ivers decided to follow the stocky, medium-sized man whom the young lady called Lopaka.

He knew enough Hawaiian to catch bits and pieces of what they'd said in their native language, but he'd been unable to hear the whispers in her ear.

He now scanned the avenue for any sign of the couple. He had lost sight of them in the milling crowd. Damned streets here were like a series of cattle cars filled to capacity. Hemmed in, Ivers used his huge purse to whack more than one person getting in his way, saying sorry in the sweetest tone he could muster.

He wasn't even sure he was following the right path when he headed east toward Fort DeRussy, but he knew there were areas around the base where you could park for a limited time without getting a ticket. He played out his cards and came to within forty yards of a battered maroon Buick as it pulled away from the curb. Inside the car, he could see the doe-eyed Hawaiian honey who'd stood at the bus stop, and her eyes appeared glazed and unseeing now, her body rigid and unyielding, a stone mannequin behind the glass. Beside her was a grinning jackal whose eyes lit on Ivers. Something in his eyes told Ivers that if this wasn't the bloody Trade Winds Killer, he'd do until the real thing came along.

Ivers raced now toward the Buick, recalling Alan Kaniola's brief description of the vehicle he'd followed the night he was murdered.

The driver gunned the old engine, and it abruptly shut down on him, simultaneously sending a smile to Ivers's lips and a black soot cloud from the exhaust pipe. The exhaust cloud blanketed a foursome of sailors in their dress whites, who instantly erupted in a flurry of curses and tossed beer cans, the missiles richoceting off Lopaka's car. Ivers was coming full speed, the sailors whistling and gawking at *him* now. He confirmed that the passenger in the car was sedated, sitting zombielike, not seeing. The driver was cursing and banging on his dash.

Ivers knew he had the Cane Cutter, and so he whipped out his revolver even as he ran toward the battered Buick, shouting, "Police. Step out of the vehicle!"

But the Buick coughed into life and tore straight for Ivers, whose approach sent him into the vehicle even as it struck him, sending him to the right of the driver's side window, stunned and unconscious, his single reflex shot striking the rear left fender, ricocheting to put a hole through the gas tank.

The smell of gasoline rose with the warm whoosh of air left in the wake of the speeding Buick. Ivers lay in the street unconscious, his dress hiked up to his thighs, some of the leaking gas lapping at his skirt, his Jockey shorts and knee-length hosiery displayed for all to see, his barrel-round legs splayed apart.

Several of the sailors converged on him, one shouting for someone to call for an ambulance, a second trying to assess the damage, when a third tossed down his cigar.

The gasoline ignited, turning one of the white-uniforms into an inferno, scattering the others. The fire raced to Ivers's prone form, engulfing him whole.

Several of the sailors sat on their burning friend and beat the flames out while Ivers screamed in pain. One sailor tore off his white jacket and smothered Ivers with it, killing the flames that'd already badly burned him.

"Call 911! Get a goddamned ambulance!"

"Forget that!" shouted the sailor who'd saved Ivers. "Run into the Army hospital! Hell, it's right here!"

In a few minutes a base hospital wagon screeched onto the scene and the medics took over. The sailor had minor burns, but Ivers was in shock.

Police cars arrived with floodlights and sirens, backing onlookers away. The call for *officer down* had not gone out, no one knowing that the big man in drag was a cop until one of the medics scooped his wallet from a scorched purse and handed it to one of the policemen to notify next of kin.

"Jesus, Steve, this guy's one of ours," the cop said.

The senior officer, Steve Fausti, stared at the badge and identification and then up at the ambulance with Ivers and the injured sailor as it raced for the nearby military hospital.

"Nate Ivers, Midtown Unit," said Phil Janklow, the younger officer.

"Yeah, he's one of their training sergeants. What the hell gives? You think he's maybe queer?"

The first cop shrugged. "If so, looks like he hustled the wrong sailor."

"What the hell happened here?" Fausti, now holding tightly to Ivers's wallet and pointing it like a weapon at the sailors, demanded of the three on the grass who were trying to sober up long enough to figure out just what *had* happened. "I want some fuckin' answers. What happened here?"

"Ivers's service revolver," said the younger of the two cops, approaching his partner with the gun. "One round discharged, still hot."

"Sure it's hot. There was a friggin' fire here," said Fausti, pointing out the remaining flames that licked up from the pavement. The place was thick with gas fumes.

The sailors helped one another from the grass, their whites stained with soot, oil, grass and what one termed *grue*. "You guys aren't going shipboard tonight," Fausti assured them, and this sent up a group groan with expletives.

"Fun and games over, boys. Now we can talk here, or you'll talk to a detective downtown. What's it going to be?"

"Follow that gasoline trail, asshole," said the sailor who'd saved Ivers from any further hurt, his white jacket missing. "That's the guy who hit-and-run your man."

A second sailor intervened, waving his arms, his freckled, Iowa farm-boy face as sooty and grass-stained as his uniform. "Your guy was playin' chicken with a '69 Buick sedan with bad tires and leakin' gas like a somma-bitch."

The third sailor, breathing into the cop's face, added, "Your guy pulled his gun, but the driver hit him before he could get a round off."

"That ain't right, Pete. He fired a shot," said the jacketless one.

"Slug must've hit the gas tank," suggested the Iowa boy.

Fausti turned to his partner and said, "You got that, Phil? This clown wants us to go away, to follow a gas leak."

"Goddamnit, that's how it went down. Your guy was trying to stop a car with his *body*."

"How many in the car?"

"Two, I think. Two was all I saw get in."

"Two?"

"A guy and a babe."

"What'd they look like?"

"Kanakas."

"What'd they look like?" Phil Janklow repeated his partner's question, ready to take notes on the answer.

The sailor shrugged. "I tol' ya, *kanakas*. They all look alike to me."

Phil came over and whispered in his partner's ear. "Maybe we ought to try—"

"Try? What the fuck're you talking' about, Phil? Try what?"

"Try followin' that trail left by the gas leak." He pointed to the lingering, scattered flames on the pavement.

"Shit, Phil, we've got a crime scene on our hands here, and the book says we sit on it until homicide detectives arrive. What's going to happen to us if we go off like fuckin' Sherlock Holmes after a fuel slick?"

"Homicide?" asked one sailor sober enough to overhear.

"Attempted vehicular manslaughter, if you're telling the truth, sailor."

"Christ, what reason I got to lie for?"

"Could maybe've happened another way."

"You can't take the word of three U.S. sailors?"

"I wouldn't take the word of the whole damn Seventh Fleet, pal." Fausti smiled, watching the sailors' dismay as they kicked about the earth and shook their heads. "It ain't in my job description. Just cool your heels until we can corroborate your story, okay?" He sent Phil into the crowd for anyone who'd volunteer as a witness, and Phil came back with a mix of white tourists, Japanese and Polynesians. They all bore out the sailors' account before the detectives arrived on scene. Fausti told his younger partner that they had done their jobs by the book, so nobody could find fault with the approach they'd taken at the scene.

"Another night of fun in paradise," said one of the HPD detectives who asked for a rundown from Fausti and his young partner.

"Yes, sir . . . well, the hit-and-run victim was a training sergeant from Midtown, HPD."

"You don't say?"

"Officer Nate Ivers, and he discharged his weapon at the assailant."

"Ivers? Christ, I know an Ivers," said the second detective to his partner. "He's been on a one-man crusade for Kaniola's killer. Damned fool's gone off the deep end, Jack."

"Where'd you say he was taken?" asked the first detective.

"DeRussy medics took him in there," replied Phil, pointing.

"Let's go see if he's conscious and talking."

Young Janklow pulled away from his partner's grasp, stopping the two detectives, informing them about the gas spill and asking, "You think maybe we ought to try to pick up the trail and follow it?"

The detectives laughed in Phil's face, and without saying a word, they walked back to their unmarked cars, where they talked and laughed as if what Phil had said was the funniest joke they'd heard in years.

"I told you to forget that shit, Phil. You sounded like the fuckin' Hardy Boys." Fausti slapped his notebook closed and put it away.

"If we'd got on it right away maybe—"

"You know how damned fast a fuel spill evaporates in this climate," said Fausti, trying to ease the bruise to his partner's ego.

"Yeah . . . well, that's the friggin' point, and all those bozos can do is laugh at us?"

"You, partner . . . they were laughing at you."

Fausti turned to the crowd, shouting, "Okay, folks, show's over. Go 'bout your business. Enjoy our fair city . . . the Jewel of the Pacific . . ."

14

Still falls the Rain—
Dark as the world of man, black as our
   loss—
Blind as the nineteen hundred and forty nails
Upon the Cross.

Dame Edith Sitwell

1 A.M., July 17, somewhere in Honolulu

Lopaka realizes when he reaches his dark little house that his tank has been emptied of gas, that the bullet fired by the cop must've put a hole through his fuel line or gas pan. It seems a miracle that the old Buick didn't explode with the impact of a .38 slug striking the gas tank. It must've passed clean through without rattling around in there. As it is, he has no way out later tonight to dispose of Hiilani's body, or tomorrow morning for that matter. He worries that someone at the fort might well have seen his license-plate number, that the authorities could be watching him at this very moment.

He steels himself and walks around the car, ready for death by gunshot if it should come. He opens the door and pulls Hiilani's rigid form from the car. She is catatonic, thanks to the drug he's injected. The drug keeps her eyes open no matter how badly she'd like to close them, and as the drug wears down, she feels more, and the more she feels, the more she suffers, which means the more he enjoys himself, and the more he feels like a person of power, filled with the manhood Kelia and his father before her had thought to strip him of.

He takes her into the killing place.

No one stops him.

No one comes crashing in for Hiilani.

A fractional part of him, deep within his long-forgotten soul, long buried in a place in his heart where no light enters, on some wasted island within him, wishes that there was someone capable of stopping him . . . but nowadays such thoughts barely mature or fully form, broken shells of thought, wisps of smoke, incapable of surviving to the surface.

He is safe to take out his feelings on Kelia once more, and the only one who has ever seen him for what he truly is now lies dead in the street in Waikiki.

"Come, my sweet, dear Kelia," he whispers in her ear as he restrains her with the human-hair coils of rope he has fashioned from the heads of earlier victims, restraints that dangle from large metal hoops nailed fast to the rack against the wall, a rack and wall discolored with the markings of his earlier kills.

He restrains only her arms for now.

Her eyes plea for mercy, but he has no mercy, only a plan for immortality.

She screams, but the drug is yet too strong to allow full use of her vocal cords. The silent scream is enough to make his penis harden and his underpants wet.

He nonetheless assures himself that what he does next is for the greater power of Ku, the power which he soon will join, to one day find his essence to be the same as the great god, to have mere mortals feeding sacrifices and offerings like Kelia to *him*.

By now there is no Hiilani. She no longer exists in his mind or eye. She is Kelia, the all-perfect sacrifice.

He makes his selection of weapons, the ceremonial sword once belonging to his father, the same one that had struck down his brother that night so far from the sight of others, save for Lopaka's curious young eyes, so many years before when he'd followed his embittered and drunken father into the forbidden forest. Later, the body was "discovered" by his father, the very assassin who had the power to cover his every step, and he did so with royal aplomb, taking the small, disfigured lump of flesh to the burning place. The bones were thrown into the sea. Lopaka pleaded for the body to be taken to the burial site. After all, Lopeko was of royal heritage, but his pleas went unheard. The body was diseased, contagious, or so the lie went.

The entire episode was cloaked in secrecy, and only the years had brought back the memories in flashes of insight long denied him by a child's abhorrence of a dread reality. Still, his memories were shrouded over, confused and disjointed. Sometimes his father used a sword, sometimes a club, sometimes a coiled rope. It mattered little, since the result was the same. Nowadays Lopaka's dead brother came to him while he slept, his bruised and torn body pleading for vengeance, telling him that his plan to gain immortality and to wreak vengeance on their father was not only well conceived, but that it would reunite them in a way they had never been united on this plane, for Ku had found Lopeko and embraced his so-called cursed soul.

His father had told the village that the boy had contracted the disease, had wandered into the forests and had died when the demons of the dark had attacked him.

All Lopaka knew for certain was that his father would one day answer to Ku, and thereby answer to him, Lopaka. That his brother would be avenged.

His mother's ghost also came into his brain and blew words of encouragement and praise for his pact with Ku. She had known the truth about his father, too, and she'd been poisoned by the devil man to protect his dirty secret.

All his life, Lopaka had lived with these *truths,* and the silence he'd had to maintain for so long erupted in violence even at a young age. He saw his enemies all around him, for many in the village where he grew up distrusted him to keep silent and his father watched him like a bird of prey considering its next meal.

He steps now toward Kelia. Her eyes give away her soul-felt fear; moist and gleaming with fright, the eyes widen even as the sword is raised above her. The sword tip eases down gently, and it snaps away button and blouse and bra, and now the tip of the cutting edge plays over her brown, firm, responsive skin, and she begins to squirm, her mouthings like an animal plea, like all the dogs he'd ever killed, and so like the girl in the village he'd killed, and so like Lina Kahala and the others before her. Each replay in his mind heightens his need to carry through with it again. Hiilani is no longer a person, she is a sacrificial offering; she is Kelia reborn, placed in his care for the sole purpose of his and Ku's delight.

"Only a few more like you," he hoarsely whispers to her, a giddy, leering smile coming to his pouting lips. "Only a few more like you, and I go to Ku." He plays out the rhyme, repeating it like a mantra. "Don't be afraid. I will anoint you, Kelia, and give your essence to Him, and you will go before me like my brother, my mother . . . to prepare my way . . . and together we will have no enemies greater than ourselves . . ."

She begins to flail like all those before her, afraid to go over. The drug is wearing down, and her scream escapes in short staccato bursts, further exciting him. His glassy eyes are alight now with a mad pleasure, his Ku taking control of him now, speaking in a voice not his: "There is no need of fear. Accept me . . . love me . . . accept your fate, Kelia."

Just as the god speaks through him, using his tongue and vocal cords, Ku also uses his hands, working quickly now to take Kelia's hair in large, long tufts. She continues to flail and kick out at him as he completes her disrobing and stares at her shivering body.

Now, Ku tells him, *we do some serious cutting.* Each cut has a purpose, a meaning, signifying the order and power over chaos Ku represents, and each cut fascinates Lopaka as blood rivulets begin to paint the child sacrifice.

Kelia's endless screams are heard only by Ku now as they mingle with the acidic screech of Suicidal Tendencies on the stereo, which Lopaka does not recall having turned on.

Ivers, unable to see and in great pain, was not a good patient. He suddenly pulled out his IV and snatched away at the bandage over his eyes while blindly shouting, "Will some goddamned somebody listen to me!"

The medics couldn't restrain him.

"Goddamnit, I said call FBI headquarters! Parry! Get Chief Jim Parry down here now. I know who the fucking Cane Cutter is! Lopaka's the name, and I got a piece of his plate number, and he's going to kill her if you don't let me the hell to a phone for Chrissake!"

Another set of orderlies came in and sat on Ivers while the doctor in charge hit him with another and stronger sedative.

•   •   •

Not three miles away, in the heart of the Waikiki district, information about the incident outside Fort DeRussy reached James Parry and scattered details were being discussed over the police band. The news had Parry instantly alert. Jessica, seeing his excitement, now listened intently as well.

"This cop, Ivers . . . I know him," Parry said. "He's a good man, but lately he's been a pain in the ass, calling every day, wanting to know the dispensation on the *Kaniola case* as he calls it. I keep telling the guy Kaniola's case is an HPD investigation, but he never bought it. He's shrewd."

"Sounds like he's badly injured."

"He's a moose of a man, but yeah . . . sounds bad. I'm going to get over to the hospital. You want to come?"

"Sure, let's go see how your friend is."

After informing the others in the stakeout party, Parry pulled away from the curb. Tony was walking the Ala Moana Boulevard route, working the street, and in close proximity to Terri Reno, checking in every hour on the hour, for what it was worth. Terri's partner, Kalvin Haley, was eyeballing them both from a nearby surveillance van, using a remote camera this time, hoping to find Terri's favorite street beau in his viewfinder, to get the creep on film.

Jessica held firmly now to the dash as Parry sped for the hospital, his strobe light flashing. Once they arrived, they found Ivers under sedation and in no condition to talk about his unfortunate experience; so Jessica went for his doctors, flashing her credentials and wanting to know the skinny on the patient in 211, while Parry held back to talk to the detectives assigned the case.

Jessica quickly located the doctor in charge of Ivers's case, a man named Flores who bitched about Ivers's behavior, saying he'd given the big cop enough sedatives to settle a horse.

"So what's the prognosis, Doctor?"

"Vital signs are remarkably stable," Flores began, taking off his wire-rims to reveal black, Hispanic eyes beneath the hospital glare. "The man's like a bull, believe me. His chances for recovery are good . . ."

"But?"

"Too early to tell about the eyes."

"His eyesight is at peril?"

Flores replaced his glasses and bit his lower lip. "We're calling in a specialist tomorrow. Can't do any more than we've already done for the moment."

"Will he be blinded for life?"

"It's my considered opinion that he will come through it in time, but who can say. There's been serious damage to the soft tissue of the cornea. If he does regain his sight, it will never be a hundred percent, no."

"Damn," she muttered.

"As for the rest of him, second- and third-degree burns up and down the left side of the body, throat, and head, but it hasn't sapped him of his strength. That much is in evidence."

"Meaning?"

"Meaning it took me and four orderlies to restrain him."

Jessica next located Jim Parry and huddled with him, informing him of his friend's condition in as positive a tone as she could muster.

Parry swallowed hard at the "good" prognosis, and then he turned back to the waiting pair of detectives on the case who'd taken the brief respite from Parry's probing questions to flip back and forth through their notes, stopping now and then to sip coffee from paper cups.

"They sedated the hell outta Ivers before we could get a word outta him," said the taller of the two.

"Hell, when we got here, they were sitting on him. He was trying to bust out, I guess," said the shorter detective with some mirth.

"He's like an ox."

Parry nodded knowingly at them, and then he stared after the two detectives as they walked away. "HPD's finest," he muttered to Jessica.

She placed a hand over his. "You all right, Jim?"

"Hell, no. How about you?"

She forced a smile. "Hell, no."

"No call for you to hang here all night. Let me take you home," he suggested. "It's damned near two in the morning."

"Fine . . . on one condition, Jim."

"Conditions . . . do you always place conditions on people who offer you a lift, Jess?" He didn't mean his tone to be quite so harsh, gesturing with the open palms for peace, flashing apologetic eyes; still, she knew that she was often guilty of placing conditions on people around her, especially those she cared about the most.

She couldn't blame him for the outburst. She momentarily thought about that well of pain she'd thrown pennies down all her life, reaching back to her relationship with her father, who was a great one for placing conditions on the people he loved. It was partially due to his military background and his own upbringing, not to mention his profession as M.E. No, Jim couldn't possibly understand fully the wellspring of fears and doubts she harbored, though he might understand the nature of her work, filled with shifty people and shifting inconstants. She was a meteorologist of murder, faced with the eddies of human "atmospheric" conditions. For in any investigation, circumstances altered constantly and prevailing "winds" were never the same if you blinked; unfortunately, it was little different in her personal life.

Jim reached out, touched her cheek and said, "I'm sorry. I had no right to say—"

"*Shhhhh,*" she replied, a finger to her full lips. "Let it go."

She briefly thought of all the men in her life, from her father to Alan Rychman. Conditions, shifting and ephemeral as nature, the sea, the clouds, the balmy trades . . . that was how she'd dealt with men all her life. Change, alter, shift them before they do it to you. . . .

Sometimes she could feel Donna Lemonte, her shrink, breathing down her neck, looking over her shoulder like a second conscience. Dr. Lemonte was an excellent psychologist and had become the closest thing she had to a girlfriend these days. Donna had made the same connection between Jessica's "conditional" professional life and her relationships with men, the fact Jessica had to be in charge, that she had to make the ground rules by which all relationships with men were to be played out.

She had become, particularly since Otto Boutine's death, afraid to truly commit herself to anything other than her career ever again, for fear of loss. She'd lost her father and her mother, and then she'd tragically lost Otto, for which she still blamed herself.

Boutine and her father . . . *tough act to follow.* She had become a cripple in more ways than one since Matt Matisak's bloody attack on her. The butcher had shaken the faith and the belief system instilled by her father, that there was a reasoning power over all and after all, a power that set into motion the human drama, as flawed and cluttered with twisted monsters as it was, a power that held a hand over the abyss and over the chaos. Matisak had made her doubt this, for she could no longer feel the pulse of that great hand as evenly as she once did. Perhaps she never would again.

Nowadays she thought more and more of a shadow self, a Jessica Coran who might have been had she never encountered Matisak, or had she not chosen her father's way of life.

She and Donna talked of shadow selves, the person or persons either of them might have been, had they been born in a different place and time, chosen a different career, met by chance the right man. Under a set of different circumstances, given other givens, other *conditions,* other choices, who might she have become? And would she not shun someone like herself, even someone like Jim Parry, *had she not been her father's daughter*?

Parry's eyes were busily studying her, and she wondered how much he knew of her from information he'd gathered on her, how much from Zanek, and how much he'd surmised just being with her for so many hours on the case. Just his fatigue talking, she decided, letting his rancor slide.

"Condition is," she said firmly, "you go home and get some rest, too."

"No . . . think I'll come back here, sit with Ivers. Want to be here when he comes around. The man doesn't have any family."

"He means a lot to you."

"A lot I owe him, yeah. He taught me how to work Honolulu."

"Aha, so that's how you know so much."

"Ivers is a white native. Came with the place. Actually, worked Maui for years before coming to HPD. He tipped me off to the disappearances there. No one knows the islands like him."

"Look. The Rainbow's not ten minutes from here. Come with me, sack out on the sofa till dawn and then—"

"I don't know, Jess." He bit his lower lip, jiggled his keys in his pocket, shuffled his feet and shook his head.

"What possible good can you do if you collapse? Think of it, you want to have your breakdown here?"

Around them, the military-green walls, cabinets and the yellow lights of the waiting room, even the cola and snack machines, seemed out of another time. "Military doctors aren't always the best," Parry said. "Thought I'd see about transferring Nate to a better facility."

"I told you, I talked with his doctor. Flores is going to get your friend through this, and the burns weren't as bad as they might've been. *He's going to come through this.*"

"Sir?" a voice at the doorway timidly called.

Parry turned and stared at a young patrol officer in uniform.

"What is it, officer?"

"My partner and me . . . we were first on scene at the incident outside the fort, sir, and well . . . I understand you want to know all the details? We got a call from the suits handling the case."

"Yeah, right, sure do, Officer ahh . . ."

"Janklow, sir, Phil Janklow."

Phil told them all that he knew, including the information regarding the gas leak which he was still brooding about. "We got an APB out on the car, but without a plate number, well . . ." He didn't offer much hope.

Jessica got a confused picture of the events, but Parry concentrated on the car, getting what he could from Janklow about the make and model of the vehicle. Much of what the police had gotten from eyewitnesses clashed and contradicted, but the car's description remained firm.

After Janklow was gone, Parry said to Jessica, "The description of the car could fit with what we know of the car that Kaniola followed out to Koko Head the night he and Thom Hilani died. Nate was looking for that car."

"So if it is the same guy . . ." Her eyes lit up. "We've got a sketch of the suspect and possibly a description of his car. Come tomorrow, he'll be feeling the noose tightening. I just hope you have all the corridors off the island covered."

"We do."

Parry, beyond fatigue now, agreed to take her up on her offer of the sofa in her room, and together they left the hospital for the Rainbow Tower. On the way to his car, Parry said, "When Ivers gets his eyesight back, I want him to have a look at our sketch of the suspect. See if it rings any bells."

"According to the doctors, he rang quite a few bells around here."

Parry attempted a laugh. "Come on, Doctor. You must be as dog-tired as I am."

"You'll get no argument there."

"An unconditional agreement?"

She only slightly flinched at the remark.

They both knew that the morning papers would be carrying the police sketch of the suspect on page one, and that things would be thrown into high gear. Anything could happen. Tips could flow in. The killer might well kill himself, or try to put as much distance between himself and Oahu as possible, which meant some form of passage off the island.

"We'll both need as much sleep as we can get if we're going to be any good tomorrow spearheading 'Operation Containment,'" Parry told her as they walked out to the parking lot and his car.

⊷15⊶

To live is like to love—all reason is against it, and all healthy instinct for it.

Samuel Butler

The Hawaiian night was calm, at peace, the wind a gentle, pulsating, cheek-caressing reminder to Jessica of the fragility of this tropical island world. Built upon volcanic rock, riddled with air pockets and underground rivers of lava, given birth by a cauldron in the boiling depths of the sea. The land mass was little more than a mighty coral reef created for the gods of Hawaiian legend whose sense of sport was often cruel.

She knew the truth, that the islands were a strange illusion created by an unruly, chaotic earth continually evolving, and that what was taken for granted here as *terra firma* was only as good as the faith people put in it, which might, faith and all, be gone with the next fiery eruption. She even imagined the river of fire come like a dragon to play out a billion-year-old game of hide-and-seek with life and death in the balance.

Hawaii was the ultimate land of illusion. Here even nature in all her lustrous, plush, enticing fantasy conspired in the deception, for while Hawaii purported to be paradise and perfection at every turn, Jessica had seen the seams, the pit viper in the garden, particularly here in Honolulu, where the darker aspects, the underbelly of the city, were as bleak and foul as anything she'd seen in D.C., Chicago or New York.

Here every illusion was forged by nature, save the sprawling city of Honolulu, yet nature conspired with the city to mask its meaner aspect. Honolulu stood a shimmering man-made Babel filled with the voices of every tongue, hugging an ocean that could destroy it at any time. The city acted as a modern jungle for such predators as the Trade Winds Killer. Nature's illusive calm and man's monuments, seemingly pleased to be in close proximity here in Oahu, left an unsettling insecurity in Jessica Coran, even as she looked past James Parry's muscular form to the lazy Pacific below.

Here was illusion, with the changing tide meeting the sky on the horizon; here the abundant cover of leaf and fruit, there light, a rainbow of shadow, lavender skies, where softly painted darkness, bird and arrow, water and drought, wind and calm, cloud and mountain, sun and rain, all mingled in a dance along a high wire of conflict and tension called life. Like the teeming sea itself, the land of the pineapple, guava, mango, papaya and sugarcane was rich in color and beauty with countless varieties of multicolored birds and flowers, some blossoms mimicking the appearance of birds. The land of the monkeypod tree, the flaming poinciana and the ancient Indian banyan represented for Jessica, and all who came under Hawaii's spell, a paradise that affirmed life's richest bounties over despair, decay and death. Yet it was an unforgiving land too, pitiless toward the foolish or uninitiated. It was a world where East and West clashed, one devouring the other.

She'd seen the ambiguity of Hawaii in the single branch of a passion-fruit tree whose flowers, symbolizing Christ's passion, flourished even as its fruit went rotting on the bough, filling the air with an acrid and sour odor which mingled with the rotting overabundance of guavas and mangoes growing wild along ancient footpaths that'd become paved highways.

She'd witnessed the same contrasts on Maui, where beauty and death were enshrined atop Maui's Haleakala summit, where the rare silversword flourished amid an arid, lunar landscape. She now recalled for Jim her visit up the winding highway to Mount Haleakala, House of the Sun, where Maui-of-the-thousand-tricks, impatient with the gods, had fooled them into creating Maui from the sea by connecting two volcanoes, Puu and Kukui, into the spectacular gorges and valleys, giving Maui the name "Valley Isle." Haleakala, at 10,023 feet, was home to the world's largest dormant caldera, twenty-one miles in circumference, and now it housed men and high-tech instruments in Science City, a collection of blockhouses and scanning devices to track NASA launches, satellites and the activity of the sun.

But the sun was far from Jim's or Jessica's mind tonight. With a near full moon, the sky over Oahu, as seen from the balcony of the Rainbow Tower overlooking Waikiki Beach and Diamond Head, was a deep, abiding cerulean, rivaling the blue sapphire of the Pacific itself.

"Beautiful and enormous, isn't it?" she said to Parry, finding him in a thoughtful mood, staring out at eternity in the form of ocean and sky as it stretched before them.

"Been a while since I've had a moment to really breathe it all in."

She'd earlier left him to his own devices while she had showered and located an extra pillow and blanket for the sofa. He'd broken into the dry bar for wine, and now he held out a glass to her and she gratefully accepted. She had on a thick white terry-cloth robe compliments of the hotel, yet she clutched the extra bedclothes to herself.

He proposed a toast, lifting his glass. "To all peaceful moments in paradise."

She smiled in return and sipped the Zinfandel. It felt oddly intoxicating, pungent, telling her that maybe she'd better go easy on an empty stomach. "You hungry?" she asked him.

"No problem," he murmured, staring out once more at the deep colors of the evening over the pulsating sea. She bit her upper lip, tentatively stepped further out on the balcony and almost turned to leave when he wheeled, his hands reaching her shoulder, his eyes smiling at her blinking stare.

"Your eyes, Jess." He began to lift uncertain fingers to her cheek. "So pretty, alluring."

She broke their stare, and while she hadn't resisted his touch, she stepped away now, her own wish to be held by him at odds with a nagging sense of duty and self-control that spoke of common sense.

She could think of nothing to say, but Jim filled in the silence. "You're as . . . as alluring as all of Hawaii and the ocean encircling us, Jess."

"Jim, we're not going to do this. It'd only lead to complications neither of us can afford right now."

"Complications." He repeated the word as if it were an alien term. He stepped back, instantly hurt, turning his eyes away, nodding. He desperately sought to change the subject. "Bet you can't imagine what Oahu was like before we whites took over," he said, setting aside his wine glass and taking pillow and blanket from her.

"Unspoiled maybe?"

"No concrete." He said the word as if it were a curse.

"No cars or exhaust," she countered.

"No liquor stores, pot or crack."

"No ice cream sundaes either," she challenged.

"There's little left of the old Hawaii. You find some of it around Hana in Maui, and of course there's Kahoolawe."

She tried to repeat the melodic word. "Ka-whoo-law-we?" she asked, smiling, fascinated with all that he knew of the unknowable islands.

"Ka-who-la-*vee*. Last of the old island tribal governments wants to rule there. It's forbidden to whites nowadays, returned to the people by the U.S., thanks to the PKO."

"PKO? What exactly does that stand for?"

"Preserve Kahoolawe Ohana. You might liken them to American Indians out to redress wrongs. They've gotten good at working in the political arena, and they have hired some damn good lawyers. They're a lot like your dyed-in-the-wool wacko environmentalists."

"I see. So Kahoolawe is now a reserve?"

"Yeah, now it is. U.S. Navy used the island for target practice with their big battleships since World War II, and this PKO group got them evacuated through legal means."

"I'm impressed, but why haven't I heard about this place?"

He shrugged, the pillow bobbing in front of him. "Nobody speaks of it much; certainly not the airlines or the brochures. Too unsettling, too political, for the tourist industry, you might say."

He stepped inside, laid the pillow and blanket on a chair arm and located the usual stash of tourist information. He quickly found a map depicting all the islands of Hawaii. She followed him back inside and looked over his shoulder. In a moment, Parry was pointing out the smallest of the Hawaiian island chain.

"That's Kahoolawe there. Only forty-five square miles across. No cars, no billboards, no hot-and-cold anything, no neon signs, football stadiums or shops. No one goes there and the islanders on Kahoolawe have shunned all Western ways, so historically there's been an understanding, but in the not-too-distant past, the U.S. made it officially off-limits to commercialization or development, and so off-limits to us, the white man." He paused thoughtfully. "The Hawaiians are holding fast to their status there, feeling the encroachment of extinction on their culture, history and laws. Even the so-called 'civilized' Oahu natives here see the preservation of the old ways on Kahoolawe as imperative to the survival of the culture. Hell, the Bishop Museum has a wing that showcases the aboriginal lifestyle, and believe me, they don't use pictures from your typical all-expense-paid TWA island luau."

"Is it part of . . . I mean, does the island fall under your bureau?"

He took a deep breath. "We don't interfere there. Leastways we haven't. Somewhere in between it gets very dull gray when we speak of jurisdictions and laws as they might apply to Kahoolawe, but suffice it to say, we're not wanted, and the State Department doesn't want us treading on their treaties. Hell, you've got the same situation on Indian reserves on the mainland. You know if the tribal leaders don't agree on FBI or even local intervention, we don't go in, any more than we would Guatemala—under ordinary circumstances, that is. Course, when things become extraordinary—"

"Yeah, I know." She studied the strange little island out in the sea to the southwest of Maui on the map he'd shown her. "So it's unofficially not part of your bureau?"

"That's about the size of it, yeah, although it shows up as part of Maui County and Maui County still wants to think of it as under their jurisdiction."

"God, I'd love to see it. It must be—"

"Pristine, wild . . . yeah, so I'm told."

"Then you've never been there?"

"I don't rush in where fools fear to tread; fact of the matter is, we've been ordered to stay out, and there's no love lost between the natives and us. But there are those who, for a price, will gladly take you to a remote side of the island, if you're willing to pay through the nose."

"Remote side? It all looks remote."

"Remote as in away from the main village. Remote as in where the wild sheep, goats and deer roam. There are some sacred shrines on the island, taboo for whites, that kind of stuff."

"Then I guess we won't be doing any diving or hunting for deer there?"

"Deer's scarce there anyway, I'm told. Maui's got enough wild lands to keep you busy for a decade. Although, I've heard what a markswoman you are. Heard about that shot you took from atop Quantico's central operations building that took out that maniac they called the Claw."

"Archer. Archer was his name, but you'd know that, having read my file. Right?"

He smiled wryly and nodded. "Couldn't help myself, matter of fact. One hell of a shot to make while you yourself were under fire from your own guys."

"Yeah, it's a shot I'd never be able to duplicate. But what gives here, Parry?"

"Whataya mean?"

"Do you really have nothing better to do? I mean reading all that crap about me? Maybe you need to get a life."

He chuckled at this. "Touché."

"You really can't find me all that interesting."

"I had a request in specifically for your help for almost a year, so when I learned you were in the islands—"

"When you learned I was in the islands? And when was that?"

"Day you arrived."

"Sneaky SOB, aren't you?"

"Comes with the chromosomes, you might say."

"And just how did you learn that I was on Maui?"

He took her in with his eyes once more. "I'm not ready to reveal all my secrets just yet—*are you?*"

She hesitated, started to answer but thought better of it.

"I have long found your work, your record interesting, Doctor, and now I simply find *you* very interesting." He moved closer, putting his arm about her waist. "Would you have me shot for my curiosity?"

She felt a wave of passion sweep through her, but still she resisted, taking his hand away and snatching the blanket from where he'd tossed it across the arm of the chair. "Better arrange this for you," she said in her most motherly tone. "Time you got some rest, don't you think?"

She busied herself with spreading the blanket over the sofa, saying in a near-whisper, "I hope you'll be comfortable here, Jim, and now, if you don't mind, I'd like just to—"

"Yes, well . . . I'm sure I'll be perfectly comfortable here, yes," he sputtered, trying desperately to regain the moment but failing to. Wanting to touch her again, but fearful of the consequences, he instead began making faces behind her back—faces that told of his frustration and anger with himself for being so clumsy—while she fluffed his pillow and pleasantly chanted, "There, there."

She smelled so clean and fresh, like the island air swirling in from the sea, and earlier he'd listened to the cascade of water from her shower, fantasizing at the time how it would be if he simply joined her. He'd step into the spray and she'd welcome him into her waiting arms, but he'd stepped out onto the balcony instead, and she had come to him in that thick robe, her robust skin shimmering against her auburn hair in the half-light. He wondered now how he could ever allow her to step away from him.

When she turned, he again reached out for her. She took his hands firmly in hers and said, "Good night, Jim. Get some rest. You're overtired, and so am I."

She quickly left, realizing how teasing and foolish she'd been earlier, having gone to him on the balcony in her robe, but she had found out what she wanted to know. He was extremely interested.

"Good night, Jim," she said in a whiskey-voiced whisper from her door.

Just as she turned, he stole a final glance to see her soft form glide off, disappearing into the adjoining room as she closed the door behind her. He then stared at the sofa, kicked off his shoes and tore away his coat and tie. In a moment he was stripping away his shirt, allowing the cool breeze coming in off the balcony to play over his naked chest. He stripped down to his shorts, grabbed a white terry robe with the Rainbow logo and went in to shower.

In the shower stall, the hot jets of water were soothing on his neck and shoulders, the headache of earlier having become a fist at his temple. He closed his eyes and stood there and suddenly his flesh trembled, feeling Jessica's soft touch against his back as she entered the stall. Drenched, he turned to face her, but his fantasy evaporated in the mist of hot spray when he opened his eyes to find himself quite alone.

He toweled off and found Jessica's Nuprin bottle, popped three of them and returned to the living area, where he dropped the robe over a chair and quickly nestled below the cotton blanket she'd given him, his head alighting on the pillow. His every nerve screaming for sleep in the absence of sex, he was immediately met with slumber.

Parry was shaken by a soft, moaning noise reverberating in his head until it turned into a panicked cry, having suddenly intensified even as he gathered his senses to realize where in hell he was: outside Jessica Coran's bedroom, in deep slumber only moments before.

Then the cry from her room became insistent. He tore himself from the covers, grabbed his gun from its holster over a chair and rushed to Jessica's side, fearing the worst.

A moment later, he stood over her bed and watched her troubled sleep. She called out the name Otto, and next she called out the single word *Father,* mantra of the frightened child, he thought. Somewhere below her calm exterior, below the veneer of the doctor, there was a scared little girl after all. "Just like me," he whispered aloud. "Like all of us, I suppose."

He felt uncomfortable seeing her like this, and so he gently sat alongside her and slowly shook Jessica into consciousness, softly and firmly repeating her name. She felt good beneath his warm, gentle touch; he smelled good, too, natural and balmy like the sea air that parted the drapes at the window. She found his eyes burning a path over her reposing form, and as she struggled for complete consciousness, she heard him tenderly say, "God, you're beautiful."

She came fully awake, her nightmare vanquished as if he'd taken a rapier to it, shredding it apart to reveal a safe reality on this side of sleep.

She gasped for air and gripped his bare arms for support. He gently wrapped her in himself and rocked slowly, telling her that everything was all right.

"I'm here, Jess . . . I'm here," came his litany of assurances.

She sobbed against his firm, wide chest, feeling foolish, caught off guard, appearing so damnably vulnerable.

"You okay?" he asked, his voice banishing the shadows and demons that'd come so near.

"No . . . yeah, I mean . . . yeah, for the moment. Bad dreams is all." She knew her voice sounded a bit desperate and rocky.

"About Matisak?" he asked, referring to her nightmare.

"No . . . about Linda Kahala . . . about the way she died. Lau and I've measured the wounds if I'm any judge of the nature of the wounds, some striated in layers, as if he'd dug out goddamned . . ."—she searched for the word—"petroglyphs against her flesh like she was stone." She'd mentioned the patterned nature of some of the cuts to him before, but she hadn't told him how it had affected her. "The . . . the bastard . . . likely placed such cuts all over her body before she mercifully gave into hemorrhagic shock, coma and death." The slow death was filled with suffering, and the nightmare felt so real.

She shivered involuntarily.

He held her more firmly. "Nothing can harm you here with me," he quietly promised, kissing her atop her head.

She tipped her head slightly upward, her mouth at his chin, and he moistened his lips and brought his mouth to hers. Their embrace was long, warm, honeyed and mellifluous; their bodies becoming fluid, each seemed to easily and wearily melt into the other, and now, for a time, they simply held firm to one another, Jim lying alongside her there on the bed, afraid to let go, a man who has reached too far, fearing a false move.

For a long time they remained quiet, but stroking his hair, she found herself exploring him, and in a moment each was exploring the other with renewed energy and needful hearts. Fingers and hands made swirls about her being, and each lover was now enraptured and wrapped in one another's longing. Each in great and passionate throes, each seeking comfort in the other . . . and suddenly there was no darkness or shadow living here, neither in the room nor inside her.

She reached around him and dug her nails into his back and wrapped her legs about him all in one flowing motion. He responded with ever more passion, his mouth cascading with a waterfall of warmth and saliva. Exploring her firm breasts, his fiery tongue stroked her like a welcomed hot poker. She raised and lowered with his rhythmic movement, their combined gasps and deep breathing their only music, enchanting and melodic.

This is what you came to Hawaii for, she thought.

"Jess, Jess, Jess," he chanted as a refrain, his unrestrained body bathing her in the oils of passion and play.

She awoke to his warmth beside her and the rich sounds of Hawaii greeting the sun. At the open floor-length balcony window here on the sixteenth floor, little island birds had come begging for morning crumbs, one of them inching into the room, cocking its head in her direction—a silent appeal for attention.

"Will you look at those beggars?" she asked. "I'll call room service," she suggested.

"For the birds?"

"For all of us!"

"Sounds good."

"Any preferences?"

"I trust you implicitly, but I'm not sure the *'elapaio* do."

" *'Elapay-o?* "

"That's what your new guests are called. Honeycreepers who've been spoiled by tourists on balconies everywhere feeding 'em Cheerios and potato chips and pizza crumbs."

"You certainly know a lot about the islands."

"Can't live here as long as I have and not pick up a few things."

"It's really become home for you, hasn't it?"

He'd disappeared, nude, into the bathroom, and in a moment she heard him call back, "What? Oh, yeah . . . well, I read a lot, too." His voice was replaced by the shower spray. She ordered scrambled eggs, bacon and coffee, and then she joined him in the shower.

After repeated raps on the door without answer, room service left the tray outside.

⟵ 16 ⟶

Life is the art of drawing sufficient conclusions from insufficient premises.

Samuel Butler

Outside the hotel, Jim Parry parted with Jessica, taking himself on a morning walk to the nearby hospital, where he'd look in on Sergeant Nathan Ivers. But just before they'd left the room, Parry had called into headquarters and been pleased with the news that a confession had been obtained from George Oniiwah's room-mate, a story of betrayal which fully corroborated their deepest suspicions regarding Hal "Paniolo" Ewelo. Jim was ecstatic, hungry for Paniolo's head, and close enough to taste it as it was skewered over the pit. Somehow, the thought of avenging George Oniiwah made Jessica, too, feel there might be justice yet in the world, and that perhaps with the noose tightening around Ewelo's ugly neck, he might just have something to share with them about what he knew of the real Trade Winds Killer, for they'd both become convinced that Ewelo knew more than anyone had at first suspected, especially since the tenuous link between Terri Reno's john on the street and the cowboy-turned-pimp bar owner had been made.

Jessica had checked for any messages left her from the previous evening, and now she was alone outside the hotel, intending to return to the FBI crime lab via cab to see if there'd been any new developments there. Suddenly she was stopped by Joseph Kaniola.

"What do you want, sir?" she asked coldly.

"I want you to come with me."

She shook her head. "I'm not going anywhere with you, Mr. Kaniola."

"I swear on my son's grave, I had nothing to do with the Oniiwah boy's death."

"I have no intention of going off with you, Mr. Kaniola. I have no reason to trust your motives, not since our last meeting."

He dropped his gaze and said, "I'm sorry if you have felt used, Dr. Coran, but now you see that we are on the same side."

She said nothing, flagging down a cab.

Kaniola persisted. "You have been long enough here now to know that everyone uses everyone in Hawaii, and that none of us are spared such . . . indignity."

"What do you want of me, Mr. Kaniola?"

"My great-granduncle is a shaman and—"

"Shaman?"

"He is a priest among the traditionals and has sent word to me . . ."

"And so?"

"He has the gift, and he has seen this Trade Winds Killer, this man who killed my son. He tells me so, and he says he has seen you with him. He says it is not Ewelo."

"Has seen me? With the Trade Winds Killer? Just how?"

"In a trance. Through here," he replied, pointing to his temple. "My great-granduncle is what your culture calls a . . . a psychic."

"Really? Look, Mr. Kaniola—"

"Will you come?"

"No."

"But he can tell you facts not presently in evidence, facts you can use against this maniac you hunt."

She shook her head. "This is still the U.S., and in a U.S. court the word of a prophet or seer isn't of any . . . use, but you know that, so why're you even pursuing this, Mr. Kaniola?"

"I do as my great-granduncle requests, without question."

She glowered at him. "What're you suggesting? That if I don't come voluntarily—"

"No, no, no, please, Dr. Coran. I only say it is imperative you meet with my great-granduncle."

"Bring him round to the Federal building then, this afternoon if you like." She tried sidestepping him, the cabbie honking his horn, becoming irate.

He blocked her way. "No, you don't understand."

"Take it or leave it, but get out of my way or so help me, sir, you will see my training firsthand."

"Great Uncle cannot make such a journey."

"What's that supposed to mean?"

"He is ancient and stubborn, like you, and . . . and he will not . . . cannot leave the shrine."

"The shrine?"

"The family shrine, where he lives in the mountains, there . . ." He pointed to the imposing array of mountains over his shoulder and looming over Honolulu. They appeared so unreal as to be painted onto the sky, the most breathtaking mountains Jessica had ever seen anywhere on earth. Kaniola continued, saying, "Great Uncle has seen you in here"—he again pointed to his cranium—"and now pleads to see you in the flesh."

She took a deep breath. "Seen me? On the six o'clock news maybe, or in your paper?"

"In his trance, and he wishes to tell you face-to-face of the . . . of an impending danger."

"Like I don't know the risks?" She almost laughed.

"No . . . you don't . . . no one knows as Lomelea knows. He is a *hemolele*."

"Would you mind? I don't have an Hawaiian dictionary on me and—"

"'*Ole, pono loa,* a perfect, a priest."

"Look, Kaniola, I'm already late and—"

"It is an honor to be asked to come before the perfect."

She stared at the waiting cab and then back at Kaniola. "Do you really think this old man can tell me anything I don't already know about the case?"

"This old man has lived for generations. He is over a hundred years old."

She dropped her gaze now. "This . . . this just better be legitimate and not a waste of my time, Mr. Kaniola, do you understand me?"

"I do, and it won't be."

"Where?"

"I will take you to him personally."

Waving off the angry cab driver, Jessica reluctantly followed Kaniola to his waiting car, knowing Jim would be furious with her when he found out what she'd done. Maybe this was why she gave in to Kaniola's less-than-persuasive plea. If she could back Jim off to arm's length, keep him guessing, keep him upset with her, then maybe she had a chance of keeping the relationship under her control—a thing that was going to be doubly hard now that they'd been intimate.

9 A.M., July 17, somewhere in the Koolau Mountains

Jessica found herself at an ancient Polynesian shrine built into the mountainside of Oahu's Koolau Range, away from the bustling city of Honolulu. The shrine was multi-tiered and draped with flowers and ceremonial leis far more beautiful and intricate than any she'd seen at the various tourist traps of either Maui or Honolulu. Kaniola led the way through a labyrinthine garden that connected with the shrine nestled here among trees. It was a shrine of light and life, of wind and bird, of water and greenery, a monument to all that seemed good in the islands. She found a sense of enormous peace and equanimity here, a feeling she'd never completely had before.

Looking back along the path they'd followed, far in the distance she could see the city of Honolulu stretching out like a serpentine creature, the skyscrapers like its knobby and horned backbone where they stood in a row along the coastal waters several hundred feet below.

If she squinted, she could make out the enormous crater called the Punchbowl, Puu-owaina, Hill of Sacrifice, where the remains of American soldiers, sailors and marines and famous Hawaiian nationals reposed in the National Memorial Cemetery of the Pacific.

Closer to her, she made out the man-made canals created in the

1800s by engineers to take the mountain rains to the sweeping flatlands of the coasts on either side, land which would otherwise be in a constant state of drought. She could see from this vantage that the islands were a playground for nature, which had created broad paint strokes of every hue.

Kaniola stopped in his tracks just ahead of her, bowed before the entrance to his great-granduncle's home and stepped through the humble little cottage door.

It was cool and damp inside, a natural form of air-conditioning, and candles lit their way to the rear where the old man, all skin and bones, lay in a cot that was little more than a rickety hammock. A Hawaiian Ghandi, she thought on seeing him. He wore the same wire-rim spectacles that Ghandi had worn.

On hearing their approach, he sat up. Bare-chested, he quickly placed a muumuu over himself the way a woman might. He didn't bother tying the baggy dress and his shape and tiny arms were lost in its billowy folds and flowered print, only the small brown face and white head showing at the top.

The models at Hilo Hattie's five-and-dime shops in Honolulu had nothing to fear from this competition, she told herself, stifling a smile at the wizened old creature.

"Forgive appearance of old men," the wheezing voice that came out of the prune face said. The man had obviously lost all his teeth and could not bother with dentures, as attested to by the sunken gums and the empty apple-sauce jars that littered his home.

"You are Kaniola's great-granduncle?" she asked, feeling a bit uncomfortable with her surroundings.

"Lomelea"—he pointed to himself—"I . . . am . . ." He spoke at a snail's pace and was hard to decipher. "And I . . . did . . . *see* you."

"Yes, in a newspaper maybe, or on television?"

He only laughed. "I live here. Do you see TV? Don't have it. Won't allow it. Western *pilau!*"

He put as much emphasis into the word *pilau* as his frail form could muster. Kaniola hadn't lied about the probable age of the old man.

"How can I help you, Mr. Lomelea?"

"It is . . . the killing one . . . You are close, but you see only his shadow . . ."

The old man had no idea how accurate that sounded, but *she* did. "We're getting closer," she simply said.

"You be near. I see you both . . . in my red dream."

"You've seen us both?"

She tried not to sound too disappointed in having come all this way for nothing.

"He is . . . one of us." The old man's head shook sadly, independent of his body, like that of a marionette, the strings moved by the wind flowing through the open-air back room where he slept.

She silently wondered how many times the old man's shrine, over his lifetime, had been demolished by the angry island gods, only to be painstakingly rebuilt like the proverbial house of straw.

"A cathedral it is not . . ." he said in shaky English as if reading her thoughts, "but ground is sanctified, and me . . . a holy man."

Wishing she hadn't come, and wishing to get this behind her, she said, "What can you tell me about the killer, Mr. Lomelea?"

"He has fire hair."

"Fire hair?"

"Red, rusty-colored, natty hair of many of our people," Kaniola explained for her.

She recalled Terri Reno's description, and the police sketch, and it fit. She realized that by now Kaniola and every other newsman in the islands had a copy of both the sketch and the description. Could Joe have cued his old relative with the information?

"You have . . . healthy doubt. Good, I respect," said the old man. "More I tell you. With heart you listen."

With that the old man squatted and called on his trance state to enable him to reveal more about the monster roaming his island. His gibberish was in Hawaiian, however, and she did not understand until Kaniola translated.

"Laulima . . ."

Kaniola said, "Community food patch, cooperation, working together."

The old man continued on, unstoppable. *"A'ohe launa ka make'u . . ."*

"No fear, friendly, sociable, yet there's no limit to the fear that is no fear," explained Kaniola.

". . . Keiki lawehala . . . lawe kahili . . ."

"What's he saying?"

"Sin, no . . . sinner, evil sinner, delinquent son of" — Kaniola hesitated — "of bearer of the feather standard."

"What does that mean?"

"Royalty . . ."

The old man seemed in another realm now, his eyes rolled back in his head so that all she could see were the whites. His speech was being taped by Kaniola, and for the first time she realized this fact.

"Can you be more specific?" she asked, wondering how she could possibly use what the old man had had to say so far. His glazed-eye trance routine had been perfected over time.

"Lawehana," he continued.

Kaniola engaged the old man in their native tongue. *"Lawehana?"*

"A me lawe hanai, eia ho'i lawehana."

"Both?"

"What?" asked Jessica.

"The killer, he says, is both a grown man and a child, a common laborer and an adopted child."

"Adopted?" she asked.

"Halfway so, yes."

How was someone halfway adopted? she wanted to scream. Still, she patiently listened as the old man continued.

Over the old man's head hung an ancient set of leis, one a *lei palaoa,* ivory pendents from whale's teeth suspended by two coils of braided human hair the texture and color of which matched the alleged killer's. Alongside this was a lei of rosary beads, known as a *lei korona* for the crown of England. A dog-tooth necklace, called a *niho'ilio,* dangled nearby as well. As she stared at these museum pieces in wonder, the old man spoke as if in her brain, saying, "Killer fashions cords from human hair," but it was Kaniola, translating, breaking into her thoughts.

"Lehe luhe, lehelehe." The old man's mouth creased in a smile over his own words.

Kaniola remained grim, saying, "The killer's lips are fat like those of the vagina, pouting lips."

"Lei palaoa, niho'illo mahine."

Kaniola visibly stiffened.

Jessica pressed him to translate the words.

"He . . . the killer makes leis from their teeth and hair. He has them in his house. He knows the ancient ways and he knows the modern ways."

"I lawa no a pau ka hana Ku, ho'i ho'i kaua," continued the old man.

"He says that as soon as the work is finished for Ku, the ancient god, then the killer will leave."

"Will leave for where?"

"To be with Ku."

"Aelo, aewa," continued the old man.

"Says your killer has no backbone, weaves back and forth like seaweed, that he is like the infertile egg that smells of rot from within."

The old man continued rambling. *" 'A'ohe Ahahui Mamakakaua."*

"He says this man is no son or daughter of Hawaiian warriors."

"What, now we're back to it's a white man?"

". . . ahiwa, ahewa . . .'aihue kanaka, ai kanaka, aikane, 'ai kapu, ai kepa, 'ai noa, ai pa'a, aiwa . . ."

"What's he saying?"

"He's not making much sense, I'm afraid."

"Tell me." She was impatient.

"Well, I'll try. He says the kidnapper is a man who seeks to find guilt and administer scorn, and that he is a cannibal, a man-eater, yet friendly or a friend . . ."

"Ahonui!" shouted the old man.

"That he has infinite patience."

"He's a stalker," she agreed, "and he knew those he killed, and it's possible they were cannibalized to some degree."

"Says he eats by using cutting blades and sometimes tears with teeth, and that he eats under taboo, yet he eats freely, ignoring taboo, without observing them."

The old man muttered in his native tongue.

"What else is he saying?" Jessica asked.

"Either that Great Uncle wants a present of cooked taro in ti-leaf bundles, or that you face a difficult problem, a mystery."

"He's got that right."

"Aka' ula . . . akiu ala kai . . ." continued the old man in a monotone.

"He is speaking now of you," said Kaniola.

She exchanged a look with Joe Kaniola, who said, "You search for answers, seek, probe, a medical person, but what you seek is a red shadow like the sunset. You can not touch it though you see it before you."

". . . alaula ala'ula . . . aloalo. 'ale'ale ho'i alelo."

"He says a canoe will take you to a flaming road in a land filled with hibiscus where no one will know your tongue—a land of kings."

Was he describing the Rainbow Tower where I'm staying? Jessica wondered, surprised at her own jaded and suspicious nature. Still, she'd become captivated by the old man's "second sight," predictions and native charms such as they were.

Kaniola listened intently for his great-granduncle's next words. There was a long silence and the old man looked faint, about to give in to his fatigue when he bellowed out yet another stream of words.

" '*Au ho'au*. Doctor . . . '*auamo, 'au'a.*"

Kaniola was reluctant to translate, but Jessica insisted he do so.

"He asks you a direct question, about your cane." Kaniola indicated the cane at her side.

"What about it?" She feared he was asking after it as an offering, a gift for his services. She hadn't seen a basket to toss folding money into.

"He says you are a strong swimmer in the sea, that you need no handle or staff or stem, that it is a burden to you, but you are stingy and won't part with it."

She gripped her cane tighter and asked Kaniola to ask the old man one question.

"Yes?"

"Ask him how many times will the red shadow kill?"

"*Ehia.* Great Uncle, *ehia*?"

" '*Ehiku,*" came the quick answer.

"Don't tell me," she said, raising a hand, "seven?"

Kaniola nodded. The old man said, " '*Ehu, 'eho kino, nuinui kino.*"

"What's that?"

"He says all the bodies are below the spray, stacked like stone markers, many, many bodies."

"How many years has the killer stalked victims?"

" '*Ehiku.*"

"Seven again."

The old man then told a tale of a chief whose son was born with many problems, from asthma to diseases that left the child crippled and deformed. The child looked like an old man who'd had a stroke. The chief adopted a foster child, a well-formed child, and had this child take the place of his only male child. With the new child in place, the chief brooded and feared that the evil-looking, obviously cursed son would infect his new son. When the sickly boy grew ill in a new bout of suffering, the chief drunkenly took hold of him and carried him out in a storm into the forest, where he destroyed the child, using a ceremonial blade. Later, telling his people that the boy had wandered away and had been mangled by the beasts of the forests, he had the body taken to the village dump, claiming it to be cursed, and had it burned in a ceremony to defeat the devils that plagued his royal house. The bones were cast into the sea, an act of disdain, an ignominious end for a Hawaiian soul. He did so before the eyes of his adopted child.

Over the years, as the adopted child grew, it became more and more apparent that while this well child did not show any physical signs of disease, he was morally and spiritually crippled in ways unapparent until one looked into his cold blue eyes.

Kaniola added, almost as an afterthought, "This child was banished from the life of the commune when his father discovered that he had killed a girl child younger than himself."

Jessica now stared from Joe to the old man, who was slowly climbing from his trance state.

"Are you saying that our killer is this same child? Or is this a quaint Hawaiian parable?"

"I cannot say," replied Kaniola. "I have heard this tale in many guises. It is possible it may be just a parable, as you say."

She asked the old man outright, and Kaniola put it to him in Hawaiian.

"It is truth at least in one eye," whispered the old man in English.

Whose eye? she wondered. His or the killer's?

"This child . . . today he is a *ho'o-haole ia* as his people say, and they banished him."

"*A ho'a*-what?"

"He apes the white people, became Americanized by the white schools and books," said Joe, "kina like me, hey, Great Uncle?"

"I don't suppose you have a name for this boy?" she asked.

"Lo-paka." The old man spewed the name with spittle.

"Lopaka?"

"That is how it come to me, yes."

"It is what you Americans and English call Robert," said Kaniola.

"He once on Maui lived . . . cowpuncher," said Lomelea.

Here was another clue that Terri Reno's Robert and Ewelo were connected. Joe pursued this. He spoke to his great-granduncle for a moment in native Hawaiian, leading him toward Ewelo, Jessica recognizing only the name.

"Paniolo, yes . . . yes," replied the old man unmistakably, "cowboy . . . cowboy . . ."

Joe frowned and now asked the old man if there was anything else he might want to add.

The old man, by now extremely weary, shook his head, pulled himself from the lotus position he'd assumed and, with Joe's help, found his hammock.

Jessica knew that much of what the old man had said about the killer might easily have been surmised from Kaniola or other sources, yet there was something genuine about Lomelea. And could it be purely coincidental that Terri Reno's strange admirer had called himself Robert? It was information Parry had withheld from the press release.

Jessica went to the old man and extended her cane to him, his eyes lighting up in response. He rubbed the silver handle between his hands appreciatively and pointed to his wall. He had already selected a place of prominence to display the gift.

17

Murder is not an instinct but an invention.

From the Notebooks of Dr. Jessica Coran

Mid-morning, the same day

It is at times like this that Lopaka Kowona feels most closely to Kelia again. Again he has her where he can control her; again he has total domination over her. He can do anything to her body; he can even make love to her body again now, if he so chooses.

Waking from the best sleep he'd had since the last Kelia, he stares up at her remains, her eyes staring vacantly back at him, her flesh crisscrossed with blood rivulets, the surface of her creamy skin looking now as if it had been turned inside out. Silently her weight tugs against the restraints and the rack sags; even in death, she fights her fate, *she wants down*.

He wants to see her come down now, too. Down and out of here, in fact. But how? His car is useless, and if he has it towed and repaired, the bullet hole in the gas pan could easily be a beacon to police after last night's near capture. He needs to know what's going on outside.

He switches on the TV in hope of finding out any information, but he has missed all the news broadcasts. It's mid-morning.

He flicks off the TV set and tries the radio. He switches from station to station for any information. He gives up, leaving on KBHT, Hawaii's hottest rock station, the D.J. spinning "Give Me That Ol' Time Rock 'n' Roll."

He then remembers to check for the newspaper on his doorstep, the *Ala Ohana*. The paper had been recently filled with news of how the cops had arrested the owner of Paniolo's bar and grill, claiming that he was a likely suspect in the Trade Winds killings, both pleasing Lopaka and frightening him, because while he despised Paniolo, the obvious conclusion was that the authorities were drawing ever closer to the truth. He'd known Ewelo back on Maui where they'd both been working cowboys on a ranch there. The man was a Samoan asshole, a creep and a bully, reminding Lopaka of his father in several salient habits and nasty practices.

Still, on coming to Oahu, he'd looked Paniolo up, asking for a job. Paniolo had put him to selling in the limited drug trade he was just putting together, but they'd had a falling out over the money exchange, Paniolo proving to be sharper than he'd let on, allowing Lopaka to dig himself into a deeper and deeper hole.

He'd finally paid Paniolo back, but for a time Lopaka had had to watch his back, fearful that the other man would come out of the next dark corner to put a knife in his ribs. That was Paniolo's style. So Lopaka had taken to wearing one of his more easily concealed knives in an ankle sheath at all times. So far as Lopaka was concerned, the arrest of this man was the best possible solution to the island's ongoing problem with the Trade Winds Killer. Still, it made him nervous to think that the cops had struck so close to home. He hadn't been in Paniolo's employ for over a year, but records could reveal his former association; hell, Paniolo might even think to implicate him, knowing of his liking for swords and knives, and if this happened, the authorities could be at his door within minutes.

He paces, telling himself nervously that there is so damned much hinging on so many things he can't control, and Kelia—her vacant eyes staring like the embers of a dying sun in the west—is now a shadow being, also uncontrollable, unless he can finish what he has started.

He lifts his camera and begins taking shots of the dead store clerk's final repose. He takes up the remaining roll, his enthusiasm for the picture-taking escalating as he goes. But his mind is still preyed upon by the mounting fears of his own exposure.

He's too close to his ultimate goal to be caught now, he tells himself. Seven years he has stalked and killed for Ku, and admittedly for his own self-gratification and lust. Seven years of seven victims minus four. He is four away from final victory, the moment when Ku will unconditionally embrace him and enfold him into His bountiful, cosmic arms to accept Lopaka Kowona as an equal.

Things just need to go on a little longer, to be brought to a final resolution, when seven victims this year would end his quest, when the power he would obtain would arrest the red flame of Kelia's life forever, He breathes deeply, inhaling death's presence deeply, thinking of the peaceful kingdom which lies ahead in which he would hold that crimson shadow in his fist in firm, godly fashion.

He goes to the door and looks outside at the bright sunlit, narrow strip of beaten tarmac, the winding, hilly ribbon-like folds where it has buckled. He absently takes in the temperature, the wind conditions, the dryness, and scans the surrounding mountainside, finding nothing out of the ordinary. It's already hot out, a promise of another scorcher. As expected, his paper has been lying there since dawn. Lopaka lifts it and pops the rubber band and hurriedly scans it where he stands in his underwear, the red hue to his skin and the smell of blood about him causing him no alarm. His front door and most of his small house are protected from view by a thick, wild border of pandanus trees.

A certain bravado pervades his mind, telling him that if there is a sharpshooter hidden up there in the mountains, then let him fire. His lazy stance outside the door is a dare he can take. Ku will protect his own.

The front page of the little newspaper strikes him as hard as any bullet. His face, or a very close facsimile, is on the front page, along with his first name, Lopaka. He's stunned, his knees wobbling. It must've come from Paniolo, is all that he can conceive. The lousy bastard has given him up as the Trade Winds Killer, obviously unable to recall his last name but not his features.

"MotherfuckingbastardPaniolo!" he screeches and darts back into the lair. He scans the paper for what the outside world knows of him. It appears at first very little, in fact, and he catches his breath.

He then sees what the paper assumed to be a separate story, that of his near capture of the night before. He scans the story to learn what *they* know, and it comes clear that the car outside his door is a major liability now. They know the make and model. They know that the fuel line or gas pan was spewing gas as the car sped away. The story relates the tale of a "heroic" attempt on the part of a beefy-faced Irish cop named Ivers to stop a hit-and-run driver, a subsequent fire and the cop's bout with his injuries. A photograph of Ivers shows a tired-looking man with thinning gray hair and a surly glare at the camera.

A scan of missing-persons reports has turned up the fact that Hiilani has not come home the night before, so the paper—not waiting the official twenty-four-hour grace period the HPD usually allows Lopaka—has put out a cry for information regarding her, an accompanying shot showing her sitting before a birthday cake in a crowded little room. Her employer has given a description of Lopaka which is startlingly close, but which the fools haven't yet put together with the description in the Trade Winds Killer story, at least so far as he can tell.

Lopaka feels his knees wobbling. They *could* stop him. They *could* put an end to his quest today, within the hour, within a minute, if someone puts two and two together; if Paniolo's memory improves, if that bastard Claxton should for once think past his nose—hell, even if his newsboy that morning smelled the gasoline odor that still lingered to the Buick . . . or if some particularly observant tourist on the bus yesterday stared too long at his mug shot on the visor.

Panic drips into his brain, filling him with an acidic fear, a consternation and dread like nothing he's ever experienced before.

He feels strongly now he *must* run, escape to finish his work elsewhere, in a safer environment. But where and how to get there?

Relatives . . . get to your relatives, he tells himself. The island is teeming with them. One of them will help you off the island; blood is thicker than anything, they say. Besides, what relative would ever imagine the enormity of his crimes, or link him seriously with the string of murders. All he need do is speak of a bad drug transaction that has gotten him into serious shit with a creep like Paniolo, who would implicate his own mother to save his own neck. That will suffice, he tells himself.

"But what about Kelia?" ask the voices in his head.

"Her remains must be cleansed and sent over."

"You can't just leave her here like this."

"I'll be back for her. I'll find a way," he replies, going for the closet-like bathroom, where he rinses blood from his hands and chest and abdomen. Using a hand rag he wipes it from between his toes and off his shins, leaving it to linger on his private parts. He quickly dresses, gulps down a glass of water and taking all of his savings, rushes out, locking the door behind him. He walks down the narrow, winding road for the main road where he can catch a bus, aware that neighbors who have seldom if ever seen him are staring from behind windows and drapes.

"I'll be back for you, Kelia," he vows halfway down the hot road when he hears the rack inside his den and inside his head sag once more with her weight, as if in reply.

Navy divers called in by the FBI had given every effort to recover any unusual objects and bones found in, around and about the area of the Blow Hole, but very little was forthcoming. Some of the bones found were not bones at all but fossilized coral, others were animal bones, but there was a human femur, an ankle bracelet, an earring, several watches and one human pelvic bone. The Blow Hole and its subterranean runway was giving up very little; it appeared that this particular purgatory was a timeless one for the victims of the Cane Cutter.

Still, Jessica couldn't look a gift horse in the mouth, so she thanked the Navy representatives who'd come bearing these questionable forensic gifts, apologizing for not being able to do more. And with Dr. Lau's help, she went instantly to work over the new specimens.

"God, what I wouldn't give for a skull," she now told Lau, her exasperation apparent.

The little man silently nodded his understanding, picking about the sad assortment of bone fragments, and clearing his throat, he added, "It would be too easy."

She knew what he meant. With a skull identification could be far more rapid and sure, with its teeth intact, for then extractions, scars and other features unique to an individual could be "hit" points on an I.D. chart. All they'd need were comparison X-rays showing faulty tooth occlusions and corrections, and a good forensic orthodontist to tell them what they were looking at. But as Lau said, nothing came easily.

Photographs of the cleaned and dried artifacts brought up by the Navy divers had to be made, but not before cleaning in bleach, soap and ammonia and then a thorough drying. Some of the bones were in a fragile condition, flakes peeling away. It would take time to air-dry them for a day or two before they could safely be handled, but who had that kind of time? She knew they'd have to allow time its due nonetheless. The waiting was one of the more maddening aspects of the work.

Like her, Lau was anxious, wanting immediate answers and so vulnerable to wrong interpretations as a result. They must do as her father had always said, "Bow to the wisdom of time."

But even so, even with the naked eye and the encrusted femur, Jessica could read the fact it bore an injury, an injury that looked like the painful rent of a powerful metal object like a cane cutter or even a sword. Lau, looking from the femur to her and back again, saw the same indelible fracture.

As soon as the bones were air-dried and photographed they'd go to work with the Butvar, a granular, dry adhesive mixed to a gel-like consistency and applied liberally to the porous bone fragments to permanently fix them. After this dried, the fragments could be newly photographed and the photos so tagged.

For any of the pieces that might be found to fit together, they'd use Florentine Red Wax to re-invent the structure. It was the same wax used by archaeologists to reconstruct pottery pieces.

The process promised only tedium without any further guarantees, but Jessica was saved from this purgatory when a lab tech called out that a phone call had come for her.

"Tell 'em we're busy here!" she countered, not wanting to leave Lau alone with the unsavory work.

"It's Chief Parry."

She frowned and Lau, with a funny little gesture of the fingers in a miniature horse race, indicated for her to run. "Chop, chop," he said.

"I won't be long," she promised.

"Take whatever time is necessary, Dr. Coran. We here can manage with these paltry bones."

She nodded and moved off at once, going for the office that'd been turned over to her. Closing the door, she took Parry's call.

"Hello, Jim?"

"We got an interesting cross-reference on a lead that could pan out to be our killer. You interested?"

"Damn straight, I am."

"I talked with Ivers. He gave me a name, a first name, Lopaka."

"Lopaka?" She repeated it, realizing that it was the same as that given by Lomelea, Kaniola's great-granduncle, when she had visited him at the shrine. "Robert," she said into the phone.

"*Hmmmmm,* your Hawaiian is coming along," he replied curiously. "Anyway, seems when Paniolo Ewelo was shown the police sketch we put together and the tapes were played for him, he instantly came up with Terri Reno's would-be protector and provider."

"That's great."

"And get this, the name's Lopaka. Ewelo calls *this guy* a creep, if you can imagine that."

"Our boy scout pointing a finger? Imagine that. Of course, you know how impressed a jury will be with Ewelo."

The sarcasm and truth of what she was saying wasn't lost on Parry, who continued. "Well, I think we can nail this bastard without cutting any deals with Ewelo."

"Really? Do you have another avenue?"

"Yeah, our fat friend, Professor Claxton, came up with the same name when Tony questioned him with the new information. Seems the creep is on one of his old class rosters, but had dropped out prior to completion."

"So now Claxton's memory is jogged. Convenient. You sure he isn't just reacting to events?"

"Sure he's reacting to events. Claxton got shit scared out of him when Ewelo and his boys killed Oniiwah; don't let the man's bravado in front of female cops and tough guys like me fool you. He seems also to have remembered someone he slept with once, someone Paniolo fixed him up with."

"Really? He slept with Linda Kahala like Oniiwah said, but not for a grade change?"

"And Kia before Linda. Seems the relationship between Claxton and the cowboy goes a lot deeper."

"Patron of the prostitutes and benefactor, I get it." She leaned back as far as the office chair would take her, interested, listening intently now while her fingers idly played with a paperweight in the shape of the islands, an odd object to say the least.

"The guy's full name is Lopaka Kowona," Parry said.

She repeated the name slowly as if doing so would exorcise all demons. She had a sense, a purely instinctual feel about the name, that it belonged to the Trade Winds Killer, Linda Kahala's murderer. "And you say Ivers picked up on the same name?"

"Nate heard the abducted girl call her abductor Lopaka. I had Gagliano check with the registrar's office at the university, and he found that there was a Lopaka Kowona registered part-time at the same time that both Kia and Linda Kahala were enrolled. Nate also wrote down half a license plate number and a check with DMV shows it registered to a Lopaka Kowona. Enough to get a warrant? Probable cause? You bet it is, and now we've got a door to kick."

"I'll be damned," she said, a feeling of relief washing over her. It was probably too late for the pretty little girl she'd read about in the *Union Jack* that morning, but this could mean an end to a seven-year reign of terror about the islands. The series of lucky strokes was almost too much to believe. "I want to be there," she demanded.

"If we can nail this guy Kowona, and Ivers and Claxton both I.D. him, we put the lid on his coffin without cutting any deals with Ewelo. That'd be the crowning glory."

She pushed aside the paperweight and realized how like a dragon the series of humps that made up the islands were.

"Don't get your hopes up too high, Jim. It sounds like we'll still need Ewelo as corroborating—"

"To hell with that."

"What?"

"Try this. A maroon sedan's sitting in this guy's driveway as we speak, and it stinks of a gasoline rupture. HPD has had an APB on the description of the car all night, and with one of their own hospitalized, they look that much harder."

"Damn, then maybe we do have the bastard dead to rights after all? I want in."

"You realize this girl, Hiilani, could well be in that house?"

"Let's hope she is. Otherwise, she's at the bottom of the ocean, and if that's the case, we'll have a hell of a time proving our case."

"Not if we can find enough trace evidence inside the car and the house."

"I'm with you." And she was. Many cases today were being

solved even in the absence of a body by virtue of the magic of DNA, blood, and serum typing, fiber and trace evidence.

"Meet me at the garage, and bring your bag, and I've got an ambulance on standby," Parry said. "I got a bad feeling about this one . . . think we're going to need a lot of plastic bags."

Everyone was in on the kill. And everyone who wasn't wanted to be.

Terri Reno and her burly partner Kalvin Haley were on hand, along with Tony Gagliano, Jim Parry and Jessica and everyone in the Hawaii FBI who had worked the case, plus a couple of HPD squad cars, one carrying Police Commissioner Dave Scanlon. They had all collected out front of the remote little bungalow on this bright Hawaiian day, the sun blinding in its intensity, the heat sending up a searing mix of gasoline and blood that mingled in the few feet between home and auto. Something about the house and the loud music coming from inside the crumbling little structure, its deserted location on a dead-end street, the terminus a crevasse looking two miles back down toward the city, and even something about the dark maroon car spoke clearly to Jessica that this was it.

At the door, there was no answer to Tony Gagliano's insistent pounding. Tony called out, "FBI, open up!"

The waiting seemed a lifetime before Parry abruptly shouted to Gagliano, "Kick the sonofabitch in."

"You got it, Boss," said Gagliano, relishing the moment. "It'll make me feel useful."

Everyone had a gun drawn. With all his might, Tony made a clean strike at the lock, sending the door in on its hinges, wood splintering going up against the door frame creating spiked lances. From within, the blare of a Hawaiian radio station hammered out an old favorite, Jim Croce's "Leroy Brown." Swelling up also from within the dark little interior was an odor like nothing Jessica had ever encountered, not even in an exhumation. The odor wafted past the door, which, swinging on its destroyed hinges, made an eerie *irk-irk-irking* sound.

"Smells bad," complained Gagliano, whipping out a large red bandanna to cover his nostrils and mouth before stepping through.

"Don't touch anything," Jessica warned from behind Parry, who quickly followed Gagliano inside, using a flashlight to illuminate the place. The incredible sunlit brightness of the Hawaiian street outside was at such great odds with the bleak hole of the doorway, so that every shadow inside was plunged that much further into darkness. Jessica's skin crawled as she stepped past the dangling door, her nostrils now flaring at the thick, pungent odor of death emanating from inside as if the odor were a living creature that had taken up residence permanently and was about to pounce shadowlike from a corner. Her eyes battled to adjust to the lack of light. When her eyes won, she found Gagliano and Parry staring back in her direction, Gagliano playing the flashlight over the wall behind Jessica's head and to her immediate left.

The place was a pigsty, she was thinking when she heard Jim's warning: "Don't turn around, Jess."

She did exactly as instructed not to do, turned and gasped at the mutilated woman dangling there, her features torn from her, making it impossible to readily identify her as the young store clerk listed as missing. Jessica's immediate reaction was one of horror and fright, but at the same time she saw the telltale signature wounds she'd come to expect from the Trade Winds Killer, each slash a meaningful symbol to the insane man. These body art marks created by Lopaka had until now been mere speculation, since all previous victims had been swallowed up by the sea.

She shuddered at the enormity of the suffering that was apparent. Parry grabbed onto her shoulders and tried to usher her out.

"No, no, Jim," she said, pulling free of him. "Have to protect the . . . integrity of the crime scene . . . learn everything we can about this sadistic monster."

"Just step out and get your bearings, Jess."

"Going out at this point'll just make it doubly hard to step back in, and it'll just make breathing tenfold harder. No." She remained adamant. "Just get me some decent illumination in here and the best equipment you've got." She was panting, trying to gain control of her autonomous reflexes. "And . . . and for God's sake, Jim, don't let anybody walk through here until I'm finished."

He looked deeply into her eyes, biting his lip and biting back his own sense of horror and insult, and recalling for a moment her tenderness of the night before, tried to reconcile that with the woman he stood before now.

"Do it, damnit. Get me some field lights in here and one of those newly developed ultraviolet reflective imaging systems if you've got one. We'll intensify the light in here seventy thousand times and maybe, just maybe we can find some usable prints in this pigsty, but whatever we do, we're going to find enough evidence to bury this bastard. The death penalty in effect in Hawaii? God, I hope so."

"Sorry, no can do . . . not even the chamber," replied Tony, shaking his head. "And if we ever needed it . . ."

"Too good for this guy," countered Jim Parry.

On the wall, on an elaborately constructed bamboo and wood "meat" rack, hanging by her wrists, her legs dangling free, Hiilani's corpse was like an agonizing, deafening scream that drowned out anything Jessica or anyone else had to say. The body, somehow like a stone object with soft, human eyes, might be made of papier-mâché and paint, ketchup and fake blood, except that the caked-on stuff was real and the flesh was responsive to the touch, the vitality of the cells having returned after rigor had come and gone, releasing the corpse from its stiffness, allowing a kind of supple "life" to return at the cellular level. Naturally, all of the lividity was in the lower extremities, all the blood having rushed there. She might appear mannequin-like, but she wouldn't feel that way, not when Jessica had to touch and prod the corpse for wound measurements, specimens and samples and slides and swabs.

She thought of the stark bone-fragment evidence brought in by the Navy guys, and now this. "You wanted evidence," she muttered to no one in particular, staring at the leis made of teeth and native hair, predicted by the old man.

"Not like this," replied Parry.

"Careful for what you wish . . ."

Gagliano had staggered about the small enclosure trying to train his eye on something—*anything* but the mutilated China doll on the wall. In doing so, like Jessica, he began to go to work, scanning for anything that might be useful. He immediately zeroed in on a rack of swords and knives on a wall the other side of the room. "Jesus, look at these," he said, pointing, about to reach out and touch one of the blades before catching himself.

"Check the refrigerator," Jessica told them.

"What?" asked Gagliano.

"Mutilation murderers . . . lust killers, they often keep 'trophies' on ice. Like the ropes he used on her."

"What about the ropes?" asked Jim, coming closer and shouting at Terri Reno, Haley and the others at the doorway to stay out, that it was already too damned crowded inside.

Reno shouted back, "Do we have the sonofabitch or not?"

"We know where he kills," Parry replied tersely before turning his attention back to Jessica, who, using a scalpel pulled from her jacket pocket, sliced one of the restraints holding the victim. This brought both victim and rack further from the wall, but everything held.

She held out the twisted rope. "It's human hair, most likely from his earlier victims."

"Jesus . . . and teeth, human teeth."

Gagliano moved to the icebox and snatched the door open to find it relatively empty, the little light coming from it reflecting off the dead girl on the wall, making her look like an odd specimen in a house of horrors display. The fridge compartment revealed a man who didn't live on food.

"Check the freezer compartment," said Jim, holding onto the black-hair rope which might well have been Lina Kahala's hair.

Gagliano swallowed hard before snatching open the freezer door. He did so a little too abruptly, and out flowed a stack of frozen female hands complete with rings and painted nails. Tony hopped back, gasping and swearing when the solid, iced hands hit the floor like so many T-bone steaks.

Parry called to the others who'd remained outside daring only to poke their heads beyond the perimeter of the broken door. He called for field generators and to have Dr. Lau dispatch all the evidence-technician support he could muster.

The men outside fought over who'd get to do this chore. Along the narrow street outside, nearby residents had begun to assemble, stare and point.

Jessica thought of the old man on the mountain, Kaniola's great-granduncle, and his predictions. How true to form was this? she wondered. Had he been speaking in symbolic epigrams? Was the red path that led to the sun here on the caked and bloodied floor of this awful place that led to the sunlight outdoors? Had he foreseen this? Hadn't he called the killer Lopaka? Had he known this Lopaka Kowona all along? Was Lopaka Kowona the child in the story the old man told of a chief who had killed one son for his deformities while another watched? Serial killers were born of man and woman, many born of much less pain than this Lopaka suffered on seeing his crippled brother destroyed in a dark wood by his father, and later burned in the village pyre-slash-garbage dump, his bones unceremoniously dumped in the ocean where the sacrilegious and demonic were cast out.

She wondered how much of this "legend" and ancient history had to do with the real killer. She wondered how much—if any—of her visit to Kaniola's seer she wished to share with Jim; wondered whether now it had any relevance or not. All Parry and company need do now was to locate the whereabouts of Lopaka Kowona. As soon as the Hawaiian community learned that one of her own had been at bottom of the Trade Winds killings, as soon as Lopaka's name was made public throughout the islands, he would either be cornered by the authorities, or murdered quietly the way George Oniiwah had been. She had no illusions anymore about Joseph Kaniola's agenda. She knew that he would be, if given the chance, the one to ram the spear through Lopaka Kowona's heart, to end the life of this vampire who preyed on young Polynesian women.

Had Kaniola known of Lopaka, suspecting him for some time now? If the university professor Claxton and the lowlife Ewelo both knew of Lopaka, then the all-knowing, nosey newsman must've had some inkling, especially after Lopaka's police sketch and description were handed to him. Joe Kaniola was among the first in Hawaii to get this description, and his very next move was a friendly visit to his great-granduncle's shrine? Had he simply been using Jessica to loosen the old man's tongue? Perhaps and maybe, she thought, recalling the tape recorder at Kaniola's side.

Kaniola had been shrewd throughout, shrewd and determined to see that his son was avenged. Revenge was best served up cold, the old saying went, and it would seem that Kaniola's every move since his son's death had been quite cool, quite calculated.

"Jim, I've got to tell you about something," she finally said, while Parry, evidence bags in hand, was scooping up the dismembered hands of each victim of the Trade Winds Killer.

"What's that, Jess?"

She quickly surprised him about her early morning visit to the guru on the mountain.

"I've heard of the old man, but I didn't know he was related to Kaniola," Parry finally said. "Explains your new look."

She stared, her shoulders rising, her eyes questioning.

"Your cane. I noticed earlier that you were liberated from it. I was just naive enough to think that maybe I'd had something to do with its . . . disappearance."

"Yeah, well . . . maybe you did. Anyway, I had to give the old man *something*."

"In return for a handful of fifty-fifty generalizations any palm reader might've handed you?"

"He was extremely close to Lopaka Kowona's description, Jim. Pouting, large lips, flame-red hair, dysfunctional."

"But he couldn't give you a name and address . . ."

"No, but he may very well have given it to Joe Kaniola."

"Whataya' mean?"

"I think Kaniola went there hoping the old man would verify his own suspicion that you and I were wrong about Ewelo being the killer, and that the old man would confirm his conviction the killer was not in custody."

"So, you think Kaniola's going after this guy Lopaka?"

"If he finds him before we do, we'll be trying Joseph in a court of law instead of Lopaka," she said with certainty. "And as for the cane, Lomelea needed it more than I did."

He nodded, understanding. "I'll see where Kaniola is and put a tail on him."

"Good idea. Meantime, I'll do what I can here."

Watching Parry lift the bag of hands to give to Gagliano before he stepped back out into the light made a powerful image in her mind. This side of the door was like being in the looking glass; this side of the door was some rung in the spirals of Hades described in Dante's *Inferno*; on the other side of the door there was light and paradise waiting. She wondered what was hardest, stepping out or staying in. In Jim's case he'd go out to his car now, make some calls on his radio, feel the ocean breeze and God's warm hand in the form of sunlight against his brow, but he'd have to climb back into this red hell a second time. She and Gagliano remained this side of the mirror, in the bleak shadow world of evil and death and madness.

Her bag was passed through to her as if she and Gagliano were down inside a deep hole and those outside were providing a source of hope and sustenance from above. Still, none of the others wanted to climb down into the hole, content to watch from the other side of the looking glass.

Gagliano reached out to her, placing his meaty paw on her shoulder, and said, "Doc, I have to admit . . . you've got some grit."

"My father called it *sand*." She was privately pleased that Jim's best friend had finally accepted her.

Jessica now forced all annoyances, images, sights, sounds and odors and her own encroaching fears and phantoms from her consciousness; she pushed Jim and Tony and the racket of the others from her mind. She snatched open her valise and pulled forth her white lab coat and gloves. She searched next for the necessary tools of her trade. It was time to do her part.

— 18 —

The test of a first-rate intelligence is the ability to hold two opposing ideas in the mind at the same time, and still retain the ability to function.

F. Scott Fitzgerald, *The Crack-Up*

Dr. Asa Holcraft and others at the academy had taught her that there was no such thing as the ideal crime scene, but here in Lopaka Kowona's murderer's den, she and Parry had come damnably close to perfection. With the help of the FBI's Major Crime Scene Unit and ident techs from the HPD, the hours-long search now under the blindingly bright lights went ahead. Throughout the lair they uncovered much that would insure that Kowona would go down quickly and efficiently, unless defense counsel saw the fantastic opportunity presented him, deciding the Kowona case would mean a major leap forward for anyone capable of proving Kowona innocent by reason of insanity. She imagined some hotshot lawyer calling in his shrinks-for-hire one atop another, to attest to Kowona's inability to know right from wrong, good from evil or pain from pleasure, muddying the waters just enough for judge and jury with sad tales of civil-rights violations to the defendant, stories of childhood molestation, split-personality syndrome and a hundred other euphemisms for animal behavior. They'd done exactly that in the Matisak case and countless others. An eager young F. Lee Bailey could make Kowona out to be the victim, leave a jury believing that the real victims here—Lina Kahala, Kia, Hiilani and countless others—didn't much matter in the grand scheme of jurisprudence. Like the photos taken by the killer himself, which would likely be labeled as inflamatory and prejudicial and therefore inadmissable. Didn't matter, she kept telling herself, struggling to do her part to counter all the possible scenarios that lay ahead of them.

In order to convict, she had to do a painstaking job here and now.

"The ideal situation is the one you don't have," her M.E. father had once confided. "Whether it's a tourist attraction at Disneyland or a Georgia swamp. All you can do is your job, which is to protect the integrity of the crime scene and the gathered evidence, even from the fools who think it's their scene and evidence, too."

She had done a fair job of keeping control here, knowing there was no such thing as total control. Fibers, hairs and minutiae from the living would find a way into Hiilani's innumerable wounds. Hell, even a single open wound at the crime scene acted like a vacuum for all the microscopic debris floating by. The CSU guys at least knew enough to strap on aprons and hair nets just like the ones she'd pulled from the side pocket of her black valise. Still, Lau and his staff would have their hands full back at the lab. Everyone remotely near the body, including Jessica, would have to be ruled out as suspects when the specimens were examined under microscopic conditions. Evidence of Kowona's hair, fibers from his clothes were what was needed here, to corroborate the gruesome photos heedlessly left by the killer. At least the crime-scene photos taken here by FBI and HPD photographers could not be held inadmissable, not since Jim had been so careful about securing a warrant to search on probable cause.

When Parry asked her if she needed help orchestrating efforts here, she'd been short with him, replying curtly, "Just be damned sure that you protect the place from *everybody*. That includes the P.C."

Harold Shore, Chief Medical Examiner for all Oahu, who had

been gravely ill, had been escorted in by Police Commissioner Dave Scanlon, who wanted some say-so and input; in fact, he wanted the scene turned over to HPD, making loud noises about his jurisdictional powers here, regardless of the fact that "discovery" came out of an FBI investigation and warrant. The P.C.'s argument was that Kowona was wanted for killing two Oahu cops and attempted murder of a third, and also for killing at least three Honolulu civilians, not to mention the fact that Kowona's bloody bungalow sat just this side of his city limits.

"This is no time to be playing your fucking little political games, Scanlon!" Parry erupted, silencing everyone in the place. "Besides, we got him on multiple murders dating back to 1987. He's our man and this is our scene."

Jessica stopped in her work long enough to insist that the two angry men take it outside, which they did, Scanlon beet red. Shortly afterward, Jim Parry returned, his jaw firmly set but still quivering with rage. Yet he'd clearly come out today's winner. Jessica knew it for certain when the P.C.'s car squealed all the way down the street. Dr. Harold Shore, looking a little sheepish and uncomfortable, was left in the P.C.'s wake as both eyes and ears for his friend Scanlon.

Shore was not ancient by any stretch, perhaps in his late fifties, but his skin tone was ashen, his near-bald pate barely covered with angel hair, white, wispy and graveyard thin. Dark age spots made a polka-dot fabric of his forehead and hands, lending a brittle appearance. He'd obviously seen a lot over the span of his career, but like everyone here, he was stunned by the condition of the body still dangling from Lopaka's rack.

Jessica knew that if she and Shore could not play well together in this macabre sandbox, then the nightmare of problems arising long after they'd both left the scene could be enough to hand that hotshot defense counselor just what he wanted to prove police bungling and poke holes in the evidentiary protocol that a Cat bulldozer could be driven through.

"Some guys you just can't satisfy no matter what," Parry now said of the P.C., his eyes boring into Dr. Shore.

"Hey, Dr. Shore can't help it if Scanlon is a hemorrhagic fart," she ventured.

Shore erupted with laughter, and she knew immediately that she could work with this man.

Meanwhile, the CSU guys stretched a twanging, metallic tape

measure from two fixed points in the room to Hiilani's body, triangulating to fix the exact spot where she was found. It would form a ghastly thumbnail sketch, which she and others could use for future reference. The body was found intact, that is in one place, the shoulders dislocated from struggling against the bonds that held her fast, impaled butterfly-like, one final sword plunge fixing her to the wall so that even her entire weight pulling on the rack could not bring it off the wall. The rack itself would also be taken in evidence. Let's see 'em try to keep that out of the courtroom, Jessica silently mused. Aloud she said, "Talk about premeditation . . ."

She and Shore both saw that the cuts and tears from which her blood had run were symmetrical, one long scar down each side, followed by two lesser cuts coming together at the center of the body. Each cut was done with some precision and care so as to not perforate a vital organ or collapse a lung, all save the final plunge; ugly rents marred each arm, each cheek, each side of the throat; each breast had two sharp, distinct slashes, all done as she'd lived as indicated in the vital reactions around each wound. No doubt, after the first of several such slashes, Hiilani had been sent into a convulsive and merciful traumatic shock with the sudden blood loss. The insults were quickly classified as incisions by both Jessica and Shore.

Shore looked as if he might faint at this point, but he was instantly alert when Jim Parry, on hearing Shore use the word incisions, shouted in his face, "What the hell do you mean, incisions?"

"Not just incisions, Jim," she cut in. "Slices, rents, cautious piercings and controlled stabs."

"This sure as hell doesn't look controlled to me."

"We'll know more when we do some molds of the stab wounds," said Shore, "determine the exact number of cuts, the depth of each, the nature of each."

"But from where I stand," she continued, "I'd say our boy toyed with her for hours before he began the deep wounds, and by then, she was already dead."

"Don't hand me a pile of crap about he didn't mean to do it, Jessica."

"No one's saying that," she countered, angry at his tone.

"This creep's not getting off on some fucking technicality or nut plea, Jess."

"No one wants that," Shore insisted.

"But we've also got an obligation to the truth here, Jim," she said. "And no one knows that more than you. Besides, the fact the first cuts weren't meant to kill, but to torture, doesn't in any way lessen the crime. In fact, it makes it that much more grisly, and it makes Kowona even more vulnerable to an angry jury. The length of time she suffered is significant, but you know that already."

"So the first sallies weren't meant to kill, lending to the abduction murder the aspects of a true lust-killing," said Parry. "The brutal bastard was flipping off as he killed her, right?"

"Right."

"You got proof of that?"

"Enough seminal fluid to bathe in," said Shore dryly.

"We can nail this bastard six ways to Sunday," she assured Parry. "As soon as your people put him behind bars."

A torture-murder case. Jessica had seen some of these "signature" channels carved in flesh earlier, in the Linda Kahala arm. The distinctive, ritualistic, ceremonial slash had been photographed. A jury, comparing today's photos of the cleansed wounds once they got the body downtown, could not help but see the patterns, the ugly precision.

"This bastard knows how to handle his knives, just deep enough to draw blood," she told Parry.

Shore, nodding, shaken, mumbled something about retiring, before he added, "She didn't feel the final plunges, the crazed hacking."

Parry, amazed by the two medical people who were able to see patterns in the serrated, fleshy wounds and blood smeared torso, was duly impressed.

"They said you were good, Dr. Coran," said Shore, "but I had no idea. It has been a pleasure in one sense." He started to get up off the floor where he'd gathered his last samples of the seminal fluids and blood found below Hiilani's body. "Now, what say we get this poor creature into a body bag and transport her downtown to my office?"

"Sorry, Shore," countered Parry. "The body will remain under Dr. Coran's care."

Jessica, also fatigued, said, "Don't be silly, Jim."

"The body—" Parry began, but she quickly cut him off.

"The body will be available to you, Dr. Shore, anytime, and I'll make sure any specimens I take, you will get a duplicate of, and as for any lab results, I'll be happy to share these with you as well."

Shore's lined face compressed into a smile and he nodded approvingly. "You know how to soothe an old man, young lady. Very well, I'll take you at your word, and thank you."

Without another word, Shore climbed from the den and was gone.

"Did you have to be so rude to him?" she asked.

"I don't trust him, all right?"

"It's not Shore you don't trust, it's Scanlon."

"Exactly, and Scanlon controls Shore."

"I rather doubt that that's a fair assumption. Anyway, you're not going to last long as bureau chief if you can't sublimate some of those feelings, Jim. Trust me, I know. Politics and hopscotch: You've got to learn both."

"Or dance around 'em, like you? Yeah, well, I get a little upset when we do all the goddamned legwork and these clowns want to waltz in and claim all the glory."

"Jim, I know that's not what you're in it for, so give it a rest and who gives a damn about Scanlon's wanting to speechify before the damned cameras?"

"Last thing he wants to do is make speeches over this one."

"What?" She was confused by the remark.

He shrugged it off. "Forget it. Maybe you're right."

"I know I'm right, but just what—"

"That's what I like about you." He stared for a moment into her eyes. "Can we close down here now?"

"Yeah, everything that can be done here's done . . . and I need to wash my hair, shower . . . get this smell off me."

He nodded, understanding.

Whole rolls of film had been taken of the place and the body. Measurements and samples had been taken, and anything remotely looking like incriminating evidence was hauled away to join the swords headed for the property room downtown. The human hands, packed on ice, were headed for Lau's freezer. The crime-scene drawings were already being fed into a computer.

On the outside, more crime-scene sketches and a thorough search that had turned up nothing had been completed, and with darkness descending no one had turned up Lopaka Kowona.

In many ways now, she had come to know Kowona primarily

through the results of his maniacal butchering, not unlike the crazed cuttings of another killer known by the public for so many terrifying months as the Claw.

Kowona's obsession with rending flesh and harvesting human hair for rope and human teeth for leis they'd found about the house, along with his liking for the victims' hands, painted him in a different hue than Archer's more "civilized" Jack-the-Ripper approach. Archer had been a medical man who'd taken a step toward godhood no one should take; he'd fed immediate impulses, cannibalizing the flesh far more than Lopaka. Still, there were unmistakable similarities: Each monster had had an overall game plan, a plan that squared with premeditation and plotting. Like Kowona, the Claw selected his victims from the faceless masses of a city, but Archer had known his victims in a professional sense, as their doctor. Kowona, so far as she could see, only saw his victims through the haze of a maniacal lust, with a savage instinct to reduce them to sacrificial lambs.

Was there a gene that dictated the evil pathways, connections and helixes in the brain, twisting, coiling, and ultimately leading one to madness, leading another to hear voices that instructed him to kill, leading another to place his own needs—body, soul and spirit—above the right of another human being to live?

All that was left to do was to maintain the integrity of the Kowona case's physical evidence. The evidence locker had to be truck size. The body, taken down with a reverential touch by a pair of silent, gaping paramedics, who'd earlier been told to go away and return in four hours, was prepared for safe transport to Lau's labs.

Lau himself, hearing of the discovery, had come on scene and remained for an hour, shaken to the core by what he had seen. Unauthorized people were kept out and the chain of custody, so crucial in any murder case, was carefully guarded. Neither Parry nor Jessica wanted a single mistake to later haunt them. To this end, Jim and Tony escorted the coroner of record, Jessica, back to property lockup at the bureau and the lab. There she placed all medico-legal evidence under lock and key. It had been the lack of such procedures in the Claw case that had pretty well allowed that New York monster to freely roam for as long as he had.

It would be a while before Jessica could shower. Throughout the evidence-gathering, she had been careful not to meet Hiilani's open eyes. In fact, after taking some fluid from the eyes, treating them—and her—like a specimen in a science experiment, she'd asked one of the CSU guys to close the lids, to symbolically put Hiilani to sleep at last. Neither had she allowed herself to feel what the child-woman had felt here at the hands of a savage slayer who'd pierced her with metal swords in one hand while ejaculating on her with the other, directing his flow at or toward her vagina. Jessica had clung to the merciful thought that Hiilani had never felt the deepest and most damaging of the stabs he'd administered in his perverted mockery of the climax to his "sex act."

The victims of this brutal monster had been raped many times over, even, it appeared, after they'd left this world, making Parry's brutal fugitive also a necrophile.

"Let's get out of here, Jess." Jim's voice broke through her thoughts, and she looked back at him, her lower lip quivering a bit, the only sign of weakness in a day that called for incredible strength born of professional detachment. But at what cost, she wondered, unable to guess what it would ultimately mean to Jim and her.

How does Jim view me now? she wondered of Parry.

July 18, FBI Evidence-Property Room

Another night passed and still no sign of Lopaka. Moments after Kowona's door had been kicked in, an APB burned over the computer landscape to reach the entire island and her sister islands, and within an hour every law-enforcement official in the state was on the lookout for Lopaka Kowona, otherwise known as Robert Kowona.

Between bouts with the forensics gathering in Lau's labs, Jessica went to the sleek FBI evidence-property room, where she felt about as comfortable as at the Department of Motor Vehicles. She had to go through a near-endless round of paperwork and doors to examine the collective photographs and photo albums of Lopaka Kowona found at the scene. A stack of unopened letters taken from the Lopaka residence caught her immediate attention. She hadn't been told about the letters, which were written by Lopaka to his wife, Kelia. Each had come back unopened, postmarked undeliverable for one reason or another, return-to-sender rectangles in blood red. She opened each with great care and began reading. Each was a great outpouring of pain, regret and pleas for her to return to him. Maybe if she had . . . maybe she'd been dead, thought Jessica. Then she thought of the innocent string of young women who'd acted as stand-ins for his rage against her. In letter after letter, his handwriting coming more unglued as he wrote, he spoke of how for seven years he'd hunted down and killed for Kelia and the gods that directed him. He claimed it was all for her. For seven years, he had been trying to kill Kelia stand-ins, and now time was coming near for her to step into the breach, to sacrifice herself, if she wished to live forever.

The madness was apparent, but so too was the timing. The dates on the wedding pictures were well after the deaths of Lopaka's early victims. He'd somehow managed to marry one of his intended victims, it appeared, and she, suspecting his insanity perhaps, had left him. The fiend had rationalized killings that had taken place years before he'd ever met or married Kelia Laliiani, who had so feared him that she had escaped to the mainland, somewhere in southern California, it appeared. As evidenced by his photo collection, all the victims looked remarkably like Kelia. Little wonder he found Terri Reno not to his liking.

"Damn," she muttered aloud. She knew the letters and the fact he kept the gory death photos in albums were the perfect arguments for an insanity plea, that the letters documented his bizarre and singular behavior. He spoke of voices that were real to him, voices that would lead Kelia and him into the afterlife, a life filled with power and strength and dominance over all living things and the elements, such as the *trade winds*. He wrote that since she would not return, he could not be whole and would not be acceptable to his gods, and that if she did not come home, he'd be forced to find another to take her place.

He didn't speak of the details of his murders or of torture; he didn't speak of a depraved, perverted sexual drive that required blood for a hard-on and an ejaculation, except to say to Kelia that he would never again make her perform any sex act with which she felt uncomfortable.

"How sweet of him," Jessica said aloud to the notes.

A handwriting expert would be called in to testify to his madness. It was evident, the expert would say, in the absence of loops and ribbons, in the missing dots over the I's, in his failing to cross his T's, and in the pinched, pained flow of every word. An expert on sociopaths and psychos would be called in to testify how the poor devil had no feelings or emotional moorings, that he could not possibly empathize with the suffering of his victims, nor presumably help himself in his own compulsion for gratification gained only by hearing the screams and seeing the blood so that he could feel *something*—even if it was just an ejaculation.

"Bastard." She moaned inwardly, shoving the letters back into the stained manila envelope in which they'd been found. She questioned how they could possibly get a conviction if Kowona was judged mentally incapable of understanding his actions.

She wished momentarily that Tony hadn't been so thorough at Kowona's place, but the place had been so small nothing was overlooked. If only the madman's letters could disappear . . . But she knew there was no way.

A lot of cops and FBI agents were thinking exactly as she was, that in a way it was good that Lopaka Kowona was still on the loose out there, because now, armed with his identity, police might find it a simple matter to do the work of the courts for them. Were such thoughts blasphemous for someone in her position? Perhaps, but they were also undeniable.

She knew Jim Parry's thoughts were goose-stepping along the same tension wire when he'd asked her to review the letters in the first place, to see if she thought they were as damaging to a righteous conviction of Kowona as Jim did on his reading.

Alongside the love letters of the lust murderer, a pathetic little photo album found in a bookcase in the dark slaughterhouse, although less than half filled with images of Kowona and his wife, revealed a lot about Kowona besides his features. Kelia—as the hastily written captions below each shot called Mrs. Kowona—even in her jeans, looked like all of Lopaka's victims. A second and newer album had photos of Kelia on the right, Lopaka's victims in various stages of undress, distress, and mutilation on the left. It was self-evident from his ghoulish gallery that Lopaka was killing and dismantling his victims out of a cataclysmic hatred for the former Kelia Kowona.

Jessica found an office and a phone to use and worked most of the rest of the day trying to run Kelia Laliiani, a.k.a. Mrs. Lopaka Kowona, down. It took some extensive help from agents in California, but finally she was patched through to a woman answering to the name Kelia Laliiani in San Francisco.

Jessica found her most cooperative, her voice quivering from time to time as they spoke. Jessica opened with a warning, believing the woman had a right to know that her former husband was at large and wanted for mass murder.

"I knew . . . I knew it . . . I just knew one day he . . . Lopaka would do something like this. I told them he would . . ."

"Told who?" she asked, surprised. "Told family, friends?"

"Yes, but not jus' them. I told the police."

"Told the police? When?"

"Four years ago, before I left the islands. I wrote a detailed letter to the Honolulu police."

"I'll be damned," replied Jessica. "Did you address it to anyone in particular?"

"A guy, yeah, a cop working on some disappearances then."

"Do you remember the officer's name?"

"Yes."

"You remember from that far back?"

"No, now I see his name all the time, in the papers, in the *Ala Ohana.*"

"You get the *Ala Ohana* in San Fran—"

"It comes late, but I never miss an issue."

"Wasn't that dangerous? He could've traced you from your subscription."

"No subscription. An aunt, unknown to him, sends hers. I am still Hawaiian, and I care about the movement."

"The movement?"

"The nationalist movement, to return Hawaii to its rightful owners."

"*Hmmmm,* then you've also been reading about the Trade Winds Killer case all this time and failed to come forward?"

"What do you mean, failed? I wrote to the police and told them everything I suspected."

"Who, who did you write to?"

"Scanlon, the commissioner, but he was not commissioner when I first told him years and years ago about Lopaka, just before I left my homeland for here. I told him again when I read about the missing girls and the two police officers who were killed, and I reminded him that I told him so before."

"Scanlon," she repeated, incredulously. "What kind of response did you get for your trouble?"

"Nothing."

"Nothing?"

"Nothing."

It explained a lot. How the HPD happened by a dead-end street to find Lopaka's maroon sedan, leaking gas . . . how they had come to zero in on him some seven years too late.

"Christ, tell me all you can remember about Lopaka, please."

"All I remember?"

"What kind of man is he? Where is he likely to hide?"

"He is an insane half-breed, mixed up in his head about his ancestry, and he talks to himself."

"Half-breed?"

"Adopted by his father, or he was a stepfather, I'm not so sure, but he always talked about one day returning to his village and killing his father. He was cruel with me. Tied me up, played . . . toyed with me . . . with his knives. Once . . . once, and I ran first chance I got."

Once again, it seemed the predictions of Lomelea, the old prophet, were coming true.

After she had gotten off the line with Kelia Laliiani, Jessica wondered what Jim Parry might make of this information; certainly it would put him in a much stronger position should the P.C. ever have the balls to go after him.

Finding her way out of the evidence lockup area, she gave a thought to the grotesque collection of hands Lopaka had foolishly kept; these could prove valuable, though long bones were always easier to identity via long-bone X-ray of arms and legs, if the victims' X-ray histories involved any of these. However, the rings still found on the hands—Lopaka was obviously disinterested in jewelry—could be identified by family members. Lau was also working on that tedious and sad process now.

She had to get back to the lab. The autopsy on Hiilani would begin at ten sharp. She'd gotten her rest, sleeping alone the night before, Parry having called her from his desk. He'd been obsessed with the case when she met him, and he was even more so now that he could smell something other than the odor of the victims' blood. Now he could smell the blood of his prey, Lopaka Kowona's blood.

19

Quarry mine, blessed am I
In the luck of the chase.
Comes the deer to my singing.

Navaho Hunting Song

July 18, FBI Headquarters

It was growing late, almost twenty-four hours since Lopaka Kowona's moldering bungalow was turned out for the world to see. Jim Parry had just finished staring once more through Lopaka's disgusting victim photos. He next examined the mildewed, dusty black binder, which revealed the man's early days with his wife, Kelia.

The photo album had shots of Lopaka on horseback swinging a rope overhead, a herd of grazing cows in the background. Parry was running it by people in the know, including Hal Ewelo in his cell, trying to get a fix on the name and location of the ranch. There were all manner of pictures of Lopaka sporting long knives and swords, several of which had been confiscated as evidence, some of which would undoubtably match the Hiilani girl's wounds, their edges and the corresponding marks on her flesh fitting together like pieces of a de Sade puzzle. There was another photo collection, separate from this album, which featured each of his swords, some extremely expensive and beautifully ornamented.

A dealer was called in and grilled about the types of weapons, their availability and prices. He was startled by one sword in particular, declaring it to be priceless, an ancient ceremonial blade that people in the business world literally cut their own throats for.

"How'd he get hold of such a sword if no one knew of its existence?" had been Parry's immediate response.

"Maybe he murdered someone for it? Most certainly it's a stolen piece, perhaps from a museum or one of the old traditionalist families," replied Arthur Early, curator of the Museum of Antiquities at the University of Hawaii, when Parry consulted him.

"Call the Bishop Museum," Parry told Gagliano after Early had left. "See if they're missing anything, but don't lead them. Don't tell them what we have."

"Hey, leave it to me," Gagliano assured him.

"What's the street word on Kowona's whereabouts?"

"Silence, nothing."

"That's bullshit. Somebody's gotta know where the SOB goes when he gets scared."

"Nobody's talking, else they really don't know. He's been a loner for a long time, and even family—and it seems he's got some on the island—aren't sure, as I read 'em. They say nobody ever went near him, especially after his wife left him. Said he didn't come around."

"Somebody's lying."

"Sure somebody's lying, but I haven't found him yet."

Parry's exasperation escaped in a sigh. He fell into his chair, stared about the room and put up his hands. "The guy just disappears off the face of the . . . islands?"

"Could've gotten a plane to the mainland. Could've done so under an assumed name, hours before we got to his place."

"Check out the museum lead. See if anybody there knows a Lopaka Kowona, if a Robert or a Bob matching his description ever worked there."

"You got it, Chief, and hey, maybe you'd best get some shut-eye."

It was getting dark again and Parry had been pulling a

twenty-four-hour shift. So long as Jessica was exhausting her efforts at the lab, he felt the least he could do was exhaust his efforts at headquarters.

Then he thought of Jospeh Kaniola and George Oniiwah. It was Kaniola's paper that had gotten Oniiwah killed, so far as Parry was concerned. Maybe Kaniola had other thug friends like the owner of Paniolo's who, for a price, would take Lopaka Kowona to a deserted beach and kick the shit and life out of him before feeding him to the sea turtles.

It was the kind of island justice that had been in operation since men first discovered the islands and set up shop; it had survived civilization, the presence of the U.S. Navy, the white man's law and courts, and it would survive Jim Parry, he reasoned. But damnit, he had a right to Kowona as much as anyone. Who was it that'd brought the case out of an officially sanctioned oblivion— *"who cares if a few* kanaka *whores are taken off the street"* —and dragged it kicking and screaming into the light? Not the HPD, not Scanlon for damned sure, not the nationalists, not Kaniola's fucking newspaper, not the FBI . . . *but him alone*. The least he deserved was to see the case through and to know Kowona's fate, and in the best of all possible worlds, to mete out that fate.

Where was the justice? Where was the bastard?

He got into his car and rushed through congested traffic, honking at the tourists buses, to get to the *Ala Ohana* storefront office. He found Joe Kaniola behind his desk, his secretary trying desperately to stop the bulldozing FBI man, but far too small to accomplish the task. She looked like a grown-up Hiilani, he thought.

"That's all right, Suzy," Kaniola called to her as he saw the train coming. "Welcome to my humble establishment, Chief—"

"Cut the *pilau*, Joe. I want to know what the word is out there on Robert Kowona, and don't give me any shit about how you don't know any-fucking-thing."

"Like I told Tony, I don't. I swear it. The street's gone stone deaf and dumb on this, almost like everybody agrees with the sonofa-bitch who killed my kid, that what he's doing is righteous, or some such fucking dog crap."

The tone of Joe Kaniola's voice and the conviction in his eye calmed Parry a bit. "Why? Why would your people—"

"First off, they're not *my* people . . . not no more. Not if they're hiding that sickening bastard. They're nobody's people. They're more displaced and disenfranchised than ever if—"

"I didn't come here for a goddamned political debate on the conditions prevailing in the islands, Joe. I came here for some answers."

"And I'm telling you that no fucking one's talking, *no one*!"

"HPD behind this? Your Hawaiian civil rights PKO guys? Who?"

"If I knew—"

"I'd be the last you'd tell, I know, but maybe if you got your goddamned dentures cracked . . ."

Kaniola whipped out a gun from his top drawer when he saw that Parry was serious. "You lay a hand on me, and there'll be something new for this town to talk about."

"Put it away! Mr. Kaniola, don't!" shouted Suzy.

The two men, staring across the desk at one another, were like a pair of bulls sizing each other up. Little Suzy stamped her foot and repeated her demand, until Kaniola, relenting, allowed the gun to softly slide back into its hiding place.

"I keep it for protection. You got no idea how often some bozo comes in here threatening me."

Parry gave a little shrug. "Likely a daily occurrence. Lucky you've got Suzy here on your side."

"This thing with Kowona, it has no sides," he replied, pulling at his facial hair, shaking his head. "I mean, everybody I speak to wants him dead; everybody is looking for him. I can't believe he just vanished, but they say he is a survivalist type, and if he had gotten up into the mountains, well . . . it'll take the entire U.S. Army on foot to get him out of there. But bottom line is, nobody's helping him, not even his family."

"Take me to them."

"Who?"

"His family."

"They're scattered all over. That would take all night, and the way you look and smell, Mr. Parry . . . why don't you go home, get some rest."

"Goddamnit, Joe!"

"All right . . . all right . . . but I got duties here. I'll get a cousin of mine to drive you round."

"Whatever and however, but I want to talk to everyone remotely related to this animal."

"I've already done it. You'll be wasting your time, I tell you."

Suzy handed Parry a cup of steaming tea. He looked into her big, oval eyes. She was pretty and petite, a candidate for Kelia's murdering husband if she were six or seven years younger.

"I am shamed to say I'm second cousin to Kowona," she quietly admitted, "and Mr. Kaniola is telling truth. No one in my family knows where 'bout he is hiding. He jus' never did come by. I don't think I would know him if I see him. My mother remembers him, but even she say she would never have nothing to do with him, that he was *ona lama, maino* and *hewahewa.*"

Joe Kaniola was blinking furiously. "You never tol' me you were related!"

"Nobody want say dey related to him, 'specially now, Mr. Kaniola." Her oval eyes drooped. "I afraid for my job here."

Kaniola asked her pointedly, "*Pupule?* You mean, insane?"

"Jus' what I say, alcoholic, crazy and cruel."

Kaniola nodded. "Come on," he said to Parry. "I'll take you to see Suzy's mother, but that's all I can do. From there, you're on your own."

Parry relented, feeling that both Suzy and Kaniola were being straight with him. Even if they had resorted to their Polynesian language, their body language spoke plainly enough.

The visit to the girl's mother proved yet another dead end, however. She knew nothing and was without guile, and Kaniola reiterated his faith that no one knew anything, and that most likely the psycho had seen from a distance that they'd discovered and turned out his killing ground, and so had fled most likely into the thick cover of the jungle in the Koolau mountain range just above his house.

"And just how long do you suppose he could survive up there?" Parry asked sarcastically, pointing to the enormous dark green range at the center of Oahu, troubling clouds at the summit.

"How long can the wild beast exist in its home?"

"He's that comfortable in the rain forest?"

"Yes, well, he grew up in the jungle."

"How do you know that?"

"Most of his family, his immediate family, lived on Molokai's remotest edge."

"Molokai?" Parry fixed for a moment on the size, shape and

location of one of the more remote and less visited islands in the Hawaiian chain. "Then maybe he's run to Molokai."

"Perhaps, but unlikely."

"Unlikely? Why?"

Kaniola stroked his small beard. "He himself was made an outcast, or so the story goes. Any of the family can always return home, that is a given, but Lopaka was officially banished from that place."

"Why was he banished? For crimes against man?"

"A series of troubles with his father, the chief, which some say began with the death of a girl child when Lopaka was hardly more than a child himself. But nothing was ever proven. When he came of age, he was sent away, lived for some time in Maui by his own wits. Later, he came here and enrolled in college without much of a plan; he'd gone to the missionary school on Molokai and there learned the white ways, and his father, a chief, had believed there was some special reason for his having conceived Lopaka with a white woman, some notion he would learn white magic. But the old chief never completely accepted the son, treating him like an orphan, an adoptee or foundling, finally claiming the boy was not his and banishing him."

"So Lopaka's mother was a white woman, a *haole*?"

"His mother was British, yes."

Parry and the others had remarked how soft and fine Lopaka's features were despite the native rust-colored skin and kinky red hair. "Go on."

"Lopaka's story was told to Dr. Coran by my great-granduncle."

"Yes, she's told me about her visit to him, and how helpful he was."

"Then you know Lopaka saw his brother killed by his father, his body burned to return it to the gods."

"Sounds all a bit fairy-tale-ish for me. But tell me, this brother was also from the white mother?"

"The brother was actually no relation, just a friend adopted by Lopaka, made his brother through a secret pact between them, but Lopaka himself considered the other boy his *twin,* or so it is told. The other boy was supposedly malformed."

"Defiled, so to speak?" asked Parry.

"One of the enticements of Christianity for my people, a casting away of such superstitions that lead to killing a retarded child, yes . . . yes, defiled."

"Then your great-granduncle knows a lot about this Lopaka?"

"He knows every important person's history."

"Every important person's history? What do you mean by important?"

"Lopaka is the son of a chief, *Chief*."

Parry's mouth swung open a moment before he continued his interrogation. "A chief? A chief on Molokai? What's his name . . . no, don't tell me. Kowona."

"Precisely."

"And so what happened? The chief banished his own son, or sent him away to college?"

"Sent him away to school, but on learning that the boy was not attending school and instead squandering his money on a young woman, and then when he married without the father's permission, he was banned from the island."

"Not because he kills young girls? But because he marries a girl here, he's banished?"

"Island law makes about as much sense as white law, my friend. Besides, the chief never believed his son truly evil."

"Everyone knew about this story?"

"It was repeated so many times it took on the quality of a legend, or as you say, fairy tale."

"Which is it? Truth or fiction?"

"Look around you, Parry," said Kaniola, waving a hand like a wand into the Hawaiian night sky. "Who can say what in Hawaii is truth, what is myth?"

"I see . . ."

"Like your white urban myths."

"So no one thought this guy anything but harmless?"

"On the contrary, you heard what Suzy and her mother said about him, but then, there's thousands of islanders, both Polynesians and Samoans, who are alcoholic, cruel and crazy."

"That's a fact."

"Just as there are as many whites with the same attributes, including your men in uniform at the bases. So why would anyone single out Lopaka Kowona as the most likely candidate to be a psychopath?"

"If someone had come forward, maybe your son and Thom Hilani and some forty-five young women would be alive today."

Kaniola hung his head at the mention of his son's name. "But you know, same as I, that nobody did . . . come forward."

"His wife, Kelia, from the mainland. You know about her?"

"I knew she ran away from here."

"Did your son, Alan, know about the Kowonas?"

"Course not. I didn't even know much. This was a long time after the first disappearance, long before DNA matching became standard practice, and there was no real evidence anyone had actually been murdered. You know how active the slave trade is around here. For long time we all thought the wife was abducted or dead. Besides, my boy wasn't even in the academy yet. I never heard the story until Lopaka's name was put on the wires yesterday. Ever'body in the family heard the wife's story of abuse and her suspicions but ever'body also dismissed it."

"Why's that?"

"The family believed Kelia was just lashing out, trying to hurt him, so they'd dismissed it."

"Same as the HPD?"

"I'm telling you that Lopaka's wife informed the Honolulu cops of her suspicions. But then the suspicions of a wife are often ignored."

"Well, Joe, thanks for the education. Dr. Coran's working on trying to get the wife on a plane back here."

"From what I hear, she'll never return; she fears him too much."

"Well, we'll see."

"If you do get her back, I'd like to interview her myself."

"I'll see what can be arranged."

They parted on much better terms than they'd ever enjoyed in the past. "Could've knocked me over with a pillow when I learned the killer was one of us *and* one of you, *hapa haole*; in a sense, from the beginning, I guess, we were both right about the racial makeup of the killer," said Kaniola, walking him out to his car. "I hope it doesn't foretell the future."

"I don't possess any crystal ball and I'm no prophet, but I'm sure Oahu hasn't seen the last of Kowona's kind. I just hope your people and mine can cooperate better than we have on this case."

He nodded. "I welcome that day."

"As I've said before, Joe, I'm sorry you lost your son to this maniac."

"When you catch him, Chief Parry, just make sure he's put away in the deepest hole you can find at Dillingham."

Once again Parry privately thought that life in the state pen was hardly appropriate. "We're going to do our damndest on that score."

"But you can guarantee nothing, I'm afraid."

Parry shrugged, saying, "What with the intricacies and complications of the system?"

"A simple justice is all we ask."

"A simple justice . . . sounds like an antiquated idea in our times, Mr. Kaniola—"

"Joe, call me Joe."

"—but as I said, Joe, we'll prosecute with everything we have, which is considerable, and we hate this bastard as passionately as you, but that's not for print."

"Understood." Kaniola managed a half smile and slapped him on the back. "I'm confident you will have him in custody within a day or so."

They shook hands and Parry motored off for his house and some much-needed sleep. Along the way, he radioed in, telling Tony about the jungle theory and that the Army should be contacted and asked to help out on a sweep of the mountainous terrain just above and around the Lopaka house. Helicopters might also be dispatched for a wider sweep.

Gagliano thought it a good idea as no evidence that the murdering Kowona had gotten off the island either by plane or boat had surfaced. "Sure," Gagliano said on the other end, "he hasn't gone anywhere. The creep's up there in the greenery like a murdering ape, ready to take up where he left off as soon as everything cools off. Bastard's become an animal, Jim."

"Any luck at the museum and where he worked?"

"Bus line acts' if he never *sat* in a bus, as if they'd fired him a year ago."

"They fire him?"

"No, hell; they just want to make out as if he didn't belong to them, get me?"

"Got it."

"Act as if they know as much about him as they do the motors under the hood, you follow? Did some cursing down there."

"What about the museum?"

"*Nada,* but they were real interested in the sword."

"You didn't give them the damned sword, did you?"

"Hell, no, just a copy of the photo. Tellin' you, Jimbo, they went like nuts for it. Recognized it, too."

"Recognized it?"

"Said it was from the *Kowona* dynasty, which I ain't never heard of, but then—"

"Get to the point, Tony!"

"The point, Jim, is this: It came from an ancient tribal group that once lived on Kahoolawe."

Kahoolawe, the forbidden isle, the island where even the FBI had no juice; the island that was now protected as a last bastion of Hawaiian culture and religion, supporting a lifestyle that had no room for deformed or maladjusted children, a land truly meant for the ancient rites and simple justice that Kaniola had referred to, a land like remote Molokai which had spawned Lopaka, a land which had spawned this beautifully ornamented, ceremonial sword he'd used on his victims, which the Bishop Museum people might kill for . . .

Parry next asked Dispatch to put him through to Lau's labs to speak to Jessica to learn what was going on at her end.

In a moment she came on a bit breathless, telling him of her bizarre phone conversation with Kelia Laliiani and the fact that the HPD had been warned years before—and quite recently—about Lopaka Kowona, but that she'd been ignored.

"Why the hell didn't she contact us?" he asked.

"I asked her that on a follow-up call."

"What did she say?"

"She was told by a brother that telling the HPD was the same as telling the FBI."

"That's some excuse."

"She also said she didn't know Hawaii had an FBI bureau."

"It's always been a fairly well kept secret, yeah. People!"

"The important thing here, Jim, and I want you not to go crazy if I tell you . . . promise?"

"What?"

"Promise me you won't go ballistic?"

"Goddamnit, Jess, out with it."

"The guy she wrote to at the time was the captain of a major precinct who'd been working the disappearances."

"Scanlon, yeah, I know he was working the original cases. Got that from my own research, but—"

"She read about him in the *Ala Ohana* and sent him a letter directing him to check Lopaka Kowona and his place out, but nothing was done, or so she believes."

"Something was done, Jess," he countered.

"What? How do you know?"

"It was filed away with every one of thousands of unsolicited letters regarding the disappearances. Scanlon was up for P.C., and the case was a drag on his career and he knew it. He found a drawer and lost the case file for as long as it took. In the meantime, each year since, there've been more disappearances, and Scanlon's been blackmailed ever since."

"Blackmailed? Christ, by whom? You don't mean Joe—"

"Whoa, whoa, I was speaking figuratively, sweetheart."

"Jeez, we don't need another complication in this mess."

"Tell me about it, but Scanlon's running scared now. You saw him at the scene. He's being blackmailed by his own damned conscience, and I can't blame him. Hell, I know he's an airhead politico with ambitions and a finger up his ass, but he's also got a decent side that has to be *ripped* by all this."

"You think so?"

"Well, yeah, I believe so."

"Then hold onto your seat, love."

"What's that?"

"Scanlon was contacted by Kelia again after his two cops were killed out at Koko Head. She tried to revive her earlier complaints against her 'crazy,' estranged husband, but once again Scanlon ignored her."

"He didn't completely ignore her the first time around, Jess. According to police reports of the time, he dispatched a squad car to look into Mr. Kowona's doings, but they came back empty-handed. Hell, I saw the same complaint and follow-up myself, but amid the thousands of others . . . well, it meant very little."

"So? What about after Kaniola and Hilani were gunned down? Scanlon ignored her again."

"It was no longer his case. He's the commish now, so if anyone was told to look into it, which I doubt, it'd have to be a direct order from him. It was probably handled as just another crackpot call."

"Letter . . . she wrote him from California."

"Mail to the police, even addressed to the P.C., goes through thirty steps before it lands on the proper desk, and with a politically involved guy like Scanlon, you're looking at weeks before he opens his mail unless it had a return address to the mayor or the governor. In point of fact, a secretary probably re-routed the letter before he ever had a chance to see it. Still, somebody in the chain must've spoken to him about it and it clicked some tumbler in his memory, because he did in the end send a squad car around to check on Lopaka, and that's how Lopaka's car was spotted. I only learned of it because I was with Ivers when that baby-faced cop Janklow wanted to personally tell Ivers about it. I immediately got HPD to hold off only because Scanlon was away, something about a fund-raiser on Maui."

"How's your friend's eyes?" she asked.

"Healing, prognosis for recovery is good. Anyway, now we both understand why Scanlon wanted control of the crime scene the other day. Why he was so damned adamant. Now he's running scared; now he really is vulnerable to blackmail, and maybe one day I'll collect on that note."

"Let 'im sweat, huh?"

"Teach him to prick around in my cases."

"I'm sure he's saying precisely the same about you right now. Better watch your back."

"Yeah, I've given that some thought. Remember what happened to my LTD? That bastard ordered his cops to stand down on that. I had a creepy feeling about it when it happened, but now I know."

"Jesus, Jim, be careful out there. Where are you now?"

"Just pulling into my driveway."

"Don't leave your car out."

"Yeah, next thing you know there'll be a ticking package in the mail for me."

"You're joking, right?"

"Just one favor, dear."

"What's that?"

"Promise me you'll get the evidence on the bastard to put him away if anything should ever happen to me."

"Nothing's going to happen to you."

"Promise?"

"Nothing's going to happen to you—"

"Promise!"

"—'cause you won't let it happen, not if you . . . care about me."

"So, anything new in the slab lab?"

"Shore and I were right about the nature of the wounds. She died of bloodletting . . . accompanying shock, after which Kowona drove the blades through her with enough force to bring down a rhino. You get a sense he gets off on seeing the muscle spasms and the body dance on impact, but first he had to draw his tattoo patterns over the flesh."

"Concerned about taboos," said Parry.

"Say again?"

"The true native doesn't make a move without blessing every this-and-that in sight; the ornamental slashes were to bless the offering, make it as pure or puree as flesh gets, I suppose, for the gods."

"Who've you been talking to?"

"Got some info from a university prof."

"*Hmmmm* . . . Sounds like Kaniola's great-granduncle."

"Yeah, well, Joseph says the streets are stone cold for information on Lopaka's whereabouts. He could be anywhere. Could be in California, going for the real Kelia . . . could be on another island, or he could be under our noses." He quickly explained Kaniola's theory that Lopaka was hiding out in the Koolau Mountains.

"God, from what I saw up there at Lomelea's shrine . . . hell, the bastard could disappear in a moment if a helicopter passes over. A foot search'll be difficult, time-consuming and costly," she said thoughtfully.

"Whatever it takes. Tony's calling out the Army-Navy guys now."

"You get some rest," she told him. "I can hear tired coming through the line."

They said good night and Parry, having parked in his garage and having cut off the motor, wearily pulled himself from the car. In the shadows, just outside the unlit garage, there stood a man as tall as Jim, staring. Unable to see anything metallic in the man's hand, Jim nonetheless momentarily wondered if he'd be found dead here the next morning, a .38 slug in his chest. The figure could be only one man, he surmised.

"Scanlon? What the hell're you doing here?"

"Been waiting for you to get home now for some time, Jim. Wanted to apologize for yesterday . . . at the scene . . ."

"Forgotten, old news, Commissioner."

"I . . . I want a truce, Jim, between you and me, I mean. I want our separate agencies to work in better harmony, you know that, you've got to know that."

"Sure, sure, I know that." There was no gun in the man's hand, only a heavy weariness in his voice. He had been sweating, just as

Jess had said, in dread fear that his *oversights* would be tomorrow's front-page story in Kaniola's *Ala Ohana*.

"You spent some time with Kaniola today," he said as if reading Parry's mind.

"That's right. Look, Scanlon, you want to come inside for coffee or something and we can sit, talk?"

"I didn't come for coffee, Parry, or any bullshit. I come to say I've been wrong, to say it like a man, to put it on the table. Maybe if I'd been more of a cop and less of a . . . a . . ."

"Ambitious man?"

". . . then maybe I'd have seen this creep for what he was the first time around."

"Or maybe the second?"

"Damnit, Parry, there were a thousand leads; you know how many women get battered by their husbands and see a story in the papers and come running to us with some wild story about how her man's a rapist or serial killer or an alien from another friggin' world?" His laugh was hollow, unfelt. "Christ, we do . . . *I* did what I could. When I was working the case, I didn't have any help, no task force, nothing, and everybody—and I mean *everyone*—treated it like a street-sweeper job."

"A street-sweeper job?"

"You know, so many derelicts off the streets, so who's going to miss 'em, right? That was the mentality I was dealing with when Price was P.C. I couldn't get manpower on the thing, and I was fucking inundated, and there were a string of high-rise robberies, a hostage deal and the visit from the damned Pope!"

It all sounded like a series of hollow excuses to Jim Parry, but he raised a hand to Scanlon and said, "Listen, Commissioner, that's all ancient history so far's I'm concerned. I haven't discussed this with anyone." He didn't include Jessica. "Certainly will never talk to Joe Kaniola about it, especially if relations between your office and mine are kept amenable."

Scanlon, ever the politician, caught the veiled threat like a pro, his mitt held at just the right angle. "Sure, sure, Jim. Just like Shore said when he got back. We can learn from one another, support one another. Anything your office ever needs just—"

"At the moment I do need every available officer for a sweep of the mountains above Lopaka's house. Whataya say?"

"I can arrange it, sure. When?"

"Tomorrow, daybreak. Have them coordinate with Agent Tony Gagliano and the Army."

"Not a problem. What else you need, Jim? Name it."

"Sleep, I need sleep, so good night, Commissioner."

"Yeah, good night, Chief . . . Jim."

Parry had moved closer and closer to his kitchen door, and now he zapped the down button on his garage door, which clattered chain-and-drumlike in Scanlon's face. It gave Parry great satisfaction, the entire scene.

— 20 —

It's like a lion at the door;
And when the door begins to crack,
It's like a stick across your back;
And when your back begins to smart,
It's like a penknife in your heart;
And when your heart begins to bleed,
You're dead and dead and dead indeed

Anonymous Nursery Rhyme

July 19, Honolulu

Dawn this side of the great island of Oahu was different from dawn in other places around the globe, and this was especially true in Honolulu. Here dawn meant a sensual softening and gradual lightening in the eastern sky while La—the sun itself—remained in hiding, invisible during this long twilight period since it rose from the windward side of the four-thousand-foot pinnacle of the Koolau Mountains, a natural border which rimmed the city on the east, and into which most people now believed Lopaka "Robert" Kowona had escaped.

It was to this sunless gray dawn light, seeping in and wending its way into his bed, that Parry awoke. He was helped along from his slumber by the shrill cry of his telephone, which he desperately wanted to ignore. And he did so until he could stand it no more.

"Parry!" he barked. "This better be good!"

"It's me, Gag."

"Tony? What's up?"

"We're in position and near ready with the search teams at the location where we think Lopaka Kowona might've gone in, Chief. Thought you'd want to be alerted."

"Where've you set up?"

Tony described the location of the command post.

"Yeah, I know 'bout where that is."

"We've been under way since before daybreak. Come join us. Should be fun." Tony's tone and emphasis on the word *fun* dripped with sarcasm.

"Dr. Coran been alerted, Tony?"

He hesitated. "I can call her after we hang up."

"Do that. Keep her fully apprised; you got that, Tony? Tony?"

"If you say so, Chief."

"I say so. Don't forget, we asked her in on this case, pal, and without her we'd still be blowing smoke."

"All right, all right. She's just . . ."

"Just what, Tony? Out with it."

Tony hesitated before saying, "Distracting."

"Distracting? Why, Tony, I didn't notice you noticed."

He grunted and said, "I noticed you two together are distracting for one another, Chief."

"Good! I'm glad your eyesight's not fully gone, buddy. Now mind your own goddamned business, okay? Just do your job, okay?"

Parry grimaced into the phone, angry with himself for losing it, half understanding Tony's concern. But the big Italiano angered him, too. Tony could be so damned stubborn, he thought. "Just concentrate for the time being on the manhunt, okay, Gag?"

"Every man and dog knows what he's looking for," Gagliano continued, wanting to add, *Do you?* but thinking better of it.

"So, what's the problem, Tony?"

"No problem . . . not really, sir."

The use of "sir" was a sure sign there was a problem. "Damnit, Tony, I got no time, and I'm in no mood for twenty fucking questions."

"Hey, I just thought you'd like to know about the word on Bethel at Hotel, and on River Street."

Parry knew each corner gathering place with its tavern row, a hotbed of street information representing the entire rainbow from truth to gossip to pure fabrication, a gauntlet for the detective to run. What Joe Citizen thought and what he knew often broke a case wide open. River Street ran through the slum areas just northwest of downtown Honolulu.

"I'm hearing the same story all over, Chief, down in Chinatown, too, and I get the same word from the wharf rats."

"Really?" Parry was instantly curious. The wharf rats were Hawaiians and half-Hawaiians who worked as stevedores and mechanics and hands along the wharves. They routinely hung about Aala Park when relaxing with a beer and a smoke. Their talk was never guarded or encumbered by fears that anyone might care enough about what they said to pay any attention. It was a far cry from the mentality of the Oahu Country Club set.

"What's the word around, Tony?" he asked, wondering if it might jibe with the information he had himself picked up on Kukui Street where local sailors and "homeboys" hung out, frequently settling differences of opinion loudly and violently. But the word he'd been hearing on the street had been directly countered by Joe Kaniola the evening before.

"Spill it, Tony. What're you hearing?"

"That Lopaka got a boat out."

"Really? Out of where?"

"Other side of the island, Mokapu Point, Kaneohe Bay."

It was one of the old ports, used by innumerable small fishing vessels, by many native fishermen who skirted the law in Hawaii with both abandon and finesse. "You think there's any truth to it?"

"If there is . . . a search of the mountainside's a really stupid idea. And you know the *kanakas*. They'd go to the mainland and back if they thought they could make a *haole* — especially one in a position of authority — look stupid, Boss."

"So people've told you he got a boat out of Kaneohe Bay and so — "

"Possibly Heeia Kea Boat Harbor, Boss."

"What kind of a boat, Tony? Did you get a fix on it?"

"Fishing vessel, in ill repair."

"Wow, that really narrows it down." Now it was Parry who was sarcastic. "What about its call numbers, its goddamn name, the captain?"

"Sorry, Boss . . . couldn't get anything specific on it, except that it sailed for Molokai."

"Molokai, huh?" Parry's thoughts came in a plethora of recall and questions. Molokai had been home to Lopaka Kowona in his childhood. It would follow that he'd race for some safe place, somewhere he felt comfortable. On the other hand, he'd been banished from that place by his chieftain father. And people like Kaniola were sending messages that were going counter to one another . . .

Tony kept talking. "Even the wharf rats were guarded about it, but I loosened some tongues with a few greenbacks and, well . . ."

"And well what?" Parry threw his legs over the edge of the bed and sat up.

"Sounds possible that whoever boarded Lopaka was maybe a family member or members."

This gave Parry pause, recalling how deftly Kaniola and Lopaka's aunt and cousin had played him. Wouldn't touch Lopaka with a ten-foot pole, huh? But why would Kaniola aid and abet his son's killer? How could he? For the cause of native rights maybe, all that self-determination crap? An order handed down by the PKO? Possibly, for some more fanatical members had already proven that they could be dangerous when they had George Oniiwah abducted, and Kaniola did have his grandchildren to think of, not to mention his wife.

"Destination Molokai confirmed by more than one?" Parry now asked.

"One or two said Maui . . . but the consensus was the closer island, yeah."

"Really?"

"That's what everybody's saying."

"Everybody?"

"Everyone that's talking, that is."

"You haul anyone in on this, do any shakedowns? Make any arrest for aiding and abetting?"

"No, nothing 'long those lines, but I'd be more'n happy to start on that course, if you—"

"What do you think, Tony? I mean about the *reliability* of the information?"

"I think it bears looking into, Chief."

"Why?"

"I dunno . . . same reason I believed George Oniiwah was innocent. 'Sides, these are *kanakas* we're talking about."

Parry let out a breath of exasperation. "What is that supposed to mean, Tony?"

"*Kanakas* have a lot of great qualities, strong hearts, pleasant manners, generous natures, even good diets, I hear, and I grant you that once a friend always loyal as hell, but a crafty ability at conspiracy? That's for us *pie-zanoz,* heh? Just isn't something I'd expect from the Hawaiians, Chief, not even the PKO."

Parry considered the wisdom being hoisted on him by Gagliano, an Italian-American FBI agent passing judgment on the entire Hawaiian race, saying they were incapable of shuffling off one of their own and keeping it a secret. And even if it were marginally true, what did this say about Parry's own foolishness, his being snookered by Kaniola's "golly gee, friendly Mickey Rooney" imitation of the night before? Sure Parry was fatigued, overworked and overtired at the time, but he should have seen through the masquerade. Joe knew that he'd be coming to have it out with him, so he'd prepared a welcoming. Reaching for the gun had been a nice touch, as was the innocent-eyed and protective secretary.

"For money," said Parry, "I don't know a lot of people of any stripe, Tony, who wouldn't turn on their own. What about that reward? Did the info get to the press?"

"A $50,000 reward was posted for information leading to the capture and conviction of Lopaka Kowona.

"This morning."

"Somebody'll turn in the bastard." Parry breathed heavily into the phone, silent a moment, giving his next move some thought.

"I know you got word to the contrary, Jim, I mean that he's somewhere in the Koolaus, but I've got my doubts now."

He thought again of Kaniola's having so completely faked him out. "Yeah, I got word to the contrary, Tony."

"You trust it?"

Without answering Tony, he said, "Look, you think you can manage with the mountain search? We've got no choice now but to see it through, and it'll give Scanlon something to do, and since we've already called out the goddamned U.S. Army . . ."

"Sure, sure, but what're you going to be doing, Jim?"

Parry had climbed from bed and was pulling on a pair of trousers, balancing the receiver between neck and jaw. "I'm going to make arrangements to get to Molokai."

"Good move, Jim."

"I hope everyone else thinks so."

"Hell, you can get clearance, if that's what you're worried about. Now that this thing's cracked open, you ought to be able to write your own ticket."

"You'd think so, Tony, but the bureau can move very slowly and in mysterious ways at times, especially if we don't have compelling evidence."

"You got clout on your side, Jim. You're the chief here. You call the shots."

"Wish it were that simple, Tony."

"Nothing's like the old days."

"No, no . . . nothing is."

They hung up and Parry wondered how best to deal with his suspicion that Lopaka Kowona was off the island of Oahu, possibly on Molokai, possibly elsewhere. It occurred to him that the information picked up by Gagliano was not so random and lucky as they might think; that it, too, could have been planted to throw them off Lopaka's trail.

Suppose the murderer did board an old island vessel at Kaneohe Bay. Who would know the boats better than Ivers? Ivers knew every scum-bucket and lowlife on this and all the islands. He'd made it his life's work to know, since he loved the old vessels and he hung about the wharves more than any man Parry knew.

Skipping breakfast, Parry rushed from his place to drive across the city to see Nate Ivers in his hospital bed, to wake him up if necessary. This morning, he'd pick the other man's brain on this score, see what popped out. . . .

Meanwhile, the County Sheriff's Office on Molokai had to be put on alert, and although it was likely too late for them to screen every boat in every harbor of that island, he made the call anyway, getting Dispatch to put him though to the other island officials, beginning with the area FBI field operative there. Parry would also have to convince his superiors that the venue of the case had shifted from Oahu to the outer islands. This would not be so simple as it appeared on the surface, because every other law-enforcement agency, plus the U.S. Army, was currently on alert that the killer had been contained on the island of Oahu and was most likely hiding somewhere in the vast Koolau Range.

The island wisdom and island mentality that still prevailed locally in many sectors also stretched all the way to D.C. when it came to Hawaii. D.C. still thought that getting away from the

Honolulu Police Department and FBI was an impossibility given the fact all escape routes were bounded by ocean.

"It's a goddamned island, Parry!" his superiors had kept repeating long distance. "Why can't you find and stop this motherfucker!" Certainly an island by definition, no matter its size, and Oahu—third largest of the Hawaiian chain with 608 square miles—held eighty percent of Hawaii's population, with seven hundred thousand people in Honolulu alone. Add to this three million tourists swelling her population annually, and it became clear that this was no Martha's Vineyard, Nantucket or circular seacoast isle with only a certain, limited number of hiding places. Never mind the shifting terrain, that areas of the landscape were lunar, mountainous or rain forest, never mind that a man could disappear here as easily as he might in the northwest Rocky Mountains, even more effectively actually, given the lush, year-round vegetation here. Still, the only means of leaving the islands was by flight or ship, and since all steamers, pleasure craft, fishers, and cruise ships had been covered along with all flights out, it followed with syllogistic logic that it must be inevitable that Lopaka Kowona would have by now fallen into their net.

Parry wasn't so sure. Lopaka was the son of a chieftain, and perhaps the people protecting him for their own misguided or perverse reasons were more cunning than most non-natives were willing to give them credit for. Lopaka knew the islands far better than any of his pursuers. Parry feared he could well have escaped Oahu, and that he might hold out indefinitely against modern law enforcement by returning to the wilds of Molokai, if not some even more remote island in the chains, say Kahoolawe, where they weren't even looking for him. Then he recalled that Joseph Kaniola had indeed suggested Molokai as a possible place where Lopaka might seek help.

Kowona had as yet to meet his yearly quota of victims. Molokai, Maui and the largest of the chain of islands, Hawaii, were all favored tourists islands where the population and bustle would help him fade into the more urbanized areas. He had harvested human lives on Maui before. He knew the terrain there. He had worked on a ranch there, subsisting as a cowboy, and a cane cutter before that. There were no major metropolitan centers to rival or even come close to Honolulu, and yet he'd managed in his grim calling there for four years. And Maui's population since he'd left had swelled to one hundred thousand, and the island remained the most popular tourist attraction alongside Oahu and Honolulu, playing host to two million visitors annually.

The other islands, and especially his homeland, would not grant the Trade Winds Killer the sort of anonymity that he required. Besides, he'd had ties before in Maui, so he could possibly take up where he left off, working and earning enough to put a down payment on a used car until *voilà,* he was back in grisly business.

The local expression on Maui was *Maui no ka oi,* meaning that in everything Maui was the best. The old expression took on new meaning for Parry as his best choice for an explanation of the disappearance of their chief suspect in the mutilation murders on Oahu.

Parry imagined the monster hiding there on Maui, changing his name and appearance as well as his habits—if he could—which could mean his total disappearance, especially if no one pursued.

Major crimes had seldom occurred in the islands in the past because there was limited access to escape, but now that was no longer true. Still, what better way to hide than in plain sight?

Parry punched the buttons to his Oahu headquarters again and asked they patch him through to Maui County authorities, getting an old friend on the line and warning him to alert all officers patrolling the island to be on the lookout, particularly the harbor patrol. Even as he said it, Parry sensed the alert had come too late. He had been in touch earlier with Maui's Mike Ulupo, who was the FBI's contact man on the island. Ulupo had researched Lopaka's background and the time he'd spent on Maui, forwarding the information to Parry the day before. This came after Hal Ewelo, owner of Paniolo's, began finally to open up about what he knew regarding Lopaka Kowona in order to save his own neck, little knowing they'd filed separate charges of murder in the Oniiwah case which precluded any deals being made. Paniolo's proprietor was going down for his part in Oniiwah's death, hopefully a life sentence. Sometimes Parry wished there was a death penalty in his state, and this, along with the Trade Winds case, was one of those instances where such a penalty was more than warranted, he felt.

He broke off with Maui now and silently cursed Joe Kaniola, whom he could no longer understand. Why would he help a man who had killed his own son? Was he that warped by his own political views? Could the man actually be harboring this monster merely because Lopaka's blood was "royal" Hawaiian? And because any apprehension of Lopaka Kowona on such atrocious charges would prove an embarrassment to the rising *kanaka* power base, the new establishment?

God, had they all sunk to such levels?

He could believe that the U.S. Government might resort to any underhanded trick possible if the killer had been shown to be a white sailor or soldier; he knew that by white standards and thinking Lopaka, by virtue of having any percentage of Hawaiian blood, was labeled a non-white and a prime example of how a man could be "tainted" by savage blood. It went without saying that Caucasian prejudices, bigotry and fears would run rampant in and out of private circles, in and out of the press. Still, what motivated Kaniola in all this? Was he a man willing to forget his own son's ruthless murder for the sake of appearances? It seemed unbelievable, yet everything pointed toward Joe Kaniola's intentionally leading Parry away from Maui as a possible destination for the fugitive by suggesting that Lopaka had taken to the mountains of Oahu.

Why? Why? he wondered over and over without answer.

"And who's going to believe it?" he asked himself aloud between calls.

It was as if Lopaka Kowona, the Cane Cutter, had been swallowed up by the earth; neither the all-points bulletin nor the U.S. Army, working in cooperation with the FBI and the HPD, could turn up any sign of the man the press was now calling the Monster of Maui, as his personal history had him in Maui for several years previous to his arrival in Honolulu. On Maui the fire-haired Lopaka had worked as a cowboy at the same ranch where Paniolo had been a wrangler. Before his cowpunching days, Lopaka had been a cane cutter on Maui.

Jim Parry had supplied most of the background on Lopaka from sources he had on Maui. Information also came down that both Lopaka and Paniolo Ewelo could be placed on the island during a time when a series of disappearances had had authorities there scratching their heads. Could the two have worked as a murdering duo? Not according to either the evidence gathered at Lopaka's grisly cottage, or Jessica's findings regarding the deaths of Alan Kaniola and Thom Hilani.

U.S. Army teams and their dogs were now scouring the jungle above Lopaka's repulsive bungalow, everyone now aware of just how dangerous this butcher could be. Jessica had remained at the makeshift outpost along a paved highway, halfway up the mountain. She now saw Jim Parry's Stealth winding its way along the road as Jim drove the circuitous path toward the command post. She walked over to greet him when he opened the car door.

"How's the search going?"

"You really want to know?" she asked.

"Tell me some good news, will you?" His plea hung in the thin air for a moment as he glanced around at the operation.

Jessica shaded her eyes against the afternoon sun, which was more intense than the noonday sun in D.C. "Only good thing is that since Kowona's gone into hiding, the killings've ended."

"So far's we know, you mean." His smile was easy and sly as he handed her a plastic thermos cup filled with black Kona coffee and a careful blend of Jack Daniel's. They were high enough up the mountainside that it was cool here, even in the bright sunlight. "Thought you could use a little kick," he warned.

"What, I'm not hot enough?" she asked playfully.

They stood halfway up the face of a mountain, watching intently a platoon of weary men in army fatigues searching alongside dogs for any sign or scent of Lopaka Kowona.

Parry studied the lay of the land and then the layout of their makeshift headquarters: an unpaved, red-sand parking lot outside a small grocery store, nestled among the foothills, serving a shy, retiring community of peaceable island dwellers, both well-to-do and otherwise up here, who'd carved out a little place of their own. Even the houses up here, tucked away behind thick greenery and blooming mango trees, seemed to be hiding from this influx of machines and human activity on the mountain. The only exception was the store and the little man who owned it, a Korean who knew opportunity when he saw it; he'd been peddling packets of peanuts, raisins, candy and Twinkies along with soft drinks and coffee to the army that had descended on the area and had bivouacked at his doorstep. He looked as if he had God to thank for his sudden prosperity, but that thanks would have to wait until after the end of a business day.

"What about the homes in the area?" asked Jim, looking over an aerial map on one of the tables here. "Have they been canvassed and cleared as possible hiding places for our man?"

"Yes, all done within a fifty-mile radius," Jessica walked him to a second rickety table below a tent where she pointed to a map held down in the wind by stones. "No irregularities, no suspicions reported, and no one's seen a hair of this guy's head."

"Then we move out to a hundred-mile radius. Give me the radio. I'll make the order."

"He's not here, Jim," she softly said.

He looked curiously at her as she stared off into the lush distance. "Just how do you know that?"

"If he hasn't been flushed by the dogs by now . . ."

"It's a bastard of a mountain range, Jess."

"The dogs've picked up no trace of him. If he were here, or if he'd been here . . ."

"Do you propose we just give in already? Tell everybody in the islands it's over, that he's given us the slip?"

"Just being practical. Don't forget, I know something about hunting, and this hunt?" She paused and pulled tiredly at her aching neck with one hand. "Just isn't panning out, Jim. We're looking in the wrong place."

"Any suggestions?" Jim's frustration was like a jagged file against his words. "He's either the goddamned invisible man or he's somehow gotten off the island."

"Bound for where?"

"We've checked and double-checked all the airlines, including the island-hoppers and chopper lines. No one boarded Lopaka, so he didn't *fly* out of here."

"Then he got aboard a ship or a boat of some sort."

"You been talking to Tony?"

"Of course I have."

"Look, the Harbor Authority wasn't alerted to the emergency as quickly as the airlines, but they claim there've been no irregularities."

"Come on, Jim."

"Regardless—"

"How many times do those guys look the other way?"

"—regardless," he continued, "we radioed every ship that left port yesterday. We're tracking every destination, and we've got agents waiting at each destination port. Each vessel will be thoroughly searched. So we've long ago assumed a correct posture there, and we've got every ship's master cooperating."

"So you covered the big ships, but what about the fishing vessels that work the islands?"

"They're all accounted for, according to the harbor patrol."

"And if there was an unscheduled boat in a slip the other night?"

"Assuming such . . . that he got a boat out. Where'd he go to?" he pointedly asked. "Best guess . . . hunch . . . anything?" Parry was feeling his way in the dark, looking for corroboration for his own amorphous theory, looking to form it into a conviction, to convince himself he was about to do the right thing.

"Some safe harbor, or where he feels at home," she suggested. "Perhaps . . . maybe Maui? He was comfortable there once."

"Again I'm ahead of you, Jess. I've already alerted authorities there. They're on the lookout for Lopaka, armed with his photo. So far, nothing."

"Now whata we do?"

"Keep our fingers crossed. Hope he makes a slipup? Whataya suggest?"

She gritted her teeth and returned the empty coffee cup to him. "That's not good enough, Jim."

"I agree wholeheartedly, dear Doctor."

"Talk is cheap, Jim. We've got to take some action and we need to do it now."

"What the hell do you think I've been doing with my days and nights? What the hell do you want from me, Jess? Miracles?"

For a moment, they glared at one another until she relented. "I'm sorry. Just have every nerve rubbed raw by this butchering bastard. Something about this beast that's primal. Savage monster's worse than Matisak and the Claw combined. I'm sorry but . . ."

"No apology necessary."

"I had no right to—"

"*Shhhhh!* Tell you what, Doctor. Maybe what we really need is a chance to completely clear our minds. I don't know about you, but what clears my soul is a good dive."

"What's that?"

Birds chirped and darted in and out of a nearby *kukui* tree grove.

"Maybe it's time for a return visit to Maui for you; you could take up where you left off. Get in some diving before you're called back to D.C."

"What, just forget about the case and go off diving? Alone?"

He smiled. "Who said anything about being alone?"

She smiled brightly and looked long into his beaming eyes. "A few days' diving does sound great," she admitted. Then with an accusatory tone, she asked, "Just what'd you go and do, Jim Parry?"

"Arranged a little excursion for us. Maybe get in a day's worth of diving. Whataya say? Come on . . ."

"How long? A day, two, three?"

"I know it's not much time, maybe get in one day's diving, but it'll be made up in quality, I promise. You haven't really seen the islands until you've seen them by helicopter."

"Helicopter? Is-sat right?"

"That's right. A few days, all expenses paid, kind of a reward for giving up your vacation for us."

"Reward? Hell, Jim, we haven't even apprehended the bastard yet, and you're doling out rewards? Some people might view it as something other than a reward . . ."

He ignored her protests. "Whataya say, Jess?"

"I'm paying my own passage," she insisted.

"That's not necessary. This is on me."

"*Ahhhh*, I don't know." Could get sticky, she thought.

"We can argue on the chopper."

"We do that well anywhere, don't we?" She smiled.

"You're getting quite good at being contrary, yes."

She gave a mock frown. "All right, when do we leave?"

"Soon as you're packed. I've cleared the way for us, and Tony's been placed in charge here, so there's absolutely nothing standing in our way." He suggested she get her things together and place them into his car, handing her the thermos he'd brought as well. She obeyed as he lifted the radio mike and called for Gagliano, looking over his shoulder to be certain she was out of earshot for the moment.

Gagliano, who was somewhere up in the mountains with the armed forces and the HPD officers sent by Scanlon to assist, acknowledged his call. "Tony, I want you to return to conduct the search from command, here at . . . at . . ." He looked over his other shoulder at the sign on the Korean's store which read *Kawaohomaenape's*. Obviously, the Korean had bought out the establishment from a Hawaiian owner but had retained the sign. "The store," Parry said, giving up on pronouncing the name. "Dr. Coran and I are outta here, Tony, and next time I get in touch it'll be from Maui. You got that? *Out*."

"Maui? Don't you mean Molokai, Boss? *Over*."

"Maui, Tony, but *you* don't know my whereabouts, understood? *Out*."

"Sure, sure, Boss." Gagliano's voice crackled over the radio. "How long do you think we should keep these boys out here, Jim? *Over*."

"Give it till nightfall. *Over*."

"And then?" *Click*.

"Call it quits. *Out*."

"*Roger that*. How long'll you be in Maui?"

"Two, three days at tops, and thanks, Gag, for setting me straight. *Over*."

"Setting you straight? Boss, I said Molokai, not Maui, remember? *Out*."

"I'm aware of that, Gag. Thanks anyway. Be in touch . . ."

"We'll cover your backside. *Over 'n' out*."

"Thanks, Gag."

She caught the tail end of his signing off with Gagliano. "Tony's going to be upset with us. You know that, don't you?"

"Tony knows we're doing the right thing. He even wished us well," he said.

She remained skeptical, her eyes telling him as much. "Well, if we're going, let's go." She started off again for his car, mumbling to herself before turning, stepping backwards as she continued toward the car and saying, "You're really serious about our disappearing to Maui?"

"Couldn't be more serious." He took her hands in his for a moment, warming her.

She started around the car, reluctantly parting her hands from his, still mumbling to herself. He pursued, coming round to her side, opening the door for her but barring her from entering, asking, "What're you going on about, Coran?"

"You . . ." She stopped to stare him down. "You know you're just flying in the face of good sense? If the newsies get wind you've split in the middle of an investigation of this magnitude for . . . for some fun in the sun with your M.E.—"

"To hell with 'em. Besides, they'll never know."

"But if they do, think of the consequences. Your name'll be mud not only with the coldly logical Hawaiians and Orientals here, but with the muckety-mucks in their homes on Diamond Head and Pacific Heights and with the luncheon set at the Pacific Club.

Think of Marshal, who'll see to it Washington knows. Think of Scanlon, who's just waiting for you to stumble."

"I'm willing to risk it. What about you?" he countered.

"Me? What about me?"

"Are you secure enough in your relationship with Paul Zanek to follow my instructions for a little R & R?"

"I'm not the least worried about my superiors, but I'm *supposed* to be on vacation, remember?"

"Stop worrying about what others will think," he said firmly. "I have."

"Oh, really?"

"Really."

"Does that include Scanlon?"

"Him most of all."

"And your superiors?" she challenged, her unerring eye pinning him to the truth now.

"They owe me," he countered, catching her mischievous glint, kissing her quickly and offering her a seat with a flourish of his hand like some coachman out of a fairy tale, she thought.

Once they were inside with the motor revved up, he spoke across to her. "Don't forget, I'm the Sherlock who uncovered this whole ugly business with Lopaka in the first place, and with your help, I'm the one who's brought it along this far; together we've I.D.'d this animal. The rest can be left up to others."

"You saying leave the collar to others? Your sure you can live with that?"

"I can. So long's he's caught. That's what matters, after all. To see him brought to justice, right?"

"You want to give Scanlon more rope to hang himself, right?"

"Maybe."

She smiled in response, feeling she understood now.

"So, Jess"—he tried diversionary tactics—"what *about* your superiors?"

She laughed lightly and then looked him in the eye. "They *really* owe me!"

"All right!" He gave a little cheer and a high-five sign.

— 21 —

Somewhere the Sky touches the Earth, and the name of that place is the End.

Anonymous Wakamba Saying

6:15 P.M., July 19, over Maui

The chartered helicopter flight was stupendous and breathtaking and spectacular all at once, revealing areas of the majestic islands that could only be reached by the eye of God or modern technology, the hovering craft. She and Jim flew over the ocean and around the island of Maui at breakneck speed, slowing and stopping at places he and the pilot alternately wished to point out to her. Jim, speaking to her through the requisite headphone set, was enjoying himself tremendously, she realized.

It was coming on dusk, and it was lovely just to watch the sun slowly dip from sight, painting the western sky with an array of lavenders and purples. Jim had been right. The helicopter trip alone had completely freed them of the hideous and offensive events left behind them in Oahu. Although they could not fully escape the horrors of Kowona's bungalow or the case, they had managed to come damned close, she felt. In fact she had all but forgotten everything during the moments they hovered beelike above an enormous, foamy waterfall on the mountainous side of Maui where there were no roads or access. Here was perhaps one of the few untouched and unspoiled areas on the face of the globe.

Maui's volcanic valleys and conical peaks were barren on one side, a lunar landscape of treacherous ridges and pitted earth where no life survived. In stark contrast, the rich and lush life of the valleys on the lee side of the island was thick with the foliage of ginger, *kamani,* ti, *hau,* coconut and breadfruit trees. Behind each valley they discovered a slender ribbon of silver in fluid motion, waterfalls everywhere, many so isolated they could only be seen from the air.

They moved on, the helicopter like a voracious bird of prey, anxious to slide away from the face of the cascading waters. Soon they were passing an occasional pastureland with roaming livestock, open-range-fed cattle and horses, and the occasional barn or ranch house. They next passed over a tiny church in the middle of nowhere, tucked among the rain forest, a small graveyard alongside it.

Jim pointed at the graveyard and said, "That's Kipahulu Congregational Church, where Charles Lindbergh had himself buried facing the Pacific."

"Lindbergh? The first solo flight across the Atlantic?"

"One and the same . . . Lucky Lindy, yes."

"The pride of St. Louis, way out here?"

"He was a resident of Hana, which is coming in view now. Was buried here in 1974. Downright murder to get to his burial site even with four-wheel drive, and it's an even bet he wanted it that way."

They swept by a series of cascading pools bounded by huge, strewn boulders. The pools and rocks had people in brightly colored clothes and bathing suits all around them.

"Tourists up from Kahului, almost sixty miles off. The place is called the Wailua Falls on the maps but the travel agencies call it the Seven Sacred Pools to lure people here," explained Jim. "Most of those fools'll be sorry if they don't get back across the Hana Highway before nightfall."

"The Hana Highway. I've heard of it."

"Hana Tarmac's a better name for it. See how narrowly the road hugs the coastline cliffs, darts and twists around blind corners, disappears and reappears?"

"So that's the infamous Highway to Hana I heard so much about while I was on the island earlier. In the shops they sport T-shirts that say, 'I survived the Hana Highway.'"

"Believe me, not everyone does. Every year or so someone goes off the edge, usually a tourist couple trying to find their way in the dark. Hell, it takes the locals two and a half hours at top speeds, which amounts to thirty-five to forty, to traverse the fifty miles between Hana and Kahului, thanks to the sheer number of hairpin and blind curves."

Each mountain valley from up here appeared to be feeding the ocean with fresh water. Here on the far windward side of the island, the great Mt. Haleakala meant for an early sunset, and nestled among the valley floor and along the quickly descending cliffs below, a small village of modern construction emerged, some homes fantastic in both size and architecture as well as location. A steeple rose from the center of the small settlement, but church and grocery stores and all other structures were dwarfed by a spectacular resort hotel.

Jim leaned into her, nudged her and pointed, saying over the noise of the chopper, through the headphone set, "Hana Town and that's the Hana-Maui, one of the world's most unique hotels."

"By virtue of its location alone," she imagined aloud.

"Have their own stable of horses for their guests, two outdoor heated pools, each room with its own sunken bath that looks out on a private garden."

"Imagine that. You've stayed there?"

"On my paycheck? Hell, no."

From above they could also see what passed for an airport here, a single strip for take off and landing, not large enough to accept any but the smallest of jets, and the pilots would have to be either crazy or extremely adept.

"Aloha Airlines has only recently gotten the okay to fly in here, Lear jets only, four and six passengers at a time, but they're restricted to one flight every three days in and out. The tower is that Quonset hut on the field."

The pilot cut into their conversation, a little static and a buzz alerting them to the fact. "Been to Hasegawa's lately, Mr. Parry?"

Parry laughed. "Not lately, no."

"Hasegawa's?" asked a curious Jessica.

"Something of a famous general store down there," he said, continuing to point.

"What's so famous about it? They got VCRs, videos, *Playboy* Magazine? L.L. Bean wear, what?"

"No, nothing like that. No TV reception this side of the island, thanks to Mt. Haleakala."

"What's with the grocery store then?"

"It's just that it's sorta become the standard by which all other island general stores must measure up, and when the original burned up in 1990, there was some suspicion that it was torched by rivals."

"I see . . . I think."

"It's just a big, quaint old, wooden small-town grocery store that sells items you wouldn't expect to find here."

"Like condoms?"

"Yeah, along with wooden airplanes, Yoo-Hoo pop, crackseeds, Jack Daniel's, Harlequin romances, and B.C. headache powders . . . you name it."

Jessica spied a simple harbor with boats. From the air she could see that each valley path, once the trek of lava flows, now supported green carpets of life which stretched fingerlike to the ocean. The shoreline had been carved out in many places by the lava flows of an ancient time, creating jagged, fantastic images.

Jim leaned over, tapped her on the shoulder and pointed to a series of monstrous driblets of the jagged rock jutting through the waves and looking like a school of dragons from an old legend. "Pahoehoe, the natives call it," he announced through the headphones.

Then Lee, the helicopter pilot, began to circle inland over the sleepy, staid, yet famous settlement known as Hana Town on the maps. They caught glimpses of the gray ribbon on Highway 36, the Hana Highway, which snaked crazily, hugging the coastline, twisting and turning along the virgin coastline where black beaches stared up at them like enormous, crescent-shaped cats' eyes.

"My first black-beach spotting," she confessed to Jim.

"Beautiful, isn't it?"

"Incredible."

"So like Hawaii to paint its beaches black. Look, would you like to go down to one of them?"

"Really?" She saw down the coast another was coming into

sight, a strip of black pebbles abutted on each side by lava cliffs. Beyond the beach lay a valley grown thick with *hau* and coconut trees. The ocean foam was stirred up wildly here in this desolate and isolated place of black sand.

"It's created by a layer of volcanic rock washed and polished by the ocean for untold centuries," he told her.

"Can we really get to it?"

"There's a trail—not a very good one—may be overgrown; leads down from the air strip."

Now she saw the small strip built here for commercial use of helicopters.

"Trail may be grown over, but I brought a cane knife," he continued.

The mention of the cane cutter reined her emotions in, reminding her of the horrors they'd so effectively and completely left behind in the powerful wake of the chopper, Honolulu now a distant memory.

The pilot pointed out a place he called the spout, another "blow hole" like the one at Koko Head on Oahu, and the sight of the shoreline geyser, sending up its powerful spray at hundreds of miles per hour, made Jessica's eyes turn to study Jim's, and there she found him out.

"You wanted me to see this, didn't you?"

"You're the one said he'd make for some place where he felt *comfortable*. There aren't too many of these spouts, and maybe it's about time we learn what happened to those missing Maui girls."

"Damnit, Jim, why didn't you tell me from the start?"

He took in a deep breath of air. "I still think we can find some time here for ourselves. I've got enough equipment and food to last, and I've got a radio. We can call it quits whenever we like."

"We're going to dive *here*, you mean?"

"That's if you'll . . . if you're still willing, yes."

"Jim, you want to come clean? Just . . . just tell me what's going on here." She was both hurt and angry.

"I planned to drop our gear here, have Lee take our bags on to the hotel and pick us up tomorrow. It's only ten minutes to Kahului, the island's main commercial airport and relative civilization, if you want to go back to Oahu, Jess."

"So, tonight you planned that we'd be roughing it, and tomorrow we'd make a dive near the Spout? Is that it?"

"It's rough, but not near so rough a dive as the Blow Hole. I plan to get in as closely as good sense and safety allow."

"Good sense, huh? On the off chance we could be more successful here than the Navy divers had been in Oahu? Just tell me, Jim, what is the nature of this probe you're suggesting?" She had to secretly admit, she was intrigued even though he hadn't been completely truthful. "Do you have any facts here, or is this a hunch you're following?"

"I've studied every inch of every police report filed on the missing girls here on Maui. One report mentioned some strange bird who was rousted for driving under the influence, caught pulling out of this area late one night. The reason it was in the report at all was that the car matched the description of one given by a witness in a later case, but a Lopaka Kowona was sought out afterwards, questioned and let go. The information was buried under stacks, and even I'd forgotten about it until we got Lopaka's name again."

"So knowing about the Spout, you came here."

He nodded, saying no more.

She asked, "Did all the missing girls live in the vicinity of the airport in Kahului or along the Hana Highway?"

"No, not really. They're from all over the island, but quite a few disappeared from Lahaina, the busiest tourist area where the old whaling sites and village are. The streets are lined with shops, row on row."

"I know, I've been there," she confessed. "Dropped a bundle."

"Of course you know already that information places our man here on the island some years ago, during which time the disappearances became frequent during the season for the trades."

"I'm more interested in recent history, Jim. What makes you think he's here and not on Molokai or elsewhere?"

He shrugged and explained his reasoning, not forgetting to tell her that whatever path Joe Kaniola had wanted him to take, he felt compelled to move in the opposite direction.

"So he says Molokai?"

"Yeah, that's right."

"So you theorize Maui, and you know about the Spout, and you come directly for Lopaka's old dumping site. Not bad, Parry. Careful or somebody's going to call you slick."

"I just put it together."

"Rather patly, don't you think?"

"Hey, two and two is always pat. The Spout's too good a connection to blow off."

"What about all those Kowona sightings we were getting all over Oahu?" she asked. "Like Elvis sightings?"

"Ever notice how nobody's seen Roy Orbison's obese ghost anywhere?" he joked.

"Suppose our being here's a mistake, Jim. Suppose one of those sightings on Oahu was correct. What then?"

"You face it. Kowona sightings have come in from every bloody corner of every island except Maui. That makes me suspicious as hell."

"Are you sure your coming here has been the right step, Jim?" she persisted. "I want to know why you're committed to this move."

"It's what Gagliano and I've been able to pick up on the street, and like I said, it goes contrary to what Joe Kaniola would have us believe."

"But why would Kaniola want Kowona to escape, to go free? Just to hurt you, Jim? That doesn't figure."

"I'm not so sure Kaniola isn't working up to another revenge hit, like what happened to Oniiwah, only now he has the right target."

"You don't really think Kaniola had anything to do with George Oniiwah's death, do you?"

"I'm not one hundred percent convinced that he didn't, no. *Ahh*, maybe not. I don't know."

"Just playing on hunches and guts, huh?"

"So whataya think?" he asked with a boyish, disarming smile. "Are you in or out? Lee can take you straight to the airport and you can be back in Honolulu in a few hours. What's it to be?"

She frowned, shook her head and stared down at the blinking black beach over which Lee had hovered as if to tempt her on. "You've thought this through thoroughly, haven't you?"

"Sometimes ideas come to me after a good sleep."

Off Hana, the night sky was telling them they had very little time to decide. Over the headphones, the pilot cut into their conversation, saying, "I can set down on the ledge at the strip, but it'll have to be now, Mr. Parry."

"Put her down, Lee," said Jessica.

Parry placed a hand over hers. "You won't regret it."

"I've heard that line before."

The chopper put down at a small strip just the other side of the cliff wall. Parry climbed out behind her, tugging at a large duffle containing much of what they needed, including most of their diving gear. The pilot opened a compartment in the belly of the chopper and began hefting out air tanks, complaining that they were the reason the bird was so sluggish. Jessica hadn't noticed a moment's sluggishness in the aircraft, and had in fact thought it capable of duplicating any aviary movement without the slightest awkwardness.

"When's somebody going to invent a lightweight air tank that's affordable?" the pilot continued, lamenting aloud for no one in particular.

The air strip, built for the heavy commercial chopper traffic that buzzed about the islands, was deserted this time of night. "Make a lot better time for Kahului without all the weight," Parry assured the pilot, slipping him a hefty tip. "And thanks, Lee."

"You give a holler when you want me back," he replied. "And I hope you'll enjoy lovely Hana and her waters. I'll see your bags go on to the inn."

"The inn," she repeated for Jim's benefit. "*Hmmmm,* you do plan carefully, don't you?" And for the first time since seeing the Spout, she realized that the charter was in fact a commercial deal, not FBI issue after all. This then refueled her earlier suspicion that Parry was doing something counter to his own best interest here.

Tugging him away from the pilot, she said, "James Parry, you're disobeying orders, aren't you?"

"What the hell're you talking about now?" he replied. "Come on, we've got to set up a tent and build a fire on the beach."

She frowned and scowled and stared at the departing helicopter as it lifted, leaving them in the wilderness of Hawaii, quite alone on their own private black sand beach.

"I've always wanted to walk on a black sand beach," she admitted, "but I want to know just what we're doing here, Jim. This *is* an unauthorized campaign, isn't it?"

"I can see there's no keeping a secret from you." He hefted as much of the equipment as he could carry. "Grab a tank, and follow me down to the beach. I'll explain along the way."

She hefted two tanks.

"Hey, take it easy. We're going to have to make two trips regardless, so . . ."

"Just move out and show me the way, and thanks for insisting I wear jeans."

He shook his head, smiled and moved out ahead of her toward the winding little footpath that would take them to the ocean edge and its volcanic, exotic black sand, which, in the approaching night, sparkled as if some magical stardust had been sprinkled by island angels, the jeweled flakes blinking under the moon. A sparkling gift of the sea.

"Talk about mixing business with pleasure," she called out to him as he moved along the footpath to the richly colored volcanic beach.

"Be careful where you step along here," he bluntly cautioned.

"Why? What're we afraid of? Scorpions, snakes, iguanas, what?"

She could hear the softly cushioned roar of the ocean as it rose up to meet them, as if it were lulling the world with some eternal hymn. A shaggy, unkempt grove of pandanus trees lined their way, each tree looking like an old man trying to get up the cliff, each bent from the effects of the ocean wind on their woody bodies. The ground was spongy with rotted palm fronds, and all around them the spiny, saw-toothed foliage crackled and tore at her with a disturbing and eerie wind giving it life. For a moment, seeing Jim ahead of her, the cane cutter strapped to his hip, she felt a mild but compelling wave of fear rush in to her.

"Careful!" he shouted, and pointed at obstacles in their way, lashing out from time to time with the cane cutter, swiping away at vines and saw-toothed leaves. *"Puka!"* he next shouted. "Large enough to swallow you whole. Careful!"

"What? What're you saying, Jim?"

"Watch out for these!"

She peered down at his feet to see a strange hole large enough for either of them to slip through; it appeared to spiral to a bottomless cavern.

"Puka, it's called. Volcanic hole carved out of lava," he explained. "I'd hoped to get here before dark."

"I can see why."

After several minutes of steady, rhythmic hacking with the cane knife, Jim stepped into a surprising and unblemished clearing, into which she quickly followed. This unimpeded area the size of a ballfield was neatly divided by ancient stones covered with spongy moss picked up by the beam of her flashlight. The clearing was bracketed by rows of slender, tall coconut trees acting as silent sentinels here, their plumed tops tilting to the wind, which seemed a refreshing but eerily constant force. She saw evidence of a graveyard in the distance and a marsh and stream beyond. A cluster of stunted *kamani* trees hung low over the setting. Behind this swampy area there was an impenetrable wall of *hau* trees that stretched back into the valley.

"We're almost there," said Jim.

"What is this place?" she asked, feeling it had a sense of haunting.

"Just a clearing."

"It's more than that."

"Well, legend has it there was once a village here, part of the Wailanos people, whose beneficent deity was the lizard. They were mostly fishermen."

"Really? I sensed there was something about this place." She imagined the simple life that had once gone on here, the sound of babies crying, of women pounding poi or beating tapa, of men telling tales as they repaired nets and others working shark tooth and shell into a lei. She pictured old women bathing their babies in the nearby surf. She could even hear the laughter of the children in the tidal pools . . . but then she realized what it must be that she was hearing: the rushing surge of the sea and its counterpoint, the outgoing flow, that timeless heartbeat of the ocean.

Still, if any place on earth harbored spirits, she sensed them here, felt them blowing lightly over her hair and down her neck. She'd felt a similar sensation once as a child, stepping lightly through a deserted cemetery. Her curiosity about headstones and what they said had gotten the best of her even as a young girl, and it had grown with age into what some considered a morbid hobby, which put off a lot of gentlemen callers along with her profession. Still, visiting old cemeteries and studying what was written on ancient headstones had always held a fascination for her. She'd taken vacation tours in New England just to get to the oldest cemeteries in the land, and one day she hoped to get to see some of the oldest in Europe, Great Britain and Ireland. She told Jim this, and added, "Just feels like we're being watched, you know."

"Hey, come daylight, if you want to check for headstones, you'll find 'em here but no markings," he said. "For now, let's trudge on, huh?"

"You're reading my mind now, Parry."

"Let's just say I'm beginning to learn."

They continued on.

"Just how often have you brought women here, Jim?"

"Don't do this, Jess."

"Do what?"

"See what I mean?" he asked without looking back.

"No, I don't see what you mean."

"Your damned FBI training takes over once more."

"That's a nasty thing to say," she replied with a tinge of indignity.

"It's better than saying you're too suspicious."

"Well, you don't deny that you've been here before, and if you've been here before, a place like this, you don't come alone, now do you?"

"All right . . . all right. You're the second, if you want the truth."

"I want the truth."

"But I've never dived here with anyone."

"Diving doesn't look safe here. Not a place for the islander dive shops to bring their charges."

"You got that right."

"Whataya mean? No one dives here?"

"No." He turned and stared long into her eyes. "We'll be the first."

"A virgin dive. That'd be something to take home. But this place . . . it's kind of a spooky, Jim," she observed. "I mean it's really desolate. If anything should happen down below . . ."

"This location can be reached from the Hana Highway."

"That doesn't inspire confidence. Isn't there something like six hundred curves?"

"Six hundred seventeen, mostly hairpins, with fifty-six one-lane bridges, but in case of emergency, go toward Hana Town, not away. There's a small hospital there."

"And I'm sure they're equipped with the latest in decompression chambers, sure. Where's the nearest phone?"

"We're not totally isolated. I've got a CB radio in one of the packs, and you saw the village of Hana as we came over, a few cattle ranches, and if things get too rough, we can always hike up to the Hana-Maui, only six hundred dollars a night to stay in the lobby's john," he joked.

She wasn't laughing.

"Come on, Jess . . . there's a dirt road pull-in the other side of the helicopter pad. We could have visitors tomorrow, and our pilot's due back by noon. In any case, it's not quite as impregnable as it looks from the air, not if you're willing to make the trek."

"Do you really think Lopaka Kowona used this place as he did Koko Head on Oahu?"

"It's worth a look-see; that's what I think. Drop one of those tanks here."

"What?" she gasped, a little out of breath.

"We go down sharply from here. I don't want you losing your footing. It's only just wide enough for one foot at a time, and if you fall, it's a straight plunge into the sea."

Protesting, Jessica said, "Only the other day I was using a cane, remember." She did as he suggested, placing one of the heavy air tanks on the ground. When she did so, she saw a place where they might climb out over the cliff ledge and stand over the Spout, which continued to blast water into the night sky like a powerful Chicago fire department boat she'd once seen battling a blaze from its moorings in the Chicago River just below the Michigan Avenue bridge.

Seeing her stare off in the direction of the Spout, he said, "Quite a sight. See what I mean?"

The ocean water roared here, a fierce lion, as it was pummeled and forced through the underwater tunnel and out through the whale-like promontory of rock at the spoutlike egress. The thunder it created was deafening, the water reaching them in a light spray even here. "Yeah . . . yeah, I do." She was beginning to feel like Fay Wray in the frightful kingdom of *King Kong*.

Below them, lava rocks jutted from the frothy foam, forming gargantuan sea monsters that seemed perched on the waves, readying for any morsel to fall into their demonic jaws. It might be insane and impossible to dive here. It was anything but the peaceful underwater crater she'd dived in on the opposite side of the island before she'd ever met Jim Parry. Here the current and the dragon rocks would make it a precarious and risky venture, an underwater Dungeons and Dragons, filled with every sort of obstacle and demon, she surmised from the murky surface.

"Tell me about the village . . . what you know of it," she called out as they continued toward the black beach.

He was some ten feet ahead of her now, his form a large shadow, his profile a silhouette against the gray-green foliage.

She checked cautiously for her footing now each step of the way. It was treacherous.

"Fifteen yards or so more now," he called back, having not understood her, his voice seemingly out of place in this wild land of sea and jungle. She could see that he'd reached a leveling-off point now ahead, laying down all the equipment he'd hauled. He then rushed back up toward her.

He'd taken the big knife from its scabbard and he held it high over his head now, and she felt her heart rise in her chest as the blade came down, tearing and hacking at some entangling branches that crossed the trail.

"Man, this stuff has no respect for people," he joked.

She breathed deeply and brought up a lopsided grin, feeling foolish, but not daring to tell him why. He sank the long knife into the earth and lifted the air tank from her, returning to the black sand and the other equipment, and there he gently placed it. He turned to find her twirling about the diamond-studded black beach, her shoes torn off.

"*Owww! Ouch! Oh,* I cut my foot, damnit." She was hobbling a bit now. "I wanted to feel it, but it's so coarse. Why didn't you warn me? I expected it to be like a white sand beach, but it isn't."

The beach glittered beneath them. "It's made of obsidian volcanic glass, for God's sake, not sand pebbles or granules, sweetheart. I was gonna warn you, but you're too fast for me, I guess."

"Don't explain too much; you'll spoil the fun."

"You did well getting down, Jess. Look, you get set up here, rest that foot, and I'll return for all the rest of our equipment."

"No way," she disagreed.

He stared into her eyes a moment, seeing some hint of her earlier fear.

"There's nobody here but us, Jess. I promise you."

Nobody but us, she thought, so why've I developed such a massive case of the creeps? Can't stand isolation because I've never had it before? Need my city lights, hum of a million volts around me, what? Is it the graveyard and encampment above, the dead? Such places don't normally scare me. . . .

She saw that Jim was staring, waiting. Finally, she said, "All the same with you, Jim, I . . . I'd prefer we stay together."

"Fine, fine." He nodded. "Sure, just as well."

He started back up. "Wait," she called after him, trying to get her shoes back onto her feet, the cut stinging and dripping blood on the onyx beach.

In a dark time, the eye begins to see.

Theodore Roethke

Jessica was exhausted by the second trip down to the lovely beach, after which Jim proposed a romantic interlude coupled with some serious business the following morning, the dive below the Spout. As for the romance, he'd thought of everything, including a tent, which he efficiently assembled. Very soon they had a fire going, and the enormity of the sky and ocean seemed closed out for a time by the circle of their flames, which sent little fireflies off in the trade winds which slapped at the tent continuously, the noise adding to that of the nearby geyser and the ocean's music.

She'd made coffee and warmed some of the canned food he'd brought, hash and beans, and they ate hungrily from tinware with small camping utensils. Nearby their diving gear and tanks stood silent sentinel to their camp.

"Jesus, it's like beyond *Deliverance* here," she softly complained. "So what's really going down here, Parry?" she asked firmly, after finishing her meal.

"Just a little excursion, so to speak."

"Unauthorized?"

He frowned and looked out to sea, his thoughts seeming to go in and out with the tide. He looked a bit annoyed that his ruse hadn't lasted any longer than it had.

She got up, walked to the nearby water's edge and said, "Great to have a ready-made sink to clean up in." She dipped her utensils and tin dish under the current, getting her feet and pants leg wet in the bargain, a little unnerved by the black emptiness of the water below her. Given the color of the bottom, the bay here was its own controlled little abyss.

"Leave it to you to call the Pacific Ocean a sink," he called out.

"Well, for our purposes, for the moment, that's what it is," she playfully parried, splashing water in his direction, sending it cascading skyward from her tin.

"Hey, cut it out!"

"So, you going to come clean, Parry? I'm here, I'm with you, I'm on your side, and I've been known to disobey authority on occasion."

He hesitated.

"You can trust me."

"I pitched the dive to D.C. and given the limited success of the Navy dive in Oahu, they passed on it. Didn't want to hear any objections from me either. Said in effect that your time and your life—*and mine,* they were kind enough to add—were more valuable than to go wasting either on what was termed an unlikely prospect in a risky environ."

"Sounds like Zanek's term for a wild-goose chase."

"Zanek and a team of think-tankers in D.C. that don't know shit about what we're faced with here. I mean if we don't nail this butchering-wacko-sonofabitch six ways to Sunday, if we don't have him on every count, and he gets some deal cut . . . well, we'll be facing some kind of race riot over in Honolulu."

"Something new for the tourists," she said.

"This isn't a laughing matter, Jess."

"I realize that. Come on, loosen up. We're here."

"Yeah, we're here, but I left out the fact Zanek kinda . . . well, he . . ."

"Out with it, Jim."

"He ordered you back . . ."

She'd been returning from the ocean edge when this news stopped her in her tracks.

"Are you saying . . . didn't you think . . . what were you thinking, Jim?"

"I wanted this time with you."

She considered this. "Well, Zanek's got a hell of a nerve ordering me back when I didn't get half my leave. Christ, the more I think about it, the hotter I get."

"Something about a Green River–type bizarre killing spree in the Northwest."

"Northwest, huh?"

"Montana, Wyoming, Idaho, Oregon and Washington."

"There're other people he can call in, you know."

"Said it was *right* for you."

"Right for me. Some rep, I've got, huh, Jim?" She sat alongside him once more, sighing heavily. The meal and the campfire reminded her of hundreds of excursions she might've gone on if she'd found a man like Parry before, a man secure enough to ask her.

Here the palms and fragrance of the exotic jungle surrounded them on all sides save the sea, acting as its own aphrodisiac in delightful addition. On one side of them lay the dense gray shadow of an *ohia* forest where the *ieie* vines with their big, sweet almond-colored flowers were in full bloom. From her reading of Hawaiian folklore, she recalled that the *ieie* plant was offered to Laka, goddess of dance.

Staring out at the flaming, pink and salmon-colored flowers of the forest, Jessica once again marveled at the interplay of what seemed a purely Hawaiian phenomena, light even in darkness, created of color. All Hawaiian life and culture seemed perched on a balance beam between childlike ebullience, innocence and warmth on the one side, and lethargy, cynicism and a stoic, dark sorrow like the carved wooden images of the island gods on the other. Not unlike the world at large, she thought. The lava rock thrown up about the cliffs here looked like the jagged edges of flames in silhouette. In another direction her eyes took in the source of the winds hurtling down from the world's largest crater, sweeping a fierce course along the ancient path of the lava that'd created the beach.

Parry, watching her, now stared at the broad face of the ascending mountain at their backs. *"Makaniloa,"* he said.

"What's 'at?" she asked.

"The long wind, it's called. Fitting."

"Here," she said, lifting the final bit of food left in the bottom of the skillet to Jim, "finish this off."

"Don't be too angry with me, Jess."

"Some cook, huh?" she teased, easing his concern. "That's something Zanek and the agency doesn't know about me. Hell, whata they care if we're human, huh, Jim?"

"You kidding? Their first concern is for our best *health*. Really. And our pensions and our old age."

She laughed in response. "I don't know what it is, but the outdoors makes me more alive, makes my senses come fully awake and my taste buds, wow."

While she had gotten busy with the prepared can foods, Jim had been cooking something that looked a bit like an exotic potato. He reached over with a skewered piece of the island delicacy as he called it and said, "Try a piece."

"What is it?"

"Taro."

"It looks like a gray boiled potato."

"Call it what you like, it's taro."

She took the offering, rolled it about her mouth and chewed. *"Hmmmm,* interesting . . . different."

"The Irish had the potato, the Hawaiians have the taro plant. If we had the time and wherewithal, we'd boil it up, ground it into a mash, and you could eat it as poi, or simply mash-fried, a real treat."

"It's good just as it is, really, Jim."

He then placed his hand at the back of her head and neck and gently pulled her toward him. He kissed her firmly before letting go. "How's 'at taste?"

"Hey, you kidding? Everything and anything—I mean anything—tastes better in the wilds."

"Including me?"

"Especially you."

They laughed together.

"To hell with Zanek," he muttered.

"You may regret all this in the morning when your Hawaiian sun is beating down on your career, Parry."

They sat curled in one another's arms for a time, silent and thoughtful until Jessica broke the stillness between them. "Once my father and I lost our catch in a torrential downpour."

"Lost your catch?"

"Twenty pounds of catfish figuring low. Anyway, we raced off, leaving the fish on the fresh line, tethered in the water to a root on the bank."

"You didn't see the storm coming?" He almost laughed, picturing the torrent.

"It just exploded over us. We were in another world. Anyway, Dad thought I'd retrieved the goddamn fish—our dinner—and I thought he had. We were in the middle of nowhere, Michigan woods, and we stumbled onto an old abandoned cabin, so we took advantage. The place was being used as an out-barn by some farmer, and it was pretty well stuffed with haystacks for his livestock. We slept on the haystacks and didn't get much sleep, let me tell you. Hay's not so soft when it's bundled and compacted; every dry stem stabbed me in the rear and back. Between us, we found two shriveled, raw potatoes. We started a fire in the fireplace and put the potatoes on the coals. It's a wonder the place didn't go up in flames."

"Best potatoes you ever ate, right?"

"I never forgot 'em."

"Maybe it was more than just the potatoes," he suggested.

"What?"

"The company wasn't too shabby either?"

"Yeah, that too, of course. Hell, we talked half the night."

"You miss him a lot, don't you?"

"Every day . . ."

"When you go back to D.C., Jess," Parry began.

"No, let's not talk about that . . . not tonight."

He took a deep breath, nodded and finished his food. "This is great."

"Go ahead and say it," she challenged.

"Say what?"

"It doesn't get any better than this. *Go on!*"

She stared off into the immense sea, the slapping sides of the tent competing admirably with the surf.

"Feels like we're the only two people on the planet, tonight," she continued.

"Glad to hear your paranoia's left you. You like the idea? I mean about us being the only two people on Earth, the only two that matter at the moment?"

"I might . . ."

"Maybe we could arrange for something a little more . . . permanent."

"What? Knock off the rest of the population?"

"I meant, maybe we could do this again. This doesn't have to be our only visit to Hana."

"Okay, maybe we can, but maybe we can also concentrate on this night?" She leaned over and kissed him. Jim passionately returned the kiss. In his embrace all her fears melted like ice under a South Pacific sun, and it did feel as if they were the only two people on the planet, at least this stretch of it on the edge of nowhere.

"Let's move into the tent where the sleeping bags are," he suggested. "As pretty as this black beach is from the air, it'll work havoc on your backside."

"Whataya mean, *my* backside?"

"Huh?"

"It's my turn to be on top."

"Just who's counting and who's making the rules around here?" he countered.

"Make no mistake about it: I am, Chief."

"What good is it then to be called Chief?"

"Come here, Chief . . ."

They embraced again and Parry lifted her into his arms, carrying her toward the tent.

"No, let's go for a swim first," she suggested.

"A swim . . ." he said as if it were a mad notion.

"When's the last time you went skinny-dipping with a girl, Chief?"

"A swim it is," he agreed, carrying her out and into the surf. As their clothes became soaked, each peeled pieces of the other's clothing away.

6:35 A.M., July 20, Maui

The lovemaking lasted well into the night. Spent and asleep in one another's arms, the couple was roused by a sudden change in the environment inside the tent which made Jessica bolt upright, causing Jim to do likewise. The incoming tide.

They'd pitched the tent too close and now water was lapping at the sleeping bags. It was dawn on Maui. Parry rousted her up and out, fighting to salvage all the equipment. Once this was done, he turned to her sleepy eyes and said, "Let's make the dive."

"What about breakfast?"

"No dice. Not where we're going."

"Are you sure this is safe?"

"No, but we're both well-experienced divers, and I wouldn't ask you to go where I wouldn't go, and furthermore, I've brought a lifeline. We'll secure it to one of the outcroppings and we stay buckled to it at all times, if necessary."

From the sound of the crashing waves, she thought it'd be absolutely necessary.

"How're we going to see anything with the sediment as stirred up as it's likely to be?" she asked.

"Look here," he said, snatching out a curious photograph. It was an aerial photo taken from a satellite in space. He pointed to their exact location.

"How'd you get this on such short notice?"

"Suffice it to say, I have my contacts at Science City. Look here." He pointed. "See here and here, these lines cutting away from the Spout."

"I do. What are they?"

"Experts tell me there's a valley on the bottom that's been cut away by the years of run-out, possibly thirty feet below the surrounding terrain at bottom level."

"Like an underwater caldera?"

"Inside which there could possibly exist a treasure of evidence against Lopaka Kowona, maybe not. Any rate, if we can make it to the bottom, locate the valley and enter it, we'll be protected from the powerful current."

"Still looks dangerous."

"Jess, if it looks bad, we'll turn around, come straight back up." She nodded. "Okay, I'm game."

"Somehow, I knew you'd say that."

Before they did anything else, Jim swam out to the jagged rocks, careful not to be caught in the incoming waves and forced against the volcanic spikes. There he tied the one-hundred-foot-long nylon cable with its anchor-end being sent into the depths below the Spout tunnel. In the meantime, Jessica began gearing up and with Jim's return to shore, they were soon both in their colorful diving outfits, tanks on their backs, wading out into the waves like a pair of alien creatures from another planet.

Out of water and flapping their fins, they were an awkward pair, like beached dolphins, but the moment they submerged they became free of weight as they expertly descended.

She knew she'd been right about the sediment here in their private little bay, for even in the protected area, hugged by natural barriers on two sides, the waves created a gray snowstorm before their eyes. It was impossible to see Jim's fins or his signals just ahead of her. She grabbed onto his left fin and held on, and he guided her. He was an accomplished diver, like herself, capable of navigating underwater with his compass alone. He'd obviously trained in dark water and night diving, as she had.

They weren't met with undersea life except for jagged coral reefs that seemed bent on reaching out to tear their suits. The current was swift and no fish would be foolish enough to be caught in it here. So they saw no other signs of life or light, save the brightness of the sun overhead, and even that was being slowly crushed as they ventured deeper and deeper.

A date with Jim Parry was a lot of things, but it was never dull, she told herself here.

He slowed ahead, the current tugging fiercely at his frame, turning him like a top. They'd both found the anchor line and were holding onto it for guidance and now dear life. She half hoped now that Jim saw what she saw, that it was more than foolish to go on, that it was deadly dangerous to be here. Still, he corkscrewed down, holding to the lifeline.

She'd let go of his fin once they'd found the line, holding to the line instead. She momentarily forgot her fright for herself and worried instead about Jim when a powerful wave overhead sent a monstrous current into her. The current forced her and the lifeline in one direction toward the coral bed and the rock outcroppings, slamming her into the volcanic base. She felt the rap against her air tank, knowing that it was dented badly by the sudden impact, the sound of the thud softened by the absorbing environment and her own labored breathing through the regulator in her mouth. She feared the next wave might send her skull into the bone-hard rock. But then she was swept in the opposite direction, toward the open ocean, the lifeline so stretched and with so much weight per ounce tugging at it, she feared it might snap. Somehow Jim had gone on, but she felt trapped between the incoming and outgoing current.

She forced herself to tug for the bottom, follow Jim, get out of the influence of the run-out.

She used all her strength to do so, her body being whiplashed by the power of sea meeting land. But suddenly, she felt free of the hostile force that had so wanted her. She was below the current's sweep, and waiting anxiously for her, his one hand on the lifeline, the other extended and waving her on, was Parry, bubbles fleeing madly around him. He was on his knees in calmer water.

She realized that the satellite photo was correct. Here was a crevice created over eons of time by the forces of this watery world. They were in the vestibule and hopefully the repository created here by the constant wash of time.

It was a large area, perhaps the size of a Little League baseball infield, handily small enough that they could scan every inch to locate what they'd come for, *if* . . . if there was anything to find. The current was still strong here, pushing them about like corks, but it was not so stalwart that they could not maneuver, if they forced the issue. She'd dived in places where the current swept by like space and stars against the porthole of an airplane, seaweed and small fish caught up in it and passing by her mask at thirty, maybe forty miles an hour, and yet she had still slowly managed to make headway against the current to return to the diving boat, using a draw line as last resort. She'd been in such a dive off the coast of Key Largo at the John Pennekamp underwater Coral Reef State Park in the Florida Keys once, when the dive-master, an enormous whale of a man whose only interest, it seemed, was his next can of beer, had foolishly taken the party beyond the barrier reef into rough waters. It was not pleasant to dive under such conditions, and it took every ounce of energy, and most of the divers that day never got off the boat, finding themselves too sick to do anything other than puke over the side.

Jim motioned for her to follow the contours of the circular field they'd discovered in one direction while he explored the other. The clarity of the water was better here than above, for it was calmer. Still, the sediment at the bottom of the reservoir was in a constant swirl, disturbed by the current, moving back and forth like milky, dirty water in a washbasin. Yet if she worked at it, she could see through this thin cloud, which hung ghostlike over the bottom, to see teeming life darting about, rooted plants, seaweed and coral and volcanic stone. A course could be determined and followed.

One thing was quite clear, with visibility so bad, they had to remain above the sandy floor, to keep their fins from swirling up the sediment even more.

As it was, they could barely see one another after a few feet of separation. Parry in fact looked like a ghost as he swam off in one direction, disappearing before her eyes. Being careful, picking her way along with great caution, fearful of swimming into a vortex, Jessica felt her stomach lurch at the thought that her last sight of Parry might have already occurred.

They were crazy to be here doing this. . . .

She adjusted her weight and descended further, getting closer for the survey of the floor, wiping aside floating debris. She followed a zigzag pattern, but not for long. She was stopped instantly by an unusually large, ivory stone with smooth contours below the sea, lichen growing on its base. Mold had so painted it over as to make it one with the surroundings, save for the top, rubbed bare, fanned for all eternity by the current. She sensed something strange about this stone immediately. It appeared bonelike.

She descended, parting small schools of fish as she did so. Nearby a sea turtle played out its underwater ballet, so at ease was it here in the depths. It came so near she reached out to touch it, but it sped off just ahead of her fingertips, as if in a teasing and familiar dance it'd danced with mankind for generations.

Below, in the sand at the bottom, she was coming to rest over what appeared the unnatural formation, a mound amid an otherwise smooth surface. Just as her knees were about to touch bottom, a UFO-shaped portion of the sand lifted off and shot away, its eyes on its head, looking angry and ratlike as it sped off.

If fish could curse, the pancake flounder would have the vilest words to say, she thought.

Jim Parry, doing his own zigzagging probe, saw her kneeling there, causing a smokescreen of sediment to settle around her. He came gliding over, curious about her find, giving her the universal hand gesture for *What?* He looked great underwater, she thought while pointing to her discovery, fearful of embarrassment now should her treasure turn into nothing, a false alarm.

She dug in with her gloved hands at the conical cap of the mound, Jim lending his own powerful hands, each scooping away sediment around the base. In an instant which made them both draw back, Jessica came away with a human skull and the neck bone from which it had so easily detached. The unmistakable skeletal remains of the skull's owner protruded now, shoulder bones and spinal column looking like a macabre mockery of the living coral around it.

Even here and through her face mask, Jessica could tell from the size, heft, contour and jaw that it was the skull of a woman. It was partially shattered at the cranium, brittle, ready to cave in. The eye sockets stared ceaselessly back at the divers. Christ help me, she thought, it's my nightmare come true, like a damned premonition. Parry went to work uncovering more bones, discarding rocks and silt, until soon, it appeared they had a large cache of human bones.

Jim had been so right it was scary, she thought.

Underwater everything was exaggerated, the five senses heightened, underscored. Colors were indescribably bright and blinding, shapes monstrous and large, and it took more effort to stare into death here like this than in her lab. Every effort made when working underwater, too, was more difficult; maneuvering the bone cache, like two spacemen lifting moon rocks in a zero-gravity environment, took its toll. Still, they worked to dig at the find with deliberate patience.

She had just begun to wonder how they were ever possibly going to get the bones to the surface when, like a magician's trick, Parry extended her a large net—*from out of thin water,* she mentally quipped—a net used for shelling or lobstering which he'd obviously brought along. Together they began filling the net with an array of bones, from ribs to femurs to skulls, some of which seemed too ponderous to be those of women—but this was no place to make such judgments. In fact, it was far too soon to tell for certain if all the bones were human, she conceded while Parry finished filling the net.

Now, the net filled to capacity, making it impossible for them to collect any more of the skeletal remains, they saw they had hardly scratched the surface of the underwater tomb. Still, it appeared that the top layer of bones was of more interest to them, since they appeared newer than most they'd found here.

Unlike the Navy divers at the Blow Hole, who'd not used satellite photo reconnaissance and had not located such a find, she and Parry had been extremely fortunate. Parry had made things happen here. She respected him for that. Forensically speaking, it appeared that they had Lopaka Kowona cornered in every sense of the word now. Just too bloody bad they didn't have the killer himself cornered.

Still, at least now they had more than the handful of bone fragments found at the Blow Hole, so skimpy as to be not enough for the usual jury, no matter how much Linda Kahala's minuscule remains might tell Jessica Coran.

Jim gave the signal that they should now find the tow rope and ascend the way they had come. She dreaded the return trip, but realized that the danger was only in one area, and when they reached that current belt, they'd have to move quickly and determinedly on. She worried about Jim and the extra weight the bone net represented, but then she saw that he had thought of everything, for he was attaching the net to the lifeline and tightly securing it there. He meant to bring it up with the anchor once on the surface, hand-over-hand.

Their little salvage operation looked to be a success when they were both successfully past the dangerous current zone and beyond any threat from the sea. The ocean was both benefactor and punisher here, depending on its whim and the foolishness of mortals like them who dared taunt the enormity of this god. Arising to meet the radiance of the upper world, Jessica was anxious to return to safety there amid the black stone beach, the sun and the silence of their private world above. She knew she'd been badly battered against the coral and lava rocks, and that her bruises would not soon heal, but they'd also be a friendly reminder of her exhilarating time here in this raw world with Jim Parry.

Even before he surfaced, Jim was looking at his watch, anticipating the arrival of the chopper and their departure. The bittersweet thought of leaving here was so strong that each of them felt it in the other's mind as they made their way out of the pounding surf to the safety of the protected bay and shore. They had yet to haul the bones from the sea. It was nearing mid-morning.

— 23 —

> . . . to the homicide detective, the earth spins on an axis of denial in an orbit of deceit.
>
> David Simon, *Homicide*

All the bones were fleshless and from the creamy surfaces and the growths and green, easily smudged life that clung to them, it appeared they were old. When Jessica mentioned this, Jim immediately wanted to know, "How old?"

"I couldn't say. I'm not a forensic anthropologist, but suffice it to say they're a hell of a lot older than Linda Kahala's was."

"Two, maybe three years old? What?"

"If I had to hazard a guess, yes . . . if not older."

"Older?"

"Yes, older, maybe a great deal older, and Jim, some of them . . ." She paused.

"What? Some of them what?"

They'd spread out some of the bones along a ledge, staring down at them, while most remained in the net.

"Some look to be male."

"Male?"

"Either that or quite large women, and Kowona doesn't do large women. He does—"

"Small women," he finished for her.

"Petite women, yes."

"Then this *has* been just another wild-goose chase, all for nothing?" He cursed under his breath and glared at one of the bones he held in his hand, making her believe he was about to hurl it back into the depths from which it had come.

"Don't jump the gun. We need to study them all. Maybe we've got a real mixed bag here. Maybe some of the pieces'll fit our puzzle, some not. It'll take some lab time."

"Yeah, sure . . ." he finally agreed, dropping the femur he held in his hand back into the net. "Come on, let's pack up and be ready for the chopper. We've got to get back up the trail with the tanks and our cache."

"If it helps, two of the skulls are definitely female, and they look relatively new, in comparison to the others, I mean, and I think they came from the top of the mound."

"That's something, but how do you explain the others?"

"Well, there once was a community here, you said."

"But they buried their dead in the earth. You saw the graveyard, the stones."

She considered this, turning one of the skulls in her hand as she did so. "What if they had some members of the village who weren't exactly *fit* for what they considered a proper burial? Do you know anything about Hawaiian religious practices and rites? Suppose they did sacrifices at one time . . ."

"To the sea? I haven't ever heard of it, no."

"To the sea . . . to the Spout?" she suggested.

He pondered this possibility. "Of course, makes good sense . . . more 'n' likely, you're right."

"And if Kowona grew up in a primal culture like they say, he'd have seen the ceremony performed, perhaps more than once. Perhaps it's the way the bones of his brother went, if the old great-granduncle of Kaniola can be believed. Maybe it's what led Lopaka to the Blow Hole, and maybe here before that?"

"Now I feel strange about taking these bones from their eternal resting place," lamented Parry. "I mean, for all intents and purposes, it's rather ghoulish, seeing as how it was their burial ground."

"We can always return the bones that belong here, but we need to know the truth about those that may not."

"Can you make good enough distinctions now, so we can return the older bones?"

"I think so, but there's no time for another dive."

"Hell, we can shoot them back through the Spout."

"And they'll likely return to within feet of where we found them," she agreed.

Just hurry. I don't want anyone seeing us. Some tourists come poking about here and see us, and God knows the consequences."

She began to cull the bones, soon finding it easy to discriminate between the newer and older, particularly the skulls. Above ground, under the illumination of the sun, she found no difficulty in distinguishing a male jawbone from a woman's, a male hipbone from a female's, and so it went. She placed all the bone parts they would keep to one side, refilling the net with the others. The amount of new bones was considerably less than the old, and as she worked with the aged bones, finding them so brittle to the touch, worn paper-thin by time and water, they flaked easily in their new, arid environment. She realized just how ancient some of the bones were; certain they must date at least to the early 1900s and perhaps the late 1800s.

She kept one ancient bone fragment for comparison and carbon-14 dating later.

While she conducted this process, Jim worked on getting all their gear back to the chopper pad. He was pretty much finished when he found her at the Spout with the net filled with returnable bones. He helped her out over the ledge with her burden and together they lifted the net and allowed the bones to return to the outgoing waters via the Spout. Standing there, Jessica could imagine the ancients worshipping this place as sacred.

Each roaring plume of the geyser was an angry godlike outburst, a counterpoint to her quiet thoughts.

Several of the thigh bones and long bones of the arm and hand got caught up in the netting and refused to return to the sea so easily. Jim fished them from the net and one by one tossed these final fragments back into the sea.

The entire time they both were drenched by the incoming tide as it flew into the funnel of the Spout and cascaded up and over them. Before it was over, they were soaking wet.

They returned to the most likely usable bones from their cache and replaced them in the net. Jim carried these up along the winding trail with Jessica following.

"I'll give you the background on the missing Maui women . . . kids really, all the medical papers, see if you can match any of the dental charts with the two skulls we've got."

"It should prove interesting," she said from behind, watching her footing as they went, seeing now just how awfully treacherous both the terrain and the *pukas* hereabouts were. One hole in particular looked like the mouth of an enormous serpent just asleep below the earth, waiting patiently for a passerby to careen down into its gut. The bottom was mere darkness. She dared stare too long into this natural abyss, feeling a dizzying disorientation wash over her. Maybe she'd gone too long without a bite to eat, she thought, regaining her composure.

After the chopper's arrival, they flew on to Kahului, where they disembarked with all that belonged to them. A rental car awaited them at the airport, the bones carefully concealed in its trunk as quickly as possible to arouse no one's concern. While still on the helicopter, Jim had radioed authorities in Maui about the find and the likelihood it might prove connected with the Kowona case. He'd made arrangements for a field operative based on Maui to meet them at the airport and see personally to the careful boxing and transporting of the evidence to Lau's labs back on Oahu while Jessica drew up instructions for Lau to go along with the bones. Working with local authorities on Maui, Parry warned that Kowona could be somewhere on their island. Patrols were stepped up, everyone put on alert, and a surveillance team was sent out to monitor the area around the Spout for any sign of a man dumping any sort of strange parcels into the ocean there.

Lopaka Kowona, Jim was assured by one patrol officer, would not slip through the hands of the authorities on Maui as he had with those "fools" on Oahu.

"That hurt," Jim said to her when the transmission ended.

From the airport they drove to their next destination, a quaint cow town like something out of a movie set in the deserts around L.A., she thought. But even though there were hitching posts along the main street and horses tied to the posts, there were also Ford,

Chevy and Dodge pickup trucks sporting gun racks and rifles through cab windows.

There were hardware stores, feed stores, millinery stores, grills, bars and taverns—she counted four within the two-block length of the little town of Makawao, where a banner proclaimed the date for the upcoming rodeo, to be held on July 4th, long since come and gone though the tattered banner waved on.

Everyone walking the concrete walks and onto the boarded steps of establishments here had chaps and boots, it seemed, and the cowboys were of every size, shape and ancestry.

"What the hell is this?" she asked.

"Kowona's home for a long time. He worked the Omaopio Ranch just outside of town here, same as Ewelo the Paniolo. People here will know Kowona, and maybe they'll talk."

"Let's do it, then. You want to canvass together or make a split?"

"Together. We might be less threatening that way."

"Or more."

"Just follow my lead." They got out of the car and instantly the locals pegged them as not the usual touristy couple. In fact, Jessica fit right in with her tomboy appearance, in two-day-old jeans, her hair stringy from the early morning dive, bruises showing on her arm as if her man had given her a good and deserved smacking around. She couldn't help but feel self-conscious, and it didn't help having the locals stare at them as if they were wearing horns. She wasn't wearing a cowboy hat, a big belt buckle or boots, and she didn't know how to square-dance, nor did she know the achy-breaky line dance. Over the saloon door a notice for tonight's dance was posted.

Parry, trying to fit in, actually sauntered to the bar, leaving her to traipse after in the best Western tradition, following her man like a heifer in heat. She wasn't sure she liked the role, even for a little bit.

"Looking for some information," Parry said to the man behind the bar.

"Tourist booth is on down the road 'bout twelve miles when you come to—"

He flashed his badge. "I'm no tourist, Slim, and I know the island. I want to speak to you about a girl named Merelina."

"Merelina?"

"Merelina Wailano, disappeared around here two and a half

years ago, last in a line of seven young women on the island to disappear that season of the winds."

The bartender breathed in deeply. "We know Lopaka Kowona's up on charges—"

"He's not up on charges, mister. He's wanted and he's a fugitive. We charge him after we catch him."

"Well, either way, we heered 'bout all this, but nobody to my knowledge has seen that ol' boy 'round these parts." The man behind the bar was white with a near black Hawaiian tan.

"Get this, Slim. I want you to tell me what you hear. We know the creep's on the island, and if I find out he's been helped out here, this whole cowboy town of yours is going to be in deep shit. There'll be so much federal in here, you boys won't have much of any fun anymore playing shoot-ups and breaking nudity and gambling laws, not to mention drug laws."

"You sure as hell don't want that," added Jessica, "do you?"

Several men who'd been seated at a nearby table, looking on and listening carefully to Parry's threats, began first to mumble among themselves, and then two of them kicked their way over in their crocodile boots.

"We're with the Omaopio," said one of the men in a deep, resonant voice. His ballcap sporting an emblem of a P within a circle. "Hain't no killing sonofabitch gonna dare set foot on the Circle P."

The other, nodding, added, "We don't none of us hold with what this monster done to those women, and Lopaka'll know our feelings."

"He knows us boys."

"He knows we ever get hold of him here, we'd likely lynch the sonofabitch even b'fore you boys—and ladies"—he stopped to tip his hat—"could do a damn thing 'bout it."

"So you're saying he's not welcome here?" asked Jessica.

Parry leaned in toward the first man and conspiratorially said, "He's got *no one* here, not even family he'd turn to?"

"Not at the Omaopio," said the first cowboy.

"And not in Makawao," added the bartender as he wiped at the bar. "People here hate the son of a bitch. Brought nothing but shame on his hometown, so far's we're concerned. Like David Koresh in Texas and Jeffrey Dahmer in Wisconsin. I reckon if he was seen on the streets here, he'd be shot down like a dog, don't you, Hiram?"

Hiram, a stocky Samoan cowboy who'd remained at the table, drinking softly from his less-than-foamy Kona beer, grunted and said, "This ain't his home no way. He come first from Molokai. I figah if anybody going take dat brah in, it be deah."

"Have you heard anything concrete about that?" asked Jessica, going to the man, her eyes pleading.

"Jus' talk is all."

"But if he was banished from that place," she began.

"Banished, yeah, but dem people who banished him ain't no now on Molokai. Dey move on."

"Moved on?" she asked. "Where?"

"Nobody can say, but dey all no stay deah now."

"Then it is possible that he's gone back to Molokai?" she said, turning and staring at Jim.

"It's possible," replied the stony Samoan, shutting down now.

The cowboy at the bar added in his broken English, "I wen talk wit' him wen he was heah. Him, he nevah sat long for a beeah or a gab. Nobody evah knew where he was or what he was up to."

"Yeah," agreed the other man at the bar. "He hated Molokai, where he was born, and he no much care for here either. Always talking about going off to Oahu, Honolulu, he said."

"If any of you see or hear of anything regarding this wanted man with a fifty-thousand-dollar reward on his head, please call this number. I'll leave it with the bar man," said Parry, tossing down his card.

"You got a place where we can call fo' you, missy?" asked one of the cowpokes.

"Jake, a classy lady like dis not going to sit your horse."

The others laughed while Parry, frowning, escorted a smiling Jessica from the bar.

"One watering hole down, three to go," she said.

"You get the feeling we're wasting our time here?"

She laughed.

"What?" he asked.

"The feeling I get here?" She looked again around the town of Makawao, seeing the white Stetsons and vests going by. "The feeling is *Twilight Zone,* partner."

"That doesn't answer my question."

She considered it anew. "Maybe we are wasting our time, maybe not. Either way, it's *sooooommme* town."

They found a small cafe, ordered a lunch of burgers, fries and

Cokes, rested from the heat and afterward continued their survey of the townspeople.

It was soon all over the little hamlet that the FBI was in town.

Their stay remained uneventful, people shying away from them for the most part, and Jim leaving word where he could be reached in each location he thought useful. Then they reached the last bar at the end of the street. Inside, they were immediately confronted by the huge proprietor, who, if cleaned up a bit, might resemble a grizzled Clint Eastwood with weight on. In his grip was a well-used and dented Louisville Slugger. He marched up to Jim and told them to get out.

"I heard how you creeps been treating my pal Ewelo over there in Oahu," said the owner of the bar, crowding Parry before he might get a word out. "And here's what I think of that."

Before Jessica knew what was happening, the man drew back the ball bat and it came at Jim with a powerful whoosh. Jessica drew her gun and went on one knee, but she needn't have. Jim expertly avoided the bat like a prizefighter. Bobbing and weaving, Parry sent several successive punches into the big man's cheek and jaw each time he swung the bat and missed, until finally Jim rained a series of small explosions into the man's eyes, forcing him back and back until he came to a wall, where Parry's fencing style of fighting took on a new nature; a serious uppercut sent the man's jaw skyward and his form slid down the wall, unconscious. It all happened in a matter of seconds.

"Christ-a-mighty!" shouted someone from a table.

"Look what he done to Big Stan!"

The others gave Parry wide berth, listened politely to what he had to say between his panting, and nodded as they left, all but Big Stan.

"Maybe this was a stupid idea," said Parry, blowing on his bruised knuckles to cool them down.

"Hey, you're just going to infect those cuts," she cautioned. "Come on, here's a water trough."

"Oh, really sanitary," he said, shaking his head, but following her orders nonetheless.

After cleaning up a bit, they went back for the car. Along the way, an elderly Hawaiian woman with squinting eyes held up a hand to them and in hurried, hushed tones she said, "You come wrong place for Lopaka. Family hiding him from you. Dey know where he is."

"Whataya mean by that?" pressed Parry, but the woman turned into a wooden creature, not daring another word, continuing on her way as if she could neither see nor hear them.

"Does that mean Molokai?" asked Jessica, but again the woman's frozen features revealed nothing.

"I think, Jess, what everyone wants us to believe is that Lopaka's returned to Molokai."

"It might seem so," she agreed, shading her eyes against the brilliant sun. The rancher town of Makawao was not at a high elevation, but rather on the fertile slopes of the lee side of the island, in the shadow of Mt. Haleakala.

"If they wanted to steer us away from Maui to Molokai, then they've got to do better than they're doing. And if they are trying to steer us back northward to Molokai, then which way is Lopaka heading? It would follow that he's going southward from here."

"What's southward from Maui?"

"The big island of Hawaii, but just southwest is . . ." Jim hesitated.

"What? What's southwest?"

"The island of death—Kahoolawe."

"Kahoolawe, but isn't that—"

"It's the closest point from Maui by boat."

She saw a light in his eyes which burned intensely. He believed he had hit on the secret where Lopaka was. "If Lopaka's not on Maui, then he's there," said Jim, leaning against the rental car, a certain finality in his voice. "Look, if that's the case, he'd have left from somewhere around Cape Hanamanioa on the windward side of the island. The channel between the other island and Maui is known as the Alalakeiki, the distance a mere ten miles."

"It's that close?"

"Just down the coast from there at Hekili Point is the only place in all of Hawaii where you can stand and see four other islands. Lopaka knows that if he makes it to Kahoolawe, he can be free. He's got to know that, and if he's being helped . . ."

She tried to decipher all this new information, recalling what Jim had told her of the no-whites policy of the Kahoolawe preserve, that even the FBI was off-limits there. "So, if Lopaka has in fact made it to Kahoolawe island, we may've seen the last of him?"

Upset now, Jim said, "Get in the car. We've got to move." He hurried around to the driver's side and got in. She slid into the passenger seat, and in a moment they were pulling from the curb, doing a U-turn on the main street of Makawao.

"What about a warrant, extradition papers?"

Parry shook his head.

"But there's got to be a way we can extradite the—"

"No go under these circumstances. U.S. authorities can't set foot on the island under any circumstances without express and unequivocal invitation. And to further complicate the situation, he could be given immunity by virtue of his lineage."

"Lineage? Whose invitation?" She was so angry she could hardly see the island road ahead.

"The head of the tribal government on Kahoolawe."

"Who is?"

"Kowona . . . the elder Kowona, don't you get it?"

"Lopaka's father?"

"Yes, he'd be one of the first to seek out Kahoolawe as a refuge from encroaching Western civilization on Molokai. He'd be one of the first to take up residence on Kahoolawe, braving whatever hardships he and his people there might face."

"You're sure you're not clutching at straws? I mean, on the word of those cowboys back there that Lopaka's people are no longer on Molokai? Is that enough?"

"When we get to the hotel on the other side of the island, I'll confirm it with our guy on Molokai."

"Our hotel's on the other side of the island? Near this bay that looks out over Kahoolawe? Then you knew all along?"

"I feared all along, the moment it sank in that the bastard had escaped Oahu, yes. It's a hole-in-the-wall, a place where a parasite like this might find refuge. There is no law there as we know it, Jess." Parry drove onward to their next destination, his teeth set and clenched.

"You've known where you're going all along . . . known about Lopaka's run for Kahoolawe all along? Hell, you forwarded our luggage there!"

"I didn't know Lopaka was related to the big muckety-muck on Molokai, not at first. Hell, over here Kowona's as common as Smith in the States. But after you told me about what the old man said, Kaniola's great-granduncle, I began to wonder and to consider the geography of it all."

"Lopaka's boyhood village was supposedly on Molokai," she

said. "And everyone's trying to rivet our attention there. So you, being of a suspicious turn of mind . . ."

"Yeah, but in the meantime, over the last year or so, his people removed to Kahoolawe. Who better to reclaim the island for the PKO when the U.S. Navy relinquished their hold over it."

"Tell me more about this unusual island and its special status," she asked. "Isn't there some way around it, given the circumstances, the dire—"

"The kid'll have diplomatic immunity there, simple as that . . ."

"God damn it!" she burst out.

He wheeled the car now back out to the main highway off which they'd descended into the town of Makawao. Back on U.S. 37, they made a beeline for the other side of the island and the Alalakeiki Channel.

"The island was used as a bloody bombing target for aircraft and naval vessels by our armed forces since 1942 and—" he began.

"Christ, it must be one helluva piece of screwed-up real estate."

"—and for a hell of a long time only wild goats and sheep lived there, but since the Hawaiians have gained in political power and influence, they've gained the island back and along with it this special status. Some of the traditionalists, the tribesmen from all the various islands in the chain, returned to Kahoolawe to re-colonize—"

"Re-establish their culture, you mean?"

He nodded, adding, "Living purely by ancient means, or so everyone says."

"You're not so sure?"

"I have my suspicions they're not about to turn up their noses at certain modern devices."

"Such as?"

"Motor boats, nautical equipment, firearms."

"Firearms, really?"

"There's scuttle that they've been amassing their own arsenal against the day when we—the U.S.—decide to reclaim Kahoolawe. Next time, they intend to fight to the death. Anyway, they're big on fishing. And they do some trading in canned goods and other foods and necessities with the Maui islanders."

"And what do they have to trade?"

"Fish mostly, exotic and authentic shell leis, some ancient

arrowhead artifacts. Couple of archaeological sites found on the island now belong wholly to the tribesmen, too."

"So, they've worked a trade for the return of a native son, and we can't touch him?"

"Who knows? Maybe we'll get lucky. Maybe he declined their invitation. Maybe he did go on to the big island south of here . . . maybe . . ."

He didn't sound convinced. The island traffic had thinned to a trickle here, the road bordered on one side by a sugarcane field through which the wind raged, setting the stalks into a frantic dance as the car sped by.

"Where to now, Jim?"

"I know some friends in the vicinity who might take me to Kahoolawe."

"What?"

"For a price."

She took in a deep breath of air and stared out at the pineapple fields on either side of the road now, wondering why Jim seemed so hell-bent on destroying his own career.

It appeared that Jim Parry meant to track Lopaka to the ends of the earth if necessary, to see justice done. Still, his obsession was her own.

"What the hell're you going to do, Jim? I mean, even if you can determine that he's on that island, you . . . we have no juice there. You can't take him off the island, not without risking your own career, not if the government says stay out, that it's not the jurisdiction of the agency."

"At this point, Jess, I just want to get my hands on him."

"To kill him?"

"Look, if I can take him alive and get him off the island without anyone's knowing I was there, then he's my prisoner."

"I see. And you think that's possible?"

"I don't know, but I'll never know if I don't get within spitting distance."

She fell silent, scanning the incredible scenery as it flew by. Jim, having been introduced to the island long ago, raced full ahead toward their next destination.

"I could use a bath, you know," she complained. "Get this seawater off my skin. I got sand in places I didn't know existed."

"There's lovely accommodations the other side of the mountain range along the ocean. Don't worry on that score."

When they arrived, she began to see familiar sights. It was the area of the island where she had dived in the marine sanctuary and a haven for snorklers and scuba divers, Molokini island and its underwater crater just off the coast and Kahoolawe just beyond; in fact, she had seen Kahoolawe island in the distance and had asked about it, but the Hawaiian dive-master had said it was no place for diving, and she'd let it go at that.

"We'll have to go in under cover of darkness," she told him.

"We? There'll be none of this 'we' stuff here, Jess. One FBI agent getting his ass canned for this kind of a stunt will be quite enough."

"I'm going with you, Jim. We've acted as a team this far, and this is no time to start acting any differently."

"Jess, this is something I *have* to do. You . . . you can walk away from it, return to D.C. tomorrow knowing you did a fine job."

"Not without Lopaka's head on a stick, no way. I feel as strongly about this damned, bloody case as you, Jim. You owe me. I'm going in, too."

"We won't be able to land a boat there. We'll have to do this frogman-style, Jess, and it'll be dangerous."

"What the hell do you call the Spout? And now you're planning to leave your diving partner behind? No way!"

"Jess!"

"If I don't go, you don't go."

"Are you absolutely sure?"

"Absolutely."

They came careening out of the mountains and around a cliff to come into view of the distant small island that was taboo to the Westerner, Kahoolawe, their next destination.

— 24 —

Man's nature is like a dense thicket that has no entrance
and is difficult to penetrate.

The Teachings of Buddha

The Wailea Sun Resort Hotel provided a place to catch one's
breath, clean up and relax until nightfall, before they would
attempt the dangerous landing on Kahoolawe. Jim had showered
and rushed out before she was even settled, saying he had to
coordinate things with the local authorities, see to it they were
doing everything in their means to locate and apprehend Kowona,
and seek out an underworld figure here who would see to it they
had passage to Kahoolawe.

The time alone, waiting for Jim to return, was passed with her
own showering and freshening up, and a brief nap after a call to
room service for a cheese and wine tray to be sent up. She'd gone
out on the balcony, put her feet up and after a few glasses of wine,
had dozed against a pillow. When she awoke, native birds had

roosted on the table and were sampling the cheese and crackers while the sky all around had softened into a cloud of lavenders and purples.

Night was descending rapidly now and she feared Jim had left her, believing she'd be safer left behind, the thought infuriating her. She lashed out at the birds, shooing them off. Then she quickly dressed in jeans and a pullover, and was about to storm out the door when the phone rang.

She grabbed for it.

"Jess, it's me."

"Where are you, Jim?"

"Take a cab and meet me at Nuekuela Point Wailea harbor. We've got passage."

"I thought you'd left me."

"Don't think I didn't give it serious thought. You realize if we're taken into custody by the local tribesmen, well, it'll be hell to get off the island, much less fax for help from Washington. You sure you don't want to reconsider, Jess?"

"I've stopped thinking about it, Jim. Let's just do it. I've got to know where this Jack the Ripper is, and if there's a chance in hell we can bring him to justice, then I say we go for it."

"We won't have a scuba in from the boat either."

"Really?"

"We're rafting in, inflatable."

"Terrific."

"And we'll have a guide."

"A guide? This is sounding better and better."

He remained cautionary. "It's not like any guided tour you've had of the much-visited islands, kiddo, so don't think it's like the little choo-choo ride through the plantation."

"Don't worry about me."

"Still, it's someone who knows the island."

"Sounds like one hell of a plus to me," she replied with enthusiasm.

"Name is Ben Awai. He trades with the locals, knows the village on Molokai where Lopaka grew up. How's that for a turn of good fortune?"

"Has he been able to confirm your suspicions?"

"Some, not all. Says Lopaka's people did move out to Kahool-awe, but doesn't know if our killer's out there or not."

A glint of suspicion like the sliver of shadow and light that runs

the gamut of a knife blade flashed along her consciousness before
it faded. But she didn't allow her suspicious nature to sway her this
time. Jim had wanted her to be less suspicious, more trusting of
him.

"I'm on my way, Jim, and don't you dare embark without me,
you hear?"

11 P.M., Wailea Harbor, Maui

At the harbor where the cab let her off, she saw Jim coming toward
her in the dark. The harbor lights were dim and pretty, reflecting
off the water, more show than functional, creating paths for lovers
to walk, not light for boatmen to work by. Still the harbor was
thick with fishing boats and men unloading large caches of fish,
carving them up over a worn, gray boardwalk long before stained
and discolored with blood.

Jim hailed her and casually said, "Ready for that moonlight boat
ride, honey?"

"I can hardly wait, dear," she replied, not missing her cue,
realizing Jim feared one or both of them might be recognized and
that their trip must remain clandestine.

He guided her down the pier, the calm Pacific lapping at the
boats in the harbor, rocking them gently against their moorings.
Ropes and lines swayed with the masts here and metal clinked so
gently against metal that the effect was of a hundred crystal wine
glasses chiming together.

A crescent moon blinked over the scene, the sea a watery blend
of turquoise, jade and azure, like an unfinished oil painting, its
colors running, except that this seascape was real. She carefully
boarded the small craft that Jim had arranged for, nodding to Ben
Awai, a thick-necked, barrel-chested Hawaiian with the familiar
knatty, red-burnished hair and grinning eyes of his race. Ship's
master here, Awai welcomed Jessica aboard with the economy of
words she'd come to expect from his race, saying, *"He mea 'ole."*

"He says welcome aboard," Jim translated.

The ship's master mumbled something in Hawaiian to the two
crew members, also Hawaiian. The other two laughed and began
casting off, wasting no time.

Jessica felt the comforting weight of her ankle holster and gun,
knowing that Jim's own weapon was safely tucked into the small
of his back below the dark green U of H sweatshirt he wore. "How

well do you know these characters, Jim?" she whispered as the boat began its slow departure from port.

"Enough. Don't worry."

"What're you saying? Situation normal, all fucked up, or have you simply gone beyond worry stage? Exit left or no exit left?"

"Awai will do right by us. I've had assurances from friends on the island that he's okay, that he's a man of his word."

"Friends?"

"In law enforcement."

This didn't quell her fears, especially when she saw one of the other crewmen glaring unashamedly at her. This was followed by more mumbling between the crewmen and more icy stares.

"What're they saying?" she asked Jim.

"Can't make it out. Something about how pretty you are, I think."

She gritted her teeth. "I don't feel entirely right about sticking our necks out so far, Jim."

"Hey, come on, you don't want a blind crew, do you? And they'd have to be blind if they didn't see how beautiful you are. As for sticking our necks out, I tried, if you remember, to leave you behind."

She frowned, paced the small deck of the fishing charter and wrapped her hands around one of the thick ropes of hemp. "Yeah, you did warn me of the risks. But now we're actually out here, sailing away from all contact with the outside world . . . I mean, anything could happen out there on Kahoolawe. We have no jurisdiction, our badges are worthless. What if we have to fall back on our weapons, Jim? You and me, we could end up on the wrong side of the law very easily."

"Kahoolawe law, yeah, quite easily."

"Just how much do you know about the people on the island? Are they as feudal as they sound?"

"They're made up of people who chose to return to a completely traditional way of life, all of them cultists in a sense—"

"Great, sounds more and more like we're stepping into a David Koresh situation without backup."

"Cultists in the sense they embrace the old ways. They've come to Kahoolawe only recently, actually, appearing from all over the other islands, Molokai, Maui, even Oahu and the big island of Hawaii itself. They're not much different from the American Indians who're trying desperately to hold onto their culture in the

States, and they enjoy the same kind of immunity from governmental pressures as do the American Indians. Sure, we could storm the reservation, but the political repercussions would cause a ripple effect that would be felt all the way back to D.C."

"And the already widening rift between the peoples of the island would be opened wider?" she added. Old scars, she thought, ripped to bleed as never before, something neither side wanted.

He put an arm around her and squeezed her shoulder firmly as the boat slipped its moorings and backed out under the power of its relatively quiet motor. "We just have to play this one by ear."

"Tell me everything you know about Kahoolawe."

"I already have!"

"Everything, Jim."

"Hmmmm, well, there's no way your prophet on the mountain, Lomelea, could be right about the so-called legend of Lopaka Kowona's having seen his brother killed."

"Why do you say so?"

"If it happened, it happened on Molokai, but records there indicate that there was no brother, that Lopaka in fact is and always has been the only son conceived by Chief Kowona, and this with a white wife who died of cholera when Lopaka was quite young. She was pregnant with a second child at the time, but no brother was born. That is according to a rough census taken."

"The old chief could've lied."

"Perhaps . . . perhaps not. I don't know a hell of a lot about psychology but I do know that killers lie, and very often they lie to themselves, to rationalize that which cannot be explained away in any other manner, if you get my drift."

"That would only prove Lomelea wrong factually; symbolically, for the killer, he did have a brother who was destroyed by his father, even if that brother was his alter ego."

"Yeah, well, that's best left to the shrinks."

"If it ever comes to that."

"Anyway, it was only in the early nineties that the U.S. Government returned Kahoolawe to the Ohana."

"The *Ohana*? Isn't that Kaniola's newspaper?"

"No, no, the PKO—Protect Kahoolawe Ohana. *Ohana* means family, but the PKO, which came into existence in '76, has turned Kahoolawe into the principal symbol of native Hawaiian consciousness. Native Hawaiians made it clear they wanted Kahoolawe back."

"But you said there's nothing there, no resources or riches."

"Still, it's been the most hotly contested piece of real estate in the islands, primarily because land is so limited and scarce in the islands—any land, even land with hundreds of unexploded U.S. Navy shells lying about."

"There're live shells all over the island?" she asked. "That's a real comfort, Jim."

"Any rate, the PKO's become a powerful political group in the islands. Hell, unless I miss my guess they were behind Ewelo's kidnapping of Oniiwah, and Kaniola's *Ohana* newspaper makes the perfect mouthpiece for them."

"Now I understand better your attitude toward him."

"Their big push on is to restore as much island land and sacred temples and burial grounds as possible, and there are some prime archaeological sites on Kahoolawe that they have their eyes on, which fortunately escaped as targets of the U.S. military over the years."

"I can see their point of view," she said, staring out toward the black mound of the island in the distance. "They've been so disenfranchised by us over the years."

"If we were to go over the island in Lee's chopper, Jess, you'd see just how desolate the place is, how awful the results of the years of bombings have been, not to mention the goats."

"Goats? Yeah, you mentioned something before about goats."

"The only thriving creatures on the island since the bombings, save for lizards, insects and maybe some mongoose."

"Mongoose in Hawaii?" she asked.

"Imported but thriving and remarkably prolific, and the goats too have been allowed to roam free and wild, and have overpopulated and devastated the topsoil on the slopes over much of the island. There needs to be a serious effort to decrease their numbers, but the PKO and the U.S. Government can't seem to agree on how it should be done; consequently, nothing's been done."

"Sounds sadly typical and political."

"You got that right. Anyway, from overhead, in the air, Kahoolawe is a uniquely Hawaiian anomaly."

"What?" she asked, turning to look into his eyes.

"An ugly, undesirable piece of property. Not supposed to be any such thing in Hawaii. Seven miles off the coast of East Maui, we come across a barren, windswept island inhabited by goats and cultists."

"Maybe you're being harsh to call them cultists, Jim. Maybe they're just what they say they are, native Hawaiians who want to live as their forefathers lived."

"Yeah, maybe I've got my prejudices, sure. Some people in the islands just see them as fools. There's barely enough vegetation on the island for shade much less raising livestock, and streams around the island dry up in the summer. Mt. Haleakala on the bigger island just about squeezes all the rain from the clouds before they reach here. The only thing Maui sends over are the dry, cold Makaniloa winds off the slopes of Halekala. Kahoolawe's hot and humid during the day, and cold at night. Much of the red-soil landscape is lunar in nature."

"Add to that fifty years of poundings by naval artillery and airforce bombers," she interjected. "Maybe it's become such a symbol for native unity because it most represents what Kaniola would call blatant *haole* disregard for his homeland? I can sympathize with the desire to see the land returned to civilian control."

"In an island state, land of any kind is valuable, Jess. All that the PKO knows is that one day Kahoolawe will be worth a fortune, and if they can squat on it . . . well, squatters' rights, you know. Hell, Jess, as a practice bombing site for the Navy and Airforce, it was perfect."

"Perfect, huh?"

"It's only one hundred ten miles from Pearl, the U.S. headquarters for operations in the Pacific."

"And you think that makes it okay?"

"In the best tradition of might makes right and given the context of the times, I don't know. Since the fifties the natives have been given visitation rights several months of each year to the island and limited fishing rights year round. It was never contested until the PKO came into prominence."

She thought Jim Parry was sounding political now, perhaps even racist, but then who could live day in and day out here without taking sides? she wondered.

"In '76 the PKO occupied the island against the orders of the Navy. It got ugly."

"There were riots?"

"More like there were arrests. It was the first of many battles fought in the name of their sacred island, and since then the PKO has scored some impressive victories. They backed their own man for Congress and he's won every year since. In 1990, Congress passed a two-year moratorium on the bombing while a federal and state commission studied the cost of clearing the island of shells and debris, its future use, and who would eventually have jurisdiction over the place."

"So what was the outcome?"

"You're looking at it," he said, pointing ahead to the dense growth in the fast approaching bay along this stretch of the island. "A return to the past."

She thought for a moment of all that Jim's phrase implied, the multifaceted levels of connotation in his words. Was going back to the past a personal affront to the white race? Did it imply that Christianity was dealt a blow, that the American way of life, Western civilization, was a poor substitute for a simple agrarian lifestyle? That democracy and the Puritan work ethic of the whites were all a fraud perpetrated on humanity by a rigid mind-set, no less treacherous in its way than that of a conqueror of another kind?

"A sacred island, they call it?" she asked. "Is it sacred, or is it like the Seven Sacred Pools, a slogan written by an ad man?"

He raised his shoulders. "I guess Kahoolawe is sacred in the native mind." But Jim wanted to talk of things associated with the island other than its sacredness to the Hawaiians. "The Ohana, with some big guns in Congress now, won their argument to have the island set aside for cultural and educational purposes. Had the island declared a national freaking historic monument. Can you believe that?" He held his voice down, obviously not wishing Awai or the crewmen to hear him on this.

"Why do they regard the island as sacred? And if it was sacred, how did they ever lose control of it in the first place?"

"They were herded off the island when the military declared it theirs. They hadn't any choice in the matter, and they weren't exactly prepared to take on the U.S., either through force or through the courts, believe me."

She repeated her question. "What makes it sacred to them?"

"Usual crap."

"Jim, why're you sounding so . . . so unlike yourself over this? Why're you sounding like a racist?"

He took a deep breath and blew it out toward the island, which was taking on more formidable size before them. "Because now this sacred place, this native Hawaiian jurisdiction, is a sanctuary, a natural haven for fugitives like Lopaka Kowona. That's why. And it frustrates and infuriates me that they hide behind a wall of sacred cows when in fact this place is no better policed than Indian Territory in the American West of the 1800s. Just pisses me off, and it hasn't got squat to do with race or sacredness."

"You still haven't answered my question."

"They think it sacred because in ancient times it was known as Kanaloa, after one of the four major Hawaiian gods. It's mentioned all the time in their chants and the legends passed down through the generations. At one time all travelers to Tahiti stopped on the island to perform rituals before journeying on, and in 1874, King David Kalakaua was personally brought here by his *kahuna*—"

"His *kahuna*? His priest?"

"Yeah, his priest . . . to purge himself before ascending to the throne. There are ancient shrines and fishing temples all over the island, and since the Navy imposed isolation, these shrines are in excellent condition, so the Ohana, naturally—"

"I see; understood. Then maybe the Ohana were right, their intentions good."

"The road to hell is paved with good intentions," he countered. "I don't know. I'm just a cop when it comes down to it, way out of navigable waters here. The PKO did force the Navy to make a comprehensive study of the environmental impact of the shelling and bombing, and a thorough survey of the archaeological sites and conditions of each. Amazingly, the shrines survived all the hits. The Ohana also managed in '81 to gain the historic site status which made the Navy's continued policy of obliterating the place appear downright un-American."

"Not to mention stupid." She laughed lightly at this. "Cunning move for the *kanakas*, heh, Joe? Chalk one up."

"Right, the beginning of the checkmate, if you ask me, because next the Ohana won the right for natives to visit the island four days a month for ten months each year. While at the same time the U.S. military stubbornly held onto its bombing schedule, at least in the abstract, since they seldom fired again on the island after this."

"Damned fools had to know that if some fool scheduled a bomb run on a day when natives were visiting shrines, well, all hell would've broken loose," she said, laughing.

He smiled at the image before continuing. "The northeast shore, where we're landing, a place called Ule Point, is where most of the visitors over the years have made pilgrimages to shrines. It's the area that gets most rainfall and has best survived the U.S. Navy assaults. Nowadays, Polynesians the islands over gather here to 'go native,' to dress in ancient clothing, celebrate ancient ritual and legends, *to talk story,* their phrase for oral histories. Some of the celebrations have been filmed and can be seen at the Bishop Museum by *haoles,* but none are invited here."

"So the Ohana won in the end."

"I don't believe that even the Ohana could've foreseen the actual return of a permanent population to the island."

"I see."

"It just happened. Pockets of pilgrims who came for the celebrations started slowly to trickle back to stay, most of them booking passage on boats like this one, refugees out of time, you might say, living anachronisms, like this Chief Kowona."

She sensed a confusion in Parry, a sense of profound sadness for these people he spoke of in such analytical terms. She asked, "Before the Navy controlled the island, it held a permanent population?"

"Yes, the diehards who from the first contact with the white man resisted becoming assimilated, and before World War II there were some flourishing ranches on the island, owned by whites who'd come in the 1870s. For a time before the cattle ranchers, King Kamehameha III had turned the island into a penal colony, which failed miserably. After the attack on Pearl Harbor, Kahoolawe fell into the control of the military, the ranchers on the island suddenly finding themselves as disenfranchised as the natives."

"Can the island support a permanent population now?"

"Doubtful, really . . ."

"Oh? Why?" The breeze lifted her auburn hair, tying it in knots.

"The island's been used traditionally as a fishing base."

"The soil no good for agriculture?" she asked.

"The soil has been determined to be excellent for modern agriculture, but for hoe and rake subsistence farming, who knows." Jim stretched, yawning, obviously tired. "Most Hawaiians are, or have been, unable to cope with Kahoolawe's changing weather, you know, cold nights and treacherous summers, so they've naturally opted for the larger, more fertile islands."

"The other native islanders still use Kahoolawe as a fishing base, then," she remarked.

Frowning now, he added, "It's going to be hell reclaiming the fragile ground cover destroyed by the wild goats and the scraffings. Soil erosion's on an enormous scale here. And without the U.S. military's help and proper management of water resources, the island's just going to continue to be parched. Much of it is a no-man's-land, like I said."

"Sounds to me like it took some courage to return here," she told him.

"No doubt of it," he nearly shouted, his voice traveling over the waters of the channel. Toning himself down, he continued. "Meanwhile, Maui County would like to control and manage the island."

"Maui County covers the island of Maui?"

"And neighboring Lanai, there in the distance." He pointed out the dark, sleeping giant in the northern sky. "Maui County also wants to return the island to human habitation; has for years, and many Hawaiians working within the system have fought for county control. They want a major reforestation effort, irrigation canals built, but—"

"But the Ohana wants control in the hands of the people."

"Exactly. They don't trust any governmental intrusion, and they've amassed a lot of native clout to push their beliefs on the rest of the Hawaiian population."

"Well, Jim, realistically speaking, if the PKO hadn't forced the issue, do you think anyone could have wrested the island from military control?"

Parry frowned, considering this, and without a word spoken she knew he had to agree.

"So, we're dealing with what, a feudal system, a native law and a local chieftain?"

"They've got their own way of doing things, now that the government has relinquished all claims to the land, setting it up as protectorate in a sense, like Puerto Rico, like the Indian Nation of Oklahoma Territory before the Civil War. The U.S. will only intervene in their affairs at the request of their elected officials."

"Is the chief elected?"

"Not on your life."

"Power by family name, Kowona?"

"Exactly, and we might assume that he doles out his own kind of justice as freely as a Hell's Angels biker king."

"*Hmmmmm,* I see." She considered this. "And given that Lopaka is the son of the chief, it follows that—"

"I wouldn't look for too much in the way of justice. They don't give a damn about our ways or our laws; in fact, they pretty much despise our way of life, and like I've said, they've harbored fugitives in the past."

"Really?"

"No one quite of Lopaka Kowona's caliber, I grant you. Thieves, crooks, scoundrels of various stripe, the occasional tax dodger, pickpocket and the like. No one's ever quite sure, because no one seeking asylum on Kahoolawe has ever been extradited or returned of his own accord, or so they say."

"They just don't play by our rules. So if Kowona has gone home, he knows this."

"Exactly."

"And if we can't return him to Maui County, we'll never see. justice done. He can never be tried for his grisly crimes," she said, finishing his thoughts.

"Any wonder Ivers pointed me to Awai when I called him?"

"Ivers? How'd—"

"The ol' fool wanted us to wait for him to fly over. He's still in hospital, half blind, but he's going to fly over. I convinced him we could get the job done."

"How'd you know Ivers would have such contacts here?"

"Ivers used to be a Maui cop for many years before going to the HPD, and he frequently visits the island both for pleasure and on manhunt. He does bail bondsman's work on the side."

The boat now moved swiftly ahead of the current in the open waters of the Alalakeiki Channel, the depths here shallow and glassy. The ship's master at the wheel wore a grim look now, the smiling eyes flat, straight-lined, revealing nothing. Jessica got the sensation of a trap being laid, a web being spun by the Jolly Roger of Hawaii and his leering crew, but maybe she was just jumpy, she told herself.

"Jim, just how well does Ivers know these guys?" she asked, her eyes going once again from crew member to crew member.

"It doesn't matter, Jess."

"It matters to me."

He deeply breathed in the Hawaiian night. "Okay, if you must know. Ivers actually suggested a boat captain named Kaupau, but his boat's in for repairs and his crew was nowhere to be found. Kaupau put me onto Ben Awai."

She sighed in sad resignation, and under her breath she cursed. "So you don't know a damned thing about Awai and his pirates?" For some reason now the filth of the boat deck bothered her far more than before, and the crowded deck also seemed to be closing in, too small for five people.

Awai's boat took on odors she hadn't noticed before. Fishing nets reeked of ancient kills, coiled as they were in all areas where she stepped, some looking in need of repair. Overhead a winch and derrick used for lifting large caches of fish tapped out an eerie requiem in the trade winds. Jim was right, the island they neared was cold. She felt a chill embrace her, nipping at her neck and tingling her most deeply embedded bones.

"I'm no longer comfortable about Captain Awai and his boys, Jim."

"They don't get paid in full until we return, and they know it. Relax, will you? Will you quit worrying?"

Another glance in Ben Awai's direction evoked a smile from the man, but she thought it forced, his yellow teeth glinting dully in the moonlight.

Ahead of them loomed Kahoolawe, out of shadow now, bathed in a blue light.

"How do we know we won't be seen, coming straight on this way? she asked.

"Ben Awai's boat trades routinely with the natives."

"By night?"

"No, by day, but if we're spotted, Awai assures me he can find a safe harbor. There're no wharves or ports, so we'll anchor and raft in, just the three of us."

"Does he know where Kowona's people are?"

"He says he does, yes."

"How far from shore's the village?"

"Not very, he says. A few miles inland, but it's a dense jungle. If you want to remain behind—"

"Not with those two, no way."

"Hold it down," he cautioned. "You never know how much English they understand."

"You're not leaving me behind!"

"Okole nani," said one of the crewmen as he passed by to get to some rigging.

"What'd he say?" she asked Jim.

"He . . . it's meant as a compliment in these parts, Jess."

"What the hell'd he say?"

"He either said you behind is beautiful or that it's in the way."

"My behind is what?"

"He heard you say the word 'behind,' and must've thought—"

She gritted her teeth and spoke through them. "I'm not staying *behind*."

"All right, all right. You've come this far."

She nodded authoritatively, effectively ending the conversation.

Midnight, July 21, the Island of Kahoolawe

They were skirting the island now, coming about into a snug bay the captain called Kanapou, an area made up of several small bays. Noticeably, with this side of the island facing Maui and the channel, away from the ocean, there were no crashing waves here. Rather, the channel waters ruled here with a tranquil peace. They put in as close to shore as Awai dared, fearful of grounding his boat, and there they came to anchor.

"Well, we're here, and so far I've not seen any spears whizz by," said Jim, lowering the inflatable over the side.

Captain Ben Awai, inspecting Jim's work, insisted that Jim try the raft first. Once it held Jim, he crooked his neck, tilted his head and gave an approving look, his smile returning. He then climbed down the rickety ladder of his own boat to the inflatable. Jessica followed, finding a seat opposite Jim, who was already pulling on the oars.

"Ben Awai gets the raft as partial payment for his help," Parry informed her.

"Aha, the plot thickens," she replied.

Ben Awai patted the sides of the fat inflatable approvingly and sputtered, *"Ko'u* . . . mine. It is soon mine."

He sounded like a child just given the biggest gift from below the Christmas tree, she thought, but then it was a state-of-the-art piece of Army issue. She wondered how the raft had materialized, how Parry had performed this nifty trick . . . but there was too much on her mind to pursue it.

Ben Awai spoke as they neared the shore. "There, there," he pointed. "Best place to hide raft. Beyond is path. I take you."

The raft silently glided in over the top of the turquoise sea which lazily lapped at the desolate island, much of which was barren wasteland as a target for bombing runs over the years, but this beach head looked as lush as Hana, or nearly so. The island was a relative latecomer in the chain of islands here, nowhere near as large as Maui's 729 square miles, which was over twenty times Kahoolawe's size.

There was also a conspicuous absence of construction. No condos here, no resorts, no paved roads. It was the antithesis of Honolulu, the primal, waiting jungle alone greeting them like stone vegetation, creating its own gaping maw where a foot-path showed the way. Until Ben Awai pointed out the near-inconsequential footpath, she could see no way to penetrate the dense wall of bougainvillea, *kedwe* trees and palms.

The raft, which Parry and Awai had pulled carefully to shore, was now quickly camouflaged.

"We go dis way," said Awai, leading them into the forest that hugged the bay. Behind them a small, warm light marked the boat at anchor, looking like a harbor buoy now. Soon, even this light was extinguished by the thick forest through which they trekked.

A quick glance at the luminous dial of her watch told Jessica it was nearing 2 A.M. Her ankles already throbbing, she wondered how long she might hold out. It had been a strenuous thirty-six hours: first the search for Lopaka on Oahu, then the helicopter ride to Hana on Maui, followed by the dive and the bone find, and now this. She almost wished she had her cane back, just to lean on.

She felt herself beginning to limp, the old pain returning. Jim, from moment to moment, looked over his shoulder from where he followed on Awai's heels. Each man had taken turns at the lead, each chopping away at the clinging vegetation on either side of the footpath.

"Seeing would be nice," she said to herself.

"What's that?" he asked.

"Nothing, never mind," she said.

"You okay, Jess?"

"Yes, damnit!" She sounded more angry than she was.

Awai just kept working at the vines ahead of him, expertly chopping away, the results visible as the foliage opened for them. Awai paid Jim and her no mind after a while, until he suddenly pulled up short, gasping for air, his hand covering his pounding heart. Parry went forward, asking in hushed tones about what had startled the big Hawaiian.

Awai pointed to a *heiau*, a religious temple with a totem carved out of the rock here. The devilish eyes of the god stared back at the party, an angry scowl forming features somewhat between those of an evil beast and a man.

The temple, restored somewhat, or at least reclaimed from the dense vegetation growing up around it and clinging to it, showed just how effectively the ancient Hawaiians had used their meager island resources of stone and wood.

"How far to the village?" asked Parry.

"That way," replied Awai as if he did not understand. "I stay here."

"Whataya mean, you stay here?"

"I stay back. I no like make trouble with the chief of these people."

"Don't do this to me, Ben."

"It's not far." The big man continued to gasp. "Go north annuder fifteen, twenty minutes maybe, Joe. Stay on path."

"You're going to take us there, Awai. We made a deal. We may need an interpreter, and we certainly need a guide, for which you're being paid well."

"I got you here. I' no interpreter."

"We need you," Jessica said, adding her plea.

"No need me. No need interpreter. Many in village speak English."

"You damned fool," Parry said, tugging at the big man. "We don't want a luau with the villagers. We don't want them to even know we're here! We just may need you in the event we're spotted."

"We might get more cooperation if you're with us," Jessica told the man.

He obstinately shook his head. He turned to find a log to sit on, and after he'd comfortably arranged his bulk there like a sitting bull, he looked up into the muzzle of Jim's .38 revolver. The metal bore he stared down needed no further explanation, end of argument.

"Get up and get ahead of us, Awai. You're being paid to guide us, so get to it."

Awai's feelings looked quite bruised, his dark, meaty face

blanched and pinched. "You *haoles* and your guns. Damn you, you no heah so good? Dey no like me over heah." He indicated the general direction of the village. "Usually trade at the shore. No like dem old ways and magic. Dem people spook me, and . . . and some I owe goods to."

"Just get us there," Parry said with bitter authority.

Awai returned to striking at the canopy of vines ahead of them. "You hard man, Mr. Parry, no *menemene*."

"No sympathy," Jim told her.

The big man was perspiring in the cold night. She worried he could turn on Jim with the cane cutter.

"Be careful of that machete, Jim," she whispered, but it was a useless warning when all around them the rain forest itself came to sudden life, painted limbs reaching out to them, dark faces and eyes following, brandishing native weapons and machetes. They took hold of Jim and her before Jim could get off a shot, and before she could reach for the gun at her ankle.

Jim was knocked down, a huge spear pinning him at the spine to the earth. Awai was likewise manhandled. All other eyes, straining from behind war paint, were on Jessica.

"Oh, Jesus," she moaned.

They were prisoners of the island, prisoners of Chief Kowona.

Awai was cursing in his native tongue, glaring at Parry and Jessica as he was being led away by the village warriors.

They were neither tied nor abused, but Jim's weapon was taken and the native men, spears in hand, forced them onward toward the village they sought.

"No chance we'll lose our way now," she joked, displaying more nerve than she felt.

"Damn me," Parry moaned. "I should've forced you to remain in Maui. I should've left you at the hotel."

"I'd hate you for a long time if you had."

"And what, you don't hate me for *this*? Getting you involved in what's bound to become a very sticky international incident if we're lucky enough to ever get off this island with all our parts intact?"

"We're not dealing with cannibals, Jim. Are we?"

"No, but I can imagine what the old chief's going to do with us."

"What?"

"Bind us over—literally—to U.S. authorities. Don't know 'bout you, but there goes my pension."

"Shut up, *haole ilio!*" shouted one of the men in paint with frightening force and venom. Jessica was told by Jim that the stocky Hawaiian had just called the Chief of FBI's Hawaii Bureau a white dog with a loose tongue.

Jessica swallowed her fear and shouted back, stunning the painted warriors. "Hey, you just tell your chief that this man you call a dog is also an important chief."

"Jess," Parry cautioned.

"No, no . . . they have a right to know who their dealing with, Chief."

"Everybody knows who Parry is," said the native coldly.

"What? How'd you know his name?"

Parry's eyes had already fixed on Captain Ben Awai.

"You bastard."

"I knew this was a setup," shouted Jessica, pulling her arm free of a native who ushered her along.

"This whole thing was engineered, wasn't it?" asked Parry of Awai. "When? When did you know who we were?"

"News travels fast around the islands, especially on the Hawaiian hot line, Chief Parry. You've been watched since leaving Oahu, and we know of your desecration of the burial site at the Spout."

"You're PKO?" asked Jessica.

"Every Hawaiian is PKO. Some of them just don't know it yet," replied Awai sternly.

"Then you do know the chief here."

"That's right."

"And you wanted your cover protected, so you wanted to wait at the shrine, or were you simply going to turn back for your boat and disappear?"

"All of the above, but it appears the chief wants to see me as well."

"I see your English has improved since we came ashore, too," said Parry, his teeth now set in anger at the man.

"You just better pray, white man."

Jessica exploded at Awai even as she fought to keep on her feet, what with being shoved forward. "You harm an agent of the FBI and your little island paradise here'll be swarming with U.S. marshals and G-men. It'll make Waco, Texas, look like a backyard barbecue! Is that what you want, you . . . you native son of a—?"

"You don't have no juice here, and your *haole* threats fall empty on Hawaiian soil, so shut up, white bitch."

"Do as he says, Jess. Hold onto your temper. We'll have to use our wits here, negotiate an agreement, some sort of amicable settlement so we can extradite Lopaka Kowona. That's all we're here for."

"I can just imagine what they'd like for a settlement. Especially Lopaka Kowona," Jess replied in defeat.

"Settlement, agreement, you *haoles*," said Awai, shaking his head sadly. "You're trying to write up one treaty while you're trampling another."

She countered, "You know why we're here! What kind of an animal we're tracking!"

"The island is off-limits to U.S. military personnel, and the entire Caucasian race. That's what was granted us, this scrap of native land. You desecrate it without a thought, and you look for leniency from our chief?"

They were forced onward to march to the village. Parry leaned into her and said, "Don't worry, Jess. They're not so stupid as to harm us."

"Who even knows we're here, Jim? Anyone?"

Parry gritted his teeth and air seeped through them in a hiss. "Only Ivers, but Tony's smart. He'll figure it out."

Just then they smelled wood fires and the lingering cooking odors of the village, and in a moment flickering fireflies shown among the wall of green darkness before them, campfires.

Ben Awai brandished the cane cutter and Parry's .38 over his head as he welcomed himself into camp ahead of the others, calling out his name repeatedly, "Awai, Awai!"

Ben was greeted by several of the children who'd come awake and wandered to the noise. Women, too, hung on Ben Awai until he shooed them off with their children in tow.

Jim and Jessica were pushed ahead, out of the dense foliage where they might have found safe hiding, a point from which to observe the village at a safe distance, spying to determine if Lopaka were actually there or not. But all those plans were dashed now, and they were forced to their knees in a neatly carved clearing where traditional huts stood about the circle of a communal campfire.

Jessica felt her stomach churn, fearing the worst lay ahead of them, getting extremely annoyed at the same time with the short creep that kept poking her ribs with a war club.

She wondered if these people were for real or if they were like the survivalists she'd encountered on the mainland, who were more obsessed with a lifestyle than committed to a way of life. The native population was crowded around them, obscuring her view, but she could hear the collective gasp that followed in the wake of Chief Kowona, who parted an Army-issue tarp acting as an entryway cover and came towards them, wearing a thick feathered headdress.

She felt Jim's hand grasp hers and tightly squeeze. "Let me do the talking. If you talk, he'll see it as a sign of weakness."

"Whose weakness?"

"Mine."

⭠25⭢

Once upon a time a man looked into the reverse side of
a mirror and, not seeing his face and head, he became
insane.

The Teachings of Buddha

They were forced back on their feet and toward the center of the
village, while the chief, acting as if they were not even present,
performed a ceremony of dancing before the fire, which was
brought to a fever pitch by the natives. But Jim suddenly stopped
in his tracks beside her, and Jessica, following his eyes, stared
across the fire and the compound to a ten-foot-high wood and
bamboo rack that looked like an instrument which normally held
fish and possibly goat meat stretched across it for drying in the
sun.

A bloodied, mangled man with dark skin and Hawaiian features
dangled from the rack, his hands and legs tied to bleeding with
thick, native thongs. The man's wounds were man-made, the
awful slashes creating a crisscross network of blood and flesh.

Below him a fire kept sending up cinders to rest in his wounds, and dogs sniffed about the dying man's feet, occasionally rising up to lap at the blood as it drained down his calves.

"Oh, my God," Jessica moaned. Her worst fears were realized before her eyes. "They may not be cannibals, but they are savages." Kahoolawe justice appeared both cruel and torturous.

Jessica was roughly forced ahead. She and Parry stood now side by side, staring at the dangling man on the rack, his face a mask of pain and blood. He'd been slashed repeatedly about the face as well as the naked torso and limbs. Jessica recognized a zigzag pattern to the wounds, realizing that each had some ceremonial significance. Her eyes then traveled to the hapless victim's private parts. His penis had been removed and the stub sewed up and burned in order to cauterize the wound and keep him from bleeding to death. A quick death would obviously end the village's and the old chief's pleasure in watching the man die at the rate of a beheaded snake.

"Oh, God, Jim," she sobbed, grabbing onto Parry for support. "I never dreamed—"

Awai, the cane cutter in his hand, jabbed it into the suffering man's chin and lifted the face, allowing for study of the features. "Here's your mass killer, Lopaka," he said.

"Look closely on him," bellowed Chief Kowona, still in as thick, feathered headdress, coming forward now. When he removed the headdress, they could clearly see that it was Joseph Kaniola.

"Why, Kaniola, you son of a bitch. You're behind all this," cursed Jim before lunging at the newspaperman and being restrained by the men around them. "Getting Oniiwah killed wasn't enough for you, no. You have more blood on your hands than you know what to do with, and now this?"

"I don't expect either of you to believe me, but I had nothing whatever to do with the abduction of the Oniiwah boy. And I regret with my soul that I used his name in my paper. It was a mistake. I should have expected reprisals, but there's not a man here who hasn't made some mistake in this ugly business."

Jessica, shaking her head in disbelief, pointedly asked him, "How could you—an educated, civilized man—be a part of this . . . butchery?"

"Like you, I am a guest here, no more, no less. Chief Kowona, Lopaka's father, shares my grief at the loss of my son Alan, as well as the combined tears of those who've lost so many daughters, all due to the son he banished from his sight years ago."

A man with regal bearing, despite being stoop-shouldered, appeared from the largest hut at the center of the village and Jessica, seeing the intricacy of the leis about his neck, the enormity of the handiwork that'd gone into his feathered *kahilis* and headdress, and his royal clothing, instantly guessed this to be the real Chief Kowona, for wherever he stepped, others hastened from his path, and wherever he pointed, others stared.

Jessica searched the old chief's wrinkled yet hard, leathery and brown countenance and the massive, swollen, heavy eyes, finding there a deep sense of remorse, shame and guilt commingling like ancient tenants. She imagined a well of withheld tears and the pain of not being in a position to allow the free flow of grief.

The old chief's hair, like Lopaka's, was rust-red and about the coal-black eyes she read a resemblance. And this place of red-earth paths recalled to her mind what old Lomelea, the prophet, had seen in his vision, that she'd find the killer in a land of raw earth, scarred not only by the foolishness of human folly, but the tears of a chief over the loss of both his son and his lineage.

"The old chief feels responsible," continued Joe Kaniola. "And whether you believe it or not, I also came here from Oahu because I knew you two were getting in over your heads."

The chief spoke in Hawaiian, Kaniola translating. "So, you now know I and my son have been sufficiently punished for our crimes. . . . Eye for an eye, as the missionaries used to say . . ."

"This is awful, Kaniola," she sternly said, pointing to where Lopaka's twitching body continued to feed the insects that swarmed about so many wounds they could not be counted. "How long has he been made to suffer?"

"What is this, mock indignation?" asked Kaniola.

"There's nothing mock about it!"

"I know the feeling among the authorities, you two included. In a state where they put people like Lopaka into a hospital for the criminally insane, you two were hoping to catch him in the Koolau Range and set the dogs on him and pump your bullets into him. So spare me your canned outrage, Dr. Coran. You see, I know about your previous cases, about Matthew Matisak, Simon Archer and others you've personally seen to eternity or wished to."

Now the veins in Kaniola's neck told of his anger with her. The chief placed a hand on Kaniola's shoulder and spoke in Hawaiian to him. Kaniola replied in his native tongue before turning back to them and saying, "The old chief wishes to answer your question, Dr. Coran, as to the duration of Lopaka's punishment."

"How many days and nights?" asked Jim.

"Shorter, I assure you, than the suffering he caused when his many victims agonized in their restraints." Kaniola's reply was a translation of the chief's words, but then he began speaking from his own heart. "Enough of your false outrage. You will take word back with you, Parry. And no one will come behind you to Kahoolawe to make reprisals on these people here. Do you understand this and agree?"

Parry exchanged a look with Jessica. His eyes and the way his teeth were grinding together told her they'd better take the offer as it might be the only one they were likely to receive here.

Jessica helplessly stared anew at the suffering Lopaka, studying closely the features beneath the bloody, pulpy mask his face had become.

"Ho'okahe wai!" shouted Ben Awai at another of the Hawaiian men, who responded by rushing forward with a leather bucket of water.

"Waiele," shouted Ben, and the other man sent the water cascading over the tortured man's face, reviving him but barely.

The water cleaned his features enough to tell both Parry and Jessica that the suffering man on the rack did indeed resemble the photos they'd seen of Lopaka Kowona.

The aged chief, barely able to straighten his spine, stood before them now in full regalia and headdress and began a river of native words which Kaniola translated.

"My son who is not my son was sought out by the Ohana and told that he would be given refuge on Kahoolawe if he came to us. The people guiding him were relatives he trusted."

Ben Awai interrupted, saying, "I myself am the boy's paternal cousin. The chief is my uncle. Returning him to his homeland of Maui and finally to here was a simple matter. He believed me when I told him that his father, now very ill and weak of mind, would welcome him back."

"So I welcomed Lopaka home. . . ." The powerful but croaking voice of the ancient man came out in English haltingly. He had patches of white hair and a broad, strong Hawaiian face below the headdress. Jessica imagined him to be in his late sixties or early seventies, but he was as rigid as wood, powerful in both size and dress. Not so spry as Kaniola's great-grand uncle, she thought. He knew enough English to get by, but apparently preferred the ancient tongue. There was a glassy stare and a tear in Chief Kowona's eye, and at his hip, as part of his ceremonial garb, was a powerful sword now caked with blood.

"You can't let this go on a moment longer, Chief Kowona," Jessica dared shout. "Lopaka is beaten. End his torment. Turn him over to us. We will see that he—"

"Men talk this talk!" shouted the chief, his eyes now darting among Kaniola, Awai and Parry. "Now quiet, *wahine!*"

She had obviously treaded on one of their many taboos, one she cared little for.

Kaniola said, "Here, women do not speak directly to a chief."

"Jess," cautioned Parry, "let me. How long's this torture gone on here, Kaniola? How long?"

"*'Elua la noa,*" replied the haughty old man.

"Two days," Kaniola translated.

"Crippling your son is not just retribution for his crimes, Chief Kowona," Parry contested.

"He will soon be beyond any misery," Kaniola countered.

Parry shouted, "He must be returned to Oahu to stand trial in the deaths of—"

Jessica felt faint at the wretched sight, unable to bear the spectacle of the dying man a moment longer, unable to close her hearing to the animal keening which welled up from deep within his frame, wracking his body to get out in a garbled plea for mercy, his eyes fixed and dilated. She suddenly dropped to one knee, and pretending her own plea for Lopaka, she slapped for the gun strapped to her ankle, brought it up and was about to end Lopaka Kowona's suffering here and now when Chief Kowona's regal hand flew into her line of fire, his huge sword leaping into his other hand as if it were alive, and in the fluid motion expected of a much younger man, he sliced off his son's head, sending shards of the wooden rack in all directions.

The head tumbled to the dogs, who at first, frightened by the old man's sudden action, crept back slowly to sniff curiously at Lopaka's decapitated and bloody head.

"Suffers my son no more," declared the old man, dropping his sword into the red earth before the malevolent son he had dispatched and going to his knees. The old man wailed, his own pain escaping openly before his followers, a punished king.

At the same time Jessica and Parry were frozen in place by the display of swift, sure justice that had come with the stroke of the enormous blade, a guillotine of finality descended over them when tribal followers wrested the gun from Jessica's hand, one of them pushing her roughly to the ground. Parry, coming to her aid, fearful the gun would go off, decked her attacker with a single blow, but this was met with a heavy war club to his back and a second to his jaw, knocking him off his feet.

Jessica crawled to Parry, clutching him, certain now they, too, would be killed by the savage justice of this cruel place. "Jim, Jim, are you all right?" Tears came of their own accord.

"Justice is served, Parry, Dr. Coran," said Joe Kaniola.

"Everything settled," agreed Ben Awai while both men stood over them.

Kaniola seemed to be acting as a bishop of sorts here. "Take them to their quarters, Awai, and then return here. We have much to discuss."

Jessica and Parry were led away to a guarded hut and told to remain peaceable and silent, and that any attempt at escape would cost them dearly.

The threat of Lopaka Kowona to the islands was at an end, but now Jessica and James Parry faced a new kind of threat. Surrounded, with no visible way out, no weapons to protect themselves with, they were witnesses to an execution-style murder here on Kahoolawe. It seemed unlikely that they would be allowed to leave with such knowledge.

At daybreak the old chief, Awai and Kaniola came into their prison. They'd obviously counseled with one another on the situation, but for now Kaniola, sitting on the old chief's right-hand side, began. "No white courts, no white law, no loopholes and no life terms, no appeals or paroles, nor endless denial of justice here, Parry."

"No hard to know tribal justice," croaked a defeated chief.

"You can both understand the pain and suffering all in this village, the shame and humiliation which these people have endured, not to mention Chief Kowona's personal loss and shame," continued Kaniola. "Can't you?"

Parry exchanged a look with Jessica. "Of course we can," he said matter-of-factly.

"And you, Dr. Coran?"

She firmly agreed with a slowly building nod, recalling that the chief liked his women silent.

"Then there is an end to it, here . . . now," said Kaniola. "No more pain . . . no more suffering, a clean end to it."

"We can live with that," agreed Parry. "Can't we, Jessica?" He nudged her.

"Well . . . yes . . ."

"Good . . . good, then Ben will take you both back to Maui. Ben," said Kaniola.

Ben Awai, looking stunned now, pleaded with Kaniola for an answer. "What? Whataya mean, take them back to Maui?"

"Just do it, Ben."

"But they'll cause trouble for us all, Joe."

"You just do as I say, Ben."

The argument obviously hadn't yet been settled, but it was now cut short by the chief, who bellowed his own orders. Kaniola translated. "Chief Kowona's talking now to Parry directly. 'Tell everyone outside of Kahoolawe that the Trade Winds Killer is dead, his body fed to the bay.' "

"Chief," countered Parry, "no one in my world will believe me when I speak of this."

"Chief you are? Among your people are you not?" he asked directly.

"Yes, but my people do not always believe in the word of their chiefs."

He nodded as if he understood this. "Sad it is when people do not trust. Married I once into your race, and result"—he indicated the outer encampment where the headless form on the rack had remained dangling all night—"is dat . . . monster."

Kaniola stared at his old friend, the chief, who struggled now to his feet, the others following suit. Parry and Jessica were told to follow. Standing now in the encampment, Parry stretched and Jessica clung to him.

Jessica could hear the flies before she got up nerve to look in their direction. Already at work, they buzzed about and perched in Lopaka's dead eyes, laying their eggs against the soft tissues, there just ten feet from her. The man's red body was suspended like a grotesque doll on the rack. With the sun bathing the entire village in a crimson dawn, reflecting back the red soil, she recalled Lomelea's prediction that she would never completely take hold of the red shadow, Lopaka, but that she would find a place like this where the sun would appear to be a blood orange in the sky and where the paths were scarlet.

"Chief," she called out to the stooped and broken men who walked ahead of them, "all peace in the islands can be kept if . . ."

"Speaks too much, your woman," said the chief to Parry.

"Yes, yes . . . I know, Chief Kowona."

She glared now at Parry, who kept talking. "But she's not an ordinary woman, Chief. She is a doctor, a medical examiner for the FBI."

"Hmmmmmmmm," he intoned, mulling this over. "A doctor woman, yes . . . and holds she secrets?"

"Many . . . many secrets, yes." Parry had found his voice and was trying desperately to help Jessica's case, feeling confident that he knew what she was driving at. "She is like your own *kahuna*—a priestess."

"Hmmmmmmmmm, and knows she the secret to peace in the islands?"

"If you will allow me . . . us . . . to return with your son's body—" Jess began, but Parry cut her short with a hand cupping her mouth.

"Shuuuuuut up!" he firmly told her.

"What will your woman doctor do with my son's body?" asked Kaniola, translating the question for Parry.

Parry cautioned her to remain silent, to allow him to do the parlaying. "She can show conclusively that this is the same man who terrorized Oahu."

"But this is well known," said Kaniola, who said the same in Hawaiian to the chief.

"Not officially. Only circumstantially. She can prove it beyond any doubt, by the bodily fluids, his DNA. You know that, Kaniola."

Kaniola relented his personal objections and spoke at length with the chief in their native tongue. Then the old chief looked to Parry and Jessica, his enormous eyes fixing them in place. "Your government . . ." He struggled with the words. ". . . requires this . . ." It was a statement, not a question. He seemed deep in thought now until he said, "No bettah way to foul Lopaka's body than give over to da fishes, 'cept for one way."

The old man stared at Jessica now, understanding now exactly what kind of a doctor she was. He had believed there could be no worse desecration of his son's body than he had already inflicted until Joe Kaniola had explained the nature of an autopsy to him.

"You are strange people. My son's body you want. For au . . . au . . ."

"Autopsy," finished Jessica, making Jim blanche and seethe through his teeth.

"Autoop-sie," the chief repeated.

Parry nodded approvingly. "Will you allow us to take your son from this soil?"

"The *haoles* will think you are a butcher, Uncle," said Awai. "That you butchered your own son. They will . . . will think our people pagans. This could cause us problems with the U.S. government."

Jessica exploded at this, pushing into the chief's face, saying, "You are a chief, and so is Mr. Parry. Between the two of you, between your governments, certain problems exist. I assure you, sir, that if you cooperate, there'll be no further prosecution of this matter and—"

"Jess," Parry interrupted her, taking her aside and whispering, "we can't make these kinds of blanket promises, not even to a chief in a protected territory."

"Not even to a chief who holds our lives in his hands, Jim? And face it, Jim, without the body we can't officially close the case; we can't prove any of this ever happened. It'll remain on the books forever."

"In the Hawaiian scheme of things, our closing our books doesn't mean shit, Jess."

Kaniola, going between the chief and the FBI agents regularly now, said, "All right, Chief Parry. You take the body back and you don't get too technical about how he died, right, Dr. Coran? Is that a compromise you can live with?"

Jess wasn't absolutely sure she could live with such a lie, and yet it appeared that lies were the only avenue off Kahoolawe at the moment. The concern clearly painted on her face was making Ben Awai edgy.

She glanced into Parry's eyes and he said, "We could say he fell off a cliff while we were in pursuit, or a pack of wild quarry dogs got hold of him and tore him from limb to limb before we could get to him."

"Dr. Coran?" asked Kaniola.

She looked around the encampment, seeing the volatile Ben Awai and the painted faces of Chief Kowona's followers.

"We . . . we . . ." she began, "we can do better than cliffs and quarry dogs, Jim."

"What's that?" he asked.

"I think it'd be fitting, even poetic, if the readers of the *Ala Ohana* and other island papers learned that Lopaka died as a result of suicide."

"Suicide?"

"That he tried leaping into the Spout on Maui where not only his body was recovered by divers, but a cache of bones belonging to his victims?"

"An excellent story," agreed Kaniola at once.

"Yeah . . . that'd make great copy, huh, Joe?" Parry asked.

"And I'll do all within my power," she continued, "to see to it that the autopsy reflects how he died."

"We'll keep a lid on the powder keg, Joe," added Parry. "Is that what you want to hear?"

"I have your word?"

"You do."

"That will best serve the press, the PKO, even the U.S., so we all remain one big happy *ohana*."

"And there's no further trouble?" asked Ben Awai.

"Chief Kowona?" asked Kaniola.

"The carcass take, but keep we Lopaka's head."

"What," asked Jessica.

"To display in the village until it rots," explained Kaniola. "Barbaric perhaps, but effective."

"You wanted his head on a stick, remember?" Parry said.

"Chief Kowona—" she began to argue.

"Jess," cautioned Parry.

"Chief, we need the entire body for this thing to work," she said, continuing her plea.

Kaniola translated. Kowona appeared crushed now. Finally, after some thought, Kaniola translated his words in a cold counterpoint to the Hawaiian he spoke. "I have personally seen enough of my son's defilement, but my followers have to know that when they take life, they will be punished harshly. This is a lesson for the generations."

"They've got to know that by now, especially the children," she harshly countered. "Hell, you've lost two sons already and—"

"Know nothing you people of this? No, one son only."

"But Lopaka . . . the legend . . . all I've learned about the story says you had two sons, one born deformed, a child *you* destroyed."

"Christ, Jess, now you've done it."

"Legend, story . . . all it is . . . all it ever was," said the chief. "It was in our village in the rain forest on Molokai."

Kaniola hastened to fill in the blanks. "Lopaka had no brother, but a friend in the village that he treated as a brother contracted a terrible illness. Some today believe it was spinal meningitis. Anyway, he was a boyhood friend, not Lopaka's brother."

"We want the entire body," Jessica insisted.

"That's not to be," said Awai.

"Take it . . . take it all," replied the chief. "If peace it will keep, take it."

"And you are going to allow these two *haoles* safe return?" Awai asked of the elder Kowona. "After their desecration of Hana where the ancient village stood?"

"The bones disturbed there were all of the sea," countered Kaniola. "You said so yourself, Ben Awai."

"So?"

"You don't know as much of the old ways as you think, Awai."

"Meaning what, Joe?"

"Meaning that sea bones tell of the damned only, the shamed, and the lawless ones like Lopaka who were not fit to be buried properly alongside the good and clean among us. We care nothing for the bones we cast into the sea. They hold the souls of men who will never find peace, whose souls wander endlessly with the tides, unable to find Ku."

Jessica realized only now that Lopaka's contempt for the surrogate Kelias in his life had naturally led him to dispose of them via the sea, that he was familiar with the Spout, and knew of its counterpart on Oahu long before he moved from Maui to the metropolis of Honolulu for fresh game.

"Ku cannot find the ones whose bones are below the waves, so he cannot take them into his kingdom, the water blinds even Ku. So it purifies his kingdom, keeps it free of the vile," continued Kaniola.

"I once knew that, Uncle," pleaded Awai, "but I forgot."

"You have done well this day, Ben Awai. You are one of us," Kaniola assured the bigger man.

"Then you will allow us to return the body?" asked Parry.

"On one condition."

"Yes?"

"That his remains be returned to the sea after you've finished all your tests."

"Consider it done," said Parry. "A burial at sea can be arranged." One way or another, he was thinking.

Jessica nodded, her eyes meeting those of the stern chief and Kaniola's grim countenance beside him. From the well of anguish she found there, she knew that both fathers had suffered and anguished over their decisions of the past few days, and that the old chief no doubt had suffered over the years in untold ways at the hand of his child.

Still, she wondered just how screwed up in the head Lopaka was that he could confuse in his mind's eye a boyhood companion with a brother, a childhood disease with the taking of a life. She remained unconvinced of the authenticity of Kaniola's version of events.

Perhaps, with the end of Lopaka's fevered brain, the ghosts of the past should also be buried with him. Either way, the old chief wasn't long for this world. She could see it in his dark, sunken eyes and the ashen and flaxen skin about the cheekbones, and in his spiritless gait.

"We will prepare for your departure with the body now," Kaniola assured them.

"I suppose you want our thanks, Joe."

"Hey, not necessary . . . only your word that you'll hold to our bargain. But I tell you this, people, if I hadn't been here, there's no telling what would've become of you two. Awai's brain isn't screwed on right, and neither is the chief's these days."

"So, in essence," she summed up, "we witnessed a monster-maker kill his own creation last night, and we just let this Dr. Frankenstein walk off to his hut and go to bed?"

"Either that or never leave the island. Remember, you aren't exactly in Kansas anymore here. You understand me?"

"Let it drop, Jess," Parry pleaded, and when Kaniola stepped off, he whispered, "Maybe at some future time, we can pursue a course of action against the old man."

"If he doesn't kick it in the meantime." She relented, feeling the return of Ben Awai's eyes on them.

She smiled sweetly at Awai. But the big man's grim look was

set in stone for the time being. Kaniola organized a party to take the body from the rack and to collect Lopaka's hacked and dirtied head.

Dawn, July 21, the Island of Kahoolawe

The body of Lopaka Kowona, reeking of blood and perspiration, was cleansed and packed in a large canvas and deposited in an enormous weaved basket along with the man's head. Such cargo could easily be misconstrued if it fell into the wrong hands, and they could be faced with many hours' delay before all was sorted out. She and Parry planned on contacting the Navy for military transport back to Pearl the moment they set foot again on Maui. The working relationship between Jim's office and the military was a close one, and they'd respond to his requests without question when he, over a pay phone, would require them to fly into Kahului Airport with an empty coffin in order to return the body of a fugitive from justice brought down at the Spout, just outside Hana.

Jessica and Parry were escorted back to the waiting boat and raft. Lopaka's body was boarded and soon they were heading back to Maui with their grim cargo.

Neither Joseph Kaniola nor Ben Awai had anything further to convey to the FBI people, and so they spoke no more, Awai accepting his final payment and his inflatable raft in stony silence. At the harbor in Maui, Parry used his badge and influence to commandeer a nearby storage locker in a meat-distribution warehouse, and there Lopaka Kowona's body was safely stored until an ambulance could be arranged for. Parry hovered about the storage facility, half afraid news would leak out, in which case their clandestine operation involving Kahoolawe would be ended. Parry also hovered over the paramedics when they arrived, bent on their handling the incident with the utmost discretion as they removed Lopaka from the ancient carrying vessel and placed him in a body bag. The medics were curious and questioning, but Parry sternly controlled them with threats nonetheless.

The medics were aghast at what they saw. They'd seen badly mutilated bodies before, heads severed in automobile accidents, but this kind of butchery was not an everyday occurrence. Still, they were Hawaiian men and with Joe Kaniola's help, they remained stoic in the face of what they witnessed. Parry instructed them to transport the body to the airport at Kahului and not to unload it until Parry met them there and directed the exchange from the ambulance to the military transport.

Jessica had little time to freshen up and change before Jim stormed into their room at the resort and told her they had to go. Everything was hinging on Parry and her now, and in a matter of hours, the case of the Trade Winds Killer would be officially closed.

All the way to Kahului, Jessica could sense Jim's primary concern was to bring an end to Oahu's longest-running serial killer case ever, and an end to the great suffering caused here by the fevered mind of Lopaka Kowona. Only a public announcement, stating they unequivocally had the body of the serial killer in their hands, and that there was clinical evidence to link him to all the murders, would quell all the fears of the Hawaiian Islands. It was ever more important that Dr. Katherine Smits back on Oahu identify the bones forwarded to her via Dr. Lau as those of victims on Maui. Such forensic truth, along with her own findings regarding Lina Kahala's arm, would corroborate the unequivocable wall of facts which she and Jim had worked so hard to uncover.

She had watched Jim at work from the moment she had met him; watched him care for his island and its people. Now, racing back across the island on the highway that had brought them here, back toward Kahului Airport, Jessica felt a great sense of well-being flood in, a feeling of closure, that it was finally over. It flooded in with her fatigue. Weak from lack of sleep and the long night on Kahoolawe, she easily dozed in the car during the one-and-a-half-hour-long drive to the only airstrip on Maui capable of handling military jets.

"You can sleep on the transport back," Jim had promised her, but she didn't even make it that far.

Even as she slept, in the back of her mind there was a nagging voice telling her that she couldn't truly rest until she proved to herself, beyond a shadow of a doubt lurking there, that she and Jim actually did have Lopaka Kowona's body in that basket.

From the disfigurement of the facial features, there still remained some doubt in Jim's mind as well as Jessica's. Could the wily old chief have been playing out a charade, his final performance? And Kaniola? Had he, too, been duped, or was he part of the masquerade? Could they've been playing out a sting operation, a magician's switch, on Kahoolawe, substituting another for the true son's life, to spare that royal blood no matter its transgressions? A hundred what-ifs remained swirling amid Jessica's dreamscape. . . .

The thought that Lopaka, for whatever inscrutable reason, might be harbored and someone butchered in his place to appease the white race both infuriated and defeated her, but a part of her mind screamed that there was no way the two of them would then have been allowed safe passage back with a ringer's body. Kaniola, Awai and the others knew that such a hoax would be impossible, that it would be discovered quickly in the lab. On the other hand, such a falsehood played out against the FBI would not only prove embarrassing, but also show that she and Jim had violated international agreements between the Hawaiian natives and the State Department. Could Kaniola be that shrewd? And could they've found such a close double for Kowona?

Such questions hounded her, and Jim as well, she suspected, all the way back to Oahu. She kept trying to reassure herself, and when she came awake only a few miles from the airport, the ambulance in the far distance ahead of them, she realized that Jim Parry had fixated on similar doubts, having had only the interior of the car to commiserate with. *Was it really Lopaka in the body bag?*

Soon they reached Kahului Airport, not the most modern facility by anyone's standard, and the waiting ambulance drivers looked on with such inexplicable eyes and nonchalance that Parry and Jessica began to wonder just what Kaniola had said to them back in Makena at the warehouse. Parry cautioned the two men once more to remember nothing of their trip from Makena to the airport. They assured him with nods and grunts that they had no problem with silence.

"Where was this body transported from?" he asked one of the men.

"Hana Town."

"At the Spout," added the second man firmly.

"Good . . . good . . ."

But Jessica sensed that Parry wanted to tear into the two youths, throw a scare into them, see what spilled out.

"If I have to come back because you men've lied to me in any way," he warned, his large finger rising to their eyes when a jetliner crashed over, drowning out the rest of his words.

"No lie, Boss."

"No lie . . ."

In a matter of fifteen minutes and two cups of coffee, the military transport came to a smooth landing on the strip and taxied over to the hangar where the ambulance waited, getting directions from the tower as to the exact number on the tarmac over which they must come to rest.

The body, loaded from the ambulance, was left in the body bag, and deposited into a Navy-issue coffin. Parry and Jessica boarded, and the plane was given immediate clearance, holding up an incoming Aloha Airlines jet filled with tourists, forcing the commercial flight to make a second pass over the island as a result.

News throughout the island—that "Parry had his quarry"— spread like wildfire ahead of them.

~26~

We must be still and still moving
Into another intensity
For a further union, a deeper communion
Through the dark cold and the empty desolation.

T.S. Eliot

Once in the air, the team of Parry and Coran felt a sense of great relief wash over them. The plane wasn't much on comfort, the seats like those of a '57 Chevy, the plane an old bucket itself. But they were airborne and as they stared down on the islands, all seemed beauty and tranquility. Jessica rested her eyes. She wanted all the turmoil, all the guessing, all the doubts over, and she wanted to believe that the natives on Kahoolawe had dealt with them fairly, that their cargo was indeed what it was purported to be.

Beside her, Parry seemed on a cocaine high. He couldn't sit. He paced the small interior of the lumbering aircraft. He sat, stood up, sat again until finally she said, "What the hell's the matter, Jim? I'm trying to catch a few winks here. Do you mind?"

"Sorry, I'm just so wired by all this."

"I understand, but you'll blow a gasket if you don't slow down."

"You know this'll kill Scanlon."

She blinked curiously at him. "Scanlon?"

"It's going to blow Scanlon right out of his office, don't you see?"

"Scanlon? Commissioner Scanlon?"

"No way he can stay on as police commissioner in Honolulu now. He'll have to go Stateside just to find someone who'll hand him an application."

"Jim, just how much pleasure are you deriving from this fact?" She fully opened her eyes to study his response.

He shrugged, but a smug look remained on his handsome face. "Some . . . some," he confided.

Her frown displeased him, and suddenly his frustration and perhaps his fatigue got the better of him, and he simply lit into her. "What, you don't think the bastard's got it coming? He's an incompetent ass, Jess, and it's bigots and assholes like him who get other people killed."

"Whataya mean? He's responsible for all of Lopaka's victims? For Lopaka's psychosis? If you want to blame someone, blame the bastard's father."

"Scanlon's got no business in such a position of power . . . it's just not right," Jim said, continuing his tirade. "*Ahh,* forget it."

"Abuse of power? You want to talk about abuse of power, think about that Chief Kowona guy, who—" Suddenly, a light came full on deep inside her brain, illuminating all the dark, fuzzy contours around Jim's relationship with Dave Scanlon. "Wait a minute, Jim, what's this really about?"

"Whataya mean? It's about a bad cop."

"A bad cop?"

"An incompetent cop. You heard what Lopaka Kowona's wife Stateside had to say about Scanlon."

"Yeah, and you knew all that long before I got her on the phone. It was all old information to you. And you didn't pay her any more attention than Scanlon had."

He looked stricken. "That's not exactly fair or correct, Jess. I had access to the records of the victims, and access to police calls relevant or otherwise to the cases in the missing-persons files. I didn't have access to anything Scanlon didn't want me to have. I didn't learn about Kowona or his wife until it was too late. You've gotta know that."

"Then tell me this, Jim. Why'd you ever begin delving into Scanlon's old caseload to begin with? What set you on his course in the first place?"

"That's obvious, isn't it?"

"No, not entirely."

He gritted his teeth. "I admit, it began as a search through Scanlon's past record."

"Why? What makes you hate the man so?"

"He intentionally screwed with an undercover operation when he was a lieutenant with the HPD, and he got a partner of mine killed as a result. He was somewhere he had no business being, Jess, and a friend was killed. Reason enough for you?"

"So you started on this case to revenge the death of a friend? All along, that's been your motive." Her tone alone condemned him.

She couldn't look at him. She turned away, staring out the porthole to see Pearl Harbor below.

"Jess, Jess," he pleaded, "it may've started out that way . . . well, yes, it *did* start out that way. But that was all back-shelved once I saw the enormity of the crimes. I cared about the victims, and I forgot my original reasons and Scanlon in the process, all before I met you."

"Really?" she countered. "And I'm supposed to believe that with you dancing the aisles here, unable to hold yourself in check because you're so jubilant over Dave Scanlon's tumble from grace?"

"Think of the number of his own cops who've died or been hurt by this, Jessica!"

"And think just how tarnished you've become over it, Jim."

She turned away, unable to speak another word, anxious for the plane to land and for their departure, anxious to get away from him long enough to sort out her feelings.

9:45 A.M., Pearl Harbor, Honolulu

When they landed at Pearl, they were encircled by brass and press there on the tarmac, including Joe Kaniola, who'd caught a chopper in Wailea near Makena and had openly spread the word ahead, labeling both Parry and Jessica as heroes worthy of the welcome afforded knights returning from a crusade. It'd become overcast and dark on Oahu. Blinding flashes of light came from both cameras and an approaching storm. There were microphones everywhere with the NBC, ABC and CBS logos and others attached to a podium. Everyone in the crowd expected a news conference on their disembarking. Jim looked from the cameras outside to the body at the rear of the transport. "Keep this body under armed guard until I—and no one but me—tells you otherwise, Lieutenant," he told the young copilot standing beside him.

"What if the brass says otherwise?"

"Nobody takes the body out of this place except me. Clear?"

"Yes, sir."

"You'd think we just escaped from Iran," she whispered to Jim. "What're you afraid of, Jim? That somebody'd actually hijack Lopaka?"

"Hey, there're people on this island that'd like to tear that body limb from limb, who'd be unhappy to know that the head was cut off before they got a chance to do it. Besides . . . not so sure I trust Kaniola."

The disembarking was met with cheers, cameras zooming in for the local and network news teams. Everyone of rank wanted to have his picture taken with Parry and Jessica. However, Parry took the initiative and simply refused to play their games, insisting he had work to attend to, and Jessica followed his lead, rushing off for the rear of the plane to oversee the disembarking of the third passenger. Hell, they had a body to attend to, she thought, and if it should suddenly disappear, who was to say whether it was or was not that of Lopaka "Robert" Kowona? If Joe Kaniola had planned this diversion and planned on hijacking the body, they might easily have played into his shrewd hand.

Parry was having none of it. He and Jessica saw to the body's careful transportation to the FBI Crime Lab, irking a number of people in the process, with Doctor Marshal, M.E., for the military, and P.C. Scanlon at the head of the line.

Later, with much help from Dr. Smits, Dr. Lau and his people, Jessica completed the various tests over the body and the autopsy report. She became convinced in the process of her work that they indeed had the man known variously as the Trade Winds Killer, the Cane Cutter and Lopaka "Robert" Kowona on her slab. The blood match was identical to blood found in his home and in the vehicle that had been impounded. Serum and bodily fluids, DNA, all a match. Dr. Smits, using her vast knowledge of cranial reconstruction, created a caste from Lopaka's head and had begun to mold and sculpt it into an exact likeness of the killer. Even unfinished where it sat in a vise in the lab, the chilling thing left no doubt in Jessica's mind that they did indeed have Lopaka. The bone structure screamed the truth and X-rays had been made, which would further prove their case.

Even before the sculpting was finished, before all the prelim tests were completed, something instinctual told her that the beheaded corpse with the fire-red hair and the dark eyes that shone like two sides of an impenetrable abyss below her light was the killer they had sought. Below his nails flesh and blood fragments that matched those of his last victim, the little woman from the liquor store, were still embedded.

She didn't believe that even Chief Kowona and Ben Awai, even if they could get help from Dr. Lau, could have planted such incriminating evidence on a decoy. She didn't believe this was a case of tampering.

As to the total fabrication that Lopaka had died of self-inflicted wounds as a result of his suicide at the Spout, choosing that end over Parry's capturing him alive, no one questioned it. Nor would they should she choose to perpetuate the story. In fact, Dr. Lau made it painfully obvious that as far as he was concerned, no one would ever know of any *inconsistencies* in the autopsy. And Dr. Smits, a bone specialist and not a forensics expert, saw no reason to question Jessica's clinical diagnosis.

Jessica felt that the lie was worth the peace it preserved and Jim Parry agreed. And now she was exhausted, and she wanted a hot shower and a bed.

Downstairs, free of her lab coat and responsibilities toward Parry and his office, free of the dreaded case that had removed her both bodily and mentally from the paradise of her surroundings, the case which had haunted her nights now for so long, she breathed in the native air as it whipped and wended its way by her, the continuing trade winds. Investigating her, the mischievous wind next moved out to sea forever. She had left extensive notes for Parry, finishing with a reminder that the body be removed now for the promised burial at sea.

There Lopaka's evil, feverish soul could wander in limbo for longer than any forever that existed anywhere else on Earth.

She hailed a cab, feeling quite alone tonight. Jim had not gotten back to her. She didn't know his whereabouts, and she had to pack for D.C. in the morning.

The taxi that pulled up to the curb was an island Yellow Cab and someone was in the backseat. She looked through the window to find Joe Kaniola waving for her to climb inside, a rare smile on his face.

Opening the door, she said, "I'm too exhausted for another kidnapping, Mr. Kaniola."

He laughed lightly, smiled and pushed the door open. "I only offer you a ride to the Rainbow Tower. That is where you're going?"

"Thank you." She got in, and even the stiff seat felt good to her. "I'm very tired."

"Everyone wishes to thank you."

"Everyone?"

"The Ohana."

"Ahh, the Family, the PKO."

"For your discreet handling of the case."

"*Hmmmm,* but you forget. It's not my case; it's Jim Parry's case."

"I've already thanked Jim, but I must say, he did not accept my congratulations as gracefully as you."

"Nobody reads Miss Manners anymore, Kaniola. You ought to be grateful he didn't find some charge to bring you in on, say, aiding and abetting, conspiracy to—"

"Chief Kowona had a right to administer his own justice to his own son. As a father and a Hawaiian, I respect that."

"Maybe . . . maybe . . ."

"We both know what would have happened with Lopaka's case here if it had gone to court. Lawyers with an eye for sensationalism would have prosecuted while others with an equal eye would defend. Before it would have been over . . ."

He allowed his thoughts to trail off, but she could read them clearly enough: Two, maybe three years would've passed before Lopaka would be sentenced, if the madman hadn't found a way to kill himself.

Kaniola said knowingly, "He would have been analyzed and psychoanalyzed and proven and disproven and proven again to be insane. His civil rights would have been proven violated by the HPD, the FBI, perhaps you, Doctor. And the best we could hope for in the State of Hawaii is that his case would end in a sentence

of life imprisonment in a federal facility for the criminally insane,
like your former Matisak case. I ask you, is that justice?"

"I don't make the laws, Mr. Kaniola."

"No, no . . . you just carry them out . . . as you did in the
Claw case in New York when you held your own execution?"

She winced at the memory, but her anger was conveyed clearly
in the bite of her words. "That was a different case, different
circumstances. It was him or me."

"Here it was him or Hawaii."

They were at the Tower and she got out, waving a final
good-bye to Kaniola, saying, "I hope you, your PKO friends and
the white establishment will fare better in the future, Joe. I pray for
it."

"Thank you. We will need all your prayers and more. The future
is as uncertain as the past, and unfortunately, we are of a species
that doesn't learn from our past, sad as it is true."

11 P.M., the Rainbow Tower, Honolulu

Jessica showered and slipped into a robe, lay down on the bed and
fell fast asleep, her mind free of everything that had been troubling
her since her first look at Linda Kahala's limb fished from the
Blow Hole. The peace descending over her felt as if it had an
island origin, a uniquely Hawaiian stamp to it: balcony window in
the sky, open to the ocean sounds, trade winds playing soft paws
over her where she slept, feelings in tune with the sway of palms
and tides.

And then a knock at the door roused her.

"Damn," she muttered, pulling herself up. At the door she
asked, "Who is it?"

"Message, ma'am. Western Union."

"Slip it under the door."

She watched the envelope creep into the room. What the hell's
this, she wondered, word from Zanek? Maybe the long-awaited
and too late apology from Alan Rychman? "Thank you, got it," she
said through the door.

But she let it lay where it was and started back for bed when the
phone rang.

"Christ," she sleepily muttered, lifting the receiver.

"Jess? It's me. Jim."

Where the hell've you been she silently screamed, but only said, "Where . . . where are you?"

"I'm in the lobby. Can I come up?"

"It's late Jim, and I'm booked on an early morning flight."

"I'm sorry I disappeared on you, Jess, but—"

She unnecessarily shook her head, saying, "That's all right. Jim. We both knew this day was . . . inevitable."

"Honey, listen, I . . ."

"I'm hanging up now, Jim, and I think we ought to make a clean break of it here and now. You and I are going to be too far apart to ever . . . really . . . to . . ."

"Jess, the State Department's asked us to stand down on the Kowona case."

"What?"

"They've asked us to comply with the wishes of the nationals. To let it alone."

"Well, that's good . . . actually . . ." Jessica imagined all that might have happened to Kaniola, Awai, Chief Kowona and his followers if the U.S. Government had actually decided to investigate. In fact, she wondered if she'd come out unscathed in such a review if anyone with the know-how were to go through her autopsy reports with a fine-toothed comb. Would they then prosecute Jim and her, according to the letter of the law? The thought rubbed her nerves raw. She feared more for Jim than herself, however, and somehow this made her breathe easier. Perhaps, if she had to, she could be something other than an M.E. and an FBI agent. The fact that she could let go if she wanted to offered its own reward and peace, and the fact that she cared more about Jim's jeopardy than her own was uplifting, hopeful and inspiring. Maybe she could love someone completely and without reservation as she had once before.

Just hearing his voice had put her at ease. "Come up. I'll put some coffee on, and you can tell me all about it."

She sleep-walked about the room, lifted the Western Union envelope off the floor and found the coffee-makings in the kitchen area. She was halfway through the fixings when his knock came at the door. She went directly to him, and helplessly they fell into one another's arms.

"You must be stone tired," he told her. "I know I am. Forget the coffee." He gently took her into his arms and returned her to the bed, where she could not have resisted him if she had wished.

He tenderly kissed her and caressed her forehead and ran his fingers through her thick, auburn hair. "Just rest, just rest," he chanted.

"I'm worried about promises we made to Kaniola and Kowona."

"Me, too, but for all intents and purposes, Jess, it's out of our hands."

"This could cause a terrible new rupture in race relations here. Do they know that?"

"Nobody knows more than our guys just how sensitive the situation is, Jess. Leave it alone. It's in capable hands. The higher-ups've had their eye on the case from day one."

"Yeah, I guess they have." She momentarily thought of Paul Zanek.

"Things are mellow."

"I'm just afraid for you, Jim," she admitted. "This could cost you big time if the details leak out."

"They're not going to. Now quit worrying."

"God, I wish we could just go back to Maui . . . hide out there . . ."

He kissed her, remembering their night on the isolated black sand beach in Maui. She passionately returned his kiss.

"One good thing'll come of this," he said into her ear.

"Oh?"

"Could mean you'll stay on longer?" It was a wishful question.

"Maybe . . . maybe I just will."

They embraced, kissing until she felt as weak as a feather drifting in the trades. She trembled childlike at his touch.

"Make love to me, Jim, and sleep with me tonight. I don't want to be alone."

Wordlessly, he obeyed and the sound of the surf outside kept cadence with their lovemaking.

What's another night of uncertainty, she told herself.

— 27 —

Instinct is not enough; emotion defies precision.

David Simon, *Homicide*

Dawn, July 22, the Rainbow Tower, Honolulu

The Hawaii dawn crept into their private world, awakening Jessica first. She turned to find Jim beside her, fast asleep. Now, she thought, I can see straight to make that coffee.

But first she stepped onto the balcony and surveyed the inviting expanse of ocean outside. How wonderful it would be to go on a pleasure dive or another excursion to one of the islands she hadn't as yet seen with Jim. She knew he'd love the idea, but she also wondered if she dared hang on here longer. She wondered, too, if she dared tell Zanek where to go when she next heard from him; wondered if she dared quit the bureau, remain here with Jim Parry, remain in paradise, made the safer for her being here. Wondered finally if the HPD needed a good forensics person on staff, or better yet on call, so she could have more time to wander the

348

beaches. Maybe that young fellow who worked for the county here had the right idea: spend more time outside instead of inside the lab.

She wandered back into the room and went toward the kitchen area to make that coffee.

As she did so, she passed the Western Union envelope where it lay, still dangling on the ledge. She now lifted it and placed it beside her as she put the coffee together. It was a simple Mr. Coffee and the brew was bubbling in no time, sending out an aromatic wake-up call to Jim. Already, she'd missed her flight from Oahu, but she'd call later and book anew, maybe. . . . It all depended on Jim.

She began peeling open the Western Union envelope along the dotted line, watching Jim turn over at the same moment, his fingertips groping, trying to find her.

She pretended indifference, looking into her correspondence instead. She turned out the tight folds of the paper and read the typed message, someone having no doubt paid extra for the red ink:

> Warm thy blood Hawaii.
> Make ready for T.
> Make it good and tasty,
> More better for me. . . .
>   Teach

Her mind and stomach crossed in a dizzying somersault as she gulped down a palpable fear. No, it's impossible; can't be, she argued with herself. If this is Alan Rychman's idea of a joke, she'd send him a response he wouldn't soon forget. But then she immediately knew better. Alan was not so callous as to sign off as the maniac who had cut her, Teach Matisak.

But who? Matisak? Christ, how could he have gotten out a Western Union from the federal pen in—

"What's 'at?" asked Parry, interrupting her thoughts.

—unless that idiot Dr. Arnold wired it for him, she silently guessed.

"What the devil is it, Jess . . . Jess?" Jim stood tall and lean in his underwear.

"Sure, that's the only explanation," she said aloud, almost convinced, almost relieved.

"What're you going on about?" Parry remained confused.

"Look at this crap. Do you believe they'd let a psycho like Matt Matisak send a Western Union to me here!"

"Must be somebody's idea of a sick joke. Look at the origin. Where'd it originate from?" He was instantly alert, his face creased with anger. "Let me see it."

He examined the origin of the message. "Says here Norman, Oklahoma. You know anybody in Oklahoma?"

"No, no one."

The phone rang and the coffee was perked at the same time. Get the coffee," she said. "I'll see who that is."

"Right, sure."

"Coran," she said into the phone.

"Don't you pick up your messages anymore, Coran?"

"What messages? Wait a minute, Paul. You send me a wire the other night?"

"No, just phone calls, several."

"I've been away from the hotel, sorry, and some weird things've been going on here, and last night I got in so late I didn't stop by the desk, so—"

"Jess, are you sitting down?"

"No, why?"

"Sit."

He said it with such command she obeyed automatically. "What is it, Paul. You're scaring me."

"It's Matt Matisak."

"What about the bastard?"

"He . . . he's no longer in custody, Jess."

"What? What? Are you . . . is this some sort of sick joke, Paul?"

"Wish it were, Jess . . . wish it were . . ."

"But if he's not in custody, what happened? Did I miss something? Don't give me any shit about his lawyer finding some overlooked loophole or I'll—"

"He escaped Arnold's asylum."

"A maximum-security prison and he escapes?"

"He escaped from a hospital ward in another part of the prison."

"Hospital ward?"

"He hurt himself . . . all part of his plot, we figure."

"Christ, Paul, he . . . the bastard . . . he sent me a wire! He's coming after me."

"He's extremely dangerous, Jess. He proved that two days ago."

"Was anyone . . . hurt?"

Parry was hanging on her every word.

"Arnold was killed, and a guard, and a nurse."

"How?"

"Scalpel to the throat . . . except for Arnold whom he took his time with."

"He stopped to drink the blood, didn't he?"

"He did."

"Anything else you want to tell me?"

"He left a message on a wall, a message in Arnold's blood."

"For me."

"For you."

"What . . . what'd it say, damn you?"

"The real thing is good, but Coran is king . . . I want her blood."

"That bastard's free and he's after my blood, Paul. What the hell am I supposed to do? You got any idea what I'm supposed to do?"

"You can't stay there, that's for sure."

"I'm going to be looking over my shoulder no matter where I am."

"Get back home, Jess. We can work out a strategy from here. If he thinks you're in Hawaii, he'll go there."

"Get back home for how long, Paul?"

"It'll buy us time . . . time to work out some strategy, Jess."

"For how long?"

"I don't know, Jess. Until we apprehend the bastard again."

"Start in Norman, Oklahoma."

"Oklahoma?"

"He sent the wire from there."

"Christ, he's halfway across the continent."

"He's shrewd and deadly. He'll be killing as he goes. Set up a command post in Oklahoma. I'll . . . I'll join you there."

"Are you sure?"

"Yes, damnit, I'm sure."

Jim interrupted. "He could be counting on that if he's as treacherous as you say."

"What?"

"That you'll come to him."

"Right, well, then he'll be right."

Zanek asked, "Who are you talking to?"

"Jim Parry." She imagined Zanek was checking his watch about now and figuring Hawaii time.

"*Ahh,* oh, yeah," he sputtered. "Sounds like he agrees with me, Jess, that it'd be best for you to return to D.C."

"Where I can sit on my thumbs? Wait and wonder and fear my own shadow? No, thanks."

"Let us take care of Matisak, Jess."

"I let you guys take care of him already, remember?"

"All right, Jess. I'll meet you in Oklahoma, but not anywhere near the bureau offices. He'll be watching the offices, if he imagines you'll come."

"Or he'll be on a flight for here," she countered.

"What's it to be, Jess?"

"Oklahoma for me, and Parry's people will watch the terminals here."

Parry stared across at her, seeing the determination in her eyes. She hung up after telling Zanek that she would wire him in Norman with her flight numbers.

"I'm going with you to the mainland, to Oklahoma," he now said.

"The hell you are. You have a bureau to run here. You're . . . you're the goddamn linchpin here in the islands, Jim, respected by both sides. With your expertise and knowledge of the Kowona affair . . . well, you're just needed here; otherwise anything could happen to this powder keg you call paradise."

"To hell with all that."

"To hell with it? No way you're going to turn your back on what you have here, Jim; what you've accomplished and built. Hell, even Kaniola has renewed respect for you and the bureau since—"

"Don't B.S. me, Jess."

"He said as much."

"I can't let you fly off after this madman alone, Jess."

"Alone? Don't be ridiculous. The entire bureau's on alert. I'll have an army of willing bodyguards and Paul Zanek'll be at the lead."

"That's supposed to put me at ease?"

"Come on. What we have found here together . . . no one'll ever replace, Jim. And maybe, when this is all over, I'll . . . I'll come back . . ."

"And maybe you won't."

"Don't, Jim . . . don't make this choice any harder than it already is, please." In fact, in her mind, there was no choice. He sensed this.

Their coffee had gone cold and the Hawaiian sky at the windows had become overcast for the first time since she'd come to Oahu.

She dialed for the airlines. He dressed. They went around one another like a pair of zombies as she packed. "Everything's changed now," she finally said.

"Everything?"

"Circumstances, but not how I feel about you . . . just circumstances. I don't *want* to go. I *have* to go."

"Why, Jess? Why can't you just stay?"

"We're not kids, Jim. That would mean giving up my career. Besides, *he* knows I'm here. I'm . . . I feel vulnerable. I have to take the offensive."

"And if it's a trap, to lure you there?"

"I've walked into traps before, once with you, remember?"

He was hurt, his insides turning over.

"Will you take me to the airport?"

"If you're sure. Okay."

"Funny this should happen now," she said.

"Funny?"

"I finally discard that damned cane, declare myself free of Matisak and the scars he inflicted on me. My nights were no longer haunted by him, and now this."

The flight out of Hawaii was long, tedious torture, the States half a hemisphere away, and it gave her too much time to wonder what might have been, too much idle questioning of her decisions until she was second-guessing herself. She thought of Jim Parry and how much he meant to her, about how dear he was, about what she was giving up.

Maybe Jim was right. Maybe she should chuck it all, turn around and return to his arms and the paradise—or near-paradise—she'd discovered there in the lush islands of the Ohana.

But if she remained it would be like a homing beacon for the evil of Matisak to invade there. If she returned to Hawaii, Matisak would be forced to find her there, and she'd be jeopardizing people there, even Jim. Matisak wanted to poison her life in every conceivable way, and how better to poison it than to destroy whatever and whomever she loved. She must never give Matisak that kind of power, the power of knowledge over her, of information that could harm her.

She feared even corresponding or talking with Jim on the phone now, for Matisak's evil genius would learn of her lover, and he would plot some awful nightmare for Jim Parry, a night of torture and death in which the psycho would slowly drain Jim Parry of his blood. This tort 9 killer, this vampire, was cunning and cruel.

She wasn't crazy or paranoid to feel this way toward Matisak. Over the years of his incarceration she'd had to make many visits to him, interrogating him, and he in turn had made numerous death threats, both direct and indirect, careful always to do so whenever her recorder ran out of tape. Still, she had fooled him once into threatening her by carrying a second, concealed tape on her person. It was useless as evidence to take to his parole board, which would be sitting in a matter of four years from now, as she'd smuggled it in and he was being taped without his knowledge, but it gave credence to her claim, and it had opened Paul Zanek's eyes to the monster.

Matisak had been careful and controlled around others, and around tape recorders. He didn't want to slip up or say anything that could be used against him when his parole board sat, but everyone except Matisak knew that no amount of good behavior and cooperation with the FBI interviewers over the years was going to win him a free walk on the first go-round.

Somehow, Matisak figured this out. Dr. Arnold, Matisak's keeper all these years, might have nastily explained it to him in a fit of his own, earning Matisak's undying hatred. Actually Matisak hated everyone, and in particular, his rage had fixated on Jessica Coran, who had unmasked him and caused his capture and eventual imprisonment.

Here on the plane with the hum of flight in her ears, she now imagines Matisak's moves there in the asylum. He manages first to slip some small item into his cage, no small trick in the maximum-security nuthouse where all transactions are handled through a revolving door in a glass cell. Then comes the injury, self-inflicted. Though Matisak is wise to medical procedures, so he may have staged a masquerade, a supposed natural injury, say a bleeding ulcer or blood frothing from the mouth. Then comes the transportation to the hospital ward, and the subsequent lapse in security, ending with three deaths and the disappearance of

Matisak, who, using a doctor's coat and badge, wallet and credit cards, waltzes out to a car belonging to the murdered doctor and drives off into the night without objection from anyone.

She now silently curses the scenario she has painted in her mind, wishing to quell it, to rest for the long haul ahead, but her mind and Matisak play on.

Then Matisak speeds across the country, no doubt leaving a trail of bloodless bodies in his wake. He exchanges cars somewhere along the way, and the fiend stops in Norman, Oklahoma, to send her a wire, having learned of her whereabouts through Dr. Arnold, who'd always taken some perverse pleasure in taunting Matisak with her comings and goings, always keeping him apprised of her whereabouts in some sick, childish game that had gone on between doctor and patient, captive and keeper throughout their relationship. This long after she had stopped visiting the asylum on a routine basis, refusing to deal with Matisak after the Claw Case, in which he had sought to undermine her confidence even from his asylum cell.

She had made pilgrimages to the maniac for only as long as he had useful information to convey, and for as long as her own tortured psyche could withstand the visits. She had made the examinations and taped interviews for the same reasons she'd conducted interviews with Gerald Ray Sims and other serial murderers, for the good of the cause, to carry on Otto Boutine's work and only because it had fallen on her to do so; Matisak would only communicate through her, at his deranged insistence, and so she had gone, playing along with his prurient game in her official capacity only in order to learn what the FBI might learn from Matisak about his fatal and instinctive working methods, his selection of victims, and the way his mind worked. Matisak got off on it, sitting opposite her, having her there to gaze at and lust for, giving him a sick sense of hope for the future, hope that he might taste of her blood a second time.

She normally wouldn't have subjected herself to such an ordeal, but she knew the necessity of learning as completely as possible the inner psyche of a creature like Matisak. Besides, it proved a useful shield against certain of her superiors who sought to remove her at the time, claiming her incapacitated, not physically but emotionally. But she had shown O'Rourke and she had proven to Paul Zanek what kind of metal lay beneath her skin. At the same time, her superiors had a case file on Matisak the size of the D.C.

phone book, and they knew as much as humanly possible about how the madman had created such an elaborate fantasy: *"I am descended from vampires, and genetically coded a vampire from birth."* The sickest thing about the belief was not that he believed it, but that he acted on it every chance he got.

Now his chances are excellent to stupendous. Now here he is in the year 1995, taking every opportunity to drink the blood of others, not content with medications to control his urges, ill content with the idea he could feed his cravings with ox blood, chicken blood, or any number of other substitutes. No, this one is bent on feeding in the manner of his supposed forebears! He should've gone the way of Lopaka Kowona, but the state of Illinois didn't see it that way.

Now, no doubt, bloodless bodies litter the trail he has blazed to Norman, Oklahoma.

Now, Jessica thinks with renewed awe, this obsessed lunatic, enraptured with me, is out there in the heartland, hunting me as if I'm some sort of filthy carrion for him; his throat and tongue and taste buds are watering for my blood a second time. It isn't going to happen.

"Warm thy blood Hawaii," he said in his sardonic message. It is clear to her that Hawaii in the poem means her, that he meant the word to mean Dr. Jessica Coran. "Warm thy blood Coran . . . Make ready for T—"

A demented, psychotic vampire is after me again.

She can think of nothing else.

She wonders if she can stand the long flight back to the mainland. Her ankles, which have not troubled her since the trek to Kahoolawe, begin to throb, and she wishes she'd kept her cane for something solid to hang onto, if for no other reason.

Matisak's insane eyes fill her mind. He's already gaining control. She feels a silent shiver run through her nervous system and she imagines the plane filled with ghosts that would crawl up from within her the moment darkness descended.

She remembers the madness of Lopaka Kowona. She recalls the insanity of Gerald Ray Sims, who'd killed himself in his cell, claiming demonic possession. She recalls Simon Archer, the notorious Claw. None of them frighten her.

But Matisak does.

She can think of nothing else. . . .